P9-DJK-880

TALES FROM THE NEW REPUBLIC

edited by

Peter Schweighofer

and Craig Carey

BANTAM BOOKS
New York Toronto London Sydney Auckland

This anthology contains stories previously published in
The Star Wars® Adventure Journal from West End Games.

TALES FROM THE NEW REPUBLIC
A Bantam Spectra Book / December 1999

ISBN 0-553-57882-0

Published simultaneously in the United States and Canada

PRINTED IN THE UNITED STATES OF AMERICA

OPM   10   9   8   7   6   5   4   3   2   1

Contents

Foreword and Acknowledgments

In recent months, the scope of the *Star Wars* universe has expanded beyond our wildest dreams. *Episode I: The Phantom Menace* has given us a detailed view of the *Star Wars* galaxy decades before the adventures of Han, Luke, and Leia. But the era in which those heroes fought and lived remains as popular as ever, and the adventures in this collection chronicle other heroes of that same era—when the Empire still cast an ominous shadow upon the galaxy and the New Republic struggled to maintain order and justice. The exciting stories contained in this anthology feature some of those heroes from the era of the fledgling New Republic; some of the adventures make their debut in this book.

For six months in 1998 I served as the editor of the now-defunct *Official Star Wars Adventure Journal*, a position previously held by Peter Schweighofer, editor of *Star Wars: Tales from the Empire* and co-editor of this volume. During my short tenure at the *Journal*'s helm, I was fortunate enough to review work from several of the most popular *Star Wars* authors. In fact, the very first draft I received my first morning in the office was Timothy Zahn's "Jade Solitaire," a new story featuring Mara Jade that introduced characters later seen in *Vision of the Future*.

For this book, our assignment was the relatively simple—but excruciating—task of deciding which stories we would choose from the scores under consideration: some previously published under Peter's direction and some from my turn as the *Journal*'s editor. Those appearing in this anthology represent the finest *Star Wars* short fiction; they are a diverse group, set in a variety of locales and starring a wide range of characters.

More people than I could list deserve thanks for assistance along the way. Chief among them are the authors—who naturally did all of the hard work and deserve the credit—and Pete, my predecessor. Pete welcomed me aboard the West End staff and not only provided me with a strong example, but also became a good friend. His diligent attention to detail and solid work ethic gave me the steady platform from which an even stronger *Star Wars Adventure Journal* would have been launched. Though those issues never came to be, I thank him for his faith in me and for the opportunity to join him in editing this anthology.

Thanks also go to Pat LoBrutto for leading the way, and our former West End associates for their input, advice, and encouragement. My wife Karrie has supported me in every endeavor and has been a constant source of strength and inspiration. My parents, my brothers Billy and Doug, and the infamous Gotham Highlanders have always been there for me and have supported my pursuits throughout the years.

And thanks finally to all the *Star Wars* fans whose support of the *Journal* and subsequent anthologies has meant a great deal to us both.

—Craig Carey, March 1999

Inspiration and support comes from many sources.

Numerous talented authors, a fine co-editor, and many

supportive friends deserve commendations for their work in *Star Wars: Tales from the New Republic.* As an editor, I helped channel others' inspiration and ideas, honing their storytelling skills so they could share these *Star Wars* tales with you. Craig and I enjoyed working with all the authors; each earned their place within these pages.

When West End Games hired Craig Carey to run the *Official Star Wars Adventure Journal* in January 1998, he brought his professional attitude, boundless enthusiasm, and a positive spirit, all of which I admire. After editing the *Journal* for four years myself, I was pleasantly surprised how well Craig learned all aspects of the job. He provided a firm hand, guiding these stories to their final form. I consider Craig a far better *Journal* editor than I ever was. It has been a pleasure working with him. As circumstances dictated, West End Games never published any of his work. I'm proud to finally see it here.

Many others deserve special thanks for *Tales from the New Republic.* Patrick LoBrutto and Evelyn Cainto at Bantam Spectra provided invaluable guidance and assistance through the logistics of producing this anthology. Timothy Zahn, Michael A. Stackpole, Jean Rabe, John Whitman, and Richard Hawran offered their constant encouragement and friendship. Numerous "dark side" and "light side" friends (and those in between) helped bolster my spirits when things seemed rough. Denise Clarkston's warmth, kindness, and late-night chats helped put everything in perspective. My family provided firm support and love, as they always have throughout my life, no matter what endeavors I undertook.

Thanks to Lucy Autrey Wilson and Allan Kausch for their official guidance at Lucasfilm. And, of course, George Lucas deserves special thanks for creating movies which inspired us yesterday, excite us today, and will enthrall us in years to come.

—Peter Schweighofer, March 1999

Interlude at Darkknell

PART 1

by Timothy Zahn

Senator Bel Iblis?"

Garm Bel Iblis looked up from his datapad, frowning with the subtle tension of prespeech jitters. The man standing in the doorway was the assistant director at the Treitamma Political Center, charged with the responsibility of smoothing any obstacles that might impede the firm step and stalwart tread of an exalted member of the Imperial Senate.

Or so the gentleman had gravely explained upon Bel Iblis's arrival this afternoon. Clearly the Anchoron reputation for flowery speech and genteel decorum had found a focal point here at the Treitamma.

Which was going to make the bluntness of his speech tonight all the more shocking. The dark truth about Emperor Palpatine and his secret agenda for his newly established Empire . . .

He shook his head briefly in annoyance. Assistant Director Graskt was still waiting patiently, and here he was letting his mind drift. It showed just how seriously this speech—and the situation it represented—had taken over his every waking thought. "Yes, AsDir Graskt, what is it?" he asked.

"A gentleman from your staff has just arrived from Coruscant," Graskt said, stepping forward and holding out a datacard. "He asked me to deliver this to you right away."

"Thank you," Bel Iblis said, the hairs on the back of his neck tingling as he reached across the desk and took the datacard. Sena would never send a package to him without making sure the courier had his private comlink frequency. The fact that there had been no calls concerning any such arrivals . . .

He slid the datacard into his datapad. There was nothing on it but a single line: "Meet me at the northeast exit. Urgent. Aach."

"Will there be a return message, Senator?" Graskt asked.

"No, that's all right," Bel Iblis said, long experience in the political arena enabling him to keep the sudden tension out of his voice and face. *Aach* was the code name of a special messenger from Bail Organa, a messenger the Alderaanian viceroy used only for top-level Rebel Alliance business.

"Would you like to speak with the gentleman?" Graskt persisted. "I asked him to wait at the main entrance."

"That won't be necessary," Bel Iblis said. The last thing he could afford was for the two of them to be seen in public together. Besides, Aach had undoubtedly slipped away by now for their more private meeting. "I'll have plenty of time to see him after my speech."

"Then the message does not in fact bespeak a crisis?" Graskt asked.

Bel Iblis felt the skin around his eyes crinkle as his eyes narrowed slightly. For someone who had struck him as having taken a double helping of the traditional Anchoroni politeness, Graskt was suddenly being uncharacteristically nosy.

Unless Aach had overplayed his hand in order to make sure the datacard was delivered. But that didn't seem likely. Could Graskt be a spy for Palpatine, here to keep an eye on him?

He felt a flash of annoyance. No—that was absurd. The man was probably just trying to be helpful. "To middle-level staffers, all news bulletins mean a crisis must be happening somewhere," he improvised, giving Graskt an easy smile. "It's important enough, but hardly a crisis. Certainly not worth delaying my speech for." He looked at his chrono. "Which reminds me, I'm due on stage in fifteen minutes, and I still have to change."

"I'll leave you to your preparations, then," Graskt said. "Good evening, sir." He bowed deeply and backed out of the room.

Bel Iblis gave him a fifty-count and then followed.

The Treitamma's northeast exit was off the group of backstage rooms to the left of the main stage, about as far away from the bustling main entrance as it was possible to get. Bel Iblis eased noiselessly down the stairway, alert for the various staffers hurrying around making final preparations for the evening's round of speeches, and slipped outside.

A landspeeder was parked in the service alleyway behind the Treitamma, gray and muted in the dim evening light. Standing on the far side of the vehicle, pressed into what little shadow there was trying to watch all directions at once, was Aach.

Bel Iblis crossed the alleyway toward him, trying to suppress a grimace and not entirely succeeding. This cloak-and-blade mentality was going to be the end of them yet. "Not being too obvious, are we?" he suggested tartly as he rounded the front of the landspeeder and stopped, facing the other.

"Your preparation room seemed a bit too public for a meeting," Aach countered, his voice as calm as his face. "Would you rather I showed up at your hotel room after the speech? That could have proved a bit awkward."

Bel Iblis felt his lip twitch. Awkward, unfortunately, was hardly the word for it. His wife Arrianya, a daughter of the old Core World families, had an unreserved and totally unwavering faith in Palpatine and his Empire, a faith that had first astonished, then baffled, then finally frustrated him. The clash of their differing political views had cast a chill over their marriage the past few months, and had dropped their two children into the middle of what was all too often a verbal war zone.

The speech he was about to make out there on the Treitamma stage was going to upset Arrianya enough as it was. All he needed was for a shadowy messenger from Bail to show up in the middle of the inevitable argument afterward. "What's the message?" he growled.

In the dim light he saw Aach's mouth twitch. "Sorry, Senator. I didn't mean—"

"I know you didn't," Bel Iblis said. "What's the message?"

Aach looked around the area again. "There's been a breakthrough," he said, lowering his voice to something barely above a whisper. "We've located Tarkin's project."

Bel Iblis felt his throat go suddenly dry. "Where is it?"

"I don't know," Aach said. "All I know is that a courier will be in the Continuum Void tapcafe in the city of Xakrea on Darkknell in three days with some inside information about it. Bail wants you to send your most trusted aide to rendezvous with him and pick up his datapack."

Courier. Bel Iblis glanced around, a bad taste in his mouth. A three would get you the sabacc pot that this so-called "courier" was in fact the thief who'd stolen the datapack in the first place. A minor military figure, most likely, either a trooper or perhaps a clerk attached to the project.

And *two* would get you the sabacc pot that his actions hadn't been motivated by anything as selfless as love of the Republic. "And how much am I supposed to pay him?"

Aach hesitated, just noticeably. "Bail basically said to give him whatever he wants. Look, we need this information—"

"Yes, yes, I understand," Bel Iblis cut him off. "If we can't get honest patriotism, we'll settle for honest greed."

"That'll change," Aach promised, a quiet fire simmering in his voice. "As soon as Palpatine's agenda finally becomes clear, we'll have the whole Republic flocking to our side."

"I'd settle for the top five percent of the Imperial Academy," Bel Iblis said sourly. Now was not the time for brooding about Palpatine's maddening talent for pulling the cloak over people's eyes. "Fine. I'll get one of my people on it as soon as I finish my—"

And with a brilliant flash, the Treitamma Political Center blew up.

Bel Iblis was lying on the ground when he fumbled his way back to consciousness, pressed up against the wall of the building across the alleyway on one side with what was left of the landspeeder looming over him on the other. Behind the landspeeder a ragged section of wall where the Treitamma had been was burning furiously, bathing the whole area with an unreal-looking blaze of yellow light and pouring black smoke into the sky.

"Senator?"

Bel Iblis blinked, shifting his eyes upward. Aach was kneeling over him, a gash in the side of his face streaming blood. "Come on, Senator, we've got to get you out of here," he said urgently, tugging on his arm. "Can you stand?"

"I think so," Bel Iblis said, gathering his feet beneath him. He looked over at the burning building again as Aach helped him to his feet—

And abruptly the haze blanketing his mind seemed to flash-burn away. "Arrianya!" he gasped. "Aach—my wife and children—"

"They're gone, Senator," Aach said, his voice suddenly vicious. "And you're going to be next if we don't get you out of here right away."

"Leave me alone!" Bel Iblis snarled, trying to push Aach's hand away and staggering as his trembling legs nearly collapsed again beneath him. "I've got to get to them. Let me *alone.*"

"No," Aach bit back, tightening his grip on Bel Iblis's arm. "Don't you see? You're the only one they were trying to kill in there. *You.*"

Bel Iblis stared at the blazing building, a jolt of fresh pain and emptiness and anger twisting together and cutting into him. No. No—it couldn't be. Destroy a whole building—kill dozens or even hundreds of people—just to get at him? It was insane.

"Looks like they used a thermal detonator," Aach said, half leading, half pulling Bel Iblis down the alleyway away from the wrecked landspeeder. "Shaped to bring down the Treitamma without demolishing the whole neighborhood. Most likely planted somewhere near your preparation room."

And Arrianya and the children had been in the private refreshment center chatting with the chief director. Only two rooms away . . .

They had reached the end of the alleyway by now. Around the corner of the demolished building, over by the sides and front, Bel Iblis could see a crowd had already gathered, their features unreadable through the smoke and heat-shimmered air. Their screams and shouts, barely audible over the roar of the flames, were like a stab of pain in his heart.

"Over here," Aach said, pulling him toward a landspeeder parked at the side of the street, its front end crumpled and blistered by the explosion. "You can take my ship—I'll get back to Alderaan some other way." He pulled open the door and guided Bel Iblis into the passenger seat.

Another layer of the mental haze suddenly cleared from Bel Iblis's mind. "Wait a minute," he protested, half in and half out of the vehicle. "Arrianya and the children—I can't just leave them."

"You have to," Aach said, his voice bitter but firm. "Didn't you hear me? *You* were the target, Senator. You still are. We've got to get you to safety before they realize they missed and try again."

He closed the door on Bel Iblis and hurried around

to the other side. "But what if they're alive?" Bel Iblis demanded, fumbling for the door release as Aach dropped into the driver's seat. "I can't just leave them."

"They're dead, Senator," Aach said quietly, his face in shadow as he hunched forward and reached up under the control board. "Everyone who was inside is gone, either from the blast itself or from the building's collapse. Whoever Palpatine sent to do the job was very thorough."

With a jolt, the landspeeder started up. "Yes," Bel Iblis murmured, taking one final look at the burning building as Aach spun the vehicle around and headed in the other direction, down the street. "He was indeed."

"And he's not going to give up now," Aach added, pulling hard to the side to get out of the way of a fleet of Extinguisher speeder trucks as they raced past toward the conflagration. A waste of effort, Bel Iblis thought numbly as they passed. There was nothing anyone could do now. "You're going to have to go underground until Bail and Mon Mothma can backtrack this and identify whoever was responsible."

"I suppose so," Bel Iblis said. His left shoulder felt cold, and he looked down to see that the top of his coat there had been torn completely away by some bit of flying debris that the bulk of Aach's landspeeder hadn't protected him from. Odd—he wondered why he hadn't noticed that before.

He was suddenly aware of a watchful silence, and looked over to find Aach eyeing him warily. "Are you all right, Senator?" the other asked. "Did you hear what I said? You have to go away somewhere and hide."

"Yes, I heard you," Bel Iblis said, the pain inside him beginning to give way to a black and simmering anger. In that single instant, a moment frozen forever in time, Palpatine had taken away from him everything he held dear. His wife, his children, his career. His life.

Everything, that is, but one. "And I'll be all right," he went on, "When Palpatine is dead, and what was once the Republic has been restored."

"I understand," Aach murmured. "You're one of us now, Senator."

Bel Iblis frowned at him. "What are you talking about? I've been part of the Rebel Alliance since it was first formed."

"But you were with us for other reasons," Aach said. "Political reasons like Palpatine's abuse of power, or idealistic reasons like erosion of personal freedom or the antialien biases drifting into the legal system."

The muscles in his jaw tightened briefly. "Now Palpatine has hurt you. Not someone else, but you. Now it's personal."

Bel Iblis took a deep breath. "Maybe it is," he conceded. "On the other hand, maybe that's exactly what he wants: to trick us into thinking we're fighting him for purely personal reasons."

"What's wrong with that?"

"What's wrong is that that kind of battle is driven by emotion," Bel Iblis said. "Eventually, the emotion burns away, and then your reason for continuing the fight is gone."

He fingered the edges of the hole in his coat. "But we're not going to fall into that trap. He can do anything he wants to me—can take anything away from me that he will. I'll still fight him because it's the right thing to do. Period."

For a few minutes they drove on in silence. On the rear display the burning shell gradually receded behind the other buildings of the city, leaving only an angry black-orange pillar of smoke to mark his family's funeral pyre. It seemed terribly wrong somehow to be running away like this, as if he were casually and cavalierly brushing aside their lives and dishonoring their memory.

But no. They were dead, and the dishonor of their blood was solely on Palpatine's hands. All that was left for him now was to do whatever he could to prevent others from dying in the same violent and useless way.

And if the whispered rumors he'd heard about this Death Star project of Tarkin's were even close to the actual truth . . . "You said I could take your ship?" he asked Aach.

"Yes, if you feel up to flying it yourself," the other said. "I was thinking I might stay around here a day or two anyway."

"Why? To see if you can find a direct link back to Palpatine?" Bel Iblis shook his head. "I can tell you right now you'll be wasting your time."

"It's my time to waste. Is there a place where you can hide out for a while?"

"There are a couple of possibilities," Bel Iblis said. "But first I have an appointment to keep on Darkknell."

"Darkknell?" Aach threw Bel Iblis a startled look. "You?"

"Why not?" Bel Iblis countered. "Who better to make the pickup than someone who's supposed to be dead anyway? My schedule is now meaningless, you know. And I have no one to miss me if I'm out of sight for a few days. Not anymore."

"But—" Aach floundered a moment. "Sir, this could be dangerous—any contact with informants has that potential. You're not trained for this sort of fieldwork."

"I did my stint in the military," Bel Iblis reminded him. "I know how to handle a blaster. And I know a bit about disguise, too. I won't be recognized."

"But—"

"Besides," Bel Iblis cut him off quietly, "I need to do something useful right now. Something to help take my mind off . . . what just happened back there."

Aach exhaled softly in resignation. "All right, sir. Before you go, though, I'll give you a letter of introduction to someone I know in Xakrea you can contact if you get in trouble. He doesn't have any particular sympathy for the Rebellion, but he doesn't much care for Palpatine's Empire, either. He's got a lot of contacts among smugglers and other fringe types on Darkknell, which may come in handy if you have to get off the planet in a hurry."

"It may," Bel Iblis agreed, noting with a somewhat

grim amusement that Aach had carefully refrained from mentioning his friend's own status within the fringe society. A smuggler himself, or perhaps a dealer of stolen goods? Or something even more unsavory?

Still, if it came to that, the Rebel Alliance certainly had its own share of unsavory characters. Some had probably been pulled in by the hope of quick profits—though those who had had most likely been disillusioned in record time on that one—but others were among the Alliance's most tenacious and effective fighters. "Do you trust him?"

Aach shrugged, a bit uncomfortably. "I think so, provided as you don't push him too hard or ask too much. Or tell him who you are or who you're working for. Anyway, he owes me a couple of favors."

"I see," Bel Iblis murmured. "It's always comforting to have allies."

"I could still go with you," Aach offered, a clear note of reluctance lurking beneath the words. "I was supposed to head back to Alderaan. Under the circumstances I know Bail would understand."

"No," Bel Iblis said firmly. "Bail undoubtedly needs you elsewhere, and I can do this myself. You just help me get off Anchoron, and then you're on your own."

Aach hesitated, then nodded. "All right, Senator. If you insist."

Bel Iblis looked back at the rear display, his eyes drawn unwillingly to the roiling tower of black smoke behind them. The shock was starting to wear off now, and a myriad of small injuries and throbbing pains were beginning to make themselves felt across his body.

But none of it could come even close to the bitter ache in his heart. Arrianya and the children . . . "Yes," he said quietly. "I insist."

The man sitting alone at the table across the crowded tapcafe was blond and fairly short, with the darting eyes and twitching mouth of someone who was somewhere he didn't want to be. Not much more than a kid, really, which could explain his discomfort at being in such a villainous lair of vile laxity as the Continuum Void.

On the other hand, his stiff back had an air of the Imperial military about it, and if there was one safe bet in this galaxy, it was that military types and tapcafes rarely needed to be formally introduced.

Moranda Savich sipped at her pale blue drink, wincing at the unfamiliar tang, continuing to study the kid even as she chided herself for letting her thoughts wander off target that way. The only reason she was on Darkknell in the first place, after all, was that it wasn't Kreeling or Dorsis or Mantarran. Inspector Hal Horn of Corellian Security had already tracked her to and chased her off all those worlds, and most likely he'd continue his winning streak by tracking her here, too. The sooner she figured out a quiet way off this rock, the better her chances of staying ahead of him until he gave up and went home.

She snorted gently. Fat chance. Horn wasn't going to give up, at least not in her lifetime. The man was one of that supremely irritating class of law enforcers who combined the menace of incorruptibility with the annoyance of not knowing when to quit.

Across the tapcafe, the kid slipped a hand beneath the left side of his jacket as he glanced around. The second time he'd done that, Moranda noted, in the past ten minutes. Must be something he was having to reassure himself was still there . . .

Stop it! she ordered herself sternly. She was on the run, and on the run was no time to be swinging for a scratch. Stirring up the locals with a score would be completely counterproductive, especially if she stirred them up enough to catch her with spice or dealies or whatever the kid was carrying that was making him so nervous.

He lifted his cup to his lips, half turning to throw a look toward the tapcafe door, his ninth such check since Moranda had been watching. As he did so, his jacket stretched momentarily against the object in his pocket, giving her a brief glimpse of its shape. It was square, slightly larger than a datacard, but considerably thicker.

A datapack? Could be. Probably with six to ten datacards, judging from the thickness, snugged together in a protective case.

Moranda swirled the blue liqueur thoughtfully in her glass. Well, now. A datapack put a very different perspective on things. Every police and security operative knew spice and other contraband items on sight or smell or taste; but a simple, innocent-looking datapack was another matter entirely. It was something anyone might be carrying, something that even the most suspicious mouth-breather would have to go to great lengths to prove wasn't her property in the first place.

More to the point, it was something that was likely worth hard, cold money. And money was what she needed if she was going to get out of here ahead of Inspector Horn and his fistful of Corellian warrants.

Which left only one question: how to get the datapack away from its nervous owner without getting caught doing it.

The glowing sign marking the 'fresher stations was against the wall on the far side of the kid's table. Refilling her drink from the carafe, she got up and ambled in that direction, putting a slightly tipsy hesitation into her movements. His jacket was cut Preter style, she noted with a single casual glance as she strolled past him, the sort with a deep inside pocket positioned beneath the armhole on either side. Possibly fastened at the top, but probably not seriously sealed. Still, with the youth hunched over the table the way he was, the only way to get at the datapack would be for her to get him to take the jacket at least partially off.

But that was okay. She enjoyed a challenge.

The 'fresher stations were like the rest of the Continuum Void: old and more than slightly dilapidated. Sealing herself into one, she set her drink down on the crumble-edged shelf and got to work.

The small tiles lining the station were the first target.

Pulling out her knife, she pried two of them off the wall, then carefully trimmed them down to datacard size. Beneath the tiles was a layer of the low-quality honeycomb that served as a passive air filter in low-tier places like this one; a double layer of that sandwiched between her two tiles added the required thickness. One of her diaphanous black scarves wrapped tightly around the pack to hold it together and it was finished. The object didn't look anything like a datapack, but it was the right size and shape and weight. With the proper distraction and the right moves, and maybe a little bit of luck tossed in, it should work.

After digging into her hip pack for a stray cigarra she kept around for just such occasions, she lit it and stuck it between two fingers of her right hand, picking up her glass of liqueur with the fingertips of the same hand. Then, with the decoy datapack concealed as best she could in her left hand, she unsealed the door and headed back into the main tapcafe room.

The kid hadn't moved in the few minutes she'd been gone, nor had the contact he was obviously expecting made an appearance. Holding her decoy datapack unobtrusively at her side, putting a noticeable stagger into her walk now, she started through the crowd toward her table, this time heading for the narrow gap behind the kid. She dodged a drunk Barrckli, sent a warning glare at an unshaven nerf herder type who looked as if he might be starting to get ideas about her, and passed behind the kid—

And with a sudden lurch as if she'd been tripped, she fell heavily against the back of his chair and splashed the contents of her glass across the burning tip of her cigarra onto the back of his jacket.

The liqueur ignited with a muffled *whoosh* into a small but very satisfying fireball.

"Look out!" Moranda gasped, dropping both glass and cigarra onto the floor and grabbing over his right shoulder for the edge of the tablecloth. She yanked it toward her, scattering glasses and tableware in all directions as

she hauled it past the side of his head toward the flames
dancing across the back of his jacket. Simultaneously,
she tugged at the left lapel with the fingertips of her left
hand. Reflexively, he swung his left arm back in response, giving her the necessary slack for pulling the
blazing garment away from the back of his neck.

And as she slapped vigorously at the already dying
flames with the tablecloth, her left hand dipped down
into the inside jacket pocket, lifting out the datapack
and leaving her decoy behind in its place.

"I'm so sorry," she repeated over and over in her best
embarrassed voice, still pounding the tablecloth across
his shoulders even though the fire was already out as
she slipped her prize into her hip pack behind her datapad. "So terribly sorry. My ankle went and—are you all
right?"

"I'm fine, I'm fine," the kid growled, twisting half
around to his right and grabbing at the tablecloth. "It's
out now, right?"

"Oh yes," she said, giving his back one final slap before letting him pull the now wadded tablecloth away
from her. "I'm so sorry. Can I buy you a drink?"

"No, forget it," he said, waving her away and trying to
turn a little farther around. Trying for a clearer look at
her? "Just go away and leave me alone."

"Sure, of course," Moranda said, easing around as she
pretended to resettle his jacket back onto his shoulders,
staying just out of his sight. Out of the corner of his eye
she saw his hand steal beneath his jacket to the pocket.
The fingers probed the shape of her decoy and fell away,
apparently reassured. "I'm so sorry."

"Go away," he repeated, starting to sound a little angry now. Clearly he wasn't happy at having all this attention focused his way.

"Yeah, sure." Moranda stepped away to his left, and as
he twisted his head in that direction, still trying for a clear
look at her face, she turned her back to him and worked
her way through the crowd toward her table.

She reached it but didn't sit down. The kid's buyer

could be here any time now, and she had no intention of being anywhere in the vicinity when he hauled her decoy triumphantly out of his pocket. Leaving the price of her drink on the table, she slouched her way to the door and out into the tangy Darkknell air. Time to find a nice, quiet place to go to ground for a while and see just what it was she'd scored.

Bel Iblis stared across the tapcafe table at the young blond man, a sense of unreality thudding through his brain in time with the pulse pounding in his neck. "What do you mean, you lost it?" he demanded in a low voice. "How do you *lose* an entire datapack? Especially from within your own coat pocket?"

"Don't use that tone with *me,* friend," the other growled back, his eyes darting nervously around the half-empty room. "And if you're hinting that I'm trying to repulsorlift my price, you'd better think again. I took a huge risk getting that stuff and bringing it here. A *huge* risk. I'm not any happier than you are that it got lifted."

Bel Iblis took a careful breath, trying to throttle back his growing anger. He might not be a Rebel field operative like Aach, but he knew how to read people, and the youth's face and voice had the ring of truth in them.

Which meant they were both now squarely in the middle of an incredibly dangerous position. The minute the thief realized what it was she'd found . . . "Is there any way they can trace it back to you?" He asked quietly.

The young man snorted into his cup. "Sure, if they really want to go to that much effort. Knowing Tarkin's reputation, they probably will."

"Then we'll just have to get it back."

The kid snorted again. "*You* can go looking under rocks for it if you want. Me, I'm heading for the tall weeds while I still can."

"You run now and they'll know for sure you were the one who lifted the data," Bel Iblis warned.

"Like that's going to matter any," the other countered

harshly, draining his cup and bringing it back dow
onto the table with an unnecessarily loud thud. "She
not going to sit on this long, you know. And the minut
she turns it in, the spaceport's going to be locked dow
solid while Tarkin's people fan out across the plane
You want to wait for that to happen, you be my guest."

He stood up. "So long, have fun, and forget you eve
saw me."

He strode across the room and vanished out the doo
"I'll try," Bel Iblis murmured after him. Taking a si
from his mug, he tried to think.

Because his erstwhile drinking companion was wrong
The thief wouldn't hand her prize over to the author
ties just like that. Someone cool enough to lift a data
pack in the middle of a crowded tapcafe would also b
cool enough to try to turn a profit from her acquisition
And that meant selling the datapack.

Which left only the question of how to persuade he
to sell to the Rebel Alliance instead of the Empire.

Fishing in his pocket for some coins, he droppe
them onto the table beside his mug and headed for th
door. One thing that *was* certain was that he wasn't go
ing to be able to track her down in a city the size c
Xakrea by himself. That meant someone with conne
tions in the planet's fringe population; and *that* mean
getting in touch with Aach's local contact.

He hoped the man owed Aach a *lot* of favors.

The room was small and dark and sparse, a sharp cor
trast to the bright lights and scrollwork and expensiv
glitter that was the norm throughout the rest of the In
perial Palace. It was a shock to most of the uninitiate
who came into it, and even those who knew what to e:
pect invariably wasted their first few minutes adjustin
their eyes and minds to the contrast.

Which was precisely how Armand Isard liked it. Of
balance people were vulnerable people, and vulner

bility was one of his favorite qualities in enemies and allies alike. For allies, after all, were merely people who had not yet outlived their usefulness to the Empire, the Emperor, and Isard himself.

Ultimately, invariably, all of them did.

His comlink pinged. "Director Isard?" his aide's voice came from the speaker. "Field Operative Isard has arrived."

"Send her in," Armand instructed, allowing himself a smug smile. Not many men, he knew, had daughters who had thrown themselves so willingly and so self-sacrificingly into their father's line of work as had his Ysanne. Already an outstanding Intelligence agent, she had time and again demonstrated a vigor and ruthlessness in her pursuit of the Empire's enemies that had put even some Moffs to shame.

An attitude, fortunately, which was solidly backed up by competence and cleverness and efficiency. Nothing, in Armand's mind, was more contemptible than a shining-eyed Intelligence agent whom smugglers and Rebels alike could fly casual rings around.

The smug smile faded. Clever and efficient, to be sure. But she was going to need every bit of her skill if she was to pull this one out of the fire.

The door slid open. "You summoned me?" Ysanne said gravely from the doorway.

"Sit down," Armand said in the same tone, feeling another flicker of pride as he gestured her toward a chair. No mention of her being his daughter, with the underlying suggestion or invitation of preferential treatment such an acknowledgment might have implied. In this room, in this building, she was an agent and he was her director, and that was the totality of their relationship. "I have an important job for you."

"How important?" she asked as she lowered herself with sinuous grace into the chair.

"It could be a career-maker for you," he said. "It also could be a career-breaker for a large number of others."

Her eyes flickered, just noticeably. She had the Isar
family ambition, too, the same ambition that had take:
Armand himself to the top. "Tell me more."

Armand selected a datacard from a stack on his desk
"An eight-card datapack has been taken to Darkknell,
he said, sliding the datacard across the desk toward he:
"This datapack must at all costs be retrieved."

"Point of origin?"

"The Despayre system," Armand said, watching he
face closely.

Once again, the brief flicker of her eyes showed that hi
long-held suspicion was correct. Despite the most strir
gent of security procedures, Ysanne had somehow man
aged to learn about the Death Star project, even to th
point of knowing where the massive weapon was bein
constructed. "So you understand the seriousness of th
situation," he went on. "Under the circumstances, I ca.
hardly declare an Empirewide state of emergency and se;
the Darkknell system with a ring of Star Destroyers."

"Certainly not for a project that doesn't officially eve·
exist," Ysanne agreed, almost off-handedly. "I presum
that also means you're not sending a full Intelligenc
force with me." Her eyebrows lifted slightly. "Or is ther
more to it than that? Is this theft somehow personal?"

Armand grimaced. "Personal enough," he concedec
"The suspected thief was given his security clearance b
a close associate of mine, a man high up in our depar
ment, who will be in serious trouble if we can't retriev
the datapack before the Rebel Alliance gets hold of i
Or before someone else in Intelligence does."

Ysanne picked up the datacard. "Is the traitor's file i
here?"

"The suspected traitor, yes," Armand said. "Alon
with several possibilities of who the Rebels might send t
pick it up."

Ysanne nodded. "So you want me to retrieve the dat;
pack, confirm the traitor's identity, and capture th
Rebel agent. Is that it?"

Armand suppressed a smile. The famous Isard famil

confidence . . . "Or as much of that as you can manage in the time you'll have," he said. "I've ordered an interdiction of Darkknell's spaceports, but I doubt the local authorities will be able to keep them sealed for very long. Just remember that retrieving the datapack is the most important part of the job."

"Then I'd best get started," she said, sliding the datacard into a tunic pocket. "I presume it's all right for me to take one of my enforcers along."

"If you have to," Armand said. "Make sure it's someone you trust, and don't tell him what it is you're actually after."

"Of course not," she said, standing up. "You'll order me a courier ship?"

"It's already standing by," Armand told her. "Goodbye, and good luck."

She favored him with a faint smile. "The Isards make their own luck," she reminded him softly. "I'll be in touch."

Interlude at Darkknell

PART 2

by Michael A. Stackpole

Hal Horn sighed heavily as the Darkknell Defense Agency officer glanced at his identification card, travel permits, and the warrants he had brought with him. It seemed to Hal that every member of the Xakrea bureaucracy had studied those same datafiles with an intensity that suggested they were digitizing the data and loading it straight into their brains. He had come to Darkknell and specifically the city of Xakrea because the local officials' legendary attention to detail and hatred for disorder made them natural allies in his search for Moranda Savich.

Now I'm not so sure, he thought. He glanced down at the smaller, slighter man. "I think you'll see, Colonel Nyroska, that all my files are in order. All I really want is for you to issue an alert that will have your people looking for my target if she tries to leave the planet."

Nyroska's dark eyes narrowed. "You realize, of course, Inspector Horn, that you have absolutely no jurisdiction here."

"I do know that, but . . ."

"And while we are willing to cooperate with fellow officers of the law, long gone are the days of Jedi vigilantes
traveling hither and thither, chasing miscreants and rendering harsh verdicts right then and there. The days of
lightsaber justice are no more."

"I understand, Colonel." Hal turned partway to the
side, so his height and bulk wouldn't seem to be threatening to the Xakrean. "As per your regulations, I surren-
dered my blaster when I made planetfall and I have no
weapons on me."

"Commendable, Inspector. And I think it good you
remain in civilian clothes, so your presence cannot be
misconstrued." Nyroska hit a button on his datapad,
ejecting the datacard that contained Hal's documents.
He toyed with it for a moment, then held it out to the
Corellian. "Your quarry, this Savich, she is not a violent
criminal? Nothing in her records indicates that she is."

"No, sir. She's just good at liberating valuables from
the unwary."

"A lifter, then?"

"One of the best."

Nyroska stood abruptly, his oversized chair sliding
back. The chair and the huge desk had helped dwarf
Nyroska, but had not needed to work very hard to do so.
He's even smaller than Corran! Hal catalogued that fact
to use the next time his son complained about being
short. The Colonel waved his hand toward the door of
the office.

Hal blinked. "That's it?"

"We really have nothing else to discuss."

"But what about putting the spaceport inspectors on
alert?"

Nyroska gave him an oily smile as he came around
from behind the desk and rested a hand on the small of
Hal's back. "My dear Inspector Horn, our spaceport inspectors are already on alert. We received a request from
Imperial authorities to be on the lookout for Rebel operatives coming here. You witnessed our thoroughness—
you fit the profile we were given. As you can imagine,

this Imperial matter is consuming much of our time. will append this Savich woman's name to the detain lis but unless you can link her to the Rebels, she will be secondary concern."

Hal closed his eyes for a moment and slowly exhale The galaxy had turned upside down in recent years, s much so he hardly recognized it. Imperial authoriti had become obsessed with the Rebellion and, while foll with Rebel sympathies could be found all over the plac on Corellia very few Rebel agents had been discovere He'd heard rumors that Garm Bel Iblis had been co nected to the Rebellion, but he considered most of th rumors the normal fallout of politics. *And with Bel Ib dead, there's no way he can defend himself against such lies.*

Still, those lies had helped brand Hal and every othe Corellian as a potential Rebel agent. While the author ties he had come to for help in finding Moranda Savic were checking him out, she could have been dancin onto any number of ships headed for points unknow Time once was when nabbing someone with her reput tion would have made a man like Nyroska jump for jo but as the Emperor focused more energy on the Rebe lion, priorities shifted.

"It would be easy for me to lie to you, Colonel N roska, and tell you she is the Rebel agent you're lookin for." Hal shook his head slowly. "She isn't—at least, don't know of any Rebel connections she has."

"Thank you for your honesty, Inspector."

Hal paused in the doorway and arched an eyebro above a hazel eye at him. "You didn't expect hones from a Corellian?"

"All I expect of you is respect for our regulations, I spector." Nyroska shrugged uneasily. "These days I nev expect honesty, from anyone."

The Corellian thought for a moment, then nodde "Have to hope for a return to the old days, then, whe those we hunted actually committed crimes. Thanks f your help. I'll let you know when I find her."

. . .

Ysanne Isard glared up at Trabler as her aide finally cleared the Immigration checkpoint. "What detained you?"

He shrugged his massive shoulders. "Profile check, I assume."

She almost snapped that he should not assume anything, but she checked herself. She'd chosen Trabler to accompany her because of his unswerving loyalty to the Empire and because she recalled his wrenching the head off a captive Ithorian with his bare hands. *He is here for his muscle, nothing more. He will do what I tell him to do when I tell him to do it. The blond hair and Corellian background of his cover identity likely did trip the Xakrean profiling system. Their tendency toward being overly thorough will only slow us down, which is why I want no official contact with them.*

"No matter. They're bringing our landspeeder around. You are confident you can navigate?"

Trabler nodded once. "I studied the local maps and always have my datapad to back things up."

"Good." She led the way to the spaceport exit and found a man standing next to a rental landspeeder. He bore a sign that read "Glasc," her assumed surname. She and Trabler made their way over to him, identified themselves, and took possession of the vehicle. As Trabler slipped into the driver's seat, she took her place in the back.

Isard powered up her datapad. "I have the files on Xakrea's fringe population and am getting comlinked updates as the locals flag files. Since the Rebel will undoubtedly be taking refuge among the scum here, we will hunt there as well. Our quarry will want to alter his identity, and there are only a few places that offer such services here. We will begin by checking them."

"As you wish, Special Agent Isard."

"There is one address on East Ryloth Street and another on Palpatine Parkway. Which is closer?"

"Ryloth Street should be." Trabler glanced at her in the mirror. "That would be your preference, then?"

"Indeed." She smiled coldly at the reflection of his eyes. "Anyone who would sell him a new identity will sell him to us. Let's go, we have a lot of shopping to do today."

Hal thanked the hovercab driver and tipped him half-again the fare he'd been charged. "Really, this is it; 24335 East Ryloth Street, right where I want to be."

The Devaronian looked around at the seedy neighborhood and back at Hal again. "West Ryloth is more your kind of place, my friend."

Hal shook his head and jerked a thumb at the curio shop. "Arky is an old friend." He gave the cabbie a conspiratorial wink. "You never saw me, hey?"

"Got it, pal. Never saw you."

The Corellian exited the cab and slammed the door shut. He watched the cab pull away, then stepped over a midden of litter and made his way straight for the shop's transparisteel door. The lettering painted on the door proclaimed the shop to be Arky's Emporium of Forgotten Treasures; Hal figured most of them were forgotten because they had to be excavated from beneath layers of dust. All the items on display in the viewports were sun-faded and cracked, hardly inviting the casual passerby to venture inside.

Not that they get many casual passersby down here, Hal thought. He opened the door and quickly scanned the place. The only other customer glanced quickly in his direction when the door buzzed as Hal opened it, then turned and seemed very interested in not letting Hal get a look at his face. That behavior would have struck Hal as odd, but the customer was likely taking his cue from the way Arky had paled when he recognized Hal.

"Seb Arkos, what a surprise." The Corellian Security

Force officer kept his voice light. "Last I recall, you'd won an all-expenses-paid trip to Kessel."

Seb Arkos snorted. He stood as tall as Hal, but had a skeletally thin build that matched the rheumy grumble that underscored his words. "Yeah, well, glitmining isn't my kind of thing. Out of your range, aren't you, CorSec?"

"I'm hurt, Arky. Here I come all this way to see you, and all I get is hostility." Hal strolled through the store, seeing only a collection of junk. He almost remarked about that fact, but he remembered that his wife had a knack for walking into such a place and rescuing treasures from it. "Dealing in antiques *is* your sort of thing now, or are those delicate hands still forging the best transport and identification documents in the galaxy?"

Arky's smile betrayed him for a second, then he scowled. "I keep my nose clean."

Hal raised opened hands. "Hey, the local snoopers are no friends of mine."

"But you are looking for a friend?"

"Someone I feel about the same way I feel about you, Arky." Hal slipped a static holograph of Moranda Savich from his pocket and flashed it for the forger. "Moranda Savich. Seen her?"

"Moranda Savich?" The slender man tapped a bony finger against his chin. "Moranda Savich?"

Hal jerked a thumb at the store's other customer. "You want me to start asking your clientele?"

Arky's eyes widened, the pale blue communicating a jolt of fear. "No, no need to do that. I seen her around, you know, places."

"She retaining your services?"

The forger shook his head. "Nope, she hasn't asked me to dummy anything up for her."

Hal caught a hint of deceit from the shopkeeper. "Let's not try to slice the truth too thin here. She's talked to you about smuggling her off this rock, right? And you figured you'd nail her for clean datadocs in the process?"

The cadaverous man's eyes narrowed, and a lank of white hair drifted down over his forehead. "Okay, straight bytes, no bits flipped. We talked. She wants to be gone, and you're the reason. She's getting very insistent."

"And you're going to let me know when you're meeting with her next?"

Arky's head came up. "Look, Horn, you know I don't play that way. You set me up to join Booster and the others on Kessel, but I didn't Vader them out, did I? I was loyal to my mates."

Hal shrugged and folded his arms across his chest. "Fine. I can wait here forever. We'll be business partners, you and I. I'll be your silent partner, checking everyone out, at least until you decide not to be silent."

Arky glowered at him, then swiped a hand under his nose. "Okay, maybe she was going to be around. Soon, maybe."

The CorSec inspector nodded. "Good enough. I can wait."

"Outside, hey?"

Hal glanced from Arky to the other man in the store, then saw a woman approaching the door. "Sure. Looks like it will be crowded in here soon anyway. I'll wait outside. She won't see me and will never know it was you."

Across the street, hidden in the shadows of an alley, Moranda Savich smacked an open hand against the wall. Seb Arkos had been the only shadow broker who had been willing to talk with her. The Imperial interdiction had scared everyone else. *Of course, you don't have to be a genius to know a Corellian expatriate wouldn't be smart enough to be afraid of the Imps.* The local authorities were ruled and regged up so badly they had to fill out Kbytes of dataforms before they could even draw a blaster. *Not so the Imps—rumor has it they get bonus pay for saving the state the cost of a trial.*

She wanted to get off Xakrea as fast as possible, and

meeting Seb Arkos the previous evening had seemed a fine stroke of luck—*luck which has soured*. As she headed toward his store to make her arrangements, who should pop out of a hovercab but Hal Horn, as big as life and too damned close for her comfort.

Closest he's gotten so far. A minute later and he would have caught me in that shop. She allowed herself a half smile. *Well, not* all *my luck is bad.*

It hadn't taken Moranda long to put together a few puzzle pieces as events unfolded on Xakrea. She'd used her datapad to take a look at the cards she'd lifted, but they were encrypted. While she was no ace slicer, she knew a few tricks and was able to determine that the files had been coded with some heavy-duty Imperial encryption routines. Given the eight cards in the set, she figured they had to be some fairly extensive military files—military files being the only thing that matched up with the courier's demeanor. The only folks who would want Imp military files would be the Empire's enemies, which meant the Rebellion. The Imperial interdict on the spaceport had a search for Rebels linked to it, confirming her suspicions.

This gave her a brand-new problem, and one that made Hal Horn a decided side issue. Moranda had heard rumors about the Rebellion, passed some on, and marveled at others, but by and large she kept away from being involved. In her line of work the face on the coin really didn't matter much, just the fact that the coin was there and could be lifted. Any government would take a dim view of how she made her living, be it Imperial, local, or whatever these Rebels would put into place. *Those folks worry about laws, where I worry about evading them.*

Having a datapack chock full of Imperial military secrets could easily be construed by local and Imperial forces as a sign that she was a Rebel. She had no idea if the rumors of what the Imps did with captured Rebels were true or not, but she'd prefer an extended stay on Kessel to what she'd heard about. Keeping the datapack was not a good idea, and she knew it. And, she kept telling herself, she was going to ditch it at the earliest opportunity.

And yet there its weight was, in her jacket pocket, slapping against her hip as she crouched down. Someone, she knew, would pay good money for the cards, and that money would take her places Hal Horn couldn't even begin to dream about finding her. She didn't see hanging on to the datacards as a gamble as much as she did a balance. Right now the risk wasn't too great, but when things got unbalanced, she could ditch the datacards.

Right, that's what I'm going to do.

Her self-mocking smile died as a woman got out of a landspeeder farther up the block. The front registration plate had a rental code on it and looked far too new to be in this part of Xakrea unless it was driven by a booster looking to piece it out for parts. The woman spoke to the driver, then set off down the street, heading for Arky's store.

Though the woman wore civilian clothes, Moranda knew she was Imperial, straight from Imperial Center, and that meant she was most probably Imperial Intelligence. The cut of her clothes marked her point of origin, and the haughty way her chin lifted as she navigated past a derelict glitbiter lying up against a building marked her as Imperial. *And she's going straight for Arky, which means Intel, and that means I'm in very deep.*

Ysanne Isard wrinkled her nose at the store's thick scent. She ran a finger across a feline statue carved from Ithorian *toal* wood, then gently brushed her hands against each other to rid her finger of dust. As she did so, she took quick stock of the store and the three men in it. Seb Arkos she recognized from a file on her datapad. The other two men seemed unremarkable until the larger one speaking with Arkos glanced at her.

Horn, from Corellia. CorSec, if the file flashed to me was accurate. It struck her as odd that a man newly arrived on

Xakrea would come so quickly to a known Rebel contact point. *Unless, like Bel Iblis, he's a Rebel, too.* She frowned. Nothing in Horn's file indicated any Rebel sympathies, and Isard dimly recalled his father being a highly placed member of CorSec, one who had been lauded for his diligence in hunting Jedi.

She turned to examine a filthy Weequay chin-harp, knowing full well it could never function without the matching chord hammer, and raised her comlink to her mouth. In a whisper she commanded Trabler to bring the landspeeder up to the store's door. Through the window she caught a hint of movement as he complied with her order, so she pocketed the comlink and walked smartly over to Hal Horn.

"Inspector Horn? I am Katya Glasc of Darkknell Special Security."

A grin blossomed on Arkos's face. "In trouble, Inspector?"

Horn shook his head. "I shouldn't be. Am I, Agent Glasc?"

Though slightly shorter than Trabler, Horn had a powerful build and a metric ton more intelligence in his hazel eyes than Trabler could ever hope for. He wore his brown hair cut conservatively short, and that revealed the gray hairs growing in at his temples. She guessed he was a half-dozen years older than she was, and someone who saw himself as a good man. *Which means he can be useful or very dangerous.*

"That depends. Your identification, please."

Horn carefully drew a datacard from within his jacket, which Isard slipped into her datapad. She glanced at his information and took in the warrants, then nodded and returned the card to him. "I wanted to make certain. Please, forgive the caution. Your investigation, we may have a break in it . . ."

Her head came up, then she frowned. "Perhaps this is not the place to discuss this sort of thing. If you don't mind, I have a speeder waiting outside . . ."

Horn watched her carefully. "You've found Savich?"

"We've found evidence of her presence. I would feel more at ease explaining outside." She hooked a hand through his left elbow, letting it rest lightly enough there to be construed as an invitation, not an order.

The Corellian nodded slowly. "Your world, your rules." He turned back and pointed a finger at the shopkeeper. "Don't let me down, Arky."

"Right, Horn." The thin man scoffed loudly. "I'll have her wait right here for you. You bet."

Garm Bel Ibis suppressed a shudder as Isard led Hal Horn out of the shop. Bel Iblis had been so careful in reaching Arkos's store that when Horn walked in, he felt certain he'd been trapped. Arkos had recognized the inspector right off and had muttered, "Emperor's black bones, CorSec, here," under his breath. Bel Iblis had braced himself not to jump when Horn grabbed him, but the man had just passed him by without so much as a glance.

As Horn started in on Arkos, Bel Iblis had begun to relax. He still had no evidence that anyone was looking for him, or that anyone thought he still lived. The anonymity of death gave him a chance to operate without surveillance, but how long it would last he had no idea. He hoped Arkos would provide him with a good set of documents to allow him to continue his search for the thief on Darkknell and, possibly, even act as a broker for any exchange.

It struck Bel Iblis as possible that Horn could be a Rebel operative sent to Darkknell by Bail Organa and Mon Mothma to recover the datapack, since neither of them knew he was alive and out to get it himself. He had no idea if Horn was a Rebel; Bel Iblis admired the efficient cell system that had been set up to deny all but those who needed to know that sort of information. He hesitated, almost prepared to make his identity known to Horn, but the direction of the CorSec agent's questioning of Arkos made him hold back.

The Senator found himself secretly smiling as Horn

worked on Arkos. One of the most galling things about being a senator from Corellia was dealing with the reputation his system had for its smugglers. Bel Iblis and the majority of the other Corellians were good people, but they were judged by association with others. While Bel Iblis didn't know Hal Horn, he knew plenty of folks like him, who worked hard to make Corellia a better place. His admiration for Horn's dedication to duty spawned his smile.

The arrival of Ysanne Isard killed that smile again. Bel Iblis had only ever met her once, at an Imperial reception. She had been on her father's arm. Bel Iblis detested Armand Isard. A little man with iron eyes and a wiry speed that made Bel Iblis feel clumsy, Armand Isard had ruthlessly ferreted out and destroyed Rebel cells, both real and imagined. His daughter, with her mismatched eyes of fire and ice, had inherited her father's singleness of purpose and, worse yet, had developed a personal devotion to the Emperor. For her to be on Darkknell meant the original theft had been discovered and that Armand Isard was sparing no effort in getting the datapack back in Imperial hands.

A cold chill sank into the Senator's bones as he realized Armand Isard had undoubtedly given the order that slew his family and almost got him. His hands closed into fists, but he didn't lash out; he didn't smash Ysanne Isard in the face with all his might, though he sorely wanted to. *No, even killing her would not hurt her father, and even hurting him is not the focus here. The datapack she's hunting for, that will help bring down the Empire. If we do that, never again will there be a place for an Armand Isard or Emperor to hurt people.*

Gaining control of his anger, Bel Iblis turned to watch the door close behind Isard and Horn. "Well, Arkos, the time we have to complete our business is slipping away. I think we should conclude it before the Emperor himself comes wandering in, don't you?"

·   ·   ·

Moranda Savich saw the landspeeder cruise down and come to a stop in front of the store and felt as if a hand were tightening around her heart. She'd spent a lot of time doing her best to avoid Imperial scrutiny, but that didn't mean she allowed herself to be ignorant of her enemies. Imperial Intelligence ops, as a rule, cast a wide web when going after a target. The fact that she could see the spider in the center of that web meant that other forces were closing in.

And that means I get caught holding a prize morsel. Again the urge to throw the datapack away nearly overwhelmed her. She reached into her pocket to get it, then noticed the landspeeder's driver's-side window sliding down into the door. The bruiser of a driver glanced around, then looked at himself in the rearview mirror. His vanity, which struck her as very human, brought her out of her panic and sparked a plan.

She pulled the datapack out of her pocket, broke it open, and pulled out the eight datacards. She stacked them one on top of another and laid them against the bottom of her datapad. Straightening up, she tugged her jacket into place, then boldly strode over toward the landspeeder. She consulted the map on her datapad a couple of times, looked around, and let a puzzled expression contort her brow.

She'd closed to within three meters before the driver noticed her, and by then she was flashing her datapad at him. "Excuse me, please. I believe I'm lost. Can you help me, please?"

The man's expression eased. "Yeah, I guess maybe I could."

Moranda leaned over and smiled broadly at him. She took the datapad from her left hand into her right and thrust it into the vehicle, stabbing toward the datapad he had mounted in the dashboard holder. "Our maps look different."

The driver studied her map, then his own, taking her datapad into his hands to do so. Moranda crossed her arms and let the datacards in her left hand slip, one by one, down into the window well of the landspeeder's door. She coughed lightly to cover the minute clicks as they descended, and was pretty certain that the driver would take any sounds he heard to be key clicks from the datapad.

The driver handed her back her datapad. "See, this is *East* Ryloth Street. Your map was showing *West* Ryloth Street. You were five kilometers off, that's why you couldn't tell where you were."

"Oh, thank you very much." Moranda studied the datapad, then shook her head and smiled. "I can't tell you what a big help you've been." She backed away from the vehicle and headed off the way she had come, valiantly resisting the urge to burst out laughing. *The prize he came here for is now ten centimeters from him and he has no clue.*

Unable to help herself, Moranda spun around in midstreet, thinking to thank the man again. As she came around, she looked up and locked eyes with Hal Horn.

Seeing Moranda Savich there, in the middle of the street, capering around in a circle like a child, sent a jolt through Hal Horn. He started to move after her, but the Darkknell Security woman's hand became a claw on his arm. Moranda had already turned and begun to run when Hal looked at his escort. "She's getting away."

"Trabler," the woman snapped, "get her."

The driver's door on the landspeeder in front of the store opened and a huge man piled out. Hal knew he was huge not only because he towered over the roof of the landspeeder, but his massive paw dwarfed the blaster he drew from beneath his jacket. Hal recognized it as a Luxan Penetrator, favored by many because of its concealability and the serious power it packed. Most models didn't even have a stun setting and that, combined with a cool sense of lethality rippling off the man, prompted Hal to act.

He took a second to focus, then used a trick his father

had taught him long ago, before the Clone Wars and before the Jedi hunters had come. He pushed his consciousness into Trabler's mind. He saw through Trabler's eyes, watching the Penetrator come up and center itself on Moranda Savich's back. He watched Trabler track her for a second and knew she'd never reach the safety of the alley in time.

Drawing on the Force within himself, he projected a blurred image of Moranda into Trabler's mind.

Trabler's finger tightened on the trigger. A red-gold beam stabbed out and caught Moranda in the shoulder just as she reached the alley. Hal heard her scream and watched her tumble down into a pile of debris. He started to go after her, but Isard held on to him again.

Hal batted her arm away. "What are you doing? She's down, either dead or seriously wounded. I need to check."

The woman's eyes narrowed and though their color did not match, the venom in them did. "We will have the locals find her and bring her to the morgue. We have more important business to attend to."

Hal frowned, wishing he could get a solid read off the woman. His use of the Force had left him a bit drained—it had been far too long since he had done anything that active, and he was grossly out of practice. As a result, he couldn't even get the menace that had to be roaring off Trabler as the man turned and aimed his blaster at Hal. "What's going on here?"

Glasc's face tightened. "I couldn't tell you in there, but we have a Rebel operative on the loose and I need your help in tracking him."

"Look, you got me out here saying you were helping me with my case, and now your man has killed my suspect. I'm not here to hunt Rebels."

Her chin came up. "But you are loyal to the Empire, are you not?"

"I serve CorSec to maintain order, so, yes, I'm loyal to the Empire."

She let her expression soften and her voice dropped

to a conspiratorial whisper. "There are members of Darkknell Special Security who are not, which is why my search is running into trouble. I have to rely on someone from outside my own service—you—to make some headway. I know this is unorthodox, but surely you've resorted to unusual methods to push cases forward before."

"Some, but I don't see that this is any concern of mine, really." Hal shook his head. "My purpose for being here is lying in a heap over there."

"So it might seem, but the Rebel we're after was involved in the assassination of Senator Garm Bel Iblis and his family." The woman's voice became very solemn. "The speech he was to give that night was one in which he was going to denounce the Rebellion. They murdered him so that wouldn't happen. I thought that you, a Corellian, might want to help us find his killer."

Hal shivered and felt his flesh puckering. As much as he couldn't believe the casual way Trabler had shot Moranda—nothing in her file warranted death as a punishment—the idea of a bomber who killed hundreds of people just to get one man filled him with revulsion. *If Bel Iblis's assassin is here, he must be found and brought to justice. Bel Iblis was from Corellia. I owe it to him to help find his killer.*

The CorSec inspector nodded. "Okay, I'm in." He leveled a finger at Trabler. "Just no shooting first, okay? If your suspect murdered Bel Iblis, we want him to talk and lead us back to the others involved in the Rebellion, right?"

Glasc nodded, then opened the landspeeder's rear door. "After you, Inspector Horn. With your help, our quarry won't get away."

As the landspeeder sped off, Bel Iblis stumbled from the shop and ran across the street. He'd seen the woman's senseless murder and though he would not have questioned the truth of someone reporting Ysanne Isard had ordered such a thing, to see it unfold before him was another thing entirely. Reaching the alley mouth he saw blood and, just for a moment, he expected to follow the trail and find his wife at the end of it.

No, she's gone. Poor Arrianya, you died for a cause you didn't even believe in. Bel Iblis choked back the lump rising in his throat, then looked deeper into the dim alley and saw the woman slumped against a wall. Her right arm hung limply at her side, the sleeve of her coat soaked in blood. A cigarra hung from the corner of her mouth, and she kept trying to strike a lighter with her blood-slicked left hand.

The woman looked over at him and grinned. "Got a spark, pal?" Then her eyes rolled up in her head and she collapsed.

The senator ran to her and knelt at her side. *The only virtue of being shot with a Penetrator is that the tiny beam makes a neat hole.* Bel Iblis saw a nasty entry wound and a smaller exit on the front side of her shoulder. He stripped off his own coat and wrapped it around the wounds, then lifted her in his arms and started back toward Arkos's store.

It occurred to him that the last woman he had carried in his arms like this had been his wife, on an anniversary getaway several years earlier. It had been a wonderful time, an escape from the pressures of his office and her duties, and they had both told each other that they would do it again, soon. *Very soon.*

Bel Iblis's expression hardened. *I lost her to the Empire; I'm not losing anyone else.* He knew, given the course the Rebellion would likely take, that resolution would never hold. *Well, at least I won't lose this woman. It's not saving the galaxy, but it's saving the part of it I can, and that works for now.*

He looked up as Arkos held the shop's door open. "We need to get her some medical help—now. That woman was Ysanne Isard, late of Imperial Center and employed by Imperial Intelligence."

"If she's here . . ." Terror choked off Arkos's voice.

The senator put steel into his voice. "Hang with me, Arkos. She's not invincible—she walked right past me, remember, and snagged someone who's got nothing to do with our business. Keep your head and we'll all keep ours."

Arkos thought for a moment, then nodded quickly. "You're right. Thanks."

"Not a problem. Let's get things going." Bel Iblis smiled. "There will come a point when Isard realizes she needs to come back here and complete her business with you. By then I want everything we need to do done, and the only thing left for her here is our laughter at her blunder."

Interlude at Darkknell

PART 3

by Michael A. Stackpole

Hal Horn's afternoon sojourn with Agent Glasc and her aide, Trabler, made one thing abundantly clear to him. These two, as efficient as they might be as investigators, were not part of Darkknell Special Security, not even whatever they might call their internal investigations bureau. *They have all the arrogance I'd expect from the Isk-isk division, but it's usually only displayed to Hutted-up cops, not civilians.*

Glasc had moved Hal from location to location, proclaiming each to be a suspected Rebel contact site. Most were sleazy little holes like Arky's store, but a couple had been more upscale and toward the west side of Xakrea. The gourmet caf shop where Hal and Trabler waited outside on either side of the door was one of the more prosperous places. Hal had enjoyed the rich aroma of the small shop, and had reluctantly agreed to wait outside as the owner took Glasc into her private office to discuss things.

Hal arched an eyebrow at Trabler. "Hard to believe the owner didn't think we'd fit in with the clientele."

The bigger man frowned, causing his blond brows to kiss each other above his nose. "You think we look like Rebels?"

Hostility poured through Trabler's voice and Hal was perfectly glad his Force senses were a bit tired, since it saved him the full force of the anger rolling off the guy. "Easy, my friend, I didn't mean to suggest that at all. You know as well as I do that the Rebel tag on this place was likely snitched by the other caf shop around the corner. Customers here seem a bit too prosperous to be Rebels."

"Think so, do you?" Trabler snorted coldly. "You'd be surprised at how highly some Rebels are placed. Then again, maybe you wouldn't."

"And that's supposed to mean?"

"Means one can't be too sure who's gone over or not." Trabler half smiled. "The Core Worlds have their share of Rebels, sure, but rimkin have more."

"Interesting point." Hal let a pair of women exiting the shop shield him from Trabler. The last time Hal had heard the word "rimkin" used, he had broken up a fight in a Corellian tapcafe where a local had beaten someone from Imperial Center to a pulp for applying such an insulting term to him. *Not too many rim-dwellers apply that word to themselves.*

The door opened again and Agent Glasc appeared. She was daubing a white handkerchief against a dark spot on her gray blouse. "She was useless. Broke down and blubbered about evading taxes, but she knows nothing about the Rebellion. Or the plot against Bel Iblis."

Trabler glanced at his datapad, then pointed on down the street. "Continuum Void is next on the list. It's that way."

Hal took the lead and found Glasc quickly pacing beside him. "The owner didn't react to any of the holographs you showed her?"

Glasc shook her head. "Ignorant, completely ignorant, as was her staff. Places like this claim to bring the latest in Imperial culture to Darkknell, but it's only what they imagine really goes on at the heart of the Empire. I mean, Corellia is a Core World—did you think the Corellian blend caf was the sort of thing you'd drink at home?"

"Well, no, but that's because at CorSec we brew it strong enough to be used for medicinal purposes." Hal shrugged. "When doing a rimstint I try not to let the indigs and their ways get to me, you know?"

"You're very charitable, Inspector Horn."

Hal smiled. "I try to be." The fact that Glasc didn't react at all when he referred to the citizens of Darkknell as "indigs" or his time on the world as a "rimstint," told him very clearly she wasn't the local she was purporting to be. *A local could no more have failed to react than Moranda could give up her cigarras. Something is not right here, and I'm not looking forward to finding out how wrong it's become.*

Trabler moved ahead and opened the door to the crowded tapcaf. Hal descended the trio of steps to the serving floor, then worked his way around past a table of boisterous Devaronians. He wanted to reach the bar before Glasc did. He managed to delay her by tapping a Devaronian on the shoulder. As the man swung his head around to see who had touched him, a horn snagged Glasc's uniform tunic, slowing her down.

Hal spotted a small man wearing a name tag that proclaimed him to be the manager and moved to intercept him before the guy could head through a doorway leading into an office marked "Private." "I'm Inspector Horn; these are Agents Glasc and Trabler. We have some questions for you. Do you want to answer them now, or *after* we lock this place down and have it searched for contraband?"

The little man gulped air audibly, and coughed half of it back up. "I don't want trouble."

Hal half turned toward Glasc. Her glare had only been partially melted by the way he'd braced the man. "Agent Glasc here has some holographs for you to look at." Hal held his hand out, and she gave them to him, then he fanned them in front of the manager. "Recognize anyone?"

The man gave them a cursory glance. "No, I don't think I do."

Hal settled his left hand on the man's right shoulder. "Look, pal, I'm just trying to give you a chance to help yourself here. The surveillance team we've got on this place has pointed out to us which of these guys has actually been through here. Now you confirm their information and answer more questions, or we send you away for obstructing justice. We can still send him to Kessel for that, right, Agent Glasc?"

Glasc nodded, her expression getting cold. "For a long time."

The little man shivered. "Kessel? I don't even know what that is."

"And that's the way you want to keep it, friend. Look at the holographs again, closely."

The man did, running a finger across the surface of each. The manager didn't let recognition flash through his eyes on any of them. Even so, with his hand on the man's shoulder, Hal could feel the tiny twitches of shoulder muscle that marked each pause over an image. Three of the five guys had actually been in the place, but the longest pause had come over the center picture, the one of the short blond guy with a military-style haircut.

The manager blinked. "I'm not sure."

"Let me help you." Hal shuffled the blond's picture to the top of the pack, then plucked it off the top and smacked it against the man's forehead. He did so with a bit more gusto than he wanted to, but the fact that the man's head bumped against the wall eased Glasc's scowl and, after all, Hal was playing more to appease her than anything else.

"This guy was in here and you remember him. How recently?"

"Um, um, yesterday maybe, no, wait, this morning. Early. Only the habituals in that early, you know?" The manager aped Hal's growing smile. "He was waiting for someone, but then he burst into flames."

Glasc pounced on that remark. "Burst into flames?"

The manager winced at the sharp tone in her voice. "Well, he was sitting there, then this woman with a drink and cigarra tripped and spilled the drink on him. Cigarra caught it on fire, I guess. She helped him put it out and he was okay."

Hal gave the man's shoulder a squeeze. "Great, and what else do you remember?"

"Well, when the guy he was waiting for showed, they talked and the blond guy there, he got agitated. He said he'd been robbed, then he took off like he'd stolen Vader's cloak, you know?"

Glasc narrowed her eyes and glanced at Hal. "Whatever he had was lifted, you figure? The woman who set him on fire must have it. What did she look like?"

The pink tip of the manager's tongue wormed its way over dry lips. "Well, she wasn't that tall, and she had brown hair. . . ."

Hal shook his head. "This is ridiculous. I have a holograph for you to look at." He reached into his pocket and slipped a holograph from his wallet, then pulled it out. He ripped the blond man's holograph from the manager's forehead and tossed it to Glasc, then showed the other holo to the manager. "Was this her?"

The manager shook his head. "Never seen her before in my life."

I should hope not. My wife wouldn't be caught dead in a place like this. Hal shrugged and slipped the holograph back into his pocket. "Thank you for your help. You're free to go."

The man scurried off as Glasc grabbed Hal's shoulder and spun him toward her. "What do you mean dismissing him?"

"Forgive me for preempting your investigation, but you know this lead was a complete bust. We're looking for the person who killed Bel Iblis, right? Well, what assassin sits around in some dump tapcaf like a jewel thief waiting for a fence? I've no doubt your pretty boy there is guilty of something, but he was a rank amateur if he got lifted the way he did. And a lifter that good has likely already put plenty of hyperspace between her butt and this rock."

Trabler frowned. "The assassin was waiting to get paid."

Hal rolled his eyes. "Then what was lifted? Proof he'd killed Bel Iblis? I would have thought the galaxywide broadcast of the state funeral on Corellia would have pretty much been taken as proof. Moreover, an assassin that good would have demanded at least partial payment up front, so he'd never have to dive to these depths again. We should be looking on some luxury resort world, not here."

Hal watched Glasc and saw her eyes flicker back and forth for a moment. He expected panic to roll off her, but he caught none of it. *Which means my Force reserves are absolutely gone, or she's just that good at self-control.* Her whole cover story, thought up on the fly as Trabler shot Moranda down, was falling apart, and Trabler's spackle job had only pointed out how absurd it had been from the start. Whatever they were really here searching for had been brought to Darkknell by the blond and lifted by Moranda. The fact that these two reeked of Core World arrogance suggested to Hal that they were most likely Imperials.

Hal shook his head. *And that means both Moranda—if she's even alive—and I are in far deeper than we ever wanted to be.*

Garm Bel Iblis looked around the threadbare apartment as Moranda gingerly shrugged on a new blouse and jacket. Her living quarters were little more than a box with a window and a small refresher station walled away toward the rear, right beside the closet in which she rooted about for clothes. He didn't see much there that made him think this was a place she'd lived long-term—and before congratulating himself on his deductive ability, he did recall that a CorSec inspector had come looking for her, which meant she'd been on the run.

The room, he thus decided, was one of those places that was the underworld's equivalent of a safe house. Governments used safe houses as places where they could hide a witness before a trial or house a spy during debriefing. There were little bits and pieces of stuff here—mismatched glowlamps, a half-dozen periodical datacards, a melange of sheets and blankets that covered a thin pad laid down out of sight of the window— that had probably been left behind by previous criminal tenants.

Now that I'm full into the Rebellion, I guess this will be the sort of place I'll be spending my time in, too.

"The place isn't much, I know. Neither am I." Moranda emerged from the closet wearing a vibrant blue tunic and a dark brown coat over it. She eased her right shoulder around in a tiny circle and almost totally suppressed the grimace that resulted. "There, good as new."

"A bacta bath would make you good as new."

"True, but the shot mostly just roasted meat—lots of aches but no breaks. Besides those Emdee droids have a nasty habit of reporting blaster burns to the authorities." Moranda eyed him closely. "Seeing as how you're a Rebel, I don't think you'd want that sort of scrutiny."

Bel Iblis stiffened, quite involuntarily, then narrowed his eyes. "How did you guess?"

"No guess about it." She tapped a finger against her temple. "First, you cared to come find me, and it wasn't to pick over my bones. Compassion is rare these days and the Rebels seem to have a lock on it. Second, you came even though you were smart enough to know the folks who shot me were probably Imperial Intelligence."

Bel Iblis nodded. "The woman was Ysanne Isard, Armand Isard's daughter."

Moranda's eyes grew wide at that, then she shivered. "I knew this was tricky business, but just how tricky . . ."

"What else made you think I'm a Rebel?"

"Arky has a rep. You're clearly a Corellian and *all* Corellians hate taking orders. The patch job you did on me suggests you've done your time in the military, which helps breed loyalty to the way it was before Palpatine got greedy. Finally, if the Imps are sniffing around for something, the folks opposing them are likely to be Rebels."

"Really?" Bel Iblis let the question linger for a moment. "Perhaps I'm Black Sun."

"Ha! There's that compassion thing, remember?"

"Hmmm, good point." Bel Iblis thought for a moment. "What makes you think the Imps are sniffing around for some *thing* and not some *one*?"

"Well, I could tell you I deduced that from the fact that Iceheart's daughter is here. For wet work they'd just send out a bunch of her drivers. She's presumably got brains, so they must want to ask questions before they shoot."

"Save in your case."

"Hey, that's a better shot than he got in." Moranda gave Bel Iblis a lopsided smile. "Fact is, I lifted something from a nervous young man here and it has Imperial property—*important* Imperial property—coded all over it. That was what you were sent to pick up, wasn't it?"

Bel Iblis shrugged as casually as he could manage. "Can you prove you were the thief?"

She nodded and pulled a black scarf from the pocket of her jacket. "The packet I exchanged for the one I stole had the mate of this tying it up all nice and pretty. Recognize it?"

He reached out and ran a thumb over the material. "Where's the package now?"

She laughed. "Not so fast, Reb. I'm grateful for the patch on my arm, but I'd like the resources to leave this mudball and get far away from Hal Horn. What's it worth to you?"

"Twenty-five thousand credits."

"How about fifty?"

"Sold."

Moranda's eyes widened again. "That valuable, eh? Can we work some bonus pay in here, too?"

"Where is it?"

She hissed and Bel Iblis felt his heart tighten. "In a very safe place."

"And that would be?"

"The reason I want to know about bonus pay." She shook her head. "I slipped the datacards into the door of Isard's rental speeder. I can see that surprises you, but don't worry. Challenges like that, they always bring out the best in me."

Hal sat alone in the back of the speeder as Glasc drove them to her operational center. Back at the Continuum Void she'd pulled Trabler aside and given him orders that sent him off on his own. She told Hal that Trabler was going to head to the spaceport to check on how things were running there, but he doubted she was telling the truth. Any information Trabler could learn in person could just as easily have been given to her over a comlink.

Hal paid little attention to the world passing in a blurred palette outside the speeder's viewports. He found himself wondering what had prompted him to show the tapcafe's day manager the holo of his wife instead of Moranda's holo. *I recognized Moranda from the description the second he started in on it—the cigarra used to roast the blond was a giveaway—but why did I protect her? Now I know she's involved, and that kills the assassin story dead. We have a simple lift from a thief here, but the presence of Imps suggests it's not that simple at all.*

By not showing the man the correct holo, Hal had killed the only solid investigative lead Glasc had. He assumed, because she was an Imp, and because she questioned his loyalty right up front, the quarry she was after was connected to the Rebellion somehow. Hal Horn had no love for the Rebels—they put themselves on the wrong side of the law and that was enough to earn his opposition—but he wasn't much crazier about the Imps. More than once he'd tried to rein in the excesses of overzealous Imperial operatives, which generally resulted in his having to clean up after them.

Trabler's actions were a perfect example of the sort of excesses he wanted to avoid. He could have easily run after Moranda and grabbed her. Instead he gave no warning, he just drew his blaster and shot. Hal hoped his messing with Trabler's aim prevented Moranda's death, but he pretty much assumed she was either dead, dying, or severely incapacitated.

Trabler's willingness to shoot to kill someone who, while not innocent, clearly was a bystander in the whole situation, told Hal that the Empire wasn't looking to take any prisoners. Whatever Moranda had lifted had to be very important—covering state secrets, no doubt. *And if I know that much, I have to assume my life may be forfeit at some point—whenever I've exceeded my usefulness, or I become enough of an annoyance.*

That realization didn't bring with it panic. Yes, Hal felt worried and hated the idea of never seeing his wife or son again, but a sense of calm overrode his emotions. He remembered back to when he was very young, not more than six, and had thrown a temper tantrum over a toy that had been broken. His father took him back out into the yard and told him that he couldn't let his emotions run wild that way, that it disturbed the universe. His father began to teach him simple exercises to calm himself and drilled Hal until they became second nature.

Calm, he could think, and he did so as Glasc slid the speeder to a halt before the door of a small house. Shrubbery screened it from the other nearby houses. An alley ran up the left side and seemed to connect via a gate to an alley or street at the back of the property. The place immediately registered to Hal as a safe house, and while he could imagine someone with Darkknell Special Security using one for her headquarters, the isolated nature of the building—despite its being in the city—made him uneasy.

Glasc unlocked the door and entered first, then shu
the door and headed down a narrow corridor throug
the kitchen toward an extension that jutted out from th
rear of the house. "This way; my office is back here."

Hal followed closely on her heels. She turned to sa
something to him as they moved into the kitchen, bu
her attempt to rivet his attention to her did not con
pletely work. A half second before Trabler emerge
from behind a door and dropped his hands on the bac
of Hal's neck, Hal sensed his presence and acted.

Hal fell to his knees and curled his body forward
forcing Trabler to bend over to maintain his grip. As th
Imperial op tightened his hands, Hal straightened u
and came up on one knee. He drove the back of his hea
into Trabler's face, producing all sorts of snappin
sounds that he was pretty sure were not his skull. Trable
yelped and released him, raising his hands to cover hi
shattered face. Hal twisted to the right, scything his righ
leg back through Trabler's ankles. The big man stag
gered, overturning a table, then crashed down.

Hal snaked a hand inside Trabler's jacket and dre
the guard's Luxan Penetrator. He snapped the safet
switch off with his thumb and triggered a quick shot a
Glasc. She ducked back with blaster in hand, firing
shot that shattered a plate on a shelf just past Hal's hea
Hal dove to his right and came up in a crouch. Behin
him Trabler, whose face was a mask of blood, had draw
a vibroblade from his boot and was scrambling to hi
feet. Hal drilled him dead center, burning out his hear
then ducked back where the food storage unit coul
give him cover.

Glasc triggered a shot that punched through the sto
age unit. "That won't protect you."

"Didn't figure it would." Hal fished the holo c
Moranda from his pocket and tossed it into the middl
of the floor. He let Glasc see it, then he fired a shot tha
melted it into a burning black bubble. "That will."

"What are you talking about?"

"You Intel types always think you're on top of th

game, but I make my living sorting truth from lies, and I've sorted enough here to know that you're here looking for something a Rebel op stole. He was the blond, and a lifter took whatever he was carrying. She has it now, and that was the holo of her."

"And you think that because you've destroyed that holo that I'll have to keep you alive to identify her?" Glasc's laughter filled the kitchen. "The warrants you brought here to Darkknell for her arrest will yield another holo of her." She punctuated her comment with another shot that spattered hot metal over Hal's jacket.

"Moranda Savich is a master of disguise, so you won't find her. More important, though, your man Trabler probably killed her. I'd guess that part of the task you sent him off on was to find out if the local police or hospitals had reported her being recovered, right? They didn't, which means she's out there and probably has help."

"And this will keep you alive why?"

"Because I know her. I've tracked her across a half-dozen worlds. I know how she operates; I know what she looks like in myriad disguises. Without me you'll never find her—or, if you do, it won't be in *time*." He stressed the last word to put pressure on the agent, since the desperate measures already employed told him time was of the essence in the recovery of whatever Moranda had stolen. "Give her a chance to catch her breath, and she'll have the prize sold to the Rebels."

"I don't know that I can trust you to help me."

"Ah, excuse me, but I'm the one here who has trust problems, given that your aide tried to tear my head off." Hal shook his head. *Pare-Imp-noia! Just never seems to stop.* "Believe it or not, I actually *want* to catch Moranda. You're my best bet for doing that. The alternative is for me to shoot you dead and hope I can evade an Imperial murder warrant. I help you, you say Trabler's weapon discharged accidentally, and we're both in the clear."

"You're right, of course. You could never escape a warrant for my murder." A very confident note entered her voice and sent chills down Hal's spine. "I am Ysanne Isard, the daughter of the director of Imperial Intelligence. You would be hunted forever and your family would disappear."

"Pleased to make your acquaintance." Hal sighed as quietly as he could. *It couldn't get much worse, could it?*

"And you are correct. I am here hunting a Rebel courier. He stole . . ."

"Don't tell me; I don't want to know. If you told me you'd have to kill me." Hal closed his eyes for a moment. "I'm here to catch a thief, and that thief has your property. I get her, you get it, I don't need to know what it is."

"Very good, very smart of you." She hesitated for a moment and Hal wanted to cringe for reasons he could not identify. "I am almost inclined to trust you, but because I don't have a full security profile on you, I will demand one condition to our alliance."

"That being?"

A thin, black, ribbonlike device rolled across the floor and unfolded as it came to rest on its side. It looked like a tiny belt with a black clasp, and Hal recognized it immediately as choke-collar. When snapped around his neck it could be given a remote command to constrict, cutting off the bloodflow to his brain, rendering him unconscious. They were often used to restrain prisoners on work details. A constriction override command pulsed out from a central control unit, so the collar constricted when prisoners moved out of range and put a quick end to escapes.

Hal picked it up and let it dangle from one hand. "You'll have the control unit and it will be a dead-man device?"

"If I give a command or my pulse stops, the collar constricts. Without a key, or without trusting someone to shoot it off your neck, you'll be dead shortly after I am."

Hal didn't want to put the collar on, but shooting her and then living a life on the run seemed to be his only alternative. "A lightsaber ought to be able to cut through this."

"Perhaps, but the Jedi are all gone. The age of Imperial Justice is here, Hal Horn."

"Of that I'm well aware." Hal slipped the collar on, snapped it closed, then raised the collar on his shirt to hide it. He tossed out the Penetrator and slowly stood. "Here I am, at your service."

Isard appeared and flashed him a quick glimpse of the control device, then holstered her blaster. "We resume our search at the place I first met you."

"Don't bother. Arky will be long gone. He knew you were Imp Intel long before I did." Hal smiled. "Back to the Continuum Void. It's the only place that stocked Gralish liqueur and Moranda's a fiend for it. Having been shot the way she was, she'll be wanting some fortification. That's the best place to begin."

Interlude at Darkknell

PART 4

by Timothy Zahn

What are you talking about?" Isard demanded, the already wintry tone of her voice dropping into subzero territory as she leaned a few centimeters further over the Continuum Void's bar. "He was here two hours ago. Where in this vat of rimspit could he have gone?"

"I don't know, Agent Glasc," the nervous-looking Devaronian standing on the far side of the bar stammered, twitching his way backward the same few centimeters Isard had moved forward. "As the Emperor himself is my witness, I truly do not know. All I can tell you is that he received a call half an hour ago, told me to handle the bar for the rest of the day, and then took off like Vader himself was after him. That's all I know. I swear."

"It probably is," Hal murmured from Isard's side, all his senses focused on the Devaronian. The species was easy enough to read if you knew what to look for. Hal did. "Offhand I'd say our quarry's been busy cleaning up a few loose ends."

"He has no idea what a loose end really is," Isard said acidly, her smoldering eyes still pinning the hapless barman to the wall. But there was a subtle change in her tone, enough for Hal to recognize that the focus of her anger had shifted from the Devaronian to Moranda. To Moranda, and her as-yet-unidentified accomplice.

And that one was starting to worry Hal a little. Fine if it was some fellow criminal, either an old friend or a new acquaintance—dangerous enough, but at least fringe types were a relatively known psychological type. But under the circumstances, her ally could instead be a member of the Rebellion.

And *that* was another vat of vinks altogether. As the late and unlamented Trabler had pointed out, Rebels came in all sizes and shapes, with profiles that ranged from opportunistic to fanatical. Fringe criminals generally avoided killing law enforcement officials unless absolutely necessary, if only because it drew too much attention their direction. All too often, in contrast, fanatics reveled in both the violence and the notoriety.

Bad enough if some loose-laser Rebel shot him through the back for no reason.

Worse if a Rebel shot Isard instead, and her dead body was the last thing Hal wound up seeing as her choke-collar squeezed the life out of him.

"Fine," Isard said, interrupting Hal's increasingly unpleasant line of thought as she straightened back up from her interrogator's lean. "If she spun him a story that he fell for that easily, it almost certainly had something to do with a relative or friend. I want their names. All of them. Now."

The Devaronian gulped. "I—of course. Let me get his profile chart."

Sidling down the bar, he escaped into the manager's office. "Waste of time," Hal murmured, turning around to lean his shoulder blades against the bar as he glanced over the handful of patrons. A mixture of simple workers and less simple fringe types, he decided, fairly typical of places like this. "Even if we find him, and even if he got a good look at Moranda, she's had more than enough time to change her appearance by now."

"The fact she and Arkos thought the manager important enough to chase out of town implies *they're* reasonably concerned about it," Isard pointed out.

"Possibly," Hal said. "Except that I don't think it's Arkos who's running around with her."

"Why not?" Isard argued. "He was right there at the scene. Probably even saw Trabler shoot her."

"Which is exactly why it wasn't him," Hal said. "I know Arkos, and he's emphatically not the type to get mixed up with a shooting. At least not without some serious pushing from someone else."

Isard grunted. "Fine; so she's picked up someone else. The point is that in setting up this wild skipper hunt they had to come at least part of the way out of the sideboards. If we can chase down the manager and backtrack the story they spun for him, we might be able to get another vector on them."

"I see," Hal murmured, throwing a sideways look at Isard's profile. It was a reasonable approach, all right, classic in its straightforwardness.

Unfortunately, it also required a data-sifting team that would stretch halfway to Coruscant to pull it off. If she really had that much manpower here to draw on . . .

"Don't worry, we're not going to do it all ourselves," Isard continued, not bothering to look at him. Apparently, she was no slouch at reading people's expressions, either. "There's an Intelligence quiet-drop tucked away in one of the better parts of town where I can tap into Darkknell Security's computers. A few properly placed orders, and the locals will have the manager's complete list of acquaintances tracked down by nightfall."

"Um," Hal said, thinking back to his own earlier interactions with Darkknell officialdom. "You'd better hope they don't tumble to what you're doing," he warned her mildly. "Colonel Nyroska, for one, struck me as something of a stickler for proper protocol. Forged orders don't exactly come under that heading."

"Colonel Nyroska will do what he's told," Isard said

oldly, dismissing Nyroska with the flick of an eyelash. That goes for the rest of this rabble, too."

And for me, too, I suppose? Hal added silently, feeling with fresh awareness and fresh resentment the soft pressure of the choke-collar against his throat. A rhetorical question—of course it went for him, too. He was just one more of her tools, after all, like Darkknell Security and Trabler and probably dozens of others whose broken lives lay scattered about in the dust of her wake. Maybe even hundreds, if the whispered stories about Armand Isard and his ambitious daughter were to be believed.

He eyed her profile again. Yes, he was a tool. But then, so was a lightsaber; and many was the overconfident would-be Jedi impersonator who had carelessly sliced off one of his own major limbs. Sometimes mishandled tools could be very dangerous.

Something to keep in mind.

The small man Moranda had pointed out heaved his travel bag into the transport's cargo area and then climbed into the passenger compartment, a vague sense of discomfort evident in the twitchiness of his movements. "He's getting aboard," Bel Iblis announced, lowering his macrobinoculars as a fresh twinge of guilt tugged at him. "Though what he's going to think when he gets to Raykel—"

"Keep watching the transport," Moranda interrupted him, her voice sounding distracted. "Make sure he's still aboard when it leaves. Anyway, what's the problem? He ought to be relieved when he finds out his father wasn't actually in any accident."

"I suppose so," Bel Iblis said, throwing a scowl at her. Seated at the apartment's battered dining table, frowning at a datapad, she was unfortunately oblivious to scowls at the moment. "On the other hand, this wild skipper hunt isn't going to come cheap for him."

"Life never has been fair," she said. "If you're worried about it, have your Rebel friends reimburse him."

Bel Iblis snorted. "The Rebellion is hardly a bottomless money pit—"

"The transport, Garm," she said, jabbing a finger toward the window without looking up. "Watch the transport."

Swallowing back a curse, Bel Iblis turned to the window and raised the macrobinoculars again. Over the past few days he'd managed to force back the sharp agony of his family's deaths into a duller ache, a quiet pain that colored every waking minute but which at least left him able to function reasonably well.

But "reasonably well" didn't mean there wasn't an edge of impatience and bitterness to his attitude, an edge this casually arrogant little thief forever seemed to be stepping on. It was a constant battle to keep from blowing up in her face over what under normal circumstances he would have shrugged off as minor personality conflicts.

But it was an effort he had to make. An effort he forced himself to make. He needed her help to retrieve that datapack, to get this vital information that could conceivably make or break the Rebellion. And besides, his black mood wasn't her fault.

Three blocks away, the transport shuddered into motion and lumbered its way down the street. "There it goes," he announced to Moranda, turning back to her again. "And he didn't get off."

"Good," she said, setting aside her datapad with an air of satisfaction, taking a draw on her cigarra, and pulling out her comlink. "He wouldn't have been much use to your friend Isard anyway, but this should give her people something to do while we stir the kettle a bit."

"Which means what?"

"Which means it's time to give the law a call," she said. "I've pulled a likely name off your pal Arkos's private list of incorruptible enforcement types. Let's hope he's also got the smarts to jump the direction we want him to."

She keyed the comlink and held it up. There was a moment's pause—"Nyroska," a crisp voice came from the instrument.

"Hello, Colonel," Moranda said. "You don't know me, but I have a small problem here and I thought you might be able to help."

Nyroska's sigh was just barely audible. "If you'll call your local Security office—"

"I have in my possession a very valuable and politically explosive item," Moranda interrupted him. "An item the Imperial Intelligence officer currently nosing around town very badly wants."

There was the briefest pause. "You're misinformed," Nyroska said. "There are no Imperial Intelligence agents on Darkknell."

"Let's not play games, Colonel," Moranda said, putting some huffiness into her voice. "You and I both know she's here. Frankly, she's pretty hard *not* to spot, what with that blond muscle-type and his Luxan Penetrator running interference for her. She's all over Xakrea, shaking the trees for a wayward Imperial datapack."

"I see," Nyroska said. His tone was studiously neutral, but Bel Iblis could hear the growing interest beneath it. "I take it the datapack is the valuable item you spoke of?"

"It is, indeed," Moranda confirmed. "Under normal circumstances, I'd get in touch with her directly to work out an exchange. Two problems: I don't have her comlink frequency, and I don't like the idea of Blondie and his Luxan lurking around the background. So I'd prefer to work the exchange through you."

"I don't know anything about Imperial agents on Darkknell," Nyroska said, his voice hardening. "But if you're in possession of stolen or misappropriated goods, the smartest thing you can do is bring everything to Defense Agency headquarters and turn it in."

"Okay by me," Moranda said. "You'll have the million ready?"

"The what?"

"The million," Moranda repeated. "That's in Impe
rial currency, by the way, not the local stuff."

"You *must* be joking," Nyroska said stiffly.

"Do you hear me laughing?" Moranda countered.
"Trust me, Colonel, a million doesn't even begin to
mark what this is worth. The Imps will be willing to buy i
from you for two million. The Rebellion, if you can find
them, will probably pay three. But don't take my word
for it—talk to the Imp and see what she says. Of course
if you turn all this over to her she'll probably cut you ou
of the profits; but hey, virtue is its own comfort, right?"

"And what makes you think an Imperial Intel agen
won't just laugh in my face? Assuming she's not just a fig
ment of your imagination."

"Oh, she's here," Moranda assured him. "And she
won't be laughing. Believe me."

Another pause. "All right, I'll make some inquirie
and see what I can find out. How do I get in touch with
you?"

"I'll call you," Moranda told him. "Remember: one
million even. Just pass on that message, and then if you
want you can be out of it."

She clicked off. "Now what?" Bel Iblis asked.

"Like I said, we hope he's smart," she said, getting up
from the table and putting away both her comlink and
datapad. "And on the assumption that he is, we vacate
the premises. Now."

For a moment Nyroska glared at the dead comlink. *Jus.
pass on that message,* the words echoed in his ears, *and
then you can be out of it.* "Not likely," he murmured to him
self. "Not flighty likely."

He looked across the room at his aide. "Lieutenant?"

"Got it, Colonel," Lieutenant Barclo reported briskly.
"It came from one of the apartments in the Karflian
Nestling block—fringe and lower-class mix, northern
end of town. I've got an airspeeder squad on its way."

"Send two more squads in as backup," Nyroska or

ered. "Then check and see if we've got Imperial Intel
perating on Darkknell at the moment."

"I'm sure we'd have heard if anyone declared him or
erself, Colonel."

"We certainly should have," Nyroska agreed grimly.
As I said: check."

"Yes, sir."

Nyroska set down his comlink and swiveled his chair
oward the large holo map of the city behind him. If
here was a foreign operative running through his city
ehind his back, he wanted to know about it.

And if said agent was chasing down something worth
million or more in Imperial currency, he most *definitely*
anted to know about it.

Accessing the spaceport's database, he pulled up the
ecent arrivals section and keyed for a search.

he manager's profile chart was short. Amazingly short.
uspiciously short.

"Sad, isn't it," Isard said contemptuously as Hal fin-
shed scanning through it.

"And they always think they're not blindingly obvious
o us."

"They do indeed," Hal agreed, handing back the data-
ad. The "personal" section of the manager's profile
ad exactly twelve names in it: parents, one brother, and
ine friends. There were Corellian fungal colonies that
ad longer associates lists than that. "Still, just because
e's gimmicking his associates list doesn't mean he has
ny particular involvement with Moranda."

"He's fringe," Isard said flatly. "That list practically
creams it. And fringe types always stick together when
he crunch begins." She considered. "Not when we start
ightening down, mind you, when they start having sprint-
aces to see who can crumble on each other the fastest.
ut up until then they stick together."

"Perhaps," Hal murmured, his gaze drifting to the city's
orthern skyline. The single red-and-white airspeeder

he'd spotted a moment ago had now been joined by tw
others, all of them scooting like their tails were on fir
Markings were impossible to see at this distance, b
he'd seen airspeeders with that color scheme parke
outside Colonel Nyroska's office. "I presume we sta
with the family?"

"Since his truly close friends—assuming he's g
any—are undoubtedly not on that list, I'd say so," Isar
said acidly. "Unless they're phonies, too. What do yo
think they're up to?"

"Who?"

Isard gestured with her datapad. "Those three Dar
knell Defense airspeeders," she said. "Don't try to te
me you hadn't noticed them."

"I noticed them," Hal confirmed calmly. "You thir
they've got a line on your Rebel?"

"Can't think what else they'd be using Defense pe
sonnel for," Isard murmured, her mismatched eyes ga
ing thoughtfully at the now descending airspeeder
"Well, if they have, we can pull it out of their comput
records at the quiet-drop."

"We heading there now?"

"Soon enough," Isard said, holding up the datapa
"I see a name on this profile that was also on Arkos
frequent-customer list. Let's go see if perhaps he hasn
had the sense to vanish like everyone else."

"Thank you for getting back to me so quickly," Nyrosl
said into his comlink, glancing over the device at Barc
and giving him a sharp nod. Barclo nodded back ar
busied himself with the trace board.

"Not a problem," the woman's voice came back. "Yo
ready to believe me yet about the Imp agent?"

"Possibly," Nyroska said. "We don't have your agen
but we do have a large blond human male in a tar
down at the morgue. The analysts tell me he was shot
close range with a Luxan Penetrator."

There was a brief pause at the other end. "Interesting."

"So you didn't know he was dead?" Nyroska probed.

"Are you suggesting I had something to do with it?" he shot back.

"No, of course not," Nyroska said soothingly. Which was, in point of fact, a true statement. He'd made a career of reading people's faces and voices, and that brief pause had been all the reaction he needed to know the news had indeed taken her by surprise.

Which meant that while she might be a thief, she was not likely to be a murderer. A point in her favor. "I merely brought it up to let you know that that part of our story checks out."

"I'm happy about it if you are," she said, with just a trace of sarcasm. "But until and unless you get to the Imp agent herself, we're no further along than when we started."

"Not necessarily," Nyroska said. "Now that I know that your story has some actual substance to it, I can hopefully persuade my superiors to take the matter seriously."

"Meaning?"

"Meaning I'd like to meet with you," he said. "No obligations or promises, except of course that I won't try to arrest you or take the merchandise. For now I just want to talk."

"Yeah, right," the woman sniffed. "All completely clear and aboveboard."

"Exactly," Nyroska said, turning up the calm trustworthiness in his voice to full power. "You have to realize you're in a seriously untenable position, especially with a dead body in the morgue that the Intel agent might well believe is your doing. I may be the only one who can help you. And you can check with your fringe friends that I keep my word."

There was another long pause. "I'll think about it," the woman said at last. "I'll call you later."

The connection clicked off. "Barclo?"

"She's moved south to the edge of Little Duros," the

lieutenant reported. "I've got three airspeeders on th
way."

Nyroska nodded. "A waste of time, probably."

"She does seem to be pretty good at slipping out c
nets," Barclo conceded. "So what now? Wait until sh
calls again?"

"More or less," Nyroska said, peering at his compute
display. The dead man's ID was being backtracked
along with that of the woman who'd arrived at the space
port with him, but so far both probes were coming u
dry. Probably another waste of time. "Anything on th
landspeeder they rented?"

"Hasn't been spotted yet," Barclo said. "Of course, a
Imperial might have altered the reg tag just on genera
principles."

"An unlikely term to use in the same breath with In
perial agents," Nyroska growled, scowling at the displa
"I think it's about time we took back some of the initia
tive. I want you to check with the General as to how fas
we could put together a sizable cash package."

Barclo's jaw dropped slightly. "You want to pay he
off?"

"Not without knowing what exactly she's got,
Nyroska said. "But if it *does* turn out to be as explosiv
as she claims, it would be nice to have some option
available."

"I suppose," Barclo said, shaking his head. "I ju
hope you're not getting in too deep, Colonel. This is In
perial Intelligence we're dealing with, you know."

"This is *my* world, Barclo," Nyroska said coldly. "*Ou*
world, not Palpatine's. He may someday be able to ru
the whole Empire from Coruscant, but until then we d
have certain jurisdictional and governmental righ
here on Darkknell. And I am flighty well going to exe
cise those rights."

"Yes, sir," Barclo said, sounding subdued as he reache
for his comlink. "I'll call the General right now."

. . .

Moranda clicked off her comlink. "Come on," she said.

They crossed the street and entered the sweets shop she had marked before making her call to Nyroska. Weaving through the mass of mostly Duros customers, she led the way back to the employees' entrance in the rear and down a flight of steps to the street at the bottom of the hill. With gratifying promptness, the street-maintenance speeder truck she'd spotted from their earlier vantage point came lumbering by just as they reached the street, and a moment later she and Garm were safely nestled into the empty debris-storage bin in the back.

"You don't think they'll search this thing?" Garm asked, looking cautiously out through the rear access opening they'd just climbed in through.

"Not when they see the bin is already full of dirt," Moranda told him, unfastening her outer skirt and pulling it off. Flipping it over so that its brown side was showing, she arranged it across their feet and knees where it would be all that could be seen through the opening without a close examination. "It's all in perception."

"I suppose." He hesitated. "So he was shot with his own weapon?"

"Unless someone else in town is packing a Luxan," Moranda agreed soberly. "What do you think? Horn, or Isard herself?"

"Hard to believe it of either of them," Garm said, shaking his head. "Unless Isard found the datacards and assumed her assistant was in on it."

"Could be," Moranda said, studying Garm's face out of the corner of her eye. They'd kept their introductions on a strict first-name-only basis; but even through the simplistic disguise he was wearing there was something vaguely familiar about this man.

His eyes in particular. Very strong and knowing eyes, they were, rich with knowledge and wisdom and some deep but very private pain. Recent pain, too, if she was any judge of such things. Or maybe it was his voice. Was he someone she might have heard speaking on the newsnets?

Decisively, she turned her eyes away. The situation piqued her curiosity, but at the moment she had more urgent things to worry about than another man on the run. "Any sign of the airspeeders yet?"

"Oh, they're out there," Garm assured her, leaning over Moranda's knees to peer out past their makeshift camouflage. "Whatever else Colonel Nyroska might be, he's also fast on his feet."

"Yes," Moranda agreed. "Well, one more call hopefully should do it."

"Do what, get us caught?" Garm asked pointedly. "Aside from appealing to your playful side, I don't know what these calls are supposed to accomplish."

"We need to flush Isard out of hiding," Moranda told him patiently. "That means drawing her to some known location. Assuming she's smart enough to notice all this Defense airspeeder activity, I'm hoping it will intrigue her enough to head to one of the Security offices to find out what's going on. The only trick will be guessing which one she'll pick."

"Probably none of them," Garm said. "Odds are she'll go to the local Intelligence drop site instead."

Moranda blinked. "Intelligence drop site?"

"Sure," Garm said. "It'll have computer access capabilities, and maybe some extra personnel she can draw on. Probably not, though—this station should be too small to be continually staffed."

Moranda stared at his profile. "How do you know about all this?"

He shrugged. "I have access to certain files."

"Terrific," she growled. "And it didn't occur to you to mention this to me before now?"

He turned those piercing eyes on her. "Before now, I didn't know what you were going for," he reminded her mildly.

She ground her teeth. But he was right. "One of these days we really have to get our act together," she said. "Fine. Where is this drop site?"

"It's a small, apparently out-of-business boutique in the main west-side shopping district," he told her. "I don't remember the name, but I have the address."

"Good enough," she said. "As soon as we're clear of Nyroska's net, we'll find a landspeeder and get over there." She frowned as a sudden thought struck her. "I don't suppose this place would have a cache of extra weapons Isard could load up with, would it?"

"Probably."

Moranda nodded grimly. "Terrific."

They'd been sitting at the back of the crowded open-air tapcafe next to the ClearSkyes Boutique for nearly half an hour when Moranda suddenly straightened up and nodded. "There she is," she said, nodding over the lip of her mug toward Bel Iblis's right.

Casually, taking a sip from his own drink as he did so, Bel Iblis looked in that direction. Barely twenty meters away a familiar landspeeder was pulling into a parking zone. And out of it stepped—

"Well, well, well," Moranda murmured. "Horn's still with her."

"I told you Isard spun him a story back at Arkos's place," Bel Iblis reminded her.

"Sure, but I wouldn't have expected him to still be tagging along," Moranda said. "He should have sliced through her story long ago."

"Or else she should have gotten whatever she wanted from him and tossed him away," Bel Iblis agreed, frowning as Horn turned slowly around beside the landspeeder, automatically checking out the area. His eyes passed over them without a flicker of recognition, the breeze pulling his collar open as he continued his turn—"Give me your macrobinoculars. Quickly."

"What's up?" Moranda asked, passing the tiny set to him beneath the table.

"Possible trouble," Bel Iblis told her. Concealing the

macrobinoculars with hands and mug, he lifted them to his eyes and focused in on Horn's neck as they crossed the street toward the boutique.

One clear look was all it took. "Make that definite trouble," he said grimly, lowering the macrobinoculars. "Horn's wearing a choke-collar."

"Oh, lovely," Moranda said. "What a pleasant woman your Ysanne Isard is."

Isard keyed the door lock, and she and Horn disappeared into the ClearSkyes.

"This changes things, Moranda," Bel Iblis said quietly, bracing himself for the inevitable argument. "That choke-collar's going to have a dead-man switch attached. I'm not going to risk Horn's death if Isard drops the thing or is injured or killed."

"I agree," she said. "On the other hand, there's no way I'm going to try to sneak those datacards out of the car if you aren't pinning them down with blaster fire—"

"Wait a second," Bel Iblis cut her off, frowning. The inevitable had failed to happen. "Did you hear what I said? Horn's a good and valuable man, and I'm not going to risk his life."

"Yes, I heard you," she said. "I said I agreed."

"But—" He floundered.

She lifted her eyebrows. "What, just because Horn's chased me halfway across the Empire you think I should be willing and eager to let him get vaped?"

"Something like that, yes."

She shifted her gaze away from and back to the boutique. "Strange as it may seem, Garm, over the past few years I've gotten sort of used to having Horn on my tail. He's a pretty good opponent, you know, well worth matching wits against. I rather enjoy that sort of challenge."

She smiled wryly. "Besides, I know that if he's the one who brings the hammer down on me, I'll be treated fairly. In Palpatine's grand new Empire there aren't a lot of enforcement types I would trust that far."

"I'm glad we're on the same side on this," Bel Iblis said, some of the tightness lifting from his chest. Arkos had known little about this woman except her name, but her airy confidence, deviousness, and pocket-picking talents had created in his mind the stereotypical fringe image, someone willing to do whatever it took to get what she wanted. The fact that casual murder, or even collateral murder, was apparently outside her ethical boundaries made working with her considerably more palatable to his own conscience.

In fact, it made her no worse than some of those he was already fighting alongside in the Rebellion. Maybe even no worse than the average. "So what now?" Moranda bit gently at her lip. "Were you able to get any details on the choke-collar?" she asked. "Design, manufacturer—anything?"

Bel Iblis searched his memory. "All I could see was that it was black," he said. "Oh, and it had what looked like a small keylock to the left of his throat."

"Interesting," she said thoughtfully. "Probably a Jostrian design, then—they use straight mechanical keylocks to keep anyone from scanning along lock frequencies and unfastening it."

"So we can't do anything?"

"I didn't say that," she said, still thoughtful. "Keep watch here—I'm going to pop into that little electronics shop over there."

"And then?"

She patted his hand. "Trust me."

"I was right," Isard said, tapping keys on the quiet-drop's computer. "Those Defense airspeeders were indeed responding to your friend Savich."

"Does it identify her by name?" Hal asked.

Isard threw him a contemptuous look. "Of course it does. And she included her ID listing and associates profile, too. If you're going to ask stupid questions, Horn, keep your mouth shut."

Hal clamped down firmly on his tongue as Isard turned back to the computer with a snort. She had been becoming progressively more ill-tempered as the day wore on, and finding that their last known link between Arkos and the Continuum Void manager had flown the nest had apparently been the last click. The anger and frustration and bloodlust were simmering barely beneath the surface, held in check by sheer force of will.

And if something didn't break soon, Hal suspected, some of that bloodlust could very well expend itself on a convenient CorSec inspector whom she was clearly starting to consider less than useful to her.

He swallowed, the movement of his throat constricted noticeably by the unyielding noose around his neck. What in the name of Vader's tailor was in that missing datapack, anyway?

And then, at his belt, his comlink beeped.

Isard spun around as if she'd been stung. "What's that?" she demanded.

"My comlink," Hal said.

"I know it's your comlink," she bit out icily, sliding out of her chair and stepping over to him. "Who knows you're here?"

"Only Colonel Nyroska," Hal said, pulling out the device. "Do you want me to answer it?"

"Of course," she said, stepping close to him. "Maybe he's got a line on Savich."

Hal nodded and clicked it on. "Horn."

"Hello, Inspector," a cheerful female voice replied. "It's Moranda Savich. How are you?"

Hal felt his breath catch in his throat. "How did you get this frequency?"

"Oh, don't be silly," she chided. "You registered it when you arrived on Darkknell, remember? Unfortunately, your friend the Imp didn't do that, at least not under a name I could find. Is she there with you, by any chance?"

"I'm here," Isard spoke up, glacially calm. "You have my datapack?"

"Sure, if you have my money," Moranda said. "The price is one million, in Imperial currency."

Hal looked furtively at Isard's face, wondering if she was approaching meltdown yet. But to his surprise, the eyes gazing back at him were as calm and cool as any he'd ever seen. With at least a potential handle on the situation now, her earlier frustration and irritation had evaporated into complete professionalism.

"You have a rather inflated opinion of what it's worth," Isard said. "I'll pay you a hundred thousand."

Moranda sniffed audibly. "That's pretty chintzy, even for an Imperial. If you don't want to play, I'm sure someone else will."

"Like Colonel Nyroska, for instance?"

"Exactly like Colonel Nyroska," Moranda said approvingly. "That's right—I forget sometimes how adept you Imps are at slicing into official computer systems. You wouldn't happen to have noticed if he's pulled together his million yet, would you?"

"He's started making inquiries," Isard confirmed calmly. "I can assure you, though, that you'd rather deal with me."

"My plan is to deal with the top bidder," Moranda said pointedly. "Still, I'm sure Imperial Intelligence can bid higher than a backwater fuel stop like Darkknell."

"Most certainly," Isard said, her voice almost silky with implied menace. "Along with that hundred thousand I can also guarantee you the chance to leave here with your skin intact."

"Don't make me laugh," Moranda sniffed. "I've eluded Inspector Horn for years—you think I can't do the same with Imperial Intelligence?

"No," Isard said flatly. "I don't think you can."

"Hear me shaking," Moranda said. "Here's the deal. I'll give you and Nyroska an hour to put together your packages—cash only, of course. Then I'll meet you both at the Number Fourteen warehouse in the Firtee Cluster north of town, and one of you will leave with the data-pack. Clear?"

"Very," Isard said softly.

"And don't insult my intelligence by trying anything cute," Moranda warned. "I'm quite good at this sort of game. One hour, and come alone."

The comlink clicked off. "Certainly we'll come alone," Isard agreed, as if talking to herself as she sat back down at the computer. "We wouldn't want the inconvenience of witnesses, would we?"

"What are we doing?" Hal asked as she began keying the terminal.

"*I* am clearing out the potential ground clutter," she told him. "Specifically, I'm sending Colonel Nyroska's entire contingent on a little impromptu training exercise."

Hal felt his jaw drop. "You aren't serious. There's no way he won't catch something that blatant."

"Let him," Isard retorted. "By the time his squawks get anyone's attention the datapack and I will be long gone."

Hal grimaced. "Leaving him with nothing to do but find someone to pin the blame on. Me, for instance?"

Isard favored him with a cool, dispassionate look, then turned back to the computer. "Think of it as your opportunity to provide a unique service to the Empire."

"Yes," Hal murmured. "Of course."

"I can't say the General's exactly thrilled by the situation," Barclo reported, clicking off his comlink. "But he *is* rather intrigued by it. He says that if you can prove this datapack is genuinely worth a million, he can have the money ready in two hours."

"Good," Nyroska said, clicking keys on his computer. "Well, well: the backtrack on our big blond cipher down in the morgue just came up empty. Which means his ID was completely phony."

"Big surprise," Barclo grunted. "Half the IDs in south Xakrea are probably phony."

"Yes, but not of this quality," Nyroska said. "His tracked all the way back to Coruscant before it petered out. That means—"

He broke off as his comlink beeped. "Here we go," he said, picking it up. "I'll bet you your next promotion this is her." He keyed it on. "Nyroska."

"Colonel?" an unfamiliar human male voice said. "My name is—well, never mind that. I'm an associate—former associate, rather—of the woman you've been dealing with on this datapack matter."

"I see," Nyroska said. "What can I do for you?"

"You can get me out of this mess, that's what," the other said nervously. "This whole thing's gotten completely out of hand. Did you know she's actually baiting an Imperial Intelligence agent? This is getting way too dangerous, and I'm ready to cut my losses and get out."

"I applaud your wisdom," Nyroska said. "Get me the datapack, and I'll see to it that you walk away."

There was a pause. "Yeah," the caller said at last, a little uncertainly. "Problem: I don't actually have it myself. But I can finger her for you, and she *does* know where it is. She'll be coming back to a tapcafe right next to something called the ClearSkyes Boutique, and she'll be back any minute now. Get over here fast, okay?"

"We're on our way," Nyroska promised. On the last word, the comlink clicked off.

"Well?" he added to Barclo.

"Could be a feint," Barclo said, frowning at his board. "On the other hand, the trace puts him in that area. I'd say it's worth checking out."

"Agreed," Nyroska said, keying his computer. He paused, keyed it again. "What in—?"

"What is it?" Barclo asked.

"My troops," Nyroska said, waving at the computer. "They've all been sent out to the spaceport."

"What? Why?"

"I don't know," Nyroska gritted, slapping at the keys. "They're phony orders—they have to be. The General wouldn't have pulled them without alerting me first. But the orders show proper authorization, and they're locked in." He swore. "And the troops are locked incommunicado, too."

Abruptly he got to his feet. "Ten to one it's a delaying tactic by our datapack thief," he ground out. "And I have no intention of being delayed. Grab Thykele from the outer office, and let's go."

"You think three of us will be enough?" Barclo asked, pulling his blaster from a desk drawer as he stood up.

"We'll make it enough," Nyroska said grimly, checking his own blaster and jamming it into his holster. "*This* time she's not getting away."

They had left the boutique and were heading across the street when Hal's comlink beeped again. "Do I answer it?" he asked.

"Probably better," Isard grunted, getting a grip on his arm and leading him over to the side of the street beside their landspeeder. "Savich may not be finished playing her little games yet."

Hal pulled out the instrument, giving the area around them an automatic once-over as he did so. There'd been some turnover in the tapcafe's clientele since they'd gone inside the boutique, and a half block farther down the street a couple of Kubaz were unloading a speeder truck, but nothing else seemed to have changed. "Horn."

"Hello, Inspector," Moranda's voice came back. "Just wanted to see if you and your Imp were still on schedule."

"We're working on it, yes," Hal said.

"Good," Moranda said cheerfully. "I also wanted to tell you that I've talked now with Nyroska, and he's ready to offer me two million."

"Is he, now?" Isard put in, glaring at the comlink in Hal's hand as if it were a display Moranda could see her through. Down the street, one of the Kubaz dropped a crate onto the street with a loud thud. "Now you listen to me, you little walking dead woman," she bit out. "And listen closely."

She began voicing an exquisitely detailed threat, a recitation Hal would normally have paid close attention to if only for professional interest. But in this case, he wasn't even listening. Isard, her full attention focused on her anger and pride and threats, had apparently missed completely the fact that the crash of that dropped crate had been echoed faintly on Moranda's comlink carrier.

Which meant that Moranda was here somewhere.

Slowly, carefully, Hal let his eyes track across the area, studying every visible face and searching windows and doorways for less than visible ones. His gaze fell on a woman about fifteen meters away at one of the tapcafe tables, her face in profile to him as she gazed meditatively at the distant mountains rising over the cityscape, a mug held to her lips. She was the right height and build, but he could see both hands clearly enough to tell there was no comlink palmed in either of them. Unless she had the device clipped to her collar or something . . .

"I get the point," Moranda put in, cutting off Isard's threat. "Here's the route I want you to follow to the warehouse. Listen closely, and don't interrupt."

She launched into a detailed list of streets, corners, turns, and backtracks. As she did so, the woman at the tapcafe table set her mug down and stood up, digging a coin out of her hip pouch and dropping it on the table. She turned toward Hal and Isard and started in their direction, glancing back and forth between the various business signs lining the street.

And there indeed was no comlink fastened to her collar, nor a telltale bulge beneath her jacket where one might be hidden. Listening with half an ear to Moranda's instructions droning on from his comlink, Hal shifted his attention back to the doorways around the area. She had to be here somewhere. . . .

"Hal?" a woman's voice called excitedly. "Hal Horn?"

He wrenched his eyes back to the woman approaching them. She was looking at him with wide eyes, her mouth gaping open in a happy grin of recognition. "It *is* you," she said, now almost bounding as she closed the distance toward him. "Well, I'll be a mynock's breakfast. Allyse Conroy—remember? How *are* you?"

"Uh," Hal said, glancing in confusion at Isard as he searched his memory in vain for an Allyse Conroy. "I'm . . ."

Isard plucked the comlink from his hand. "We've got trouble," she cut into Moranda's monologue. "Call us back in ten minutes." Without waiting for a response, she clicked off.

"Imagine running into you here on Darkknell, of all places," the approaching woman said, her grin if anything even bigger than it had been. "How are Nyche and Corran? He's what, sixteen years old now?"

"Eighteen," he said, flinching back as she raised her arms for a hug. But her ebullience was hardly to be stopped by anything as simple as a flinch, and the next thing he knew she had her arms around him, pressing her body tightly against his. "Ah—Allyse—"

"It's so good to see you," she said, her voice oddly muffled as she spoke into his shoulder, her face pressed against the left side of his face, her breath disconcertingly warm on his neck. "How have you been these last few years?" Hal glanced past the side of her head. Isard had now stepped around behind her and was giving Hal the same kind of look she'd just been giving the comlink. "Actually, Allyse, I'm kind of busy right now," he told her, trying to diplomatically ease her away from him. A waste of effort; her arms merely tightened all the harder around him. "In fact, I'm in the middle of something very important. I have to go."

"Imagine finding you here," she repeated. "Is this destiny, or what?"

Isard's eyes were starting to throw sparks. Bracing

himself, Hal took a deep breath and got a firm grip on Allyse's ribs.

And abruptly froze. Faintly detectable with that incoming breath had been two distinctive aromas: the pungent tang of cigarra smoke, plus the more subtle scent of Gralish liqueur.

Moranda Savich?

He opened his mouth to speak; but before he could get the proper words lined up, the arms pinioning the two of them together loosened and she stepped back. He caught just a glimpse of the slender lockjim between her lips before it vanished again into her mouth and belatedly noticed the pressure of the choke-collar around his neck had disappeared—

And with her grin still in place, Allyse backed full tilt into Isard.

"I'm so sorry," she gasped, twisting around with feline speed and grabbing Isard's jacket in time to keep her from falling backward. "So very clumsy of me," she added, busily brushing down Isard's jacket where her grip had momentarily wrinkled it. "Are you all right?"

"Get away," Isard snapped, putting a palm against Allyse's chest and pushing her away. The shove sent her sprawling back against the side of the landspeeder, her hands scrabbling for balance and finding a grip across the top of the door.

"Well, sure," Allyse said in a subdued tone.

"You don't have to be so rough," Hal reproved Isard gently, his eyes probing Allyse's face. Usually he was able to pull Moranda's features out from under the mask of her many and varied disguises, but here, at first blush, anyway, he couldn't seem to find her anywhere in that indignant expression. Maybe it wasn't her, after all.

"She should be thankful I *didn't* get rough," Isard countered acidly. "Now get away from our landspeeder. We have business to attend to."

"I don't think so," a voice called from Hal's right.

He turned. Colonel Nyroska, flanked by two uniformed Defense officers, was striding in their direction.
All three had blasters drawn. "Colonel Nyroska," Hal
nodded. "What brings you down here?"

"Your friend there, Inspector Horn," Nyroska said,
his gaze shifting over Hal's shoulder. "She and I need to
have a long talk."

"My friend?" Hal frowned, turning back to look at
Allyse.

But she was not, as he'd expected, waiting with the
wilted, defeated look of a criminal or fugitive who'd finally been run to ground. Instead, she was standing tall
and proud, an almost haughty expression on her face. "I
commend you on your excellent timing, Colonel," she
said in a voice that matched the face as she gestured at Isard. "There's your thief, and my Rebel agent. Arrest
her."

The sheer effrontery of it caught Isard completely
flatfooted. "What in the—?" she sputtered. "You little—
back off!" she snapped as one of Nyroska's men reached
for her arm. "Back off, all of you."

Her hand dived beneath her jacket, then froze in
place as three blasters suddenly lined up on her face.
"You're making a big mistake, Colonel," she said quietly.
"A big mistake. I'm Imperial Intelligence Field Operative Ysanne Isard."

"Indeed," Nyroska said calmly. "You have ID, of
course?"

"Of course," she said, shifting her hand elsewhere beneath her jacket. Her hand paused, her face changed,
and she spun her head around at Allyse. "Give it back,"
she snapped. "My ID. Give it back."

"Nice try," Allyse said patronizingly, lifting her arms.
"As you're welcome to confirm, Colonel, I don't have
anything of hers. However, if you'll escort us back to
your headquarters, I'll be happy to have my staff trans-
mit the credentials she mentioned."

Isard's mouth dropped open. "You'll *what?*"

"Present my credentials," Allyse said, turning a glacial

ook on Isard. "You see, Colonel, I am Field Operative Ysanne Isard."

"This has gone far enough," Isard snarled. "Horn, tell the Colonel exactly who I am."

"Inspector Horn?" Nyroska invited.

Hal hesitated. "She did tell me she was Field Operative Isard," he conceded. "But the only ID she showed me identified her as Darkknell Special Security agent Katya Glasc."

"Did it, now," Nyroska said, his voice suddenly cold as he looked at Isard with heightened interest. "Impersonating law enforcement personnel is a class-one offense on Darkknell. And is she by any chance the one who put that highly illegal device around your neck?"

Hal reached up and pulled the loosened choke-collar away. "Yes," he said, handing it to the colonel.

Isard's eyes were simmering pools of death. "You're dead, Horn. Dead."

"I can only say what I know," Hal said. "Anything in the way of further proof is up to you."

"Indeed it is," she breathed. "All right, Colonel, you win. Let's go to your headquarters and sort this out." She looked at Allyse. "Let's *all* of us go."

"Of course," Nyroska said softly. "I wouldn't have it any other way."

Bel Iblis waited five minutes after Moranda and the others had left the scene before cautiously approaching the now abandoned landspeeder and letting himself in. No one shouted in triumph at his appearance; no one, so far as he could tell, even noticed him. Two minutes later, working awkwardly in the cramped space, he had the inner door panel off.

The datacards were there, all right, jumbled together at the bottom of the narrow space. Nestled in among them was an extra datacard, this one bearing official Imperial markings. Ysanne Isard's missing Intelligence ID, no doubt.

For a moment Bel Iblis considered taking it with him, decided it wasn't worth the risk of getting caught with it, and left it where it was. Besides, if Moranda was right about being able to talk her way out of detention—though how she was going to do that he couldn't even begin to imagine—she might want to track down the vehicle and borrow the ID herself.

He refastened the panel loosely back in place, feeling a twinge of stung conscience as he did so. Yes, this had all been Moranda's idea in the first place, a challenge she'd seemed eager to take on, but this was his mission, and the Rebellion's, and yet it was Moranda who had ended up doing most of the work and taking all of the risks.

And not for the flat million in Imperial currency she'd demanded from Isard, but for the relative pittance he and Arkos had been able to throw together. Someday, if they all lived through this, he would have to find a way to make it up to her.

And the first step in the survival process, he reminded himself, would be to rendezvous with Arkos and get himself and these datacards off Darkknell and back to the Rebellion. And there to find out what exactly Tarkin's Death Star project entailed.

"Good luck, Moranda," he murmured as he climbed out of the landspeeder and closed the door gently behind him. "May the Force be with you. May it be with us all."

Hal would have bet money that Isard's eyes couldn't have gotten more wild than they had been outside the ClearSkyes Boutique. He was wrong.

"What do you *mean* she's gone?" she thundered looming over Nyroska's desk like a berserk storm cloud "How could she be gone? You locked her in a *cell*, for Palpatine's sake!"

"I'm sorry, Field Operative Isard," Nyroska said apologetically, clearly trying to press as far back into his chair as he could manage. "My people assured me she was properly secured. Apparently they were wrong."

"Apparently they were idiots," Isard shot back. "And what precisely are you doing to recapture her?"

"We have an all-planet alert out," Nyroska told her. "If she's still on Darkknell, we'll get her."

Isard's snort concisely delivered her opinion of that. "And you," she bit out, turning her glare onto Hal. "If I find out that was Savich—and that you knew she was and didn't say anything—I'll have your head for shockball practice. Clear?"

"Clear," Hal said. "And I repeat: I don't see how it could have been her standing there hugging me when she was on the comlink at the same time giving us directions to the warehouse. Best guess is that it was her ally running interference for her."

"In that case, you'd better hope Nyroska catches her," Isard said. "Because if she or anyone else gets off the planet with that datapack, I'll have *both* your heads."

She turned back to Nyroska. "I'll be at my ship," she ground out. "You've got my comlink frequency. Let me know if anything turns up on either woman. *Anything.* Understood?"

"We will, Field Operative Isard," Nyroska said humbly.

Spinning around, she stalked to the door and stomped out.

Nyroska exhaled raggedly. "We're in trouble now, Inspector," he said quietly. "The whole Empire may be in trouble if that datapack gets off-planet," Hal agreed. "At least, if her reaction to the whole situation is anything to go by. But to be honest, I don't think you and I are going to take the brunt of it, not from her anyway. Isard has about three TIE squadrons' worth of pride, and bringing official Intelligence wrath down on us will put her in an embarrassingly bad light."

"As bad a light as it would put us in?"

"Probably not," Hal conceded. "But people like that only risk losing face if the potential rewards are worth it. Frankly, neither of us qualify." He shook his head. "No, whatever shrapnel comes of this is going to hit elsewhere."

"Against members of the Rebel Alliance, perhaps?"

Hal shrugged. "Or those Isard decides are members," he said. "Whether they are or not."

Nyroska tapped his fingertips against the side of his desk. "A mess, indeed," he said. "I wouldn't want to be in her boots when she has to go back and report this to her father."

Hal nodded soberly. "I'll drink to that."

"What is this?" the barman demanded, frowning at the two small items resting in the palm of his hand.

"They were inside the mug at that table over there," the young cleaner said excitedly, pointing across the tapcafe. "The one where the dark-haired woman was sitting."

"Which? The one involved in that Defense Agency to-do down the street?"

"Yes, her." The cleaner pointed at the comlink in the barman's hand. "See, the comlink is still on. I tried talking, but no one answered."

"Cut off from the other end," the barman grunted.

"That's what I thought," the cleaner agreed. "But that recorder is the really strange part. Go ahead—play it."

Throwing the kid a speculative look from under his bushy eyebrows, the barman plucked the wafer-thin recorder from his palm and touched the play button.

"Next, you're to cross the street and pick up a north-bound transport," a female voice came from the device. "If there isn't one there, just wait—there will be. You ride it to the corner of Pontrin and Jedilore, then get off and go into the clothing store you'll find on the corner—"

"You hear that?" the cleaner said. "It's like a treasure hunt, isn't it?"

The barman sniffed. "It's a prank," he declared, shutting off the recording and thrusting it and the comlink back at the cleaner. "Here—you can keep them."

The kid took them uncertainly. "But what if it isn't a prank?"

"It is," the barman assured him with a sniff. "Trust me, lad. There's no treasure worth hunting for on Dark-knell. Never has been; never will be."

Epilogue

by Michael A. Stackpole

Armand Isard looked up from his desk, slightly more angry that his daughter had left the door open behind her than that she had entered without requesting permission to do so. She advanced toward him too quickly, her mismatched eyes ablaze. He held up a hand, then pointed to the chair before his desk. "Please, be seated."

She glanced at the chair, then looked at him. "Can I be sure it is safe?"

"If the result of this operation was for you to be killed, you'd already be dead, Agent Isard." Armand tried to keep his voice as cold as he would when addressing any insubordinate operative in his organization, but a hint of anger bled into it anyway. "Please."

She settled herself onto its brown synthleather cushion, though her body seemed as tense as if he were asking her to sit in a chair bristling with sharp transparisteel fragments.

He tapped the datapad on his desk. "I've read the report you sent about the action on Darkknell, and I have spoken to the Emperor on your behalf. You won't be killed despite your failure."

Her posture eased a bit, but not quite in the way he would have expected. She leaned forward, less stiff, more supple, like a predator getting ready to pounce. "I do not fear for my life at the Emperor's hands, Father."

"No?"

"No. He read the report on Darkknell, the full report on Darkknell."

Her words froze his heart in his chest, and the appearance of two Royal Guards slipping in through the open doorway started it beating again, very fast. "What do you mean? What full report?"

Ysanne snorted. "Did you think I wouldn't see what was going on, *Father*? You send me off on a mission of incredible delicacy—one you clearly would give only to an agent you had the utmost trust in. It was also a mission that would get that operative killed if she failed, and that was your aim all along."

"This is nonsense!"

"Hardly." Ysanne let a smile slither across her lips. "You see, Father, your plan succeeded. The information you wanted stolen has been communicated to the Rebels, and we know you had a hand in it. I found fingerprints and other trace evidence that identified the Rebel agent sent to retrieve the plans. It was Garm Bel Iblis."

Armand Isard's stomach folded in on itself. "Bel Iblis? Impossible. He was blown up. The bomb killed his whole family."

"Oh, well acted, Father, very well acted, but we both know that's not true, don't we?" She laughed lightly. "You got word to Bel Iblis and got him out of the bomb's range. You didn't mean it for him anyway: you wanted his wife, Arrianya, dead. She was the last link he had to the Empire. She was devoted to the Emperor, so at the bidding of Rebel Masters you had her slain, forcing Bel Iblis to ally himself fully to the Rebellion."

"That's absurd, completely untrue and absurd." Armand forced himself to breathe normally. "You have no proof of any of this."

"You approved the operation that was supposed to kill Bel Iblis, so you clearly knew how to thwart it. And you sent me out on a mission you knew would fail so I would be eliminated. You would use my death at the Emperor's order as an excuse to go over to the Rebellion. With you there to reveal the Empire's secrets to them—and the Death Star datacards were proof you could deliver—they would welcome you. You would overthrow the Emperor, then betray your Rebel companions and take the throne yourself. It's a brilliant plan, Father, simple and yet so effective."

Armand shot to his feet and pointed at the Royal Guards. "Arrest her. Clearly she has gone over to the Rebellion and has concocted this story to remove me, crippling the effort to find and destroy the Rebels."

Neither of the scarlet-armored Royal Guards moved.

Ysanne Isard stood and slowly smoothed her tunic. "They're here, *Father,* to conduct you to the Emperor. I believe he wishes to discuss with you the course of the rest of your life. It is to be a short conversation."

Armand Isard stared gape-jawed at his daughter, then closed his mouth and sighed. "I had expected this someday, you know, Ysanne."

"Of course; I *am* your daughter." She came around the side of his desk and gave him a kiss on the cheek. "It's over for you now, Father, but fear not." She dropped herself into his chair. "The Isard legacy is in very good hands."

Jade Solitaire
by Timothy Zahn

Excuse me, folks—I'm looking for Talon Karrde."

Mara Jade looked up from the engine monitor, peripherally aware that, on the other side of the board, Chin was doing the same. The voice coming from the direction of the *Wild Karrde*'s bridge door was completely unfamiliar to her.

As, she discovered, was the face that came with the voice. "Captain Karrde isn't here at the moment," Mara told the stranger, eyeing him narrowly. Just because they were in a familiar docking bay in a familiar port was no reason why strangers should be wandering loose around the ship. "How did you get in here?"

The man waved vaguely behind him. "Oh, Dankin was back at the hatchway, and he let me in. Karrde and I are old friends—he and I go way back. Any idea when he'll be showing up?"

"I really couldn't say," Mara said, throwing a glance at Chin. Someone who went way back with Karrde should logically go way back with Chin, too, given how long the older man had been with the organization. But there was no recognition on Chin's face, either. "If you'd like, you can leave a message."

The man sighed deeply. "No, I'm afraid that won't do." He waved toward the viewport behind them and the bustling spaceport scene beyond it.

Abruptly, the back of Mara's neck tingled with subtle warning. Her right hand dropped to the blaster holstered at her side—

And froze there. The intruder's waving hand had abruptly split open down the middle, revealing the blaster that had been hidden inside the prosthetic shell. "And I don't have time to wait for him, either," he said, his voice as unconcerned as ever. "My employer would like a word with all of you. He'd prefer you arrive undamaged, but he'd understand if that's not possible."

Mara hissed softly between her teeth. On her own, she knew, she could take him easily, trick weapon or no. But she wasn't alone, and Chin didn't move nearly as fast as he used to. And whether by accident or design, the intruder's weapon was pointed squarely at the older man. No, better to find out what this mysterious employer wanted and wait for a better opening. "I'd hate to disappoint him," she said, lifting her hand away from her holster. "Especially after such a gracious invitation. Please, lead on."

Though if he had harmed any of the *Wild Karrde*'s crew getting inside, she promised herself darkly, her cooperation would be coming to a quick end. A painfully quick end.

Fortunately for him, he hadn't.

"Sorry, Mara," Dankin apologized, looking rather sheepish as he and the rest of the crew piled out of the group of black-windowed landspeeders in which their captors had brought them here. "They got the drop on us at the hatchway."

"Don't worry about it," Mara said, glancing around as

hey were herded toward the side door of an ornate and
vell-guarded mansion. There was no indication of who
he owner was or even exactly where they were, though
rom the sounds of spacecraft in the distance they
probably weren't more than a few kilometers from the
paceport. "Let's see what all this is about. We can always
get annoyed about it later."

They were ushered through the front door, up a stair-
ase, and along a corridor to a huge office whose luxury
evel left the rest of the mansion in the dust. A group of
hairs had been set up facing a massive desk that looked
o be nearly half the size of the *Wild Karrde*'s entire
ridge.

And seated behind the desk, peering at them like a
neat-buyer assessing a passing herd of bruallki, was a
arge, heavily built man. "Thank you for coming," he
aid, his voice penetrating the distance without giving
ny impression that he was even pushing the limits of his
olume. "Please be seated."

"Your invitation was hard to ignore," Mara told him,
hoosing the chair directly in front of him and sitting
lown. "You might want to consider trying a more polite
pproach."

"If I'd had the time, I would have," the round man
aid, glancing over them again. "Where's Karrde?"

"He's not here," Mara said. *And not likely to bump
nto this meeting any time soon, either,* she added silently to
erself. He was over in the Gekto system making some
hipping arrangements, and wasn't due to return until
omorrow. She could only hope he wouldn't be as easily
abbed as the rest of them had been. "I'm Mara Jade,
urrently in command of the *Wild Karrde.* What do you
ant?"

The man's eyes narrowed. Mara met his gaze evenly;
fter a few seconds, his face cleared and he even smiled
lightly. "Mara Jade: I've heard a great deal about you,
oung lady. Yes, you'll do nicely."

Beside Mara, Dankin stirred as if he was about to
peak. Mara shot him a quick glance, and he subsided.

"Very good, indeed," the large man murmured. "Perfectly in command, both of yourself and of your people. Yes, you'll do."

He took a deep breath. "First, some introductions. My name is Ja Bardrin. Perhaps you've heard of me."

Mara kept her face steady, wincing inwardly at the ripple of surprise that ran through the rest of the crew. Of course they'd heard of the industrialist—half the sector had—but that was no reason to play into this false modesty, ego-stroking game of his. "I think I've noticed your name go by once or twice in a footnote," she told him calmly. "Under weapons and ship systems, if I recall correctly. Usually dealing in market areas Uoti hasn't gotten to yet."

She had the small satisfaction of drawing a flash of annoyance from him on that one. The Bardrin Group and the Uoti Corporate had been jockeying for market position and prestige for over two decades now, a rivalry that was deep and bitter and showed no signs of being resolved any time soon.

Unfortunately, Bardrin's brief flicker of anger subsided too quickly for her to use the lowered mental guard to pull any insight from his mind. "But enough of this chitchat," she continued. "I'll ask again: what do you want?"

Bardrin locked eyes with her. "My daughter Sansia has been captured. I want you to rescue her."

Mara frowned. "I think your information sifters need a refresher course in how to do their job. We don't handle military operations."

"The mission requires a woman," Bardrin said. "A resourceful, competent, combat-trained human female."

"So go hire a Mistryl."

Bardrin shook his head. "There's no time to contact them, even if I knew how to go about it. I have to get Sansia back now, before her captors realize who it is they have."

"What are you talking about?" Odonnl spoke up. "You said they kidnapped her."

"I said they captured her," Bardrin countered, pin-

ing Odonnl into his chair with a single contemptuous
glance. "Kindly pay attention."

He brought his gaze back to Mara. "She and the Soro-
uub three-thousand luxury yacht she was flying were
taken by a pirate gang while in port on Makksre and
given to a slaver consortium headquartered on Torpris
and run by a Drach'nam named Praysh." He lifted his
eyebrows slightly. "I presume you've also come across
that name in your footnote perusals."

"Once or twice," Mara conceded, suppressing a grimace. In the circles the *Wild Karrde* moved in, the name
of Chay Praysh was even more well known than Bardrin's. "I understand he makes the late and unlamented
Jabba the Hutt look like a fine, upstanding citizen."

"Then you understand why I want Sansia and her ship
out of his hands," Bardrin said, his voice suddenly low
and with an underlying edge of desperation. "I know
Karrde would have been willing to help me, but Karrde's
not here. You, Jade, must make the decision."

"What about the authorities?" Dankin spoke up. "The
Sector Patrol, or even the New Republic?"

"And have them do what?" Bardrin shot back. "Request an audience with Praysh? Mount an attack on his
fortress that will leave it in ruins and everyone inside
dead? Besides, their security leaks like rock sifters. If
Praysh learns who Sansia is, he'll bleed me for everything I own. And then kill her anyway."

He looked at Mara, an almost pleading look in his
eyes. "Sansia will have been sent to work in the slime pits
in his fortress," he said. "He sends all human female cap-
tives there—some deep desire to humiliate them, I presume. You'll have to get them to take you in as another
prisoner—"

"Wait a minute," Mara cut him off. "I've already told
you we don't do this sort of work."

"Then you'd better learn how quickly," Bardrin rumbled, his earlier desperation changing abruptly into ominous threat. "There's no time for me to get anyone else.
You're it."

Mara crossed her arms, bringing her hand close to the tiny blaster concealed inside her left sleeve. "And if I refuse?"

"There are twenty-four blasters concealed in the walls of this room," Bardrin said. "Three trained on each of you. Before you could even pull that weapon clear, you'd watch your crewmates die around you."

Mara flicked her eyes across the room, stretching out to the Force as she did so. He was right; she could sense the alert presences hidden behind the ornately carved walls all around them.

And if she hadn't been willing to risk Chin's life earlier, she certainly wasn't going to play games with the entire *Wild Karrde*'s crew now. "You didn't answer my question," she said, unfolding her arms.

"You won't refuse," Bardrin declared, leaning back in his chair. "You see, you've just now given me all the leverage I need. You'll go to Torpris and bring back Sansia and her ship . . . or I'll execute your entire crew."

Someone off to her left inhaled sharply. "You can't be that stupid," Mara said, trying to put confidence she didn't feel into her tone. Through the Force she could read Bardrin's intentions, and knew he was deadly serious. "You kill Karrde's people, and Karrde *will* come after you. And I guarantee he's not an enemy to trifle with."

"Neither am I, my dear," Bardrin said darkly. "A contest between us might prove quite interesting."

He leveled a thick finger at her. "But regardless of the outcome, you would still have to live out your life with the knowledge that it was your obstinate stubbornness that had sent them to their deaths. I don't think that's a burden you really want to carry."

"There's no need to be quite so melodramatic," Mara said, forcing her frustration and anger deep down where it wouldn't show. To find herself being so easily manipulated was infuriating.

But she had no choice. She was Karrde's second-in-command, and she'd seen the concern and respect he

onsistently showed toward his people. She wasn't about
o lower those high standards, and she certainly wasn't
oing to risk her people's deaths by refusing Bardrin.
nd everyone in the room knew it. "I'll see what I can
o. What can I have in the way of equipment?"

"Anything you want," Bardrin said, standing up and
aving a hand. Behind them, Mara heard the doors open.
My people will escort your crewmates to their quarters,
here they'll remain until you and Sansia return. You and
will go make whatever arrangements you need."

"Fine," Mara said, falling into step beside him as he
assed between the entering lines of guards.

But that didn't mean the matter would end with
ansia's rescue, she promised herself silently. Not by a
ong shot.

ardrin had told her that Praysh's mansion and grounds
ere set up near the center of one of Torpris's larger
ities. He had failed to mention, however, that that par-
icular section of the city was otherwise composed en-
irely of slums.

Or at least that was how it seemed to Mara as she
naneuvered her landspeeder down the winding streets
oward the high walls of the compound, wincing at the
arbage and debris piled in alleyways between the dilapi-
ated buildings and trying not to hit any of the ragged
lerelicts shuffling along the street. A dozen different
pecies were represented here, all looking equally hope-
ess, and she found herself wondering how much of it
vas a result of Praysh's presence in the city.

Passing one final clump of huddled beings, she
eached the side door she'd been told to come to. Flank-
ng it were a pair of Drach'nam guards, looking even
nore massive than usual for the species in their heavy
ody armor. Each of them held a neuronic whip, with a
olstered blaster and long knife standing ready in re-
erve. "Hey, there," she called cheerfully to them, eyeing

the whips with the sort of contempt she reserved for un necessarily barbaric weapons. "I have a package here fo His First Greatness Chay Praysh, a gift from the Mrahash of Kvabja. May I enter?"

There was an almost chuckle, quickly strangled off from one of the guards. "Really," he said, lumbering toward her. "Bring it here and let's have a look."

Mara slid out of the vehicle and pulled the packing cylinder from the storage compartment in back. It wa large—a good meter tall and half a meter in diameter— but fairly light, most of its bulk consisting of cushioning material for the delicate floater globe she'd borrowed from Bardrin. "It's some kind of expensive art object, think," she said, setting it carefully down in front of him

"Oh, it's that, all right," the guard agreed, looking Mara up and down. "Just a minute."

He went back to the door and busied himself with a comm panel built into the wall. There was a breath o movement beside Mara—

[Leave it and go,] an alien voice spoke quietly from behind her.

Mara turned. A Togorian female was standing at the rear of the landspeeder, her fur matted and dirty, clearly just another of the derelicts loitering on the street. Bu her yellow eyes were bright and alive, and her teeth were bared slightly toward the guards. "Excuse me?" Mara asked.

[I said leave it and go,] the alien said, mouthing the Ghi trade language words with some difficulty. [You are in great danger here.]

"Oh, don't be silly," Mara said, shaking her head with casual unconcern even as she wondered at the Togo rian's courage in sticking her neck out this way. Clearly she knew or suspected what happened to human fe males who wandered near Praysh's fortress; but to try to chase a potential prize out from under the slaver's snou this way bordered on the suicidal. "I'm just delivering a present to His First Greatness, that's all."

The Togorian hissed. [Fool—you *are* the present,] she snarled. [Flee, while you still can.]

"Okay, we're set," the guard said, keying off the comm unit and walking over to Mara. She turned back to him, making sure to keep a pleasantly blank expression on her face. If he even suspected the Togorian had tried to warn her, there might be unpleasant repercussions. "You can take it right in."

"Thank you," Mara said, stooping to pick up the cylinder—

A gauntleted hand came down with a thunk onto the top of the package. "*After* we unpack it, of course."

Mara felt her muscles tighten. "What do you mean?" she asked cautiously, straightening up.

The guard already had his knife out, a nasty-looking serrated weapon with a handguard consisting of a series of thick, needle-sharp spikes alternatively curving up and down from the base of the blade. "I mean we unpack it out here," he said, digging the blade in beneath the lid. "Never can tell what someone might try to slip inside the packaging, you know."

Mara flicked a glance over his shoulder at the second guard, a sense of things gone suddenly and terribly wrong rippling through her. Nestled in its hiding place between the inner and outer shells of the cylinder, she would have bet heavily that her lightsaber could slip through any standard weapons scan Praysh's guards might have put the package through. But unpacking it outside the fortress was not a possibility she'd expected. "But what if you break it?" she asked anxiously.

"Don't worry—we do this all the time," the guard assured her. "H'sishi, I thought I told you scavengers you were supposed to stay behind the mark line."

[Your pardon,] the Togorian said, her tone almost groveling. [I saw the shiny metal—]

"And hoped you could get first grabs, huh?" The guard finished slicing off the top and peeled away the first plate of packing foam. "Here you go, scavengers," he called loudly, hurling the lid and the foam down the street.

Abruptly, the gathered loiterers exploded into action, diving toward the flying pieces as if they were prize jewels instead of unwanted garbage. The guard continued digging down, throwing more foam plates into the melee, until he reached the floater globe at the center. "There it is," he said, reaching in and carefully pulling out the globe. "Nice. Okay," he added, handing the globe to Mara. "*Now* you can go in."

Mara swallowed, glancing down at the cylinder as the guard continued to unload the packaging from the bottom and throw out the pieces. She looked up—

To find H'sishi's yellow eyes steady on her. Mara felt her lip twitch; and then, to her surprise, the alien bared her teeth slightly, as if she'd found a hint she'd been searching for. There was a movement from the side, and Mara looked back just as the guard hefted the cylinder itself over his head and hurled it toward the seething, quarreling crowd.

A dozen of the derelicts abandoned their fight for the foam scraps and charged toward the spot where it would land. But H'sishi was faster. With a single leap she got under the cylinder, snatching it into her arms and hissing a warning at the two or three who tried to grab it away. Another hiss, and the crowd reluctantly fell back.

"I guess she really *did* want the shiny metal," the guard said with a sneer. "Okay, human, let's go."

Despite the fortress's sleek and modern exterior, the interior was dark and decidedly dank, its twisting and rough-floored corridors clearly modeled on the hiding-tunnels much prized by Drach'nam on their home-world. Mara didn't bother to keep track of the route as her five-guard escort took her ever deeper into the fortress, concentrating instead on evaluating Praysh's overall defense structure and gradually increasing the level of nervousness she was displaying in her body language and infrequent attempts at conversation. Her lightsaber was going to be severely missed, but even if she'd been able to smuggle the weapon inside, she'd already concluded that the best hope of getting out would be in Sansia's impounded ship. Fighting their way back along the tunnels and out into the grounds was not an option she was interested in trying.

Still, that lightsaber had been Luke's once, and he was going to kill her if she lost it. Hopefully, when this was all over, she'd be able to track H'sishi down and buy it back from her.

They reached Praysh's audience chamber at last, a large, high-ceilinged room that by its gloom, smells, and general repulsiveness brought back unpleasant memories of Jabba the Hutt's throne room on Tatooine. His First Greatness obviously lacked Jabba's egalitarian sensibilities, though; the only beings in the room were more of Praysh's fellow Drach'nam.

"Well, well," Praysh called, swiveling his throne around to face the incoming group. "What have we here? A present from the Mrahash of Kvabja, is it?"

"Yes, Your First Greatness," Mara said, putting a nervous quaver into her tone as she glanced surreptitiously around. There was a pair of camouflaged blaster ports in the false wall behind Praysh's throne, but other than that the only defenses were the handful of guards standing between her and the slaver chief. Unlike the door wardens, this group carried no blasters, but were armed only with the same type of long knives and neuronic whips. Probably the intent was to keep the more dangerous weapons away from rioting prisoners or slaves; still, it was an overconfidence she might well be able to exploit. "He sends you greetings and—"

"Take that bauble, someone," Praysh cut her off, waving a gem-encrusted scepter toward her. "You—human—step forward."

One of the guards took the floater globe and nudged her forward. Stretching out with all her senses, Mara walked toward the throne. Somewhere along here there would undoubtedly be a test to make sure she was nothing more than the useless slave she appeared. . . .

She'd gone no more than three steps when it came Abruptly, one of the guards ahead pulled his whip from his side and with a casual flick of his wrist sent the lash snaking toward her.

Mara gasped and threw her hands uselessly in front of her face, forcing back the reflex to dodge or duck or do something—anything—that would be more effective.

To her relief, the lash cracked a few centimeters short of her face. "Your First Greatness," she gasped, taking a quick and unsteady step backward. "Please, sir—what have I done?"

The only answer was the sound of another whip from behind her. She half turned—

And suddenly the lash curled itself around her knees and a wave of pain surged through her body.

Mara screamed, an explosive sound that was only partially role-playing, as she toppled onto the floor, the whip's current arcing agonizingly through her body. She clawed once at the lash, screaming again as the current burned at her fingertips. "Please—no—please—"

"Here—defend yourself," a voice called out, and she looked up as a small blaster landed on the floor beside her legs.

She grabbed at the weapon, forcing her fingers to fumble as if dealing with a totally unfamiliar object clenching her teeth against the waves of pain as every part of her being screamed at her to *do* something. The blaster was undoubtedly useless, just another part of Praysh's sadistic test, but if she swiveled on one hip swinging her legs hard around, she might at least be able to yank the whip out of her attacker's hand.

But if she did that—if she showed any sign of combat skill whatsoever—she would probably die.

And then so would the *Wild Karrde*'s crew.

She got a grip on the blaster at last, bending awkwardly around to try to bring the weapon to bear on her assailant. The muzzle wavered uncontrollably, and she tried to prop her elbow on the floor to steady it, sobbing now like a child. The blaster sagged and dropped from her paralyzed fingers—

And abruptly, thankfully, the current shut off.

Mara lay there, unmoving, still sobbing through clenched teeth as she worked out the sudden cramps in her leg muscles. If she'd misjudged Praysh's intentions—if he'd decided to kill her for sport instead of putting her down in the slime pits . . .

"That was an object lesson," Praysh said conversationally. There was a movement beside her, and rough fingers began unwrapping the lash from around her legs. "Now that you've seen what a neuronic whip feels like, I'm sure you won't ever want to provoke its use again."

"No—please—no," Mara managed, the words coming out mangled through her gasping sobs. A pair of hands grabbed her upper arms and hauled her up onto her feet. She took a second to confirm that her legs were recovered enough to hold her weight, then let her knees wobble and collapse again beneath her. The two Drach'-nam pulled her up again and turned her to face Praysh. "Please—" she whispered.

"You belong to me now," Praysh said quietly, his colorless eyes staring at her. "Your safety—your well-being—your life—are all in my hand. If you serve well, you will survive. If not, there will be neuronic whips around you for the remainder of a short and excruciatingly painful life. Do I make myself clear?"

Mara nodded quickly, dropping her gaze and hunching her shoulders, the helpless terror of a beaten animal. "Good," Praysh said, waving off-handedly toward a different door leading out of the chamber. The show was over, and already he was bored with the performer. "Take her to the slavekeeper," he ordered. "Enjoy your new life here, human."

Halfway down a long flight of stairs her escorting guards apparently decided they'd had enough of carrying her and cut her loose to walk on her own. Aside from a lingering tingle in her muscles Mara had completely recovered, but she was careful to maintain a weak-kneed stagger for their benefit the rest of the way down. Neuronic whips were the ultimate glorification of savagery and degradation, just the sort of thing Praysh's thugs would use as their primary persuader, and she had no intention of letting them know how fast she could recover from their effects.

The slime pits were in the lowest level of the fortress, composed of a series of interconnected trenches about two meters wide and a hundred meters long set into the floor. On the walkways between them strolled the Drach'-nam guards, idly fingering their whips or playing with the hilts of their knives. Perhaps two hundred women, most of them young looking, slogged slowly through the waist-deep gray muck in the pits, bent over double with their arms dug into the slime, their faces bare centimeters above the surface. All those Mara could see wore identical expressions of blank hopelessness that sent a shiver through her.

"I'll explain it just once," the slavekeeper said, gesturing almost genially toward the pits. "The nutrient slime in there is home to the pupal form of the krizar creatures His First Greatness uses to patrol the grounds. The pupae are hard-shelled and ellipsoid, about the size of one of your pathetic little thumbs. Your job is to find the ones that are starting to break out of their shells and put them up on the walkway where they'll be retrieved and moved to the main hatchery."

"How do I know when they're ready—?"

"You'll know when they're ready when they start to wiggle and chew their way out," the slavekeeper cut her off sharply. A couple of heads turned at the sudden harsh tone; most of the women didn't even bother to look up. "And don't try just pulling out every one you find. If the pupae are out too long before they're ready, they'll die."

He waved his whip in front of her nose. "And dead pupae make us *very* unhappy. Understood?"

Mara swallowed, forcing herself to shrink back from him. "Yes, sir," she murmured.

"Good," the slavekeeper said, his tone back to genial again, a being who clearly enjoyed his work. "Your head fur is an interesting shade of color. It will be of no use to you in the pits; perhaps you would like to sell it to me."

"In exchange for what?" Mara asked cautiously.

"Favors. More food, perhaps, or other kindnesses."

Mara fought back a grimace. The thought of her hair hanging from a slavekeeper's trophy wall was utterly abhorrent. But on the other hand, he could probably take it without any payment at all if he chose. Hopefully, she wouldn't be here long enough for him to get around to that. "Can I think about it?" she asked timidly.

He shrugged. Clearly, this was just a game to help him pass the time. "If you wish. Oh, one more thing. If you *don't* get the pupae out fast enough, they'll start digging through the shells on their own. No problem with that; except that their mouth palps are always the first things that come out. If they get those into your skin, you'll need a trip to the med facility to get it taken off."

"Oh," Mara said in a small voice. Now, *that* was very useful information. "Does it hurt?"

He gave her one of those evil smiles that Drach'nam did so well. "No more than the whip. Now get in there."

Mara looked down at her jumpsuit. "But—"

She didn't even get a chance to finish her protest. Putting a massive arm around the back of her waist, the slavekeeper swept her off the walkway into the nearest of the trenches.

She managed to hang on to her balance as she landed, keeping her head and most of her torso up out of the slime. But the impact sent a wave of thick muck splashing outward at the nearest workers. "Sorry," she apologized.

One of the women looked up at her, a dab of the slime oozing slowly down her cheek. "Don't worry about it," she said in a voice that sounded more dead than alive. "Don't worry about getting dirty, either. You'll never be clean again."

A neuronic whip cracked warningly overhead. Mara shied back, but the other woman didn't seem to notice or care as she dug into the slime again. Stomach twisting with revulsion, Mara eased her arms into the muck and got to work.

It took her three hours of nauseating, backbreaking sifting before her search pattern finally paid off. "Your name Sansia?" she asked quietly as she came up beside the woman whose holo Bardrin had showed her earlier.

The other woman looked up at her, eyes narrowing suspiciously. "Yes," she acknowledged warily. "What about it?"

Mara glanced casually around. None of the Drach'-nam were in earshot at the moment. "A close relative of yours asked me to get you out of here."

She'd expected elation, or barely contained joy, or at least a certain amount of surprise. But Sansia's reaction wasn't any of those. "Did he really?" she said, her voice dark and scornful. "How very kind of him."

Mara frowned. "You don't seem very pleased."

"Oh, I'm overjoyed," Sansia said sarcastically. "The joy is merely tempered by a somewhat cynical disbelief. You're what, some kind of mercenary?"

"Not exactly," Mara said. "Disbelief in what?"

"In Daddy dear's motivations," Sansia said, digging down into the slime. "Let me guess. He told you about my terrible plight, and how important I am to him and the business, and that he would do anything and give anything to get me back. Once you were properly teary-eyed, he turned up the heat and either talked, maneuvered, or bribed you into charging here to my rescue. Right so far?"

"Close enough," Mara said cautiously.

Sansia's hand came out of the slime holding one of

the krizar pupae. She glanced at both the long ends, then tossed it back in behind her. "But though he desperately wanted his darling daughter back, he also made it clear—subtly, of course—that he wanted the ship back even more. In fact, he probably gave you all the access and command codes you'd need to get it flying whether I was with you or not. Am I still right?"

Mara felt her throat tighten. "He said I needed to be able to fly the ship if you were incapacitated during the escape."

Sansia snorted. "That sounds like him. Plausible straight to the top, but phony as Imperial confidence. The fact is, merc, that he doesn't care about me one single bit. If he did, he wouldn't have sent me to Makksre on that half-daft run in the first place. He wants the *Winning Gamble* back, pure and simple."

Mara glanced around again. One of the guards across the way was eyeing her, and she dug her arms again into the slime. "What's so special about the ship?"

"Oh, it's just about three levels past state-of-the-art, that's all," Sansia said bitterly. "It's got an incredible flight system, an unbelievable weapons targeting array, and a crazy, one-of-a-kind defensive shoot-back system I think Daddy must have stolen from somewhere."

Mara studied her face, stretching out with the Force to try to get a feel for her mind. The same bitterness she could hear in Sansia's voice was indeed roiling through her emotions. "So what are you saying?" she asked. "That you don't want me to try to get you out of here?"

Sansia's eyes slunk away from Mara's gaze. "I'm just telling you how it is," she muttered. "Maybe warning you that somewhere along the line he's probably going to try to force your hand. Try to get you to run without me. I guess I thought you should be ready for that."

And was hoping against hope that, unlike her father, her rescuer had a conscience? "Thanks for the warning," Mara said. Her fingers touched something hard in the slime: one of the elusive krizar pupae. "It just means we'll need to move up the timetable a little," she added, pulling the pupa to just above the surface where she could examine it. The entire shell was solid; clearly, this one wouldn't be poking its jaws out any time soon. Perfect. "Where will they take us after we're finished here?"

"Across the hall to a really disgusting barracks-style sleeping room," Sansia said. For the first time since their conversation began Mara could sense the faint whisperings of cautious hope in the other woman's voice and emotions. "They'll let us wash up, then feed us."

"Showers or tubs?"

"More like animal watering troughs than real tubs," Sansia said contemptuously. "Once they bring you down here, you're never clean again."

"Yes, I've heard that," Mara said. "All the more reason not to hang around any longer than we have to. Are there surveillance cams in the room?"

"There are a couple of obvious ones near the door. Probably a whole bunch of non-obvious ones hidden around, too."

"Okay," Mara said. "One more question: how long to the shift change?"

Sansia peered across the room at a set of glowing emblems embedded in the wall. "Not long. Maybe ten minutes."

"Good," Mara said. "I have a couple of things to pick up first, so I'll catch up with you in the sleeping room. Get washed up fast, and be ready to move as soon as I get back."

Sansia was eyeing her suspiciously, but she nodded. "I'll be ready," she said. "Good luck."

Mara nodded and moved on, holding the krizar shell she'd found beneath the surface as she slogged along, wanting to put a little distance between her and Sansia before she made her move. Out of the corner of her eye she saw one of the Drach'nam walking purposefully down the walkway toward her, flicking his whip into the air as he came, no doubt preparing a comment and object lesson about idle chat while on duty. Mara let him get almost within whip range . . .

And with the most spine-curling scream she could muster, she swung her left arm up, clutching the forearm with her right hand. "It's got me!" she yelped, flailing around and sending bits of slime flying through the air all around her. "Get it off—get it off!"

The Drach'nam reached the edge of her trench in a single bound. "Get your hand out of the way," he snapped, leaning precariously over her as he caught her left wrist and hauled her bodily up out of the pit. The movement brought her up against his belted knife, and she winced as the needle-sharp spikes of the handguard dug briefly into her ribs. "I said move it," he repeated, dropping her onto her feet on the walkway and prying her right hand away from its grip.

To reveal the krizar shell hanging from the underside of her left arm.

Or at least, that was what Mara hoped it looked like. Her Force-manipulating skills might not be as good as Luke Skywalker's, but it was no big trick to use the Force to hold the shell pressed firmly against her arm as if the creature inside were hanging on. The only danger was that the guard might brush off the glob of slime strategically placed at the intersection point and notice that there were no krizar palps linking the shell to the arm.

But after all the times this had undoubtedly happened, the guard was clearly uninterested in the details. "Got one there, all right," he growled, shifting his grip to her right hand and pulling her along the walkway toward the door. "Hey! Your Seventh Greatness?"

"Yeah, go ahead," the slavekeeper told him, gesturing the guards flanking the door to open it. "Tell Blath to be careful this time—His First Greatness isn't going to like it if he loses another one."

The door opened. A second Drach'nam stepped to Mara's left side as they headed out, taking her left arm and holding it in an iron grip at the level of her waist—

probably, Mara decided, making sure she didn't knock the krizar off against her side. The door slammed shut, and the three of them headed at a fast walk down the corridor.

Mara didn't know where the med facility was, but odds were it wasn't very far away, which meant she had to move fast. She continued to moan and cry like a helpless and broken slave as the Drach'nam half dragged her along, struggling ineffectually in her supposed pain against the casually unbreakable grips of her two escorts. Under cover of her attempted flailings, she glanced down to her left. The second guard's knife was bouncing along only a few centimeters from where he was holding her left arm pinioned.

And here was going to be the riskiest part of her plan. With both of her arms under their control, the two Drach'nam wouldn't be expecting any trouble from her and should therefore be less watchful than they might be otherwise. But if that assumption proved false, there was going to be some serious and immediate trouble.

But there was nothing for it but to try. Stretching out to the Force, she slid the knife partially out of its sheath, monitoring the alien's mind closely to see if he would notice the sudden change in weight at his belt. Carefully, trying not to jar the weapon, she eased the spiked hand-guard up against her left forearm near the spot where she was still holding the krizar pupa in place. Two quick jabs—two stabs of genuine pain against the backdrop of her agony act—and she eased the knife down into its sheath again.

Just in time. The knife was barely back in place when the guard on her right brought her to a halt at a side door, shoving the panel open with his free hand. Shifting her attention to the krizar pupa riding her arm, Mara sent it spinning away down the dingy corridor ahead of them.

After the darkness everywhere else inside the fortress, the medical facility was something of a surprise: bright, clean, and reasonably well equipped, with a tiled floor and even some sections of wood paneling. And the reason for the altered decor was immediately apparent: the medic wasn't a Drach'nam.

"Sit down," a tired-looking Bith in a slightly shabby medic's tunic said, coming around a desk and gesturing them to the room's lone treatment table. His tone was brisk, but his face and hands betrayed the edge of nervousness that Mara suspected was probably a common condition among non-Drach'nam in Praysh's employ. "Where is the pupa?"

The guard on Mara's left lifted her arm. "It's right— oh, *pustina*. It's gone!"

"It must have fallen off," the Bith said, the tension in his voice suddenly jumping sharply. His eyes flicked guiltily toward the wall to the left—"You two had better go see if you can find it."

The two guards didn't argue, but charged immediately back out into the corridor. "Did you notice it fall off?" the Bith asked, turning Mara's arm over and starting to clean the residual slime away.

"No, I didn't," Mara said, putting some whining fear into her voice as she looked past the medic's large head. Through an open doorway in the back of the treatment room she could see a large supply cabinet. Stretching out to the Force, she eased the transparisteel cabinet doors open a few millimeters. The labels on the vials were too far away to read, but if the colors and bottle shapes followed conventional New Republic pharmaceutical standards, the three she was looking for were there. Lifting one of the vials off its shelf, she slid it quickly down along the wall to the floor. There was no way to know where the surveillance cam back there was located, but there was nothing she could do about it from out here anyway. She could only hope the bottle's sudden movement wouldn't be noticed by whoever His First Greatness had monitoring the spy displays. Getting a grip on the second bottle, she lowered it to the floor beside the first . . .

"Odd," the Bith said. He had that section of her arm

clean now and was peering at the two puncture marks she'd made with the guard's knife. "These don't look like krizar palpal indentations at all. Are you certain that was what grabbed you?"

"I don't know," Mara moaned, moving the last of the three vials to the floor and then snagging a couple of small squeeze bottles and adding them to her collection. "All I know is that it hurt. It hurt a lot."

She could sense the sympathy and frustration in the Bith. "Yes, I know," he murmured. "It is not an easy life for you down here."

"No," she said, half sobbing as she moved her prizes across the floor to the examination room doorway. Whoever was on surveillance duty might reasonably be expected to ignore an empty supply room, but a room occupied by a human slave and Bith medic was another matter entirely. She had to take out the surveillance cam in here before she could bring the bottles the rest of the way to her.

"Ow!" she gasped suddenly, half pulling her left arm out of the Bith's grip as she quickly studied the wall he'd glanced at earlier. The cam, clearly designed to be hidden, was fairly obvious to someone of Mara's training and experience: a small lens masquerading as a knot hole in the wooden paneling.

"I am sorry," the Bith said, and she caught his mixture of concern and puzzlement as he immediately eased his grip on her arm. "There should not be anything where I was touching that should hurt."

"Well, it did," Mara said petulantly. With the fingers of her right hand, she surreptitiously dug a wad of slime from the hardening mass caking her legs. "They were whipping me earlier up in that big open place—*ow!*" She snatched her left arm away from him again, flailing this time with her right as well. The motion sent a half-dozen small globs of slime spinning across the room—

And with a little help from her Force abilities, the largest of the globs splattered into the wall squarely over the hidden surveillance cam.

"Again, I am sorry," the Bith said, glancing over at the wall. He took a second look, his whole body stiffening suddenly as he realized what had happened. "Excuse me," he said, grabbing up a towel and hurrying over to the wall.

And with the cam still covered, and the medic's attention elsewhere, Mara brought her vials and squeeze bottles flying across from the doorway and dropped them smoothly down the front of her jumpsuit. By the time the Bith finished his cleanup job, they were safely nestled in the folds of material at her waist.

"My apologies," he said as he put the towel in the disposal and returned to her. "The nutrient can damage the wall material, you see, which His First Greatness was kind enough to allow me."

And he would be in serious trouble if he allowed the cam to stay covered too long? Probably. "It's okay," Mara muttered.

Once again, she was just in time. The Bith had just taken her arm again when the two Drach'nam guards clumped back into the room. "Nothing," one of them snarled, glaring suspiciously at Mara. "What did you do with it? Well?"

Mara shrank away from him. "Nothing," she said, her voice frightened and pleading. "Please—I didn't do anything."

"Then where is it?" the Drach'nam demanded, taking a threatening step toward her, neuronic whip in hand.

"Perhaps it was a krizar which was still immature," the Bith spoke up, holding a hand up protectively between Mara and the guard. "Its grip was weak and not completely firm."

"Then where is it now?" the second guard put in. "It was attached to her—I saw it."

"If it's not in the corridor, it must still be in the growth room," the Bith said reasonably. "Perhaps it fell off again into the nutrient pits."

The guards continued to glare, and Mara held her breath. If either of them had actually looked at the pupa after they left the room . . .

But apparently neither of them had. "Yeah," the guard said with ill grace. "Maybe."

The Bith glanced at a wall chrono. "At any rate, the work shift is over," he said. "Why not escort her back to the communal, and then you can search the walkways in the growth room."

"Don't tell us our job, Bith," the other guard growled, baring his teeth as he grabbed Mara's arm in a none-too-gentle grip. "Come on, human. Time for your slops."

The mass sleeping/eating/cleanup room Sansia had spoken about was directly across the corridor from the slime pits. It was also fully as disgusting as her tone had led Mara to expect. About half of the woman had finished their cleaning by the time Mara arrived, leaving the liquid in the long troughs looking more like a runnier version of the slime than anything resembling water. Mara joined the crowd of women waiting their turn, and under cover of the bodies pressing around her, she worked the vials out of her jumpsuit and confirmed that they did indeed contain the chemicals she wanted. Once again, the comprehensive saboteur training the Emperor had given her so long ago was going to come in handy.

"I thought you were kidding about going to pick up some things." Sansia's voice came softly from behind her shoulder, too low for any of the other women around them to hear. "Where did you get those?"

"Medic supply cabinet," Mara told her, concentrating on the task of pouring the first vial into one of the squeeze bottles, keeping them both at waist height where the activity would be shielded from prying eyes.

Sansia made a sound in the back of her throat. "I suppose it's too late to mention this, but the med facility probably has surveillance cams, too."

"I know," Mara said. "Don't worry, I took care of it. Here, hold these."

She passed over the empty vial and full squeeze bottle, giving Sansia a quick once-over as she did. Despite the other woman's efforts to clean up, her hair and clothing were still badly streaked and stained with the slime she'd spent the day in. Whatever Praysh's reasons for hating human females, Mara decided darkly, he'd honed his campaign of degradation to a fine edge.

"I didn't think you were going to come back," Sansia said, her voice sounding a little odd as Mara began filling the second squeeze bottle from one of her other vials. "I'm glad I was wrong."

"I'm used to being underestimated," Mara assured her. "You think you can find your way to where your ship's being kept?"

"As I would the road back home from an execution ground," Sansia said feelingly.

"Good. Describe the route for me."

Even without looking she could sense the sudden tension in Sansia's mind and body. "Why do you need to know?" the other woman asked cautiously. "We're going to be together, right?"

"We could get separated," Mara pointed out patiently. "Or you could be hurt or otherwise incapacitated. I don't want to have to lug you around and look for the way out at the same time."

There was a short pause. "I suppose that makes sense," Sansia conceded reluctantly at last. "Okay. You head out the door over there and turn right . . ."

She went through the whole route, describing each turn and intersection in precise terms. Clearly, the woman had an eye for detail. By the time she finished, the second squeeze bottle was full.

And they were ready. "Okay," Mara said, handing Sansia the second empty vial and taking the full squeeze bottle back from her. "Ditch those empties somewhere out of sight and then move over toward the door. You ever have fire drills in here?"

Sansia blinked. "Not since I arrived, no."

"Well, you're going to have one now," Mara said. "When the Drach'nam come barging in, make sure you don't get run over. Other than that, just wait near the door until I come for you."

"Understood." Sansia took a deep breath. "Good luck."

She moved away from Mara, easing gingerly through the press of still slime-covered women. Mara stayed with the crowd, moving slowly forward as places at the trough opened up, running through a slow mental countdown and wondering if she could risk cleaning up a bit herself before they made their break. Probably shouldn't take the time, she reluctantly decided. The Bith would notice the missing vials the first time he looked into the supply cabinet, and he'd probably be as quick to report the loss as he'd been to scrape the slime off the surveillance cam.

The last woman in front of her moved away, and Mara was finally in position. Palming her last full vial, she stepped to the trough, and, with a smooth wave of her arm, she poured its contents into the filthy water.

And with an angry hiss, the trough abruptly erupted with a sizzle of flame and a cloud of yellow smoke.

There were a half-dozen piercing screams as women whose minds had been systematically reduced to near-catatonia woke up enough to claw their way back from this sudden and inexplicable danger. The smoke continued to billow up and out, and within seconds the room was impossible to see across. There were more screams and shouts, the thudding of feet and colliding bodies, as a sudden panic gripped women who had nearly lost the ability to feel emotion of any sort. There was no place to go, no place to hide, and they all knew it.

Praysh's guards were faster on the uptake than Mara had expected them to be. She was barely halfway to the door, pushing her way through the chaos, when the heavy panel slammed in and a dozen of the Drach'nam thundered into the room. Mara caught a glimpse of heavy extinguisher canisters as they passed her on their way to the smoking trough—

And then she'd made it to the door, and Sansia was at her side. "What did you *do*?" the other woman hissed.

"Just a little chemical diversion," Mara said, peering through the smoke at the doorway. Not all the guards had charged to the rescue of Praysh's precious slave laborers: two of them were blocking the corridor just outside the room, neuronic whips held ready for any attempt by the slaves to take advantage of the confusion. "Stay behind me," she added, getting one of her squeeze bottles in each hand and stepping out the door.

One of the guards snorted at this slim human female apparently challenging them. "Where do you think *you're*—?"

He never got to finish his question. Raising her hands, Mara squeezed a shot of liquid from one of her bottles into each of the guards' faces. They sputtered, lunging forward even as they tried to turn away from the stream of spattering fluid. Crossing her wrists, Mara switched aim and gave each guard's face a dose from the other bottle—

And with howls that shook the corridor, both Drach'-nam dropped their whips and staggered back away from the women, hands clutching at their faces.

"Come on," Mara snapped to Sansia. Ducking between the Drach'nam, she snatched up one of the fallen whips and headed at a dead run down the corridor.

She reached a cross corridor just as another pair of Drach'nam came around it. Gaping, they grabbed for their whips, but before they could get them into position, Mara's lash snaked out, wrapping around both of their necks. They bellowed almost as loudly as the last pair had as they fell into a tangle of arms and legs onto the stone floor. Mara plucked a replacement whip from one of their hands, and continued past.

"This way," Sansia called, in the lead now. "At the next corridor we turn right up the stairs—"

"Stop them!" a voice bellowed from behind them. Mara glanced back over her shoulder, her senses tingling with sudden danger—

And ahead of her, Sansia screamed.

Mara twisted back around, her whip already in motion. Two Drach'nam had appeared from ambush out of doors on opposite sides of the corridor, both their whips now wrapped around a violently twitching Sansia.

Mara snapped her whip at the attacker on the left, catching him a glancing blow across shoulder and back as he ducked away. He snarled something vicious as the current shot briefly through him, but he managed to keep his grip on his own whip. Mara brought the lash back over her shoulder and sent it toward the other Drach'nam—

And then, without warning, the weapon abruptly seemed to catch in midair, the sudden loss of momentum nearly yanking it out of her hand. A movement above her caught her eye, and she looked up.

To see that the rocky ceiling overhead had vanished, replaced by a forest of thick, multi-barbed spines pointing down toward her. Her lash had hung up on them, hopelessly entangled among the barbs.

"Foolish human," Praysh's voice purred from some hidden speaker amid the thicket. "You didn't really think I would rely solely on neuronic whips and Drach'-nam muscle to keep my slaves in line, did you?"

Mara ignored him, heading toward the two guards still pinioning Sansia in place between them. With their whips locked around her, they had only their knives left in reserve. . . .

"Stop," Praysh ordered, all the levity gone from his voice. "I don't particularly want to kill you, human, but I will if you force my hand."

Mara kept going. Both guards had their knives out now, and had half turned to point them at the suicidal human charging toward her death. Mara stretched out toward the blades with the Force, preparing to twist them aside at just the right moment—

And then, behind her two opponents, the corridor was suddenly filling with Drach'nam.

Mara came to a reluctant stop, the sour taste of defeat

in her mouth. Force skills or not, Imperial combat training or not, there was no way she could take on the entire garrison by herself. Not here, not now. "I'm willing to make a deal," she called toward the ceiling.

"I'm sure you are," Praysh said, purring again. "Guards: release the second woman and bring them both to my audience chamber. I have some questions I want to ask our scrappy little fighter."

With Sansia still suffering from the partial muscular paralysis brought on by the neuronic whip, their progress up the stairway and along the stony corridors was decidedly slow. Mara supported the other woman as they walked, the guards glowering around them the whole way. Several times Mara asked for their help in carrying the injured woman, requests that went ignored.

Which was, of course, precisely the response—or lack of it—that she'd hoped for. With the task of supporting Sansia falling totally on her, she was able to adjust the timing and stall off their arrival at Praysh's audience chamber until Sansia was mostly recovered from her ordeal. Any fresh escape attempt they were able to make, after all, would be considerably simplified if they were each able to do their own running.

It was quickly clear, though, that Praysh had no intention of making any such attempts easy for them. From the number of Drach'nam lined up against the walls or standing in a protective ring around Praysh's throne, it looked like His First Greatness had half his garrison in here. "Looks like you're having a party," Mara commented as she and Sansia were led to within a couple of meters of the inner guard ring. "Are you that afraid of us?"

"Oh, the guards are merely here in hopes you'll give them an excuse to avenge what you did to Brok and Czic outside the slave quarters," Praysh said offhandedly. "I'm curious: where did you obtain the acid you sprayed into their faces?"

"I borrowed the ingredients from your dispensary," Mara told him. There was no point in deflecting the question; if they hadn't noticed the thefts yet, they would soon enough. "It's just a matter of knowing which chemicals to mix."

"Interesting," Praysh said, leaning back in his throne and regarding Mara with a mixture of curiosity and suspicion. "Hardly the sort of knowledge a slave sent by the Mrahash of Kvabja should be expected to have."

He shrugged elaborately. "But of course, that's an irrelevant comment, isn't it? Given that you weren't sent by the Mrahash of Kvabja."

Mara felt her throat tighten. Bardrin had assured her that the Mrahash was currently out of the sector, and that there was no way Praysh could check out her cover story. "Of course he sent me," she said, stretching out to the alien's mind, trying to figure out if this was some kind of trick.

"Spare me your lies," Praysh said, his voice suddenly harsh. And no, there was no trickery in his thoughts. "I have a communication from the Mrahash himself, saying he's never heard of you. In fact, I was just about to send for you when you made your pitiful escape effort."

"I told you Daddy would try to force you to leave without me," Sansia murmured.

A whip cracked from the side, and Sansia jerked, inhaling sharply in pain. Mara glanced at her, saw the bright streak of blood across her cheek. "If you have something to say, you will say it to me," Praysh said coldly. "And you will start by telling me who you are and exactly why you're here."

"And if I don't?" Mara asked.

Praysh's gaze shifted to Sansia. "We'll start the persuasion with your friend here. I don't think you want to hear the details."

Mara looked around the room, searching for a chink—any chink—in Praysh's defenses. But there wasn't one. About all she could do now was refuse to talk and hope there would be fewer guards to deal with in whatever torture chamber they took her and Sansia to.

Unless they didn't plan to let her watch. Or, worse, let her watch on a monitor from a different location entirely. That would mean letting them put Sansia under a knife. . . .

A quarter of the way across the room, one of the guards at the chamber's main entrance door abruptly stepped forward, a comlink in his hand. "Your First Greatness, a word if I may," he called toward the throne. "I've just received word that there is new evidence of who this spy is."

"Excellent," Praysh said, swiveling his throne around to face that direction. "Bring it to me."

The guard spoke into the comlink, and the door opened to reveal two more Drach'nam and H'sishi, the Togorian scavenger Mara had met briefly outside the palace wall. Clutched in H'sishi's hands was a section of the packing cylinder Bardrin's floater globe had been in.

The section that had had Mara's lightsaber concealed in it.

Mara clenched her hands tightly as the trio marched through the assembled guards toward the throne. Any chance she and Sansia might have of escaping was going to depend heavily on the fact that Praysh didn't know about her Force abilities. If H'sishi showed the lightsaber to him, that advantage would vanish in that same heartbeat. She had to make her move before that happened.

But there was still no chance. A Drach'nam on either side of her, more of them crowding the room, the packing cylinder section too far away for her to rip out the inner lining and get the lightsaber out . . .

"Who is this?" Praysh demanded.

"A scavenger from the street," one of the guards said. "This is a section of the packing cylinder which the human brought your gift in." He reached over to take the cylinder section from H'sishi—

The Togorian pulled it away from him. [It is mine to show,] she hissed. [My discovery. My reward.]

"Just let her bring it," Praysh said, gesturing impatiently. "Show me this supposed evidence."

Deliberately, Mara thought, H'sishi looked over at the two women. Then, stepping through the inner ring of guards, she held the cylinder section up in front of Praysh. [You see here,] she said, pointing a claw to the bottom. [It is the marking seal of the Uoti Corporate.]

"What?" Sansia muttered as Praysh leaned close to look, and Mara could sense her sudden confusion and suspicion. If her would-be rescuer was actually from their Uoti competitors instead of from her father—

"Quiet," Mara muttered back, frowning in some confusion of her own. There hadn't been any marking seals on the cylinder—she'd made sure of that. Had the Togorian mixed her cylinder up with some other piece of garbage?

"That is indeed the Uoti symbol," Praysh agreed, taking the section from H'sishi and turning his gaze on Mara again. "So that's what this is all about, is it? Uoti wants their new toys back."

Mara didn't reply, her eyes on H'sishi as she tried to figure out what was going on. But the Togorian's expression was totally unreadable.

"Yes, that must be it," Praysh decided. "And I suppose I should have expected this. I must congratulate you on your speed and efficiency in locating me—it's been, what, only a week since that particular acquisition?"

"Yet perhaps the efficiency is only an illusion, Your First Greatness," one of the Drach'nam spoke up, eyeing H'sishi suspiciously. "Recall that all the packing from the Uoti acquisition was similarly thrown to the scavengers. This alien could have obtained one of the marking seals and transferred it to this cylinder."

"No," Praysh told him. "The seal has the proper edge engraving carved into the metal around it. It's genuine."

He gave Mara a smile that sent an involuntary shiver down her back. "Besides, why else would a warrior of such skill deliberately step beneath my hand as she has?"

Mara looked back at H'sishi. The Togorian was gazing back at her now, and as their eyes met, she lifted a hand to casually rub at her neck, stretching her claws a little further from the ends of her fingers as she did so. Was she trying to show Mara how she'd faked the edge engraving? Or was there some other message there?

And suddenly, Mara got it.

"I don't know what kind of trick this is supposed to be, Your First Greatness," she called, putting an edge of scorn into her voice. "But it's a pretty feeble one. I can tell from here that's not part of the cylinder I brought."

Praysh face darkened. "Can you really," he rumbled. "What remarkably good eyes. Or what a remarkable wretched memory. Perhaps that memory needs some encouragement."

[Perhaps a closer look at it would help, Your First Greatness,] H'sishi suggested.

"I think not," Praysh bit out. "The preliminary games are over. She's refused to play." He glared at Mara. "Your last chance, warrior, to do this the easy way."

H'sishi glanced at Mara, her expression suddenly looking stricken. Mara lifted her eyebrows, nodding fractionally toward the cylinder. . . . [May I have the cylinder section back, Your First Greatness?] the Togorian asked.

"When I'm done with it," Praysh said shortly, his attention still on Mara. "No? Very well, then. Guards—"

And abruptly, H'sishi leaped up to the throne in front of him. Slashing her claws across the faces of the two bodyguards flanking Praysh, she snatched the cylinder section from his hands, slammed it across his head hard enough to stun, and reached her hand in to the inner lining. Above the roar of multiple Drach'nam bellows came the screech of tearing metal; and just as the inner ring of guards reached H'sishi and threw themselves on top of her, she flicked her wrist over their heads—

And Mara's lightsaber came spinning across the room toward her.

There was a warning shout from someone; but it was

already far too late. Mara grabbed the weapon in an iron Force grip, yanking it through the Drach'nam hands trying to slap it out of the air. "Down!" she barked to Sansia as she caught and ignited the weapon, in the same motion cutting down the two guards flanking her.

And the entire audience chamber collapsed into pandemonium.

The nearest of the Drach'nam, too close to use their whips against her, went for their knives instead. They died holding them. Those further back lived a little longer, but not much. With no time to organize, too densely packed together for efficient use of their whips, and facing a weapon that could cut through the lashes with ease, they had no chance at all. Mara slashed through their ranks like a mowing machine, littering the rocky ground behind her with their bodies, a haze of righteous fury clouding her vision. Retribution for Sansia and the other degraded women in the slave pits; retribution for piracy and robbery and cold-hearted murder; retribution for the danger they'd put the *Wild Karrde*'s crew in—

And suddenly, or so it seemed, it was over.

She stood in the middle of the room, lightsaber held high, gasping hard with her exertion. All around her were piles of Drach'nam bodies—

[I would not have believed it.]

Mara spun around. H'sishi was pressed against the wall behind the throne, staring at Mara with an expression of stunned disbelief, a half-dozen oozing wounds scattered across the matted fur of her face and torso. "How badly are you hurt?" Mara called, crossing the room toward her. None of the injuries looked serious, but she wasn't familiar enough with Togorian physiology to know for sure.

[Not badly,] H'sishi assured her. [They lost interest in me very quickly.]

"Lucky for me they did," Mara said grimly, focusing on the false wall behind H'sishi, the wall containing the two hidden blaster ports she'd spotted on her first trip through the chamber.

Only now there was a second hole, knife-blade-sized, just beneath each of the ports. And gripped in H'sishi's hand was an appropriated Drach'nam knife, its blade stained with the pale pink of Drach'nam blood.

"Thank you," Mara said, gesturing to the wall. "I wondered why they never fired at me."

[They never had time,] H'sishi said simply.

"I see that. Thank you. What about Praysh?"

[I believe he escaped,] H'sishi said. [Along with many of his guards. But we must hurry—your companion is already gone.]

"What?" Mara demanded, looking around again. Sansia was gone, all right. "Did Praysh take her?"

[No, she left alone, by that door.] H'sishi pointed.

Heading for her ship, no doubt, all set to take off and leave Mara and H'sishi stranded here. "Blast it," Mara snarled. "Come on."

The corridors, not surprisingly, were deserted. Mara led the way, lightsaber in hand, silently berating herself for not expecting a last-minute back-blading like this in the first place. Like father, like daughter . . .

And then, almost before she was ready for it, they pushed open one final door and stumbled into an open courtyard filled with yachts, small freighters, and rows of deadly, spine-winged starfighters. Midway across the yard, a single ship was just lifting off into the air.

A SoroSuub 3000 luxury yacht.

[Is that her?] H'sishi asked.

"Yes," Mara said sourly. Like father, like daughter, all right.

But there was no time now for the luxury of anger. "We'd better find a way out of here before Praysh gets what's left of his thugs organized," she told H'sishi. "Let's see if any of these other ships are unlocked—"

She paused, frowning. The yacht, contrary to her expectations, wasn't heading for the sky as fast as Sansia could push it. Instead, it had moved on repulsorlifts to a hovering position a few meters over the center of the courtyard.

And even as Mara wondered what in the worlds Sansia was doing, a pair of turbolaser blasts blazed outward from the underside of the craft into one of the parked starfighters, blowing it into a violent yellow fireball.

H'sishi snarled something Mara didn't catch over the roar of the flames. Still firing, the yacht swiveled slowly around in a circle, methodically turning the rest of Praysh's potential pursuit craft into scrap metal. Then, maneuvering across to where Mara and H'sishi stood, it dropped again to the ground and the hatch popped open. "I thought you two would never show up," Sansia's voice called impatiently from the direction of the bridge. "Come on, let's get out of here."

The guards who'd been watching the outside of Bardrin's mansion during Mara's first visit were nowhere to be seen as she and Sansia parked their landspeeder and headed inside.

And, as it turned out, for good reason.

"Welcome back, Mara," Karrde said, rising from his chair beside Bardrin's massive desk as Mara and Sansia entered. He was smiling, but Mara could sense the icy anger simmering beneath the pleasant expression. "Excellent timing, as always. We've just secured the mansion, and I was about to start putting together an attack force to come after you." He half bowed to Sansia. "You must be Sansia Bardrin. Welcome home, as well."

"Thank you," Sansia said, nodding back. "I'm impressed—the people who designed this little fortress for my father claimed it would be impossible for anyone to take it. Not intact, at least."

"I had some professional assistance." Karrde looked at Bardrin, seated in glowering silence behind his desk. "As well as considerable motivation. You may want to explain to your father later that playing games with my people this way is not a way to maintain a long and healthy life."

"Don't worry," Sansia promised darkly. "He and I have a great deal to talk about. Starting with his willingness to leave me to rot in Praysh's slime pits as long as he got his precious *Winning Gamble* back."

"You wouldn't have been there more than another six hours," Bardrin rumbled. "I already had a team assembled to come in after you."

"Through Praysh's outer defenses?" Sansia snorted. "They'd have been cut to ribbons before they even hit atmosphere."

Mara cleared her throat. "Actually, I think you'll find he's been even more devious than you thought," she said, stretching out with the Force to Bardrin's mind. She had most of the pieces now, but his emotional reactions would help confirm she was putting them together in the right order. "I think he set you up deliberately to be captured by those pirates, knowing they'd send you and the *Winning Gamble* straight to Praysh."

Sansia frowned at her. "You can't be serious. What would he gain by that?"

Mara smiled tightly at Bardrin. "Some brand-new, high-tech prototypes Praysh stole from the Uoti Corporate."

Bardrin's expression remained solidly under control, but his guilty mental twitch was all the confirmation Mara needed. "I don't know what you're talking about," he growled.

"But continue anyway," Karrde invited, a sly smile touching his lips. Mara had been with him long enough, she knew, for him to recognize that she never used this tone of voice when she was just guessing. "This is most interesting."

Mara looked at Sansia. "You remember that Praysh mentioned it had only been a week since the Uoti theft. Your father heard about it and decided to steal it from them before Uoti could get organized to retrieve it themselves. He knew that when the pirates gave you to Praysh they'd also give him the *Winning Gamble*; and so he rigged that fancy targeting system you told me about to make a complete sensor recording of Praysh's defense array on the flight in."

Sansia's face had turned to glazed stone. "Why, you vac-hearted, manipulative nerf belly," she breathed, her eyes locked on her father's face like twin turbolasers. "You deliberately put me *through* that—?"

"I thought someone of Jade's skills would have a better chance of getting out alone," Bardrin cut her off brusquely. "*And* she would have an easier time getting to the *Winning Gamble* from Praysh's audience chamber instead of the slave quarters, which is why I sent that anonymous tip suggesting he contact the Mrahash of Kvabja about the floater globe. Once we had the *Winning Gamble* and could analyze Praysh's outer defense array, our private troops could have swept in with ease, rescued you, *and* destroyed Praysh's operation in a single blow."

"And the Uoti prototypes?"

Bardrin shrugged. "A small bonus. A reward, if you like, for our civic-mindedness in eliminating a particularly noxious slaver. We *are* business people, Sansia."

He looked significantly at Karrde. "And I taught you better than to vent business disputes in front of outsiders."

"Yes, you certainly did." Sansia took a deep breath; then turned to look at Mara. "Whatever he promised to pay you, you deserve more. Name your price."

Mara looked coolly at Bardrin. "You can't afford to pay for what he put me through," she said. "But I'll settle for a copy of the *Winning Gamble*'s tracking record. There's some serious justice I intend to rain on Praysh's head, and I don't think I want to trust your father to do it for me. Civic-minded or not."

Sansia threw a malicious smile at Bardrin. "I'll do better than that. Take the whole ship."

"*What?*" Bardrin leaped to his feet, oblivious to the blaster that had suddenly appeared in Karrde's hand. "Sansia, you are *not* going to give *my* ship to these—these—"

He sputtered to a halt. Sansia gave the silence a couple more heartbeats, then looked back at Mara. "You already know the access and operating codes," she continued as if her father hadn't spoken. "It's a good ship. Enjoy."

"Thank you," Mara said. "I will."

"There's also the matter of *my* fee," Karrde spoke up.

"What are you talking about?" Bardrin demanded. "She already gave Jade more than—"

"I'm not talking about payment for your daughter's rescue," Karrde cut him off coldly. "I'm referring to my fee for not killing you outright over your kidnapping my crew."

He looked at Sansia. "Unless you'd rather not make such a deal, of course. I can certainly take my fee in blood instead if you prefer."

"It *is* tempting," Sansia admitted. "But no, I'll deal with Daddy dear in my own way." She smiled thinly. "Out of sight of outsiders. What sort of fee do you want?"

"We'll work out something later," Karrde told her, putting his blaster away. "I'll be in touch. Come, Mara. It's time to get back to clean air again."

They left the room and headed through the strangely deserted mansion; and it was only as they were descending the final staircase toward the vestibule that Karrde's earlier comment about having had professional assistance finally became clear. Lurking in the shadow of a carved support pillar where he could cover both the stairway and the door was a silhouette she remembered all too well.

"I called in a few favors from Councilor Organa Solo," Karrde murmured in explanation from beside her. "It was a very profitable trade."

"Yes," Mara said, shivering involuntarily as they passed the Noghri warrior and headed down the stairway. "I'll just bet it was."

.   .   .

"Mara?"

Blowing a drop of sweat off the end of her nose, Mara keyed off the combat practice remote and shut down her lightsaber. "Come in," she called.

"Thought I'd find you here," Karrde said, glancing around the *Wild Karrde*'s exercise room as he walked in. "H'sishi said you'd been spending a lot of time alone in here. Making angry sounds was how she put it."

"I've been working out a few frustrations," Mara conceded, snagging a towel and wiping the moisture off her face. "How's she doing?"

"Mostly healed," Karrde said, crossing to one of the resistance benches and sitting down. "It was her very first time in a bacta tank, as it happens. She's rather impressed."

"We need to do more for her than just get her back to health," Mara said. "She really put her neck on the block when she brought my lightsaber into Praysh's palace."

"I agree," Karrde said. "Though oddly enough, she doesn't see it that way at all. She told me that once she found your lightsaber and realized you were a Jedi, she had no doubt at all that you could handle Praysh's legions with ease."

Mara grimaced. Jedi . . . "I trust you disabused her of that notion?"

"Not really. As far as I'm concerned, you're a Jedi in everything but name."

It wasn't that simple, Mara knew. Not nearly that simple. But it also wasn't a subject she wanted to get into right now. "Were you able to dig anything out of her as to what sort of reward she might like?" she asked instead. "I couldn't make any headway at all on that subject on our way off Torpris."

"According to her, all she's ever wanted was to get out of that demeaning scavenger life she'd been forced into," Karrde said. "It doesn't sound like she has much in the way of marketable skills, though, so I was thinking of offering her a course of study in starship operations at our training center on Quyste."

"I think she'd like that," Mara nodded. "She seemed fascinated with everything about the *Winning Gamble* during the flight."

"Good," Karrde said. "If she proves competent enough after her training, I thought I'd also see if she'd be interested in joining the organization." He smiled. "Though whether that would qualify as a reward or a punishment is probably debatable in some circles."

The smile faded. "Actually, I was wondering if you were finding yourself in one of those particular circles at the moment."

Mara felt her lip twist. "You do find convoluted ways to bring up these subjects, don't you?"

"It adds variety to conversation," he said. "Particularly when the other party to the discussion seems inclined to avoid the issue."

Mara sighed. "I don't know, Karrde. I've been feeling—I don't know. Squeezed, I suppose. The responsibilities have been weighing more and more on me lately, and this thing with Bardrin seems to have brought it all to a head. I don't like the fact that he picked on us in the first place because we were smugglers and couldn't go to the authorities over the kidnapping of the *Wild Karrde*'s crew. And I really don't like the fact he was able to manipulate me so easily by threatening them that way."

She waved the lightsaber. "I feel like I need to get out somewhere. Anywhere. At least for a while."

"I understand," Karrde said quietly. "It is a crushing responsibility sometimes." He cocked an eyebrow. "Fortunately, like all good employers, I've come up with a possible solution. How would you like to go into business for yourself?"

Mara frowned. "Are you throwing me out?"

"Oh no," Karrde assured her. "Certainly not unless you yourself want to leave. I was talking about setting you up with a small trading company of your own for a while. A totally legitimate one, of course, which should help keep opportunists like Ja Bardrin off your back. You'd get a chance to relax away from the perennial intrigues and back-blading of the fringe, get some experience with small-business management, and possibly even gain a little more respect among the high-noses on Coruscant."

"That last one's pretty low on my list," Mara said, glowering down at her lightsaber. "What do you get out of it?"

Karrde waved a hand casually. "Oh, just the satisfaction of helping out a loyal and trusted colleague. And, of course, getting back a more experienced and relaxed lieutenant when you return to the organization."

"And if I decide not to come back?"

A muscle in Karrde's cheek twitched. "I would hate to lose you, Mara," he said quietly. "But I would also never try to hold on to you if you truly didn't want to stay. That's not how I do things."

Mara fingered her lightsaber. Freedom. Real, genuine freedom . . . "I suppose I could try it for a while," she said at last. "Where would we pull the start-up money and resources from?"

"From Sansia Bardrin, of course," Karrde said. "She still owes me, after all. And now that she has an effective veto over the family's business decisions, her father can hardly do anything to block it."

Mara shook her head in disbelief. "I really would have expected her to do a lot more to him than just appropriate some of his stock," she said. "Certainly given the way she was looking at him when we left."

"They're business people," Karrde pointed out. "That's what warfare looks like in those circles. And of course, you already have a ship. The *Winning Gamble*."

Mara blinked. "I thought that was the organization's."

"Sansia gave it to you, not the organization," Karrde reminded her. "And you're certainly not going to make a case that you didn't earn it."

"No," Mara murmured, an odd feeling trickling

through her. She'd never owned her own ship before. Never. Even when she was the Emperor's Hand, all the ships and equipment she used were Imperial issue and property. Her own ship . . .

"Anyway, start thinking about what exactly you'll want and we can work out the details later," Karrde said, standing up. "I'll let you get back to your exercises now." He headed for the door—

"Karrde?" Dankin's voice came over the exercise room intercom. "You there?"

"Yes," Karrde called toward the speaker. "What is it?"

"We've got an incoming transmission from Luke Skywalker," Dankin said. "He reports the New Republic raid on Praysh's fortress is over and all the slaves have been rescued unharmed. He wants to thank you for sending him the defense array data, and to discuss your fee for it."

"Thank you," Karrde said. "Congratulate him, and tell him I'll be right there."

The intercom clicked off. "You sent *Luke* the data?" Mara asked. It didn't seem like the sort of thing a Jedi Master would get personally involved in.

"I thought he'd be able to move on it faster than if I tried going through the New Republic command structure," Karrde said. "Apparently, I was right."

"It must be terrible to be right so often," Mara murmured.

"It is a heavy burden," Karrde agreed with a smile. "One just has to learn to live with it. I'll see you later."

He left. Wiping her face again, Mara tossed the towel aside and ignited her lightsaber. A new job—even if it was only temporary—and her own ship. Her very own ship.

Though of course she would have to change its name. *Winning Gamble* sounded more like something Solo or Calrissian would use. No, she needed something more personal, something that would hearken back to what she'd gone through to earn it. The *Jade's Whip*, perhaps, or the *Jade's Sting*.

No. She smiled. The *Jade's Fire.*

Keying on the practice remote, feeling more relaxed than she had in weeks, she settled into combat stance and lifted her lightsaber. Yes, this was going to be interesting. Very interesting, indeed.

Gathering Shadows

by Kathy Burdette

For the first time in years, Harkness couldn't stand the silence.

He had two options: he could lie with his good eye open and think, or he could lie with his good eye shut and think. It didn't matter either way, because the cell was pitch black and the only indication that he wasn't having a strange dream was the smell of something dead or dying in the same room.

Maybe it was him. All during the interrogation, Harkness had kept his focus away from the pain and the questions, and where he had put his focus he could not remember, but he wasn't required to do it anymore. It hurt to breathe; it hurt to be wearing clothes; it hurt to swallow. The nicest thing the Imperials had done for him was not to put his boots back on his stinging feet.

Moreover, there was a humming sound in his head. It could have been something to do with where he had placed his focus, or it could have been an aftereffect of the drugs. Which brought to mind the image of the round, black interrogator droid that had administered them. Which, in turn, had left him with a vision of sickly colors, distorted sounds, and a sensation similar to that of having needles in his brain and his eyes and the whole inside of his head. That thought, coupled with the humming sound, sent him into a near panic, and he decided to drown both elements out entirely.

"Hey!" he said. His voice was hoarse and thick, but it echoed and that made him feel better. At least he wasn't floating in some infinite vacuum. "Hey, yeah. This is great. Way to be, Harkness."

He thought about all the stories he had heard about prisoners who had been locked up alone for decades and gone insane. He had expected that any time in solitary confinement would be paradise, but now he could see himself in two years, drooling, talking to himself all the time. People would look at him funny and whisper about him. On the other hand, wasn't that their normal practice anyway? Harkness decided he would probably be fine as long as he never answered himself.

"Well," he said. "Maybe it could be worse."

"I doubt it."

Harkness froze. He had been answered by a female voice a short distance away.

"Hello?" he said tentatively.

"Yeah?" said the woman. Her voice was raw, and its thick, nasal quality suggested that she had a broken nose, but her tone was steady. The sound of a person in the comfortable situation of things not being able to become worse.

"Who's there?" he asked.

She slurred her words together, and it took a moment for Harkness to extrapolate what she had actually said: "Master Sergeant Jai Raventhorn, Alliance Infiltrators."

Harkness absorbed that. "I thought High Command dissolved the Infiltrators," he said.

"Rub it in, why don't you," said the woman.

"Hah!" said Harkness. It wasn't a real laugh, but it was the only positive response he could come up with. Raventhorn's voice carried the depth of the numbness, the pain, the humiliation, and the relief that was in Harkness right then, and he dismissed the automatic assumption that she was some COMPNOR agent planted in the cell to get him to talk casually.

It also sounded as though she were shivering, as Harkness was. Most likely she had been done exactly the same way he had, and that made him furious. But he didn't want to tell her that because she might think he was being patronizing.

"So what do you do now instead, Sergeant Raventhorn?" he asked.

"Who wants to know?"

"Harkness."

"Harkness what?"

It suddenly occurred to him that he couldn't recall his first name. If he had one at all.

"Harkness what?" Jai asked again.

"I . . . think it's just Harkness," he said. More enthusiastically, he added, "I'm a mercenary."

"A merc. Really. I don't think that's what I am."

"Try to remember. We're just experiencing the aftereffects of the mind-probe."

This was just a guess on Harkness's part. But it made him feel better, and Jai evidently believed it because she took a few moments to think. Finally she said, "Oh, wait—I work in Intel now."

"Intel? Were you with Red Team Five?"

"I think so. Yeah, I was," she said, and there was no trace of pride in her voice on admitting that. But then came a sudden spark of interest. "Are you one of the mercs who tipped us off about this place?"

"No, but guess what?"

"What?"

"I think there might be an Imperial garrison here on Zelos."

She gave a half-amused snort. "You think?"

"Is the rest of your team around here?"

"They're dead," said Jai.

"Oh," Harkness said. "I'm sorry."

"I'm not." She gave a heavy sigh. "I don't suppose you told them anything."

"Who?" asked Harkness. He was feeling confused. His lips had started to feel numb.

"The Imperials."

"No," said Harkness, and then he was struck anew. "Hey—"

"What?"

"I didn't tell them anything!" He had completely shut it out of his mind, but his interrogators had realized that mind-probing him was useless and therefore the interrogation was a failure, and they had tortured him just to make themselves feel better. Suddenly Harkness felt positively warm inside. It was the ultimate test and he had passed it. He could actually feel himself grinning. There was not a lower place that could possibly exist, and his situation could only improve if they had him killed now. He didn't remember ever feeling so secure in his life.

"Yeah," said Raventhorn, "I heard you the first time."

"How about you?" he asked. "You tell them anything?"

"No. Nothing."

"Good for you."

"Yeah, good for me," she said unenthusiastically.

"Doesn't that make you feel great?"

"Not especially."

"You know how many people can't make it through interrogations like that? If they don't talk, they usually just die from the physical punishment."

"I know."

"My point is, the Imperials could have done worse things. They could have run a catheter straight up your nasal cavity into your brain. If you didn't die you'd be jelly."

"You're a lot of fun to have around," said Jai.

"I'm serious!" Harkness said, although he didn't know what exactly he was feeling. It was almost giddiness. "Listen, you can go back home and tell everyone you didn't crack, and they'll give you a medal or something."

"Yeah, they *would*," Jai said in complete disgust. "That's what's wrong with the New Republic."

"What is?"

"Medals. Glory. You know. These days they give stuff out if you remember not to wipe your nose on your sleeve in front of General Madine."

Jai's voice was fading and Harkness's vision seemed to narrow to a pinhole. There was a sensation of a cool, gray fog beginning to permeate his body from underneath him.

"I can't feel my hands," said Jai.

"Me neither," said Harkness. He didn't want to talk anymore, but he knew the silence would seep into the fog, into his body. And the humming! Why wouldn't it stop? "Do you know him?" Harkness asked.

"Who?"

"General Madine?"

"Do I?" asked Jai.

"I don't know," said Harkness.

It got quiet again. Harkness was finding himself less panic-stricken about it. He was cold all over, but he was getting comfortable. He knew he should have tried to stay awake, but he hadn't been so relaxed in a very, very long time. He felt free. He wanted to savor it, even if it meant dying. Especially if it meant dying.

In fact, he would have let himself drift off entirely, except that Jai said, "I wish they would have."

Her voice seemed to ring, not off the walls but all through Harkness's head. "Would . . . what?" he asked.

"I wish they would have turned my brain to jelly."

Silence. Harkness's mind immediately cleared itself out. "Wait a second. What's that mean?" he asked.

"I just have this feeling," Jai said.

"Like what?"

"Like there's nobody waiting for me to come back."

"What is up with this place?" said Platt for what was about the third time in fifteen minutes.

Tru'eb glanced up from the information console. "I said I don't know," he told her irritably, although he could understand what Platt was talking about. Passengers and flight crews were roaming throughout the spaceport, checking their cargo specs at public maintenance terminals, slumped in chairs still waiting for their ships to pass muster, rushing to catch the next shuttle. Perfectly normal. But the locals—the maintenance people, the desk personnel, and the green-eyed humans—all had a raw, shaky look about them. Tru'eb usually associated expressions like those, and the scent they gave off, with sheer terror barely held in check.

"I mean we've been waiting for four hours now and nobody knows anything. Dirk could be dead somewhere."

"Harkness strikes me as rather resilient," said Tru'eb. "I doubt he ran into any serious opposition."

"Like what? That Imperial garrison nobody knows anything about?"

Tru'eb didn't answer. The whole point of the mission had been relatively simple; there was a stash of Imperial-issue weapons being transported in, disguised as ship parts. Platt, Tru'eb, and Harkness had planned on liberating the weapons for their own personal use. Platt had a couple of smuggler friends who were only too happy to provide a distraction. At a place like this, with the spaceport personnel totally clouded over by fear or whatever, nobody saw Tru'eb and his friends take custody of the alleged ship parts. Or nobody cared.

The hitch in the plan came with Harkness, after they had the weapons. Platt and Tru'eb hadn't worked with Harkness for very long, but it wasn't hard to gather that he had some sort of personal vendetta against the Empire. Where Platt and Tru'eb would not have bothered to ask where the weapons came from (as long as they turned a fair profit), Harkness had to know. Which had led them to some of his contacts within New Republic Intel, and somebody leaked him the information that there was currently a team investigating a probable hidden Imperial garrison on Zelos. While Platt and Tru'eb were discussing terms with an arms dealer at the south end of town, Harkness had rented a repulsorlift vehicle and told them he would be right back. That was four days ago.

"He's crazy, but he's a good man," Platt said. "I like working with him. Despite the vendetta thing."

"I agree, but I was hoping this trip wouldn't be—"

"Excuse me, folks?" somebody said. Tru'eb and Platt turned around; standing behind Platt was a green-eyed starport official in a light green uniform, holding a datapad.

"I've got the—right here, here's the—" He held out the datapad.

"Oh, right, you're the guy I talked to earlier," said Platt.

"Yes . . . about the information you requested? First of all, I'm sorry that took so long."

"Don't worry about it. Although I wouldn't have thought skiff rentals would be that hard to track down," said Platt.

"Well, we've had security problems before . . . there was a shipjacking about four years ago, and some crime lords got involved—"

"What did you find?" asked Tru'eb.

The man swallowed and held his datapad close to his chest. "I don't know how to tell you this," he said.

Platt and Tru'eb exchanged glances. "What?" said Platt. "The skiff blew up? What?"

"No, but there's been a. . . ."

"A what? Tell us!"

"A—a mistake. On the readout."

Platt visibly restrained herself from striking the man.

"What do you mean?" asked Tru'eb, reaching up and putting a hand on Platt's shoulder.

"Well, it says here that the gentleman you're looking for rented a spaceport skiff that he took out past the badlands . . . all the way north, into the mountains."

"So what?" said Platt.

"It's impossible. Nobody goes out there. Ever."

"Why not?"

He hesitated. After looking over his shoulder a couple of times, he drew himself in close toward Platt and Tru'eb, who drew in close toward him. Their heads were almost touching.

"There," he said in a low voice, "is where the dead can walk."

A week earlier, Jai had been sitting in the communications tent at a flimsy metal table, with the comm unit placed in front of her, when her C.O.'s voice came over the channel.

"Raventhorn?" he said. "We're in Sector Three now. Looks like there's a couple of scout troopers guarding a bunker."

Jai put down her protein stick and swallowed. "Well, whatever you do, sir, don't—"

"Moving in to attack."

She put a hand over her face. Her C.O. was a Rodian lieutenant who had somehow slipped past Officer's Candidate School during the New Republic's post-Endor barrage of promotions. The rest of her teammates had little or no field experience—just training. Great. Three hundred and twenty-seven combat missions, and I never got a splinter. I move to Intel and these idiots are going to get me killed on the first day. "Sir, negative! You shouldn't compromise your position, is that clear? It's probably an—"

A shout came over the comm channel, but it wasn't directed at Jai. "This one's for Mon Mothma, guys!"

There were faint rallying shouts from the other team members. Jai could actually hear the blasterfire, quick little shots being fired off somewhere off in the distance. Then there was a louder shot, followed by an explosion.

After that, the exploding never stopped; within minutes, the Imperials had moved in and surrounded the command post.

Jai ran outside into the cold, wet mountain air. A flickering glow lit up the sky in the distance.

—*ambush*.

Seconds later a massive blaster bolt, artillery grade, slammed into the tent where Jai's remaining team members were sleeping. The whole thing was immediately swept into flames and took the munitions tent with it.

Jai didn't hear the explosion. She just felt herself rising up in the air, and then a numb sensation shot through her body. She never remembered hitting the ground, but suddenly she was lying on her stomach, blinking furiously and spitting out dirt. When she looked up again, there was a bright, artificial light shining into her streaming eyes.

"Get up."

A gray shape stood over her. His voice was muffled, and the rest of what he said was lost to the ringing in Jai's ears. She could feel an unbearable heat coming from the burning tents, but the gray-clad person stayed where he was. Several moments later there were about twenty of him all around her. She was jerked to her feet.

"Hands over your head. Do it now."

Jai had never been cornered before. She should have lunged for somebody, should have made them kill her right then and there—because if there was one cardinal rule about being an Infiltrator, if there was one thing you made absolutely sure that you did, it was to die before you got taken into custody.

But a face flashed into her memory, and she hesitated. Before she had a chance to register who she was thinking of, or to change her mind, one of her captors took a fast step toward her, the butt of his blaster rifle swinging at her face.

Suddenly Harkness shouted her name, and she started.

"What?" she cried. "What is it?"

"Are you still there?" Harkness said.

"Where would I go, idiot?" she said, annoyed.

"I've been calling your name for twenty minutes here!"

"Really?"

"Yes! What happened to you?"

"I was just thinking."

"Well, you could have answered me!" Harkness sounded almost furious.

"Hey, look, I didn't do it to spite you! I just got to thinking. I'm trying to remember stuff."

Harkness backed off. "Well . . . but . . . I was just—" He floundered for a second. "Okay. As long as you're not dying of shock over there."

"Only when you yell real loud like that."

"What were you thinking about?" Harkness asked.

"Just stuff," said Jai. "Did it get warmer in here?"

"No," he said. "Listen—mind if I ask you something?"

"Yeah?"

"You don't care about your team. You don't seem to care about the Rebellion anymore."

"I do care about the Rebellion. It's the New Republic I hate."

"And you say you can't remember if you have any family."

"Are you taking notes or something?"

"I'm just curious; what made you resist interrogation?"

"Look, just because I don't like what happened to the Alliance doesn't mean I'm willing to turn on it."

"That's not what I mean," he said. "What did you focus on?"

"I focused on not telling anybody anything."

Harkness gave a terse sigh. "Sarge—"

"What is your problem?"

"You are not listening to me." Harkness slowed his voice down. "In that moment . . . in the interrogation room . . . when the drugs had worn off . . . and you tried to feel sorry for your interrogators . . . and you tried to hyperventilate yourself into a trance . . . and you realized that it didn't matter what you did, because those Imperials were living out their life-long dream of making an Infiltrator scream, and they were having so much fun they might never stop . . ."

Jai stared at where she thought Harkness's face probably was.

"Yeah," she said.

"What was it that you focused on? What image came to your mind?"

"I don't know."

"Then think! Come on! Was it a person?"

"Yeah, it . . ." Jai stopped herself. "Yeah!" she said. "It was my little sister."

Harkness shifted around. "You're somebody's older sister?"

"You sound like you think that's funny."

"No, no. I can just imagine you ordering some six-year-old around."

"Well, she's a little older than that. She's a major in Special Ops."

"So she gets to order you around."

"She wouldn't dare."

"Major Raventhorn," said Harkness. "That name sounds familiar."

" 'Course it does," she said.

"When's the last time you saw her?"

"I don't know." Jai's brain clouded up as easily as it had cleared, and she felt a throbbing tightness all the way from her shoulders up into the back of her head. "I thought I hadn't seen her since she was about twelve. But I can see her with an adult's face . . . I thought I just talked to her a few months ago . . . or last week. . . ."

"Keep thinking," said Harkness.

"What about you?"

"Me?"

"No, the other beat-up merc across the room. How come you didn't talk?"

"I don't know."

"Keep thinking," Jai said, with more than a trace of sarcasm.

"No, really, I can't . . . but I feel like I knew a minute ago. . . ."

"I'd love to know what they did with our heads," Jai said irritably. She found that she could lift her arms now, and kept trying to massage the tension out of her shoulders with one hand. After a while she began to notice that the pain wasn't just in the muscles but in the skin, and her hand came away wet. She forgot all about the tension and felt the burning all across her shoulders and her back.

Suddenly Harkness yelled, "Dirk!"

Jai felt her whole body tighten. If she could have sprung to her feet, she would have. "Who? What? Who?"

"Dirk! That's my first name!"

Jai's body relaxed, and her limbs shook from the tension release. "Will you quit screaming out like that?"

"Dirk Harkness," he said. "I'm Dirk Harkness."

"Dirk Harkness?" Jai finally said, primarily to get him to stop chanting it. "What kind of name is that? You don't sound like a Dirk."

"So don't call me Dirk." He made some shuffling noises again; Jai imagined that he was lying on his side now.

"Fine, Harkness," she said. "If you remember your first name, then tell me what kept you from talking."

Dirk was silent.

"Well?"

"I think," he said, "it has something to do with this humming in my head."

"Well, well, well," Platt said, peering over the ridge. "Our boy Harkness certainly knows how to sniff out Imperials."

"How many?" Tru'eb asked. He was a short distance below her in the gully.

Platt slid down the steep rock wall and handed him the macrobinoculars. "Look for yourself. I make it about two, maybe three. See them?"

Tru'eb got a foothold in the crags and hoisted himself up into the thick, tufted grass on top of the ridge. "I can't see anything," he said. "The fog is even worse over there."

"The yellow switch polarizes the lenses. See the hill directly across from us? It runs into that cliff, you can't miss it. Now look at the a ledge sticking out of the cliff, out over the hill. You see the Imperials?"

"No . . . just trees and plants . . ."

"They're sitting in a dugout under a camouflaged lean-to."

"Ah, yes," Tru'eb said after a moment. "Army scouts. But I don't see a garrison."

"I don't even see any valley," Platt said.

Nonetheless, Platt's chrono indicated they were some 1,200 meters above sea level. This neck of the mountains was permeated by rocky ground and sheer cliffs topped with conifer trees. The Bare Forest, the locals called it. Or at least that was what their guide had called it before he had bolted with the repulsorlift a day earlier. At least he had left them some supplies and a one-person emergency inflation shelter, the latter of which had been an awfully tight fit last night.

Still, Harkness had left a trail of blaster-charred trees and discarded rations. Those clues led Platt and Tru'eb straight into the remains of the Rebel camp—a flat, razed area with scattered ashes, melted tent frames, and smashed comm equipment. The trees were bent and broken, probably crushed by AT-ATs. Platt was hard-pressed to imagine where one of those would have come from. All around was the acrid smell of burned flesh and spent blaster packs; Platt had to avert her eyes from the scattered bodies. Most of them had been shot in the back, Tru'eb told her. The rest were charred beyond recognition.

"Those scouts have an E-web, did you notice?" Tru'eb said, adjusting the sights. "But there are, let's see, one hundred-thirty meters between us and them. I doubt they would be able to see us from there."

"They wouldn't, if I weren't wearing red. Duck back down."

"You really ought to rethink your wardrobe one of these days, Platt," Tru'eb said dryly.

Platt grinned. "I thought you appreciated my keen fashion sense."

"I do. It's my whole reason for living."

Platt took back the macros. Then she looked up at the murky sky. "Say, Tru'eb . . ."

"Yes?"

"Did everything around here just go really quiet, or is it me?"

They listened, and looked at each other. All morning there had been a constant chattering and hissing of birds, which had suddenly stopped. Platt pulled out her blaster.

"Did our Green Boys notice us?" she whispered.

"Let me have a look—"

Something came crashing through the underbrush behind them. Platt and Tru'eb spun around, but when the thing came out of the mist, they just stood where they were, frozen.

It was a Sullustan in New Republic military fatigues. But something about him was not quite right, and horribly surreal: his eyes were a milky gray and his head tilted at a grotesque angle. His arms hung at his sides, waving around slightly at each step as the head jarred and bobbed.

"Walking Dead!" Tru'eb hissed, backing away from the Sullustan, who seemed to be headed purposefully toward him.

Platt fired a blue stunbolt into the Sullustan's chest. He gave a wild spasm and then flopped to the ground.

Silence. Platt and Tru'eb looked at each other.

"Was that real?" she whispered, and looked at the ground again. The Sullustan still lay there with his face in a mud puddle. In his back was a week-old blaster wound.

Platt scrambled up the ridge again. One of the guards was situated at the front of the dugout, leisurely wiping down the barrel of the E-web; the other sat off to the side, staring into space, waggling his foot. Occasionally he would lean out and look up at the gray afternoon sky.

"Doesn't look like they heard," Platt said.

Tru'eb gingerly approached the Sullustan. He fumbled for a pulse, and then stepped back.

"Come look at this, Platt. It's incredible."

Platt gave the guards a final look before sliding back down.

"What?" she asked.

"Look," he said, pointing.

The Sullustan lay twitching, but not breathing. On closer inspection he turned out to be completely immobile; the appearance of twitching was caused by the presence of hundreds of tiny wormlike creatures swarming around the hole in his back.

Platt felt her gorge rise. She backed away, but there was no escaping the stench of the body or the memory of the worms; she leaned against a tree and vomited.

Then she stood up and coughed a couple of times. "Thank you, Tru'eb. Thank you for sharing that with me. I'm just going to go far away from you right now."

She ventured a little ways into the woods, until the smell dissipated somewhat. Tru'eb followed her. "But don't you see?" he said. "This is the source of the Walking Dead illusion. Some parasites can release enzymes which provide electrical stimulation to the brain of a dead host. So this fellow may be biologically deceased, but there are artificial signals going out to his body."

Platt turned around. "Get outta here."

"Do you have a better explanation?"

"Worms operating a complex bioelectrical system? You're making that up."

"All right, so I'm just guessing. But you know," said Tru'eb, studying a worm perched on the tip of his index finger, "I have actually heard about a similar incident. Do you remember when I was working on Big Quince's ship?"

Platt rolled her eyes. "You think I could ever forget?"

"This was before I met you. I was not privy to a great deal of information, of course, but I recall a story that was going around. Apparently some Imperial friends of

Big Quince's were quite traumatized after seeing a squadron of dead stormtroopers stagger across a battlefield. At the time I assumed that the storytellers were spiced. Now I wonder."

Worms inside your armor. Platt felt her entire body start to pucker.

"Supposedly," Tru'eb went on, "each corpse walked around aimlessly for a while, then went back to the place where it had been killed."

"And this guy here was walking toward the Green Boys over there."

"That does not necessarily mean he died there."

"No, but something's definitely up with those guys," Platt said. "I mean, look at them. If it weren't for the fog, they'd have the best vantage point in the whole mountain range. You wanna tell me they're just sitting around guarding nothing?"

Tru'eb held up his hands. "Furthest thing from my mind."

Platt looked at the Sullustan again. For a moment she thought she was going to vomit again. But instead, she stopped herself and broke into a slow grin.

"Hold on just a second," she said. "I have an idea."

When Harkness opened his eyes this time, it was still dark, but his body felt almost weightless. Not dizzy and thick, not drugged; just light. It was because there was less pain in his body now.

He didn't feel as though he could sit up yet, but at least the possibility of moving didn't fill him with trepidation anymore. And the humming sound lingered at the back of his head in a muted, almost pleasant way. He entertained the idea that it might be a fraction of a song Chessa used to sing; she had been on his mind for what seemed like hours now, although he couldn't remember her ever singing in front of him.

"Hey," he said. His voice was stronger, clearer. "Hey, Sarge."

"What?" said Jai, still across the room.

"How you feeling?"

"Better, I guess," she said.

"Me too. I don't know why."

"How long have we been here?"

"Dunno. A few days. Maybe a week."

"Maybe an hour."

"Maybe."

"Has this ... uh ... ever happened to you before?" she asked.

"Getting captured? Yes," he said. The memory of it appeared out of nowhere and surprised him; nothing about his current ordeal had seemed familiar until now.

"Oh," she said.

He expected her to ask if that was how he had lost his eye, and then remembered that she still couldn't see his face. In all the time they had been there, their eyes still had not adjusted to the darkness.

"Did they work you over that time?" she asked.

"Yeah. Worse than this."

"Can't imagine that."

"Well, maybe not by much," he said. "Is that what you were thinking about over there? My prison record?"

Suddenly he recalled something he had said earlier, regarding the gray boys in the interrogation room. Living their lifelong dream of making an Infiltrator scream. Maybe Jai had been done the same way as he had, and then again—

"Jai?" he said tentatively. "Do you—still have both eyes?"

"Huh?"

"I mean ... did they put your eyes out?"

Jai laughed, a surprising, loud, sardonic cackle. It took her a couple of minutes to rein it in, and then she said, "Hey, Dirk—who can tell?"

Harkness felt his lips twitch slightly.

Then he heard more laughter, both of their voices, ringing off the walls, choking through the pain, and eventually dying down to a few stuttering gasps. When it was over, his ribs ached and his throat hurt, but he felt an unfamiliar satisfaction.

"Why'd you ask me that, anyway?" asked Jai around a final chuckle.

"Forget it. Long story."

"Oh, well, you better not get started. I have to be somewhere in ten minutes."

"Yeah, I have a date myself."

It occurred to Harkness that he did have someplace to be, and people to be with. But where, and with whom? When the walls stopped ringing, the humming came back.

"Is that what you've been thinking about?" asked Jai. "My eyes? If it makes you feel better, Harkness, I'm told they're stunning."

"No," said Harkness, and he sobered. "I was actually thinking about Chessa."

"Who's that?"

"My girl." Harkness thought about her face the last time he had seen her. It was a nice, normal day, full of routines, loading the ship, the two of them flirting over the cargo load. But he had known, somewhere on the odd fringes of his mind, that she was about to die. He always knew when somebody was about to die. There was a softness to his or her features on those days. He would see it all through his stint in the Alliance, and he saw it for the first time in Chessa, standing there in the docking bay.

"Do you think about her a lot?" Jai asked.

"She's dead," said Harkness in his usual blunt, conversation-ending tone. Dirk, how's Chessa doing these days? She's dead. Oh. They always changed the subject after that.

But not Jai. "I know," she said.

"No, you didn't."

"Yes, I did. It's the way you said her name."

Harkness didn't know how to respond to that. Jai had spoken with such confidence, and he hated it when people thought they could dissect him. Like all those Alliance counselors he never wanted to go to.

"How did I say her name?"

"Like it was sacred."

"So what? That's how you said your sister's name."

"Yeah, but—"

Jai broke off, so abruptly that Harkness thought she had disappeared altogether. In her place Harkness imagined a deep black hole generating silence, threatening to suck him through, too. Harkness could actually hear it, ringing, clouding his ears.

Then his mind cleared out and he realized what he had said. And what it had meant.

"Sarge?" he said.

"Yeah." Her voice took on a heavy, listless resignation that was very familiar to Harkness. He wished that she had the energy to crawl across the floor and smack him across the face. Or that he had the energy to do it for her.

"When?" he asked.

"Two months ago."

Endor. No wonder the name had sounded familiar. Harkness remembered briefly meeting a tall, dark-haired officer named Morgan Raventhorn shortly before the battle. A kid, really. He imagined that girl lying on the floor across from him, with a slightly older face.

Jai remained quiet, but her breathing hadn't changed. She wasn't crying. He wondered whether she had cried over her sister at all, and if not, whether she would anytime soon. That idea puzzled him; up until that moment, he had guessed that Jai's mind worked much the way his did, and that their experiences were similar. But he had never been so numb he couldn't mourn.

Harkness's usual course, as a practiced loner, was to give other loners a fairly wide berth. If they wanted to be left alone, he knew it, and he would honor it. But Jai was different. Certainly Harkness had lost his faith in the New Republic, had lost his faith in love, and sometimes had lost faith in himself and his purpose. But he couldn't imagine what you did when you lost your faith in everything all at once.

"Chessa was killed by a bunch of stormtroopers," he told her. "All she was doing was loading crates, but they started a firefight with her. They knew she was a Rebel sympathizer."

Jai was silent. Harkness went on, "I had been thinking about marriage at the time. I was an idiot, you know; I was young, I thought I could have everything."

"I had a fiancé myself," she said.

"What was his name?"

"Krül."

She said it the way she had said Morgan's name.

Harkness didn't think he should say anything else after that. He felt embarrassed at having told Jai so much about himself. Even after four years in the Alliance among people he trusted without question, he had not told anyone about Chessa. To those who had known her he never talked about what she meant to him.

The silence seemed to fill up all around him like some invisible snow, and he thought about the absolute last time he had seen Chessa. Pasty, bleeding. Not even a person, really. Some dead people looked like they were sleeping; Chessa's expression was frozen, her eyes staring up at the docking bay ceiling, surprised and horrified. He shook that image away and pictured her alive and healthy. Then he pictured her lying in a dark cell with a bloody nose and nothing to live for.

At that moment, Harkness came across a part of himself that he did not like to acknowledge, and his stomach tightened. It was the part that had already begun to dissolve the security of his prison, and his sense of unparalleled freedom. It was the entire reason the interrogation officers had seen fit to beat him. He had yet again discovered, to his dismay, the part of himself that wanted to survive. Whole. Undefeated.

Harkness sighed heavily. Well, it was cozy while it lasted. He shut his eyes and took a few deep breaths, willing his body to heal itself, willing the pain to stop. It wasn't that he had any flair for manipulating the Force or anything like that; he just knew that the reason he had survived all the injuries and setbacks and impossible missions that had marked his military career was because he had willed it. And that was why he wasn't going to die in this cold, rank little cell. Just by wanting to heal, willing himself to live, he'd find some way to save himself from whatever the Imperials had planned for him.

Saving Jai, on the other hand—that was the part he feared he couldn't do anything about.

"Radlin?" said the taller of the guards, thoughtfully giving the E-web a final wipe and sticking the rag in his back pocket. His voice echoed off the mountainside. "Radlin, I'm bored."

"I guessed," said Radlin, still sitting and waggling his foot.

"I mean really bored. Really really. What are we even here for? There's no more Rebels."

Radlin said, "It's procedure. Procedure is this thing you do where you follow orders so you get that promotion thing we talked about?"

"I'm just saying we should think up something to do."

"You're just all antsy 'cause that merc guy showed up looking for the Rebels."

"*You're* just all mad 'cause we weren't the ones who caught him. Look, Rad, let's just go hunting or something. Pick off some more of those Walking Dead Rebels."

Behind a nearby tree, Tru'eb caught his breath when he heard them mention the Walking Dead. But it was too late—right on cue, Platt came stumbling up the hill toward the guards. She was trying to imitate the Sullustan's jerky walk and his glazed expression, but her steps were exaggerated and her tongue was hanging out of her mouth. Tru'eb put a hand to his face and shook his head.

Nevertheless, Radlin leaped up, knocked over his chair, and stumbled backwards. When the tall one turned around and saw Platt, he visibly tensed, but he gave a terse, macho laugh. "Radlin, you want this one?"

Platt stopped when the guards' ledge was at her chest level. "Excuse me, gentlemen," she said, clasping her hands behind her back. "Is this the way to the spice mines of Kessel?"

Radlin gave a shriek and opened fire.

"Honestly, Platt," Tru'eb said, as Platt put on Radlin's camouflage jacket, "I don't know how you talked me into that. You know there's nothing more dangerous than a blaster being handled by someone in a panic."

"Yeah, but there's nobody more fun to pick off than somebody in a panic, either." Platt surveyed the area. "You think there's any more patrols roaming around?"

"Yes. So let's be quick about this."

The dugout was actually situated in front of a deep, man-made fissure that ran straight through the cliff and out the other side. Tru'eb and Platt were pleased to discover that this end of the fissure gave way to a relatively flat area of the forest.

For twenty minutes they made their way over fallen trees and scrub and large rocks. Platt was becoming increasingly nervous. From what she had seen, this end of Zelos didn't really have dusk; the sun just seemed to wink out in the evening. Moreover, the fog was still thick enough that she could see no more than two meters in front of her at a time.

"What are we going to do," she said, stepping in front of Tru'eb and walking backwards, "if we don't find the garrison before nightfall? I don't think that cheap survival shelter has another night's worth of—"

Tru'eb stopped. "Just a moment," he said. "Do you hear that?"

"No. What?"

"Almost a rumbling noise."

"I didn't—" Platt said, and then the ground underneath her disappeared.

She felt herself falling, tried to scream through a dry mouth and clenched lungs, felt a violent surge of blind panic shooting through her entire body—and then a yanking sensation through her right arm as she stopped and dangled where she was. Tru'eb had her by the wrist.

"What . . . what was . . . what just happened?" she said when Tru'eb had hauled her back up and she was on her knees on solid ground. "Did I just fall off the . . . how come I didn't see . . . Tru'eb, what happened?"

Tru'eb didn't answer; he was staring over her shoulder, awed. Platt turned around just in time to see a black TIE fighter come *whooshing* up out of the ground about four meters in front of them.

Both of them fell back in a shower of dirt and leaves, the deafening sound of the TIE roaring overhead, and Platt thought the sheer momentum of the thing might blast her into the mountainside. Then, just as abruptly, everything went quiet.

They looked up. The TIE fighter sailed just above tree level and then disappeared.

When the pounding in Platt's head subsided, she looked at what she had stepped off of. The ground ahead looked like an overgrown clearing. But now Platt saw that she had walked right off the edge of a sheer rock face that descended hundreds, perhaps even thousands of meters.

Tru'eb was next to her, staring into the gorge. It was impossible to make out the bottom of the valley, a dark well with layers of fog drifting above it. Plunging down into the darkness, the cliff wall was a marbled gray with steplike ridges naturally chiseled into it. There were also outcroppings along the way, so heavily overgrown that the plants and trees hung precariously out over the valley; waterfalls poured out of the rock face in a number of places. After several dozen meters everything disappeared into a bluish-gray soup.

Far below, winking on and off through the fog, there was a small blue light. And another, and another, and a hundred, neatly lined up. Platt shut her eyes and then looked again.

"Running lights," she said, amazed. "But it's too dark to make out the garrison."

"Hence, the Valley of Umbra," Tru'eb said.

"Yeah, I get it. Look at the waterfalls. Twenty credits says that's a leaky aqueduct."

"Look there," Tru'eb said. "Do you see that? There, and over there—all around."

Platt looked. Weaving in and out of the cliff was a series of metal ladders and walkways, probably leading to maintenance ducts hidden in the rock face.

Tru'eb took her macros. "Six hundred meters down." He looked up. "And the distance across is twice that. I suppose we can safely say we know where Harkness is."

Mist oozed up over the edge of the valley. Platt wasn't sure whether she should be excited or appalled at knowing Harkness's location.

"There must be a turbolift or a flatbed loader leading down." Tru'eb said. "You have code cylinders in that uniform, correct?"

"Yes, but I'm not keen on explaining why we're not at our post. Or why one of us grew head-tails and fangs and the other decided he was much freer as a woman."

Tru'eb shrugged. "Then it's straight down."

"How?"

"We'll take the maintenance ladder wells. They must eventually lead all the way to the bottom."

"Suppose somebody's working on them, genius?"

"Why would they? They have repulsors."

"Yes, but I'm trying to delay this as long as possible." She looked at him. "I really don't want to go down there."

"But you will."

"But I will." She sighed and slid down on her belly, wedged her foot into the cliff face and hoisted herself down. The nearest ladder was about five meters below, according to the macros, but it wasn't hard to get a foothold on the crags. Before long the two smugglers were standing on a solid, grassy boulder that jutted out over the valley. One of the rusty maintenance ladders, dripping with moisture, stuck out of the rock face nearby.

"I'll go first," said Tru'eb, dusting up his hands with dirt and taking a step toward the ladder.

Platt grabbed his shoulder. "Tru'eb."

"Yes, Platt."

"Why are we doing this?"

"Harkness is our friend."

"So what? We have lots of friends."

Tru'eb stepped onto the ladder. "No, we don't."

Before Morgan had died, Jai had experienced several incidents in which she had forgotten who she was.

The most prominent of them had happened about eighteen months earlier, when she led a five-man Infiltrator team to Bevell Three on a supposedly well-planned assignment. They were to capture four Imperial agents, but somebody had tipped off the Empire; a squadron of TIE bombers appeared out of nowhere and razed the area. Everybody fell, except for Jai, who walked away without even a bruise. As usual, she got everybody out. But for the first and only time in her SpecForces career, she didn't get somebody out alive; Leong, the team's comm specialist, died en route to the medical frigate.

Jai went through the next week completely numb, not responding much to anything or having any sort of recognizable emotion. High Command promoted her to master sergeant and she didn't object, even though she knew it was a propaganda tool. No Infiltrator assignment should ever have garnered that much attention, but this one had, and on her watch. Still, she accepted the promotion and went on about her routine business.

Then, one day, rummaging through her locker, she found one of Leong's gloves and her heart shattered into a million pieces.

Now, lying on the floor in the dark, Jai recalled that moment with a great deal of distance. As if it had happened to somebody else. The memory was vivid, and she could access the sounds and smells and visions of the time with clarity. No matter how hard she tried, however, she couldn't access the emotion.

What would Leong say if he could see that Jai had let the Imperials take her? Surely he'd be disappointed. But after two months of feeling nothing, suddenly there had been an onslaught of pain, rage, fear, shame—every bit of which was preferable to numbness. For a couple of blissful days, her brain had been so ravaged by the interrogation that she had forgotten to be numb. And now she was back in the same old rut, wishing the pain across her back, the dried blood on her face, the memory of the Imperial soldier swinging the butt of his blaster rifle at her face, any of it would jar her back into emotion.

"I'm starting to wonder if we've been forgotten. Personally I'm kind of hungry."

Harkness's voice, coming out of another world. Jai had to mentally adjust herself. "Huh?"

"I said I'm kind of hungry," he said.

"Hmm," she said dully.

"And that maybe they forgot about us."

That got Jai's attention. "What—you think they left us to rot?"

Rotting away, that was something that wouldn't grant any real emotion, either. Her thoughts drifted back to Bevell Three.

Several minutes later, there was a scraping sound next to Jai's head. Harkness let out a quick, pained gasp.

"What?" asked Jai.

"Sorry. That hurt my eye," he said.

"I don't get what you—"

"Didn't you see the light?"

Jai hadn't seen anything.

"The hatch by the door, it opened for a second—" said Harkness.

"I'm not facing the door," Jai told him.

"But you're near the door?"

"Yeah."

"I think somebody slid something in here," he said.

Jai lifted a sore arm and felt around where she thought

she had heard the scraping noise. After a moment she touched something soft and wet. Burrowing her finger down into it, she touched metal.

"I think it's food," said Jai. "On a tray."

"Taste it," said Harkness.

Jai licked her lips; they were metallic and salty with dried blood. "I won't be able to. Anyway, I bet it's drugged."

"You think?"

"You're the prison veteran here. Maybe they want us doped up for some reason."

"For what—another interrogation? They don't need to sneak us drugs for that, not in our condition. They could just come in and—"

Harkness stopped.

"And what?"

"Is it me, or did that food come awfully quickly?"

He was right. It came as if he'd asked for it.

"Oh, great," said Jai. "We've been monitored."

How could they have overlooked that? She tried to think whether she had told Harkness anything about her past missions, or where she was stationed, or anything at all that could be of use to the Imperials. While she was still racking her brains, she heard the door open, and then footsteps vibrating through the floor, right next to her head. Light flooded into the room, and Jai shut her eyes.

Somebody grabbed her by the hair, hoisted her under her arms to a near-standing position.

"Get up, Rebels," said a man's voice.

It was familiar, but Jai couldn't place it, even as she was dragged from the room, even as Harkness began shouting, and his voice trailed off behind her.

Platt and Tru'eb came straggling across the valley floor sometime close to 0600 Standard, Tru'eb estimated. Somewhere beyond the fog and the overhangs he thought he could see the sky turning pink.

Working their way down the cliff had taken the entire night, although everything had blended together in the end; Tru'eb didn't really remember what the journey had felt like or even looked like. They had just pressed on and on, barely speaking to each other, and when they thought they just couldn't take another step, they'd do it anyway. Then one more. And one after that. And another. Most of the night had been eaten up in that fashion, and now that the climb was over, Tru'eb felt dazed and dreamy.

He looked to Platt, clambering unsteadily over the rocky ground in her oversized Imperial army boots; she was covered in dirt and white rock dust, and her face was almost gray with exhaustion. Getting across the valley floor was no less difficult than the trip down, as the ground was covered with small, wet, rocky crags.

Platt caught him looking and gave him a wink. Tru'eb smiled back; Platt's eyes were tired, but clear. The approach of morning was making both of them feel sharper. Moreover, they were both filled with wonder and a sense of brilliant accomplishment. If they didn't have a greater mission in mind, they would have considered the climb alone to be story fodder for years to come.

Right, let's not blow it now, Tru'eb thought as he heard a loud, raw voice echoing across the valley. He grabbed Platt's sleeve and pulled her behind a boulder. A few minutes later the yelling got louder; a squadron of drilling Imperial soldiers came crunching by, the sergeant screaming out cadence. His voice rang off the canyon walls and floor and disappeared way, way overhead.

His men marched on, yelling back in unison. They clambered easily over the rocks, past Tru'eb and Platt, across the deep stream where the waterfalls let out, and finally the troops jogged underneath a landing platform and disappeared around a corner. On a distant cliff wall, a massive flatbed lift sat with an AT-AT on top of it. Two army grunts stood off to the side giving hand signals to the pilots. Standing in the base's weak spotlights, they were a sickly yellow color.

"Small operation," Tru'eb said.

"Pathetic operation." Platt indicated the landing platform. "If this is a standard garrison, there should be a droid maintenance hatch near there."

"Will the droids give us any trouble?"

"No. They're maintenance droids."

"And the humans?"

"We shouldn't have any real trouble finding an unmanned security station. This Sergeant Radlin guy should have enough clearance to at least get a look at a prison roster."

"And then?"

"No idea."

Tru'eb sighed.

"Don't fade out on me now, Tru'eb. You're the one who made us start down the cliff."

"I know. Come along."

They made their way over the rocks and across the stream with considerably less grace than the soldiers had done. But it wasn't long before the landing platform glowed blue over their heads, and Platt struggled to get a code cylinder out of her jacket sleeve with her numb fingers.

The only light source they had had throughout the journey down the mountain was one glowrod, which had gone out shortly before dawn. With the platform overhead, it was almost pitch-black where they were. Platt felt around the wall for what seemed like an incredibly long time before she found a slot and inserted the code cylinder.

As Tru'eb's eyes adjusted to the dark, he began to see a weak seam of light where the door was located.

Something suddenly occurred to him. "I say, Platt—"

"Oh, yessss," Platt said happily, as a swishing noise heralded their way into the garrison. "Let's hear it for the servants' entrance."

"—Don't you think this door is a bit large for just a—"

Both of them winced as the garrison's blinding light shot out of the doorway; Tru'eb was just starting to see again when he heard somebody yell, "Hey! Who's out there?"

Tru'eb's entire body tightened. There was a long silence as he focused on who was speaking: a man in a green Imperial uniform, like Platt's. Beyond him, there were two rows of what looked like a patrol, maybe ten or twelve men, standing in a small docking bay. Beyond them were speeder bikes, neatly lined up and resting on maintenance cradles.

"Um . . . coming through," Platt said, stepping inside and pushing past the soldier nearest to the door. Tru'eb followed, his head down. He knew that was completely pointless. There was no way they hadn't been made already, and yet the troopers were shocked into indecision for a moment as Platt made her way past them with stunning audacity.

Finally one of them grabbed her by the arm and said, "I don't think so."

"Run!" Tru'eb shouted, charging ahead. The Imperials around him were still confused, but the ones by Platt were already drawing their blasters. Platt jerked free, right out of Radlin's jacket, and stumbled forward. When she had gotten her bearings enough to run at a decent clip, she started kicking the speeder bikes off their perches.

Tru'eb followed suit. Blasterfire spattered behind them, over their heads, into the speeder bikes. The soldiers who had gathered enough sense to run after Tru'eb and Platt came roaring blindly across the docking bay and tripped over the vehicle in their paths. *This really is a pathetic operation,* Tru'eb thought as he ducked behind a bike and fired a couple of shots.

Still, the Imperials had numbers on their side, and he could see some of them digging comlinks out of their belts. In a few seconds the whole station would know what was going on.

Tru'eb looked over at Platt, who had situated herself

at a computer terminal near the turbolift. He squatted down, got one fist around the handlebar controls of the nearest bike and his other hand on the foot pedal. Then he pressed the activation button and set a random automatic course. The bike lifted off of its maintenance cradle, shook for a second, and plowed straight into a pile of its brethren strewn around the floor. There was a loud popping noise as the whole mess burst into flames.

The blasterfire stopped for a moment. Tru'eb ran over to Platt and ducked behind the terminal.

A voice over the comm unit announced to the entire station that there was a fire in Docking Bay Three.

" 'Droid maintenance hatch,' indeed!" Tru'eb shouted, reaching around and firing at those troopers who weren't busy running for an extinguisher. "Where did you get that one from, Platt? 'Palpatine's Military Guide for the Recently Lobotomized'?"

"All right, so they changed a few things!"

"A few, yes!"

"Calm down!" Platt shouted. "I found out that there's only one detention level at this place!"

"Where?"

"Level Eight! I already called the turbolift!"

Tru'eb glanced behind them; several meters away the turbolift door was open and waiting. Ahead of them, some of the troops were still trying to return fire and the rest were shouting orders at each other or into their headsets.

"You know it says here that the whole station only outnumbers us a hundred to one? They must have captured Dirk out of sheer paranoia! What do you wanna bet they don't even have a shield generator?"

"Just keep your head down and think up some other grand plan," Tru'eb said, and ran into the turbolift.

Behind him, Platt called, "I already thought of one."

"Fight back! Fight back! Fight back!"

The interrogator's voice came through between waves

of dull pain across Jai's stomach. Her hands were free, but she didn't try to stop him.

"In the face of the Empire, you are nothing. The Infiltrators were nothing, and you were a noncommissioned nothing because you didn't have enough brain power to become an officer of nothing."

The pain stopped. Jai heard the interrogator step back and then begin pacing by her head. "Well, I guess this is getting us nowhere," he said loudly to somebody else. Jai lifted her head enough to see the reflections of several gray-suited people across the polished floor. The room wasn't very big; there was a massive desk against the far wall, and most of the rest of the space was taken up by computer terminals. The lighting was soft, almost relaxing. An atmosphere of both utility and comfort. Somebody's office.

The interrogator pushed her head back down with his boot and stood there for a moment. "I am taking my blaster out and setting it on 'kill,' " he announced. "Now I am aiming it at your head, Sergeant Raventhorn."

A moment or two passed.

"I said I'm aiming this blaster set on 'kill' at your head."

Another moment passed.

"Here it goes!"

Pause.

"It's on 'kill'!"

"I heard," Jai said.

He lifted his boot from her head. "Okay, I've decided not to kill you," he said in a tight voice. "But I will when I feel like it."

Another moment passed.

"Oh, get on with the interrogation," said another, exasperated voice. A woman's voice. "I haven't got my whole life to spend watching you annoy her into submission."

"This is how you conduct an interrogation, Major. You show them who's got the power."

"Currently it doesn't appear to be you," the major

said. "Interrogation takes control and skill. Which means you're hopeless for starters."

"Oh, aren't you hilarious. Look, I don't care if this is your garrison—interrogations are *my* forte. Why are we even doing this in here? I say we take her downstairs and do this properly."

Footsteps across the floor, coming closer to Jai. "This isn't the same as before," the major said. "I've got a different plan. Did you not read the mind-probe data results?"

"Who needed to? Take one look at her! She doesn't care about anything!" the interrogator said. "You could set her on fire and she wouldn't care!"

"Of course she wouldn't care, idiot. You could set her planet on fire, you could blow up the New Republic and she wouldn't care."

Jai was curled up in the fetal position. The voices of the Imperials disappeared into a loud ringing, which Jai thought was in her head; but then there was a deep, tinny voice in the room announcing a fire in one of the docking bays, and she recognized the sound of a fire alarm.

After a few moments, the alarm died down. The major was finishing off a sentence.

". . . See what happens when we bring her mercenary friend in."

Jai focused on the floor again. There were a few drops of blood near her head, a couple more now, a blemish on the spotless Imperial war machine. It made Jai's head clear out a little bit. In fact, she suddenly felt lucid.

Bring her mercenary friend in.

Jai looked up, past the face of the interrogator and into the face of the major. Their eyes locked for a second, and Jai saw the major's face register that a fatal mistake had been made. In that instant, it was no longer a question of whether Jai was going to talk. It was now a question of who was going to reach the major's blaster first.

. . .

At that moment, Dirk's world was the mezzanine across from him and the ground floor eight stories below him, the view divided by vertical black metal bars. One of the Imperials was trying to bang Dirk's head on the rails in a vain attempt to get him to keep still. Apparently Jai's indifference had led the guards to believe that her cellmate would be just as easy to drag to the interrogation chamber; as a result, several blasters lay scattered across the corridor, two officers lay unconscious by the cellblock door, and somebody was screaming for reinforcements over his comlink. Harkness wasn't sure how many there had been to start with or how many were left. He just knew that he couldn't manage to get hold of anybody's blaster, not with his burning, slippery feet sliding out from underneath him anytime he tried to stand on his own, and not with a terrified, unarmed guard shaking him by the collar. Harkness wasn't sure he could prevent his head from being shoved right through the bars. But then it got worse: the guard gave up on the bars and started ramming Harkness's head against the floor. There was a resounding pain through Harkness's skull, a blinding ache that shot through his temples, his teeth, his neck.

Then there was the sound of a blaster being fired—no, several blasters—and some shouts. The guard hesitated. That was all Harkness needed. He reached back, got his fingers underneath the guard's helmet, and yanked the guard's helmet clean off.

Now Harkness had something better than a blaster. The guard turned out to be a stocky, blond kid, whose face took on an expression of unadulterated panic as Harkness got up on his knees and started bashing away with the helmet.

"Stop, he's out already, take it easy!"

Someone grabbed Harkness by the shoulder. He looked up, blurry-eyed, at someone wearing white and green, and an unmistakable Imperial cap.

"Back off!" he shouted, swinging the helmet at the person's knees. Whoever-it-was managed to dodge out of the way, and said, "Hey, whoa! It's me! Take it easy!"

Harkness stopped himself. His vision cleared; the Imperial was a platinum-haired woman wearing a fancy white smuggler's shirt and half a trooper uniform. He looked wildly into her eyes, which shifted nervously back and forth as she took him in. "Remember? We're your partners. . . . We brought you to Zelos."

Someone else appeared behind her, a Twi'lek wearing dark glasses and gray robes caked in dirt. Harkness wasn't sure what their names were, but their manner was familiar; he felt his whole body relax.

"You . . ." he said after a moment. "We went to the— didn't you help me nail down a shipment of Imperial blasters? You're Tru'eb . . . and Platt."

"Actually, we're Platt and Tru'eb," Platt said.

"You came all this way to get me?"

"We're funny that way. Do you think you can stand? We're going to get you out of here, okay?"

Harkness jerked away, as if he suddenly remembered to be crazed. "No! They took her down the hall!"

"Who?"

"Jai! One of the New Republic agents—they were taking both of us down to the chamber, but she wouldn't even fight—"

"Which chamber? Where?" Tru'eb asked, grabbing him around the waist and pulling him to his feet. Harkness leaned on Tru'eb's shoulder with most of his weight; Tru'eb didn't seem to strain at all.

Which door? Harkness looked down the corridor at the row of black doors to his right; the guards had taken Jai through the one with the large white Imperial seal painted on it, although Harkness could have sworn he remembered being shoved through two red-stamped doors before his own interrogation. Moreover, this white-stamped door turned out to be labeled "Command Center."

As Platt worked at getting a code cylinder into the

slot, Harkness found himself looking at his reflection in the metal doorframe. In fact, several seconds passed before he realized that the reflection was actually his; it blinked when he blinked and moved its head when he moved his. But its face was pale, with a mangy light brown beard sprouting around the hollow cheeks, and the white eye patch was now a filthy gray.

Platt turned around, scowling. "I lost the other code cylinders with the jacket. Anyway, there's no way Radlin had this much clearance."

"But you did say you had thought of a plan?" Tru'eb said.

"Yeah, but it had a hitch in it," Platt said.

"Who cares?" said Harkness. "Tell us!"

"Okay—first, I pretend I'm a prison guard and I tell everyone I'm bringing Tru'eb in as a prisoner. Then we get into a heated fight in front of the Imperials, so that they're totally confused for half a second, which is all the time we need to stun everyone, get into the cell block, and free Dirk from his cell."

Dirk and Tru'eb looked at each other, and then back at her.

"Of course that's somewhat irrelevant now," Tru'eb said tersely.

"Yeah, see, that's the hitch."

Harkness leaned his head against the door. He couldn't hear anything going on inside, which made him feel worse. He should have known something like this would happen. It wasn't like it was with Golthan's people: pick a prisoner, teach him respect, and then forget about him. That was why Harkness's eye couldn't be replaced— the subsequent infection had destroyed the nerves. It wasn't the pain of the torture that hurt the most to remember; it was the sense of being nothing, a brief amusement to be thrown into a cell like a heap of garbage and then forgotten for three months. Certainly he hadn't been left in solitary, but his cellmates that time were Alliance intentions wimps, and not part of his team. They wouldn't even help him make any escape attempts.

The sound of Tru'eb's voice brought him back to the present.

"Oh no. They're here."

The four turbolifts on the opposite side of the mezzanine arrived almost simultaneously. One after the other, the doors opened, and Imperial troops and officers came pouring out, all of them armed, all of them running, all of them shouting. Within seconds, Dirk, Platt, and Tru'eb were surrounded.

"Drop your weapons! Now!"

They obliged.

Harkness's head started throbbing. This is not happening, not after all this, not after I made up my mind. . . .

"Stand down!" somebody shouted.

A new voice. Everyone froze. Two figures were standing in the doorway to the command center.

Harkness blinked a couple of times. He saw a female Imperial major with a red-spattered uniform; her face had flashed into his mind several times since his interrogation, but he hadn't recognized it until now. Then he saw her.

Jai was as bloody a mess as Harkness. Her eyes squinted in the combination of bright lights and, probably, a splitting post-interrogation headache. There was a thick, red seam across the bridge of her still-bleeding nose; an arm locked around the head of the barely conscious major; and a heavy, Imperial-issue blaster aimed at the major's right temple.

"Stand down," Jai said again. "I have a proposition."

A young, skinny lieutenant spoke. "Let her go, Rebel," he said. "Drop your blaster, put your hands on your head."

"You can't afford to waste time taking us back into custody," Jai told him.

"And why not?"

"Because the Major and I made a little call to the planetary government."

The lieutenant blanched. A faint murmur started up amidst the troops.

Jai went on, "Apparently they aren't amused to find

out what's been lurking here in the Valley of Umbra. I think you'd best evacuate your troops before Governor Nul sends a full-blown air strike."

"Don't you think that would be a little paranoid, Rebel?"

Now Platt spoke. "Don't you think the entire population on this planet is a little paranoid, buddy?"

"Aside from all that, I'm giving you an order," Jai said. "Because as of three minutes ago, Zelos II belongs to the New Republic. Isn't that right, Major?"

The major took a deep, rattling breath and nodded faintly.

The lieutenant stared at Jai for a minute, his eyes darting from her to Harkness to the major. It was obvious the boy had never made an executive decision in his life.

"Cut your losses, son," Harkness told him. "Do what the nice lady says."

The lieutenant looked at the floor.

Then he turned around and signaled the troops. "Initiate evacuation procedure. Come on, do it now! Let's go!"

Nobody seemed to object. Some of the grunts closer to the turbolifts had already put their blasters away when Jai had said "air strike." Within seconds the troops had begun to disperse, some of them swearing, most of them trying to shove through the crowd.

"What about the major?" the lieutenant asked Jai.

"I think she'll be coming back to my base with me. I also think she'll be loaning us her shuttle to get out of the valley. You don't object, do you, Lieutenant? Unless you'd like to come along?"

"It doesn't appear as though your troops are interested in stopping us," Tru'eb said.

The boy licked his lips and mumbled something about Docking Bay One, and clearance; then he turned and walked away.

Harkness untangled himself from Tru'eb's shoulder, leaned against the wall, and took a few excruciating steps toward Jai, who was visibly struggling to keep her adrenaline going in order to hang on to the major. Aside from Jai's injuries, nothing about her appearance surprised Harkness at all. She matched her voice exactly. And she did look like her sister, a taller, blond version, with the same ice-blue eyes. The only difference was what seemed to be behind the eyes; Morgan's had been clear and knowledgeable, a window to the brilliance beyond the absentmindedness. Jai's were bright and painful and hard to look into. Across her left cheek was a long, pink scar, testimony to a wound that had never seen a bacta tank; but in a strange way, it didn't seem ugly or out of place.

Something inside of him felt oddly settled, seeing her for real.

And in those troubled eyes, he saw a glint of recognition as she finally took a second to focus on his face.

"Harkness."

"Sarge."

"You're . . . just as I pictured you."

"You mean happy and handsome?"

"Here, I'll take Major Psycho," Platt said. "You guys lean on Tru'eb. Just concentrate on staying conscious until we get inside the shuttle."

Jai seemed to noticed Platt and Tru'eb for the first time. "Who are you people?"

"Your ticket off the planet," Platt said, taking Jai's hand and shaking it.

At first, Harkness had resisted the idea of being injected with a heavy sedative. He needed to remind himself that he was on board Platt's ship, the *Last Chance*, already light years away from the garrison, and that the major was imprisoned in the hold. At least that was what Platt had told him. He didn't remember anything beyond hobbling into the major's *Lambda*-class shuttle and sinking down into a shiny black passenger seat.

Beyond the concept of taking the sedative, however, he just didn't want to sleep. In his experience, sleeping drugs tended to pull you down into heavy fever dreams you had a hard time waking up from. And he knew what kind of dreams he was going to have.

"Sorry I don't have a bacta tank on board," Platt said, rummaging through the cabinet next to Harkness's medical bunk. "But it's only a couple days to Wroona from here. Jai, I've got a couple of Rebel friends out there. They can help you contact your base."

"Thanks," Jai said. She was lying in the bunk across the room, on her stomach.

Tru'eb came in. "No medpacs in the forward berthing compartment," he said.

"You're kidding. I thought we just stocked up on . . . oh, here we go." Platt tossed one to Tru'eb.

"I don't want to sleep," Jai said.

"This really isn't a strong mixture," Tru'eb told her, sitting on the edge of her bunk. "It's actually designed to kill the pain while improving the quality of your sleep. That way your injuries don't interfere with your normal sleep pattern. Which means you are less likely to have vivid dreams."

"Oh. Okay."

"And listen," Platt said, "it's not a big ship. If you need anything at all, press the green button on the side of the bed. Yeah, that one.

"Okay, Tru'eb and I are going to get a little shut-eye— is there anything else you two need?"

"Leave the lights on," Jai said.

After Tru'eb and Platt had gone, Harkness said, "What will you do when you get back?"

"Are you kidding? I just inducted an entire planet into the New Republic. I've got lots of desk work to do."

"Eh. Bag it. Make somebody else fill out the forms."

"Yeah." Jai was quiet for a moment; then her voice seemed to slur. "Maybe when I get back I'll tell General Madine what he can do with this Intel assignment."

"Maybe you should."

"Maybe."

Harkness felt the sedative seep into his limbs, warm and heavy. The room seemed to mist over, in the same blue-gray fog as the one that hung over the Valley of Umbra.

"Sarge?"

"Yeah?"

"You ever think about becoming a mercenary?"

"Sometimes," she said. Then her voice seemed to gather a little strength. "Yeah, I think that would be pretty nice."

"You said you don't care much about fighting for the New Republic."

"Why? You proposing something?"

"Maybe."

She seemed to drift off after that. Harkness felt the silence tugging at him, but it seemed to be easing him into a warm darkness, not a bottomless well.

Then the humming noise came back.

Harkness started; he felt a surge of dismay. But then he settled back and closed his eyes. It hadn't been a song, or anything to do with Chessa. The humming was the sound of the engines on Platt's ship.

Hutt and Seek

by Chris Cassidy and Tish Pahl
with Special Thanks to
Timothy Zahn

Fenig Nabon searched the skies for the ship she knew was on its final approach. But, from her vantage at a grimy window, all she saw was Ryloth's tortured land-scape, empty and desolate, stretching into darkness.

She shifted from one foot to the other. The move-ment betrayed her uneasiness and stirred choking dust in the stifling heat of the port control room. As the vet-eran of seedy spaceports too numerous to be counted, the Corellian smuggler knew she should be entirely in her element. Instead, the whole deal about to go down left Fen with a queasy stomach and three not so minor questions. Why was she here when she could have been making a simple raava run between Socorro and Corus-cant? Why was her beloved ship, the *Star Lady*, docked systems away on Nal Hutta? And when, in over twenty years of traversing the stars, had she irrevocably and irre-trievably lost her mind?

There was one answer to all these questions—Ghitsa Dogder, her current partner of circumstance. Feeling another bead of moisture weave its tortuous way between her well-worn flight suit and her sweat-soaked back, she wished for the millionth time that she had followed her first instinct two years ago and just blasted the little con artist right out of her wildly impractical high-heeled shoes. It would have truly been an act of galactic altruism on par with the destruction of both Death Stars.

Squinting, Fen finally spied a speck of fast-moving light. It materialized into the midsized, heavily armed freighter she and Ghitsa had hired for passage to Nal Hutta. The ship arrowed up and disappeared overhead to cruise above the cliffs housing the Twi'lek clan warrens of Leb'Reen.

Always the victims of pirates and plunderers, the reclusive Twi'leks never made even the legitimate landings easy. For the Leb'Reen approach, a pilot had to fly down a narrow rift carved into the plateau to emerge into the landing cavern five hundred meters below. Harsh gouges made by disrespectful pilots marred the unforgiving rock walls. Fen doubted the Mistryl piloting the inbound ship would make the same mistakes.

Mistryl. These enigmatic women warriors would do desperate things for their impoverished people. And in a universe of uncertainty, getting on the wrong side of a Mistryl was a sure way to meet a really certain, and completely lethal, end.

"It would be a pity if they damaged the ship," said a cultured Coruscantan voice.

Fen didn't bother to look down at her diminutive partner. "They won't. Shada D'ukal's a good pilot."

"High praise from you, Fen."

"Simple fact. I didn't say she was a great pilot."

"Or as good as you think you are?" Ghitsa taunted softly.

Fen was too tense to argue with her. "I told you before, conning a Hutt is a bad idea; using Mistryl to do it is a really bad idea."

"Such uncharacteristic understatement for a Corellian." Ghitsa sighed, smoothing back a tendril of spiky blond hair that dared to be out of place. "We have been

over this. Mistryl possess a peculiar, tarnished nobility.
And . . ." she screwed her perfectly applied face in concentration, "they are likely to identify with the seeming
predicament of our cargo. We could not count on anyone else to be as predictable."

"They also carry heavy weapons, know how to use
them, and don't need a blaster to do permanent damage to a body."

"A Hutt is a big mark in a blaster sight, and a very
small one in a con," Ghitsa replied evenly.

They turned from the window as the hum of repulsorlifts echoed in the landing cavern behind them. With a
whoosh, the ship burst through the gaping hole in the
roof of the Leb'Reen landing bay. Fen studied its descent intently with a professional's eye. *Watch out for wind
shear,* she cautioned the pilot mentally, as the ship
bounced to a final, unsteady stop.

Her partner's crisp words interrupted Fen's musing.
"I will finish the details with the Shak Clan." Straightening the shoulder pads of her tailored ensemble, Ghitsa
took in Fen's own tattered flight suit and ragged, nut-
brown hair pulled into a sloppy braid. "Must you always
look as if a rancor dressed you?"

Fen slapped her head in mock horror. "And I ever
so wanted to squeeze in an appointment with your
designer."

Ghitsa rolled her eyes with amused disgust and, as always, got in the last pointed barb. "You are as hopeless as
a Mistryl's cause." Pivoting on a sharp, stylish heel, she
walked away.

Fen positioned herself precisely so that the ramp of the
ship extended to rest at her big toe. From the bottom,
she studied the two Mistryl at the hatch. Tall and not so
tall, dark and light, mature and young, they bore vibro-
blades, blasters, and the easy confidence of those accustomed to using them.

"Shada, you're lucky you didn't lose your rear deflector when that wind shear caught you," Fen said, in her equivalent of "Welcome to Ryloth."

"It's nice to see you, too, Fenig," the older of the Mistryl returned, calm and unruffled. "I'm sorry to hear the *Star Lady* is still dry-docked. We'll try to make you as comfortable as possible on *The Fury*."

Fen scowled. Shada knew nothing pained a pilot more than playing passenger on someone else's ship. "You know me, Shada. I'll be comfortable anywhere."

Shada moved down the ramp to stand next to Fen. Fen made a point of ignoring the younger Mistryl who followed. To Shada, she muttered, "New sidekick, I see."

"Dunc T'racen," the younger woman identified herself. "And we of the Mistryl don't refer to subordinates as sidekicks."

"My mistake," Fen replied, her voice flat. Dunc bore her Mistryl heritage proudly, but not yet with Shada's smooth competence. Possibly a novice, she speculated. "My partner's over there," Fen continued, with a tilt of her head. "Hammering out the final details with the Shak Clan representative."

Across the Leb'Reen landing cavern, they saw Ghitsa in an earnest, close exchange with an immense, cloaked Twi'lek. Abruptly, Ghitsa spun about and trotted away, swallowed quickly in the darkness of the spaceport. With a flick of his head tails, the Twi'lek stalked after her.

"Where's the cargo?" Shada asked.

"And how much ryll are we talking about?" Dunc added.

"Ryll?" Fen scoffed. "Who said anything about ryll?"

A frown creased Dunc's delicate face. "Given the cost of your Ryloth cargo, we assumed you were moving ryll kor for bacta use."

Fen barked crudely, *"Saltan valoramosa n telval mord."*

"What's that supposed—?" A subtle hand signal from Shada, and Dunc swallowed the rest of her question unasked.

"It's old Corellian," Shada said, measuring Fen with a cool gaze. "It means 'assumption is the first step into a shallow grave.'"

"Very good, Shada," Fen responded, trying to sound casual or even a little sneering, no small feat under that gaze. "But I would have expected better language skills in your younger mercs."

"We're not mercenaries," Dunc uttered with the firmness of one who still believes what she has been told.

Heels tapping a staccato rhythm on the stone floor interrupted them. Ghitsa emerged from the gloom of the landing bay; one by one, five Twi'lek females followed her. Subdued, head tails limp, each shouldering a heavy pack, the Twi'leks padded forward, as if links in a chain, one after another.

"You're shipping Twi'lek females?" Shada moved closer, her sheer physical presence crowding Fen back a step. "To Nal Hutta?" she added, her voice chilling still further.

"I have a contract, executed by your leadership, that guarantees our passage to the Hutt homeworld," Fen said, again striving for offhanded casualness. She drew her datapad from her pocket, careful to keep her movements slow and nonthreatening.

"Ladies, is there a problem?" Ghitsa asked pleasantly.

Shada ignored her. "You know we won't run slaves," she said icily, her eyes still on Fen. She threw a quick glare at the approaching Twi'leks, who took the cue and stopped.

Ghitsa held out her hand; Fen wordlessly slapped the datapad into her palm. "It's Shada D'ukal, isn't it? Pursuant to our agreement, the Mistryl are bound to provide passage from Leb'Reen to Nal Hutta for myself, my colleague, and our cargo." Her intricately wrought bracelets clattered against the display. "Fee of twenty thousand, nonrefundable deposit of five thousand, contract void if done in aid of the former Empire . . ."

"The Mistryl won't deliver anyone into slavery," Dunc bit out.

Ghitsa spared Dunc a slitted, reptilian glance before returning her attention to Shada. "Of course you wouldn't slave. Slavery is illegal under New Republic Senate Resolution 54.325." She deftly manipulated the pad again. "This is my contract with Brin'shak, the Twi'lek talent agent. He is providing the services of a Twi'lek dancing troupe to Durga the Hutt. Durga will pay these dancers."

Shada shifted her measuring gaze to Ghitsa. Not that the diminutive con artist would require that much measuring. "Sure he will," the Mistryl said, her tone clearly indicating how much she believed that.

Ghitsa proffered the datapad. "And pay them very well. Datapage eight, paragraph twelve."

Shada took the pad and reviewed the contract entry. Not satisfied, she scrolled through the document from beginning to end. Dunc, in a tribute to her training, remained watchfully silent.

The seconds seemed to be dragging on toward forever before Shada finally looked up again. "According to this, eighty percent of the dancers' pay reverts back to the Shak Clan," she pointed out.

"The Twi'lek method of compensation is not your concern, Shada," Ghitsa said loftily. "And if you back out now, you'll forfeit the deposit, lose the contract, and pay a ten thousand penalty."

Fen winced inside herself. That was the right lever for moving impoverished Mistryl, all right. And Ghitsa had done her usual expert job of pulling it.

Shada didn't react, at least not visibly. Her younger partner, though, wasn't nearly so good. "Shada, we can't be party to this," Dunc urged quietly. "Not in good conscience."

"Conscience?" Ghitsa asked blandly.

Fen couldn't let that one pass unremarked. "Do you need to look up the word, Ghitsa?"

Ghitsa waved a gilded hand. "No, Fen. I have a passing familiarity with the costly phenomenon known as conscience. Still, if this conversation is going to drift into ethics, I might point out that our hirelings should not be trying to renegotiate an agreement their leadership executed."

"The contract appears to be both legitimate and legal." Shada shoved the pad back to Ghitsa. "But of course we all know what appearances are worth. So I'm going to go talk to Brin'shak and your alleged dancers. If they show any indication of coercion, the deal's off. Period."

Shada gave Ghitsa a smile that didn't make it anywhere near her eyes. "I suppose I could also threaten to report your activities to every law enforcement agency you've ever heard of, plus a few you haven't. But I won't bother. I'll just mention that you'll be in trouble with us. Serious trouble."

She looked at each of them in turn, as if daring them to protest. "And if the whole thing is legitimate, you'll pay thirty-two thousand, not twenty," she added. "Or you can back out right now, we leave, and the contract is void. Your choice."

"No problem," Ghitsa said airily, waving toward the Twi'leks still waiting off to the side. "Satisfy yourselves as much as necessary. We have nothing to hide."

Sure we do, Fen thought grimly. *Sure we do.*

"Did you really have to say that the Twi'leks could just rattle around in the cargo hold since they are trained to endure physical pain?" Fen grumbled, strapping herself in for the ride to come. Her partner had quickly moved to Phase Two of their plan and was determined to make the now-committed Mistryl rue the day they contracted with Ghitsa and Fen.

"I did see the wisdom of seat restraints," Ghitsa conceded, struggling to squeeze her shoulder pads into a passenger seat of *The Fury*'s main cabin. "None of them have been off-planet before. We don't want them panicking and injuring themselves."

"Of course not," Fen said. "Incidentally, the next time you feel an urge to spout off about how an injured dancer depreciates in value, either don't do it when Dunc's hand is anywhere near a hold-out blaster, or wait until I'm not around. Okay?"

"Given what we have heard of their unarmed combat skills, a blaster would make little difference to a motivated Mistryl," Ghitsa pointed out.

Fen swallowed her retort, preferring to savor instead the familiar thrill of a ship lifting. She felt every pitch and roll as *The Fury* fought the Leb'Reen cavern wind shear, only to emerge into the blistering wind and driving sand of Ryloth's brutal lower atmosphere. Fen counted down the minutes of that wild ride in anxious anticipation.

The moment the ship surged into hyperspace, Fen slipped free of her seat harness. She rose from her seat with a grace borne of thousands of hours logged in flight while Ghitsa was still fumbling with the clasps of her restraints. Eyes darting to the winding passage leading forward, Ghitsa whispered, "You go check on the Twi'leks."

Ghitsa was curled in the most comfortable seat in the cabin, filing a perfect, pink nail when her partner returned. Fen responded to Ghitsa's unasked inquiry, "They're fine." Fen turned her attention to the cabin's computer station, wondering if all of it had been passworded.

A moment later, Shada and Dunc appeared in the cabin, without the slightest sound to warn of their approach. Nodding a greeting, Fen started her mental countdown. She made it to three—a new galactic record—before Ghitsa asked the inevitable question. "So, what do you have in the way of recent holovid recordings?"

"We're not here to entertain you," Dunc said scornfully.

Shada leaned against the bulkhead, crossing one long leg over the other. From this vantage, she was, Fen realized, able to observe both the burgeoning spat and the score in Fen's own battle game.

"Come now, last we heard, Princess Leia had been kidnaped by that rogue smuggler." Ghitsa rose, and moved across the cabin to a small holovid recorder. Pawing through the cataloged disks, Ghitsa asked in a pout, "You do not have anything more recent?" She withdrew a disk from a pocket, "How very fortunate that I purchased the last two weeks of downlinked *Coruscant Daily Newsfeed* before we left."

The trip had just taken a horrifying turn for the worst. The Mistryl would be demanding combat allowances.

"Have you checked on your passengers yet?" Shada asked.

"The cargo?" Ghitsa asked airily. "Why?"

Shada sent a cool look her direction, then turned without a word and left the cabin. "How very humanitarian," Ghitsa commented, just loudly enough. "For a mercenar . . ."

Annoying electronic theme music interrupted any rejoinders. "Ah, there we go." Ghitsa sashayed across the cabin, forcing Dunc to shift slightly out of her way. "I confess to being an avid Imperial Palace watcher," she divulged.

An image of a human man appeared on the screen. "Welcome to the *Coruscant Daily Newsfeed.* Today's top story, the dramatic kidnaping of Princess Leia Organa by her former flame, Han Solo."

"White is simply not her color," Ghitsa clucked.

Dunc threw Ghitsa a look of obvious disdain as the vid droned on. "And now Organa's brother, Jedi Knight Luke Skywalker, and Hapan Prince Isolder have gone in search of the errant Princess."

"He'll never find them," Fen declared. "Not a chance."

"Of course he will," Dunc countered, clearly being drawn into the conversation despite herself. "A Jedi Knight using the Force—"

"Force, my blaster," Fen retorted, pulling on a loose thread on her flight suit. "He's just a farm boy from a dust bowl."

"A very lucky farmer," Ghitsa murmured. "I wish I'd taken those odds on the second Death Star. . . ."

"I'd say Skywalker has a better chance than anyone of finding his sister," Shada put in.

Fen had not even heard Shada return from the cargo hold. "Unless her ladyship doesn't want to be found," the smuggler sneered.

They all started at Ghitsa's loud outburst of laughter. "Why would that be, Fen? Not everyone is as smitten with the astral General Solo as you were."

Fen stiffened involuntarily. "Me? Smitten? He could only wish."

"Is that why there is still a Wookiee-sized bunk on the *Star Lady*?"

"You know I had that bunk installed specially to accommodate your shoulder pads, Ghitsa." Fen slipped out of her seat. "I'm going to go check on the cargo, make sure they weren't damaged."

"I've just checked," Shada told her. "They're fine."

"Glad to hear it," Fen said shortly. "You don't mind if I look for myself, do you?"

Fen headed out of Ghitsa's line of verbal fire. Prowling down the passage, she took a turn, stopping at the plate concealing the shield generator. She popped the panel out, pulled a multitool from her pocket, and waited for Shada to arrive.

She didn't have to wait long. "I don't think you'll find the Twi'leks in there," came the Mistryl's calm voice.

"No Sithspawn?" Fen peered at the deflector matrix. "Must have taken a wrong turn."

"You must also be feeling particularly foolhardy today," Shada warned.

"Oh, come on, Shada. You know I know what I'm doing."

"Perhaps." Shada lifted an eyebrow. "On the other hand, would you allow me to tinker with the *Star Lady*?"

"Not while fully conscious," Fen conceded, pocketing the tool. "Fine. You check the rear shields."

Shada stepped to the wall and punched a button. A hidden panel slid open at Fen's elbow, exposing a row of tools. Waving Fen out of the way, she selected a scanner and probe tip and set to work. "So tell me, Fen," she said. "What is going on here?"

"Should be obvious," Fen said, craning her neck to see over Shada's shoulder. "With that wind shear slamming the ship down stern first and the rough ride out, I figured the shield had probably gone weak back there."

"That's not what I meant."

"What did you mean?" Fen asked, trying to sound innocent and sly at the same time.

Shada glanced up at her. "I meant what are you doing with . . ." She seemed to struggle to find a suitable word, finally gave up. "Her."

"Ghitsa?" Fen laughed. "She's not bad with a datapad, and she can cook."

"And she's got Coruscantan Imperial stamped all over her," Shada said bluntly. "What do you really know about her?"

"Probably no more than you do," Fen countered. "Come on, Shada. I know the Mistryl have her mapped out. Her entry is probably right next to mine in the 'useful but untrustworthy' category."

"She's not Jett, though, is she?" Shada observed quietly, the question really a statement.

A thick, tense silence hung in the air. "That's the whole point," Fen finally replied, her voice dead.

Shada's next words were careful, like a sculptor gently carving a piece of limestone. "Jett Nabon was a man of great compassion."

"And look where that got him," Fen spat. "Dead on the floor of an Ord Mantell cantina, with a bunch of drunks stepping over his carcass for last call at the bar. He might have lived if someone had bothered to pull the vibroblade out of his throat, but nobody showed him any *compassion*."

"His compassion also brought trade to the Mistryl when almost no one else would," Shada continued, ignoring the outburst. "I think that's why the Eleven agreed to this contract with you, despite their misgivings about your partner. Because we honor his memory."

"And look where it got you." Fen pointed over Shada's shoulder at one of the flux rods. "Make sure you tighten that one," she said. "It can jar loose sometimes."

"Already did." Shada picked up the panel and snapped it back in place before speaking again. "That same compassion compelled Jett to pull a young, abandoned pickpocket off the streets of Coronet and adopt her as his own."

"Guess you could say that was another one of his mistakes, huh?"

Silently, Shada returned the tools to their wall case. Still silently, she headed forward, leaving Fen alone with her memories.

Since Leb'Reen, Fen could but marvel at how Ghitsa managed to sneak the word "mercenary" or "Imperial" into every exchange with Dunc lasting more than two sentences. It kept the conversation entertaining and far more dangerous than Fen normally preferred.

She and Ghitsa were now waiting in the cabin. Dunc and Shada were forward for their first course correction. The itch to be in the cockpit became an ache as Fen felt the ship drop into normal space. Just when she thought the whole process was taking a bit too long, Shada's voice called over the comm. "Fen, get up here."

She was out of her seat and halfway up the passage before Ghitsa caught up.

As they ducked into the cockpit, Shada swiveled around in the pilot's chair. "I want your opinion on something the sensor sweep turned up."

A few degrees off the bow a metal cylinder turned lazily on a spindle. An antenna protruded from its top. *Stang*, Fen swore silently. The trip had just gotten a whole lot more interesting.

Shada was watching them closely. "It looks like a relay

buoy," she said. "Apparently, it's picking up ship signatures as they drop in here."

"Blast it," Fen uttered curtly.

Shada was already bringing *The Fury*'s laser battery to bear on the buoy. "Yes. I intend to."

"It's probably too late, though," Ghitsa opined as she eased into the cockpit's rear seat. "Whoever put it there will know soon enough we were here and where we're headed."

"Who would care?" Dunc challenged.

For once, Ghitsa favored her with a straight answer. "Anyone interested in what travels on the smugglers' hyperspace lanes between Ryloth and Nal Hutta."

"Ryll pirates," Shada said, making the name a curse.

"Or worse," Fen said.

Shada deftly moved the targeter on her board. A sure punch and the buoy exploded, for an instant a brilliant orange glowing flower on the canvas of space. "Any particular 'worse' you had in mind, Fen?" Shada asked.

"The Karazak Slavers Cooperative springs to mind," Ghitsa put in grimly. "The KSC used to ambush ships along this line looking for Twi'leks to sell."

"Anyone who does this run will know that a ship from Ryloth will normally change course here," Fen added. "Usually for a jump to the Naps Fral cluster—"

"—And then a set-up there for the final jump to Nal Hutta," Shada finished for her. "Which means that a relay buoy here implies a trap waiting at Naps Fral."

Ghitsa nodded. "The KSC was once very active on this route. Jabba stopped it because he thought too many valuable slaves were dying in the ambushes."

Shada gazed at both of them, her dark eyes thoughtful. Dunc could learn much from that knowing, quiet surety, Fen thought. It was probably why the younger Mistryl had been paired with Shada in the first place.

"Jabba died four years ago," Shada pointed out. "Were you expecting the KSC to have moved back in here since then?

"There were reasons we wanted Mistryl," Fen responded truthfully. "The possibility of the KSC returning was one of them."

Turning back to her board, Shada nosed *The Fury* in the direction of the Naps Fral cluster. "Well, there's no going back now," she said simply. "Looks like you may get your money's worth after all."

"No!" Ghitsa protested with a stamp of her shiny boot. "I am going to ride up front. I'm a perfectly capable copilot—"

"Forgot to take your antidelusional medication today?" Fen cooed, pushing past her and into a cockpit seat.

Since the last course change, Ghitsa had harped endlessly on about wanting to be in the cockpit when they dropped into the Naps Fral cluster. She now curled her hands into tiny fists, reminding Fen of an extremely petulant toddler.

"She can stay," Shada said calmly as she slid into the pilot's chair. Ghitsa smiled like a child just presented with a space pop. "However," Shada added in the same tone, "if she says or does anything to annoy me or distract us, I'll cripple her."

"Unless I beat her to it," Dunc added, her eyes on the monitor readouts.

"Give you a cool thousand if you let me do it," Fen offered.

"I can *too* fly," Ghitsa stated for the official record, dropping into her hard-earned seat.

"Sure you can, Ghits," Fen mocked. "Just like the time your nav coordinates would have put us into Corellia's sun?"

"We would have just grazed the corona," Ghitsa said defensively.

"How about the time you were shooting at dust because you thought it was draining the shields?"

"It *was* draining the shields."

"It was *dust*! Blasting dust will just make *more* dust."

"Put a cleaning rag in it, both of you," Shada cut off the growing argument. "We've got work to do."

Ghitsa bridled, but fell silent. "Sorry," Fen said.

"As I see it, our worst-case scenario is that we'll find an armada waiting for us when we drop in," Shada went on. "They may try to hit the engines with surgical turbolaser blasts; more likely, they'll have a heavy ion cannon ready for a saturation disabling."

"After which they'll board us, take the Twi'leks, and kill us," Fen nodded. "Which means they'll try to be right in front of us or else aligned on our probable exit vector."

"That was my reading, too," Shada answered. "So our obvious countermove is to simply come in two or three seconds early."

Fen swallowed as she pulled up a chart of the Naps Fral system. Most hyperspace entry coordinates had a built-in "safety zone" of a second or two. In-system pilots knew to stay out of the zones to keep from having a ship pop into real space on top of them. Studying the chart, Fen realized Shada had, once again, done her homework. Three seconds would put the ship just outside the zone, probably not too close to anything lethal. *Probably. Hopefully.*

Ghitsa was clearly thinking along the same lines. "Isn't altering your hyperspace entry point . . . dangerous?" she asked in a small voice.

"Very," Dunc said absently.

"It's definitely a maneuver with a warning on the box that says, 'Don't try this at home,' " Fen forced a quip.

"Stay sharp, everyone," Shada said. "At my mark. Fifteen, fourteen . . ." At five seconds, she squeezed her hand over the levers, and star lines melted to the milky cluster of Naps Fral.

A flash of blue ion fire cut across their bow, the proximity alarm pealed, and Shada pulled *The Fury* around in the direction of the threat. In the span it took for the sensors to tell her what had just tried to paste them, Fen reached over and switched off the alarms, wondering why anyone even bothered with the prijgin things. If you needed them, you were already dead in space anyway. "Kuat *Firespray*–class ship," she announced through clenched teeth.

"Switching over," Dunc said, her voice unreasonably calm. *The Fury* shook as a pair of concussion missiles blazed off in the direction of their welcoming committee.

"Fen, find out what the computer knows about Firesprays," Shada ordered.

"Right."

The Fury jerked to port, then rolled starboard as Shada bounced between bursts of ion energy.

At Fen's elbow, the computer display began spewing technical information. " 'Puter says this model's got a ticklish spot in the port shield," Fen called. "Right below the stabilizer fin."

"Stang," Dunc muttered. "Wouldn't you know we'd come in on their starboard."

Shada pushed on the throttle. Still dodging between bursts of ion fire, she lunged straight for the attacking ship. At the last moment, she hauled on the rudder, bringing *The Fury* under the belly of the Firespray. There was a sickening crackle of ion discharge and a lurch—

"What does that red light mean?" Ghitsa asked, pointing over Fen's shoulder.

Fen shoved the other's rigid arm out of her face. "It means bad," she spat. "We took a hit to that weak aft shield," she added for the benefit of the others. "Another hit and we're in trouble."

"They won't get the chance," Shada gritted as they burst clear of the Firespray. Yanking on the throttle, she reversed the forward thrust hard, and flipped *The Fury* back over. The Firespray's left fin magically appeared before them, jutting out from the ship, small and vulnerable. "Dunc?"

"Got it," Dunc said, fingers flying across the console as she tracked the quivering Firespray and, from the sound of it, emptied an entire magazine into the left fin.

The Firespray's shield rippled with the force of the blasts, plasma ebbing and flowing across the ship's hull like a flooded river. Dunc let fly another barrage, and this time the missiles pierced the other vessel's weakening shield. Fire exploded on the ship, scorching its armor. Plates began peeling off the hull like a reptile shedding its skin.

Dunc switched over to the heavy turbolasers. The hot lasers carved through the Firespray's collapsing shield, strafing the ship along its diagonal. Two explosions, one at the cannon and the other near the reactor, and the Firespray, true to her class, erupted in a brief and blazing shower of white, yellow, and red.

For a moment they all sat in silence. "Well," Shada said at last, her voice calm as ever. "That seems to be that. Well done, both of you."

"Not a bad piece of flying, Shada," Fen conceded, trying to get her breath back and wondering why she was so winded. "Though of course I would have done it without losing that aft shield."

To Fen's surprise, Shada laughed. "Fen, you have to be the most arrogant pilot in the galaxy. You want to see if the computer was able to pull an ID before we blew it into the next sector?"

"Let me check," Fen said, keying the computer. A name came up. "Surprise, surprise," she muttered in disgust. "It was the *Indenture*."

"Well, well." Ghitsa murmured.

Shada and Dunc exchanged glances. "Explain," Shada said.

"You need to get out more," Fen said bitterly, "if you haven't heard about the *Indenture*."

"Mistryl don't move in the same exalted circles we do, Fen," Ghitsa scolded, her customary tinge of superiority returning.

"And you can't imagine how pleased we are about that," Shada countered. "Fen?"

"That ship's had more names and ID codes than a

Gamorrean has morts," Fen said. "Last I heard, it was traveling as *Salvation,* doing hit and runs for the Karazaks out on the rim."

"Firesprays are mostly used in law enforcement," Ghitsa added. "I understand Krassis Trelix really appreciates the irony of using that kind of ship for slaving."

"And Krassis Trelix is?" Shada waved out at the still glowing dust cloud. "I'm sorry: Krassis Trelix was?"

"Karazak logistics coordinator," Ghitsa amplified. "A very nasty person, even for a smuggler."

"Couldn't have happened to a nicer guy," Fen added. Shada nodded with comprehension, and maybe satisfaction, too, Fen thought.

"Dunc, let's get those coordinates," Shada said. "Next stop, Nal Hutta."

Fen rinsed the anxiety of the battle from her body. The water was flat and recycled, washing over her like a ritual cleansing that was really nothing more than a tepid sponge bath. She let her head fall forward and rest against the wall, taking a deep breath.

The KSC encounter had not been entirely unexpected. It had been a lucky break in some respects, and disastrous in others. She had done her part. Now it was up to Ghitsa to get them out of this developing jam.

Stepping into another battered flight suit, she ran a comb through her wet hair, slicking it back in what Jett had called her drowned womp rat look. Having already been to Mos Eisley numerous times by age fifteen, she had long ago ascertained how rare a commodity water was there. Her adoptive father had laughed until tears ran down his red face when she had explained that, in the Tatooine desert, water was too precious to be wasted on drowning rodents. Only belatedly had she understood that that had been his point. She quickly checked the small grin threatening to pull at her lips.

At the cabin entrance, she paused, taking in the sight.

Dunc was straddling a chair, watching Ghitsa seated near the back primly apply a new coat of nail polish. The omnipresent holo viewer hummed lightly in the background.

Fen eased back over to the computer terminal. With Dunc distracted and Shada tending to the shields, now was a good time to complete a certain task still on her checklist.

The first eighteen times Shada had caught her, Fen had appeared to be doing nothing more than playing battle simulations. Shada had her suspicions, but, as every female on that ship knew, there was a galaxy's difference between doing something and actually getting caught doing it.

Ghitsa delicately applied a streak of vibrant red to replace the pink adorning her fingertips. Dunc watched with suspicious fascination. "Why are you using such an obvious color?" she asked.

"Ohta su marvalic plesodoro," Ghitsa responded.

"Which means?" Dunc countered.

"Huttese," Fen said. "Let them marvel at our splendor."

"It was a favorite phrase of Jabba's." Holding out her hand, Ghitsa admired the gaudy red shade. "Jabba understood the importance of flaunting prosperity to demonstrate power. Since Mistryl have nothing, this is something you cannot understand."

Ghitsa sure wasn't wasting any time. Fen subtly shifted for easier access to her blaster, wondering if a stun setting would stop a truly enraged Mistryl.

But Dunc merely cocked an eyebrow, the same gesture Fen had noticed Shada using on occasion. "You seem to know a lot about Hutts," she said. "One might wonder how that happened."

"Oh, I don't think you're wondering at all," Ghitsa said with a smug, evil smile. "Surely you've read the Mistryl backgrounder on me."

"What backgrounder?" Dunc asked. *Score one for Ghitsa,* Fen thought. Although Dunc's light skin would probably always betray the slightest stress, the young Mistryl was going to have to learn to lie better. She would have to remember to mention that to Shada . . . from a couple of light-years away.

Ghitsa had obviously noticed the reaction, too. "Oh, come now, Dunc. Fen's dear-departed, noble partner dealt with the Mistryl for years. As has Fen." Her forefinger joined her thumbnail, both colored red. "So what does it say?"

"Why don't you tell me?" Dunc suggested, her voice dark.

"If you insist," Ghitsa sighed irritably. "Among other things, it says that I am a Hutt counselor. Do you understand what that means?"

Dunc's mouth twisted in contempt. "It means you're authorized by one or more Hutts to conduct business on their behalf," she said. "Like this dancers' contract between Durga and Brin'shak."

"A nicely standard textdoc answer, shadow guard," Ghitsa said approvingly. "But it doesn't even scratch the surface. Shall I tell you what it really means to be a Hutt counselor?"

Dunc nodded her head slightly to the side. "I'm all ears."

"Hutt clans appoint counselors to conduct their business," Ghitsa said. "The skill and loyalty required to manage their complex schemes, plus a Hutt's own longevity, dictate that counselors remain within a single unit, preferably a family. Dogders have orchestrated Hutt infiltration of Core World businesses for over one hundred and fifty years."

Fen lifted an eye from the screen. This was news to her, too, if it were true.

"I see," Dunc said in a cold voice. "What a splendid and honorable family history you have."

"I don't need to justify myself to you," Ghitsa said loftily. "My motivations, and those of my clan masters, should be perfectly comprehensible to you." Her left hand now completely painted, she switched the brush from right to left, and began reddening her right nails. "Money, profit, security—things even Mistryl ought to understand."

Dunc snorted. "Except that our principles aren't for sale to the highest bidder."

"But that's the irony of it. They are for sale. They have been sold, you have been sold, like any cheap trinket." Ghitsa laughed with merry scorn. "Do you really think Mistryl are immune because they don't deal with former Imperials, refuse to assist in patently illegal ventures, and charge more for the questionable ones?"

Under the terminal, Fen slowly and silently slid her hand down and released the safety on the blaster at her hip. She had no idea how much of this was show and how much the twisted truth. What she did know was that Ghitsa was trying to push the young Mistryl to the snapping point. And that she might succeed.

"For all your exalted justifications of saving your desperate people," Ghitsa went on, "you're delivering the Twi'leks to servitude and death as certainly as any Karazak slaver."

Slowly, deliberately, Dunc uncoiled from her chair and stalked over to the table, her face calm and deadly. Fen got a grip on her blaster butt, but Dunc made no move against her partner except to stand and tower over her like a storm cloud.

"The contract said they were being paid, Hutt," Dunc bit out, making the word a curse. "You said they weren't slaves. You've lied to the Mistryl."

Ghitsa raised her eyes to Dunc. "I didn't lie. They will be paid. And then they'll be charged; for costumes, board, room, and expenses. At one time, they might have saved enough to buy out their contracts. However, because Twi'lek mortality hovers near seventy percent, Durga now withholds an additional sum to cover the cost of a burial shroud."

"Shada questioned Brin'shak," Dunc hissed. "She asked each of the Twi'leks if they wanted to go."

Ghitsa held her hands out, admiring her work. "In a uniquely Twi'lek way, these dancers do indeed go willingly. They know some Twi'leks must end up in Hutt throne rooms. This is the price they all pay for a lack of power. A Hutt commercial agent will see that the clan is compensated. The alternative is indiscriminate Karazak slaving raids on their enclaves."

Dunc's lip twisted. "I'd heard that Twi'leks sell a few of their own to buy a greater peace for them all," she conceded reluctantly. "But you make it sound as if your altruism keeps Karazaks from plundering Ryloth."

"*Our* altruism, Dunc—we're all in this together, you know." Ghitsa blew lightly on her perfectly marked claws. "I advised Durga it was more cost-effective to go this route, rather than contract with the Karazaks. The KSC is expensive and their slaves tend to be poor quality." She began capping the little bottle. "As I see it, the Hutts purchased Mistryl morality for thirty-two thousand. Karazaks would have demanded at least forty-five. But then, they aren't as desperate as the Mistryl."

Fen cringed at Ghitsa's attack. Perfectly crafted in the words of commerce, she was a humanoid vision of repugnant Hutt excess.

And it had worked, all too well. Dunc stood above her, color rising, the slow boil of a jump's worth of taunts and insults bubbling over, threatening to ignite the fire beneath. She stirred, perhaps about to go for a weapon, perhaps to simply pick Ghitsa up and hurl her bodily across the cabin—

"Dunc, *in aiente,*" came a quiet order from the door.

Fen jumped. Ghitsa didn't even twitch. "Hello, Shada," the con chirped innocently. "How long have you been standing there?"

"Long enough," Shada said, her eyes on Dunc. *"In aiente."*

Dunc took a careful breath. Then, wordlessly, she pivoted away from Ghitsa and strode from the cabin.

For a moment Shada studied Fen and Ghitsa, her face

stiff and unreadable. "We drop out of hyperspace at oh-one-hundred hours tomorrow," she said and followed Dunc out into the passageway.

Ghitsa finally broke the long silence that followed. With uncharacteristic, doubting hesitation, she asked, "Do you think I went too far?"

"Hard to say," Fen said, working moisture back into her mouth. "If we get out of this alive, I'd say no. If they slash our throats in our sleep, then, yeah, probably so." She hesitated, weighing her words carefully. "You said some pretty reprehensible things. How much of it was true?"

She grimaced. "Enough. Too much."

Seeing the little grifter shift uncomfortably in her seat, Fen asked, "Ghitsa, could that be your conscience bothering you?"

Ghitsa made a show of examining her nails. "Of course not, Fen. Merely indigestion. Ship's rations, you know."

Fen slipped back into the main cabin just in time to see the holovid system sputter. Spewing smoke, it coughed out the smoldering remains of Ghitsa's *Coruscant Daily Newsfeed* recording. Perhaps there truly was a higher power in the universe and she had a sense of humor, Fen thought.

"We'll be adding the repair costs to your bill," Shada said, examining the unit.

"By all means," Ghitsa replied, moving to the holographic game table. "How about a round, Fen?"

"I'll pass."

Ghitsa shrugged. "I don't see why you won't install a holobeasties game on the *Star Lady*."

Fen laughed, stretching her arms high. "Let's just say that the last time I allowed a round on board, my droid ended up with his arms ripped out of their sockets. Besides, we're about to come out of hyperspace, aren't we, Shada?"

"Five standard minutes," Shada said over her shoulder as she exited the cabin. "I've already seen to the Twi'leks."

Ghitsa waited, then whispered, "You didn't run into her, did you?"

"No," Fen replied wearily, strapping into her seat. As Ghitsa did the same, Fen let her eyes slip shut. "Won't be long now."

"No, it won't," Dunc's voice agreed quietly next to her ear.

Fen's eyes flew open. Dunc was standing to the side, pointing a blaster at the two of them. Fen's blaster, she realized suddenly, belatedly missing the weight at her hip. Her vibroblade, for good measure, was hanging loosely in Dunc's other hand. The girl definitely had talent. "What is going on?" she snarled.

"There's been a change of plan." Dunc said. "Dogder, I'll take that blaster in your boot. Slowly."

"Certainly," Ghitsa said calmly, reaching into her boot and removing a small hold-out blaster Fen hadn't even known she owned. "I don't recall a contractual provision about a blaster in our faces," she added as she slid the weapon across the deck.

"The contract's been changed, too," Dunc said, settling in a seat facing them.

Fen felt the ship tumble into real space. A minute later, Shada joined them. "We protest this treatment, of course," Ghitsa said, getting in the first word.

Shada ignored her. "From the beginning, Fen, your behavior on this trip has been completely irrational," she said. "You convinced us to take this passage; then, at every opportunity, have hounded us that what we were doing was a moral outrage. I want to know why."

"We're just chatty," Fen muttered sourly.

"You wanted us to break the contract, didn't you?" Shada persisted. "That's the only explanation. But why? You can hardly bring suit against us—legally, we don't even exist. Blackmail? Ridiculous."

Ghitsa spoke up. "This is a perfectly legal operation.

You renege, and the Eleven will be extremely unhappy with you."

"Having others unhappy with you isn't as bad as being unhappy with yourself," Dunc put in. "We'll take our chances."

"Ah, yes—the wonderful view you get from the high moral ground," Ghitsa said sarcastically. "Not that you gain much of that high ground by shooting two un-armed people."

"We won't deliver the Twi'leks into slavery, Fen," Shada said. "Not even a carefully disguised slavery. If you won't tell us what's really going on, you leave us with no other alternative."

She paused, waiting for a reply. Fen kept her mouth closed, her heart thundering as she wondered if Ghitsa had finally made her last miscalculation. If Shada de-cided that murdering a pair of would-be slavers did in-deed count as high moral ground . . .

"Very well," Shada said after a moment. "Time's up. Unstrap—you're making the rest of the trip without us."

The Mistryl silently ushered them aft. It was worse than Fen had imagined. "You can't be serious."

Shada swung open a tiny door. "It was your choice, Fen. Into the escape pod."

Ghitsa climbed in without protest. With her own blas-ter hovering somewhere behind her back, Fen ducked in after her.

"Good-bye, Fen," Shada said.

The door slammed, shut and sealed. Like our fate, Fen reflected, before turning on her partner. "Fine mess you've gotten us into."

"What are you talking about? This has worked perfectly."

Before Fen could utter a properly acidic reply, *The Fury* belched the pod into space. She shouldered Ghitsa out of the way to get to the controls.

Just as she had suspected. There was a tiny ion engine cluster with enough reaction mass for orbital insertion, re-entry burn, and, maybe, something left over for deceleration before touch-, correction, make that *smash-down*. Typical. In her experience, the best pilots always had the worst pods.

The odds of a controlled landing in this vessel were minuscule. The odds of making it alive were only slightly better. All Fen knew for certain was that she planned on bracing herself with Ghitsa's ample shoulder pads on impact.

"Shada?"

Shada turned her head as Dunc stepped into *The Fury*'s cockpit. From the tone of her voice . . . "What is it?" she asked. "Something wrong with the Twi'leks?"

"Not at all," Dunc said, sliding into her seat and handing Shada a small holo tube. "They're quite happy. And they seem to have known all along that they weren't going to Nal Hutta."

"Really," Shada said, examining the holo tube. "That's very interesting."

"That's what I thought." Dunc gestured to the tube. "One of them, Nalan, gave me that. Near as I could figure through her accent, she said that 'Fenig-who-is-brave' gave it to her to give to us."

Shada looked out the viewport. The pod had disappeared, caught in Nal Hutta's gravitational pull. "I'll check out the tube," she said. "You'd better run a fast diagnostic on the ship's systems."

"You think we've been conned?" Dunc asked, keying her board.

"We were being conned from the minute we landed on Ryloth," Shada said, carefully filtering her emotions out of her voice. It wasn't proper for a Mistryl to show frustration and bitterness in front of a subordinate. "The only question was in what direction we were being taken."

"Well, whatever direction that was, our former employers seem to have gotten what they wanted," Dunc said sourly. "Except maybe for the escape pod part—oh, *Sithspawn*."

"What?" Shada snapped.

"*The Fury*'s ID code." Dunc was furiously pulling up the stored nav coordinates for an emergency leap out of Nal Hutta space. "Fen must have reprogrammed one of the comm systems to create an overlay. We're broadcasting as that Karazak slaver ship, the *Indenture*."

Shada spun *The Fury* around. A blinking comm light signaled a hail from Nal Hutta; she ignored it. "What are we going to do?" Dunc demanded.

"Get out of here, of course," Shada said. "I have no particular desire to get caught in the crosshairs of Hutt slave politics."

"No argument on that one," Dunc said. "What I meant was what are we going to do about our two former employers?"

Shada grimaced. Yes, the Mistryl owed Jett a debt of honor for his friendship to them. But no one misuses such a debt this way. No one. "The galaxy is big," she told Dunc darkly. "But not that big."

Dunc nodded. "Understood."

A Hutt patrol ship appeared, heading in their direction. With a final glance at the muddy planet, Shada pulled the hyperspace levers.

Fen wrestled with the pod, trying to align it so the aft shields bore the brunt of the re-entry burn. "Impact in one minute."

"Aren't we going a little fast?"

By way of response, Fen squeezed everything she could from the poor pod's deceleration system. White, hot fire burned out the window.

"Uh, Fen? The large brown area we are plummeting into? I suggest you try not to land in it."

"A swamp might cushion our landing, if we don't drown. Get ready for the cheapest mud bath of your life."

"You simply cannot be serious."

"Fifteen seconds," Fen replied, as she attempted to aim the pod toward a large, muddy swath.

With a terrific, teeth-shattering jolt, they splashed down.

Fen shrugged out of the harness. "This thing's got flotation pads. They may keep us from sinking right away." Tugging on the release bar, Fen popped the hatch open. The dreary, gray colors, fetid odors, and mud of Nal Hutta poured in.

Fen clambered out first, and looked quickly around. Swamp. Oozing, oily goo. She jumped in and was immediately enveloped in slime up to her waist. Ghitsa, however, was stalling at the hatch of the rocking pod.

"Gotta do it, Ghits," Fen called back to her.

She looked out across the swamp. "Well, at least we don't have far to go. I only wish I weren't wrecking a pair of designer boots." With a weary sigh, Ghitsa jumped into the bog.

Slogging through the tangled weeds and stinking mud, they trudged toward a landing facility they had both spotted, some five hundred meters away.

As they staggered onto blessedly dry, hard duracrete, a tusked Whiphid lumbered out of the building. His manner was so casual, Fen concluded that two women missing the landing pad to crash in the swamp was a near everyday occurrence.

Ghitsa and the Whiphid exchanged a rapid-fire mix of Basic and Huttese, and the Whiphid ambled off.

"Now what?"

"With your best efforts, we have, however miraculously, crashed in Durga's Clan territories. I told him that I am one of Durga's counselors."

"He believed you?"

"Of course. This kind of mishap is not uncommon if you deal on behalf of Hutt clans." Ghitsa seemed bemused by Fen's incredulity. "Durga's estate is less than three hundred kilometers from here. He will be here right away to inspect his new dancers. So we wait."

They found a cold, pitted bench at the edge of the pad, and sat.

"Fen?"

"Yeah?"

"Are your affairs all in order?"

"My *what*?"

"Affairs, your will, estate, and such, in the event Durga feeds us to his pet dianoga."

I definitely should have plastered her on Socorro two years ago, Fen thought viciously. No money was worth this. "I thought this was going to be the easy part."

Seated on the bench, Ghitsa's feet were swinging several centimeters off the ground. "Easy?" she echoed. "Whatever made you think that?"

"I assumed . . ."

Ghitsa's reminder about assumptions and shallow graves was cut off as a low, loud hum reverberating across the sullen marsh. They scrambled to their feet. Squinting, Fen spotted a sail barge moving fast over the quagmire. Its size and sure, smooth movement evidenced the Hutt opulence which was always, to Fen's mind, incongruous with the dank misery of Nal Hutta.

What had appeared in the distance to be blobs on the barge's deck devolved into a full complement of heavily armed and undoubtedly fiercely loyal guards of various slobbering species. As the sail barge skimmed to a stop before them, Fen's fingers twitched at her side, instinctively looking for the blaster that was probably still in Dunc's hands.

In a mimicry of how Fen herself had met the Mistryl, Ghitsa walked forward to stand at the bottom of the barge's ramp. An immense Hutt with a large mark stretched across his forehead slithered down the plank.

"Counselor Dogder," Durga finally rumbled, with a glance at Fen. "I doubt my dancers are hiding in the escape pod I saw on our clan's property. I expect an explanation for my missing Twi'leks."

Fen watched in fascination as her partner bent into a

low bow. "Your Magnificence, thieving knaves stole your dancers from your most humble agent."

"Stole?"

With an effort, Fen did not flinch at the malodorous smell wafting from the Hutt. Was it something expelled when a Hutt was angry, she wondered? Or just the remnants of breakfast?

"Yes, Your Corpulence. We were betrayed by those we hired for passage from Ryloth. When we arrived into Nal Hutta space, they overwhelmed us and forced us into the escape pod."

It was over before Fen could comprehend it had even happened. Durga snapped his grasping, stubby fingers, and five guards surrounded Ghitsa. Fen was now standing squarely, and without cover, in the sights of an E-web repeating blaster mounted on the barge.

"Counselor, I will hear your explanation. And whether it pleases me will determine whether you die quickly, or very, very slowly."

Fen willed composure. Ghitsa, however, seemed perfectly calm. Or maybe, after a lifetime with Hutts, she was so warped that five slobbering aliens with BlasTechs aimed at her was simply all in a day's work.

"Durga," the con artist said smoothly, "if I give you two reasons why you will not kill me, will you pay me seventy-five thousand credits?"

"I will indeed, counselor."

"First, I hereby invoke the Hutt Commercial Laws, section C, subsection 12.4e, and the protections it affords all counselors and messengers."

Fen had never been able to read Hutts well, and though she had never seen it before—and doubted she would see it again—she knew that Durga was shocked.

Ghitsa plunged ahead. "You kill me, Durga, and every deal I have brokered on behalf of our Clan is forfeit. At my last calculation, that sum exceeds one-hundred million."

Anger rippled over the Hutt. Durga bellowed, "You dare cite our own laws to me?"

"You know the law, Durga." Now, Fen heard steady reason in her partner's voice. "Counselors and messengers are not to pay the price for those who would use them to embarrass or cheat the Hutt Empire."

Durga gave his little counselor a long, calculating look, then finally said, "If memory serves, those laws were enacted after the early and violent deaths of twelve counselors and innumerable messengers."

"Your memory is faultless, as always. You will doubtless also recall what occurred when a young, skinny, and very foolish Hutt of the Vermilic Clan forgot this prohibition two years ago and disintegrated his counselor."

Fen was startled to realize even she had heard of that incident. The Vermilics were bankrupted and no Hutt traffic moved for three months. She wondered now if the counselors had refused to broker the Hutt deals.

A long, humid pause strung out before Durga spoke again. "I believe, Dogder, you had a second reason?"

"If you kill me now, you will never regain your Twi'leks."

"Ohhh, ho, Dogder." When Durga laughed, Fen was reminded of a restless, rolling sea. "And just how will you return my dancers?"

"I can give you the ID code of the ship we retained, its itinerary, and ownership registry. You will be able to trace those who have truly wronged you."

Durga's face folded into frowns. "And how will I know if the information you provide me is useful?"

"You may pay me fifty percent now, and the remainder within one standard week," Ghitsa replied. "You will have sufficient time to verify if the data is valuable."

"Do you trust us so much, counselor?" Durga seemed amused. Fen was not.

"I trust you, Master."

Under Durga's thoughtful, raking scrutiny, Ghitsa stood impassively. Then, with a snap of his fingers, the guards lowered their weapons, and Fen found she could breathe again.

Durga put a companionable arm around Ghitsa's mud-encrusted shoulders. "After so many years of loyal service, counselor, you understand that should you prove unfaithful, I am confident that the galaxy will be too small a place for both you and my anger."

"I understand, Master."

"Although I remain disturbed with your failure, I am pleased with your efforts to foresee possible betrayal." He held out a tiny, groping hand, and Ghitsa gave him the disk Fen had taken from *The Fury*. "You may transfer the sum from our Coruscant account."

Ghitsa bowed slightly.

Durga's tail twitched violently, serpentine. "You also know that for the sake of our interests, we permit only credible counselors. Once this transaction is completed, we will look elsewhere for an advisor."

"You have always wisely insisted that counselors not be the victims of other predators, Master. I ask for no exception in my case." Fen would wonder for some time whether Ghitsa actually sounded wistful at that parting.

"All right," Shada said, easing the holo tube into the player. The scan had showed it was a normal holo tube, with no surprises attached. But that didn't mean she entirely trusted it. "Here we go."

A two-meter-tall likeness of Fenig Nabon appeared. "Hello again, Shada," the figure said. "Since you're watching this, I presume Ghitsa and I are gone. Hopefully still alive, though you're now probably regretting that you didn't send us out the airlock without the benefit of vac suits."

Dunc grumbled in her throat, but said nothing.

"Ghitsa has maintained that you would want to deliver us to the Hutts for their own peculiar punishments," Fen continued. "If this went down right, she'll be selling to Durga the Hutt a datacard with detailed information on the ship responsible for the theft of his dancers. A competent slicer will trace that information back to the *Indenture* and the Karazak Slaving Cooperative."

The image grinned, a little shamefacedly. "I'm sure

you've also noticed that *The Fury*'s ID is reading as the *Indenture*. That was my own touch, in case someone on Nal Hutta spotted you. The overlay program is buried in your backup comm system. You'll probably have to go in through the battle game I was playing to get to it— that's how I got in—but it shouldn't be any real trick to disable."

She sobered. "On the more serious side, you can probably predict what will happen when Durga reaches the conclusion that the KSC stole his dancers."

"Gang war," Dunc murmured.

"Ghitsa thinks that in the resulting turmoil both the KSC and the Hutts will leave Ryloth alone for a while. Durga's slicer should also find certain inconvenient payments the KSC has made to Brin'shak. This will likely be the last Twi'lek acquisition Brin'shak will make for the Hutts."

The image shifted, foot to foot. A little embarrassed, perhaps? "We've told the dancers that you'll return them to Kala'uun on Ryloth. The Dira Clan is expecting them and can be trusted. The Shak Clan may howl about it, but you shouldn't get anything but noise from them. They were discredited two years ago in Kala'uun after trying to scam the New Republic over some ryll kor and are generally trying to lay low.

"Finally, assuming you haven't killed us, Ghitsa will transfer twenty thousand into your account, as agreed. I know you're expecting thirty-two, but if you play it right with the Dira Clan, they may pay you some ryll kor for bringing the dancers back." The image smiled, a little smugly. "Ghitsa urges you to sell quickly, as she believes the market will top out soon."

Fen raised her head, looking out into nothing. "Jett always really admired the Mistryl, Shada. But sometimes he was uncomfortable with what you would do for money. Poverty makes people desperate, he would say. But sometimes, it's better to be poor. Ghitsa, of course, disagrees."

The image of Fenig Nabon flickered out.

• • •

Durga escorted them to the port city of Bilbousa where Fen had berthed the *Star Lady*. They set course for the nearest New Republic facility with a decent banking exchange.

As soon as the ship jumped, Ghitsa slipped out of her cockpit chair. "I'm going to get cleaned up."

When Fen emerged from her own long, hot shower, Ghitsa was already in the cabin, sitting at the cabin's table, intently watching the final chapter in the wooing of Leia Organa. Fen grabbed a bottle of Corellia's finest and two glasses before sitting across from Ghitsa.

"So," Fen began, pouring and sliding a glass across the table to her partner. Ghitsa said nothing, but did accept the drink.

"Did Durga buy it?"

"I doubt it," Ghitsa scoffed. "But he is cautious. He won't part with one-hundred mill without proof and thirty-seven and a half is a small price to pay, for now. All the proof will point to the Karazaks. They are more likely to cheat him than I am."

"But you aren't a counselor anymore."

Ghitsa visibly brightened and took a sip of her drink. "Rather convenient, I thought."

"You wanted this?"

She sighed, tilting her head back against the booth. It was the first time in a while Fen had seen Ghitsa look normal—a simple flight suit, damp hair, nothing caking her face or nails. "You remember how I said that mortality among Durga's Twi'leks was around seventy percent?"

"Yeah."

"It's even higher for Hutt counselors. Even if a counselor's own clan won't kill her, we tend to be excellent acquisition targets for Hutt competitors."

Ghitsa, Fen suddenly realized, would not have taken these kinds of risks for a mere seventy-five thousand. "And those twelve dead counselors?"

"Two of them were Dogders." Ghitsa stopped there, lips pressed into a thin, firm line.

Fen veered to safer ground. "Will Durga pay the rest?"

Ghitsa took another swallow. "Maybe. Probably. He'll be very happy when he finds out about the Karazaks. I expect he'll give me a bonus."

They watched as the *Coruscant Daily Newsfeed* gushed about Princess Organa's impending nuptials.

"Pity about Han Solo," Ghitsa said.

"Waste of a pretty good smuggler," Fen sighed, staring into her drink.

The Princess appeared, again in her regal white, announcing that Dathomir would now be open to Alderaani exiles. The program intoned, "And Organa announced today that the New Republic has appropriated two-hundred million in financial assistance for displaced Alderaani. Low-interest loans will also be available to aid in resettlement. . . ."

Fen whistled appreciatively. "Too bad you have to be Alderaani to be eligible."

They stared at the screen.

"You know," Ghitsa began, "I've always wanted to play impoverished nobility."

Fen glanced from her partner to the vid, and back again. "True," she finally said. "And Leia Organa may not look good in white, but, Ghitsa, I bet you do."

The Longest Fall

by Patricia A. Jackson

The Imperial Star Destroyer *Interrogator* maintained its support position, matching coordinate planes and acceleration bursts with its nav computer specifications. From the observation deck, several levels beneath the flight bridge, the commanding officer stared through the transparisteel platform as the *Imperial II*-class Star Destroyer maneuvered into the mouth of a vacuous, black nebula. Gliding from the sinister shadow of undistinguished space, the *Interrogator* was an impressive sight, a precisely honed dagger tip against the starless backdrop of space.

An advanced point ship, his vessel was moving in to investigate a little-known area of space known as the *Nharqis'I*. The term, despite its romantic appeal, was a crude variation of a word in a lingering smuggler dialect, which he understood to mean "the death place." Starless, featureless, menacing—the foreboding nebula was a testimonial to seemingly endless continuity.

Chewing nervously at his lower lip, the young captain

stared into the faceless void, wishing he could lose himself inside it. The *Nharqis'I* could be no colder or more forbidding a place than the anonymous darkness of Lord Tremayne's waiting room. And the *Nharqis'Al*, a hideous, mythical leviathan said to lurk within the nebula, could certainly be no more terrifying an entity than the Emperor's leading High Inquisitor himself.

In the midst of the sparsely furnished, cruelly antiseptic interior of the waiting chamber, the young captain noticed only one chair sitting against the far wall. He wondered how many Imperial officers had sat in that chair and how many had lived to tell about it. The numbers were quite disproportionate to each other, he was certain, and he congratulated himself on his decision not to sit in it.

Though he was not a superstitious man, the captain was confident that he enhanced his chances of survival if Tremayne should come and find him standing in anticipation of this meeting. He had, in fact, been standing, respectfully at attention, for the past three hours, waiting for the Dark Adept to address him personally.

And if his diligence had no bearing at all upon the outcome of their meeting, at least he would have the satisfaction of meeting High Inquisitor Tremayne and his own potential execution with a small measure of dignity.

The others died on their feet, his subconscious told him. Admiral Ozzel. Admiral Ranes. Captain Needa. His esteemed mentor and friend, Captain Nolaan. And there were others who did not directly come to mind. *What makes you so different?*

The inability to answer that question brought a hollow, unsettled feeling to the bottom of his stomach. Clasping his hands tightly behind his back, the young captain swayed back and forth on his heels, an impatient habit learned on the bridge and honed by the daily stresses of commanding a ship in the Emperor's most prestigious war fleet. It was a peculiar fixation on motion that he was working to eliminate and had regulated it with some success. In any case, the swaying did not trouble him quite so much as the violent tremors that shook his hands.

The captain brushed his fingers over the front of his uniform and straightened the insignia, chiding himself for allowing a physical manifestation of his concerns to appear. The last impression he wanted to make before leaving this world was the empty illusion of fear.

Fear. That was not the way to run a ship or motivate its crewmen and support personnel. Fear inspired mistakes, tension among the crew, which accounted for more mistakes and erroneous decisions in judgment. Ultimately, the end result of such tension was failure and more fear. Respect was what they taught in the Academy, respect and subject to authority.

Discipline is the immediate compliance to all orders, undeviating respect for authority, and above all self-reliance.

The young captain grinned as the memorized definition came to mind—a recurring echo from his days at the Academy. He remembered the fear of those early days of training, when everything had seemed so beyond reach. He remembered his initial clumsiness with orders and superior officers, the ambiguity of doubt, and the gradual breaking down and reestablishment of his pride. There was indeed a certain arrogance in the mastery of discipline, the mastery of self. There was incalculable self-satisfaction in obeying orders, respecting the High Command, and in being recognized for the ability to think clearly in a crisis. These things combined evoked respect, not fear. High Inquisitor Tremayne knew little of the former and enlisted too heavy a hand in the latter.

The captain nodded in complete confidence. He regretted nothing he had done in the course of his military duties to dismantle, or at least dilute, the fear that High Inquisitor Tremayne inspired. His service record and that of the personnel aboard the *Interrogator* was without blemish, asserting, at least in his mind, that respect was a superior motivation to fear.

Meeting Tremayne's orders with a thin smile and consummate bowing of the head had made him one of the most distinguished officers in the Fleet. No other would be so bold as to even meet the Jedi's menacing face, with its equally sinister cybernetic replacements. And while the captain's efforts were met with cold disdain and neutrality, he persevered, hoping to influence the Emperor's infamous servant with a small measure of his loyalty and willingness to serve.

"What did it matter?" he whispered, startled by the sound of his own voice. The captain paused, cocking his head to one side as the echo reverberated between the narrow walls of the waiting chamber. Chiding himself for the outburst, he pursed his lips as that hollow feeling dug itself deeper into the pit of his stomach, where the root of all his suppressed fears had lain dormant, until this ignobling day.

Indeed, what did it matter? His relationship to the deceased Captain Nolaan was an unwritten blight on his reputation, one that would inevitably doom him. And his fate would be no different than the others who had been Nolaan's trusted advisors and formal companions. High Inquisitor Tremayne had made that distinction very clear, starting with Nolaan's summary execution on the bridge of the *Interrogator*. And in the aftermath, not one who had called Nolaan friend and mentor was alive to mourn him, except for himself. And that was soon to change.

Vharing swallowed convulsively, remembering Tremayne's wrath. He shuddered with the recollection of Captain Nolaan's gray, stricken face as the troopers dragged his body from the bridge and into the corridor for expeditious disposition. If Tremayne's justice was as predictable as the black void of the *Nharqis'I*, he was next in line.

He straightened the collar of his uniform and adjusted the tilt of his cap. A patriotic cant learned during his tenure at the Imperial Naval Academy came to mind and the young captain took a sudden rush of optimism from the words. The power of those memories instilled him with the courage to face Tremayne as he would face any man in a position of power—with respect and defer-ence rather than fear. After all, it was not his command that had sent a full squadron of Imperial TIE bombers to the cloudy, defenseless world of Qlothos.

His subordinate, the ambitious senior lieutenant, had picked up some peculiar signals from the nearby planet. It was a frequency that nearly matched a set of earlier transmission codes that had been intercepted from an Alliance operative. Suspecting a hidden Rebel garrison, the senior lieutenant sent the TIE bombers to destroy it.

All this had transpired while the captain lay asleep in his bed. He was only awakened by the lieutenant after the facts were collected and the casualties calculated. There were only minimal injures to report, no damages to craft or equipment. But nearly sixty civilians, most of them prominent Imperial citizens, were dead—among them a high-ranking Kuat Drive Yards engineer, his wife, and two sons, who were on holiday in the capital.

Evidently, the cloudy blanket of atmosphere covering the planet played havoc on the identification beacons built into the concussion missiles. One went astray and demolished a secluded section of the residential com-munity, which lay only a kilometer from the suspected Rebel compound. Hours after the fatalities were counted, Lord Tremayne's summons had come through directly. And without the added apprehension of his military aide to share in his inner torment, the captain came to meet with the High Inquisitor alone.

But now, he regretted that decision. The briefest con-tact with another human, however succinct, might have eased his anxiety and given him something to dwell on besides this impending meeting.

The industrious senior com-scan officer would have been an excellent choice. A family man and father, he was an incessant talker—one reason the captain had over-looked him as his military aide. A loyal and competent leader, the com-scan officer always had time to devote to the love of his wife, nearly three hundred light-years away, and to the newly born child he had never seen, except through holos and rare face-to-face transmissions.

The balance seemed to anchor the talkative officer in a way the captain had come to admire and finally resent. But after today, all that would change. After assuring High Inquisitor Tremayne that the ambitious senior lieutenant would be punished to the fullest extent—court-martialed, convicted of manslaughter, the destruction of Imperial property, and harassment of loyal Imperial citizens—the captain would promote the com-scan officer as his new advisor and begin to share in this esoteric life.

The door to Tremayne's chamber abruptly opened. The captain turned curtly on his heel and saluted as the Jedi stepped into the room. "High Inquisitor Tremayne, I have a full report into Senior Lieutenant Leeds's blundering—" His voice was arrested by the lancing pain that assailed his throat.

As the invisible grip intensified, the captain fell to his knees. He winced as the small bones at the base of his skull cracked audibly under the pressure. Unable to breathe, he found himself sprawled on the cold glare of the waiting room floor. He closed his eyes in an effort to compose himself.

His mind began to flounder for lack of oxygen, and he remembered the stress exercise at the Academy where his colleagues and he were subjected to a panic test in a room full of noxious fumes. Half blinded and nearly unconscious, he was the last to emerge—the only one with the courage, or foolish pride as many called it, to remain longer than any of the others. But in this new test, there were fatal consequences. Here the captain was fully cognizant of what was happening to him. There would be no noxious fumes to dim his senses and lessen the blow. He could feel every sensation in vivid detail, from the cold kiss of the deck plate against his palms to the coarse fabric of his uniform as it chafed his elbows and knees.

Unable to raise his head and beseech Tremayne for a

second chance, the young captain could only stare into the flowing black hem of the Jedi's robes. As his consciousness waned, he imagined himself being drawn into that black fabric and into an alternate world as dark and starless as the *Nharqis'l* nebula surrounding his ship.

What a fitting end to my life, he thought with numb pleasure. The first small bone broke beneath the pressure and he felt his body relax.

Born into a prominent bloodline and class, Jovan Vharing attended the Imperial Naval Academy, a decision made for him by traditional family dictates rather than of his own accord. But there were no regrets to that course, and he delved deeply into the best of himself to impress mentors and superior officers alike. For his concentrated efforts in detail and accuracy, he graduated in the top two percent of his class—a distinguishing achievement. Newly commissioned as a lieutenant, he went on to a prestigious posting as senior tracking officer aboard a *Victory*-class Star Destroyer.

His ambition and eye for competent and cost-effective action made an early reputation for him—then a newly graduated officer, serving in the desolate Outer Rim, in the area of space commonly referred to as the wild frontier. And while it was no auspicious duty for an officer of his caliber, it was to be a short-lived tenure with many notable accomplishments that would earn him the sympathetic eye of Captain Nolaan. Having also served on the Outer Rim as a junior officer, Nolaan took an instant liking to Vharing. To spite several of his junior officers, Nolaan called in several favors and arranged for Vharing's transfer—to the bridge of the *Interrogator*, where he made no attempts to shield his partiality.

Within one year, Vharing would live up to the high expectations set for him by his ill-fated mentor. After Nolaan's untimely execution, Vharing became one of the youngest men to achieve the rank of captain. As such, he would be one of the youngest officers to ever receive command of an Imperial II Star Destroyer. And with it, he inherited the burden of Tremayne's exacting demands and the resentment of every Imperial officer on the bridge.

Death was a shadowy cloak surrounding the captaincy of the *Interrogator*. Promotion was by succession—the kind of succession one sees in a toppling house of sabacc cards. Vharing's promotion to captain was simply a complicated ploy by his executive colleagues to stay well out of Lord Tremayne's omniscient shadow. Vharing, as did his predecessor, would serve as a buffer. When the next blunder surfaced, when the next inaccuracy arose, his would be the name spoken by Tremayne and his would be the neck crushed by the wrath of the High Inquisitor.

So, as with all things, Vharing threw himself, mentally and physically, into the endless pursuit of perfection. His was the highest efficiency rating in the fleet and his men the most steadfast and loyal. At a formal dinner for the executive staff of the *Interrogator*, Vharing was forced to fend off the curious inquiries of his fellow officers, who for the last six months had stood by and gawked in envy of his ability to motivate men and support staff, even under the most extreme circumstances. When asked what was his single, greatest achievement, Vharing replied, "Serving under High Inquisitor Tremayne."

A moment of quiet met the comment; the jovial atmosphere usurped by a darker, fearsome mood. Staring at each other and then at Vharing in turn, the assembled Imperial officers were speechless and deferred to the talents of their more outspoken members.

"Are you insane, Vharing?" General Parnet whispered. The disgruntled officer glanced over his shoulders, as if expecting High Inquisitor Tremayne to be nearby in the shadows, listening.

"Oh, come, gentlemen," Vharing scolded, raising his goblet in a toast. "The man is not so dreadful as all that—oppressive, demanding, unforgiving. He's no different than our drill mentors back at the Academy or any of the superior officers under whom we served before our grand appointments to executive commission."

"And there's your mistake, Vharing," Parnet said evenly. His cruel, handsome face was as expressionless as the shadows flanking the corners of the room. "Failure at the Academy was expulsion. Failure in the line of duty oft times means reassignment to some shameful task, demotion, perhaps court-martial in the worst cases. Here—" He put his goblet down to candidly decline the toast to Tremayne. "Here the penalty for failure is death. And that my friend, is the longest fall any man can take—alone or with his friends." Parnet paused and glanced around the table at each of his colleagues in turn, waiting for a consensus from the group.

"Well spoken," Lieutenant Uland concurred. He swallowed the entire portion of his wine and set the goblet aside as the first warm charge rushed through him, warding off the intoxicating chill brought on by Tremayne's name.

Vharing met Parnet's statement with a thin smile, marveling at the black mockery of fear behind the General's insipid eyes. "Then to Death, gentlemen," he raised his goblet, "the longest fall."

As Vharing's face met the cold embrace of the deck floor, he was as a dead man. Hot surges of agonizing sensation lanced through his battered skull, and he awoke from that desperate state—alive by every indication of the pain that swept through his heightened senses.

With a child's wondrous delight, he experienced the sharp agonies of living—the nagging aches and stiffness of his joints, the twisted pinch of his uniform, chafing uncomfortably at his skin. One of his insignia pins had broken in the fall and was piercing the muscle of his chest. *Dead men do not bleed,* he thought to himself, feeling the warm adhesive of his blood against the fabric of his uniform.

There was a dull roaring in his ears as his physical faculties returned. A momentary stab of pain confessed itself to be a separated rib, possibly two, suffered in the fall to the waiting-room floor. His right index finger would not move on command and any effort to coerce it brought a secondary wave of sensory anguish. And there was more. Something was terribly wrong—he could not breathe.

In desperation, Vharing searched the room, his lethargic eyes slow to focus on his surroundings. The delay in his vision brought terrifying images back to his bewildered brain, making the few objects in the immediate area seem gigantic in comparison to his frail, battered body. This appalling effect redoubled his terror, prolonging the agony of his asphyxiation.

Why doesn't he finish it! Vharing demanded in his mind, unable to speak. His throat was on fire. The salted aftertaste of blood repulsed him and caused him to gag, aggravating his desperate circumstances.

Then as his will to survive conquered the army of dull sensations numbing his brain, Vharing opened his mouth. The frigid chill of the waiting room sliced at his tongue as he took his first gasp of air. The experience was a miserable agony to endure; the icy sting swept through his mouth and then into his nostrils.

Vharing coughed, continuing to wheeze as his lungs began to function. "Alive?" he rasped, startled by the hoarse growl of his voice. *Had Tremayne left him for dead? Impossible.*

Slowly rising from the floor, Vharing swallowed with deliberate caution. He closed his eyes, near fainting, as the agony in the back of his neck intensified. There was undoubtedly some damage caused by Tremayne's wrath, but nothing the surgeon droids in the *Interrogator*'s sick bay could not fathom. Spreading his fingers wide and wiggling his toes inside the hardened leather of his boots, Vharing grinned and turned for the door.

Pausing momentarily, he stared at his reflection in the observation glass, noticing the thin trickle of blood

unning from the corner of his mouth and from one
nostril. Quickly pulling the handkerchief from his pocket,
he moistened the corner and dabbed at the wound. The
injury at his chin would bruise by morning, but he was
not worried. He would wear the bruise as a mark of dis-
inction among his colleagues.

Hurrying through the bulkhead door, Vharing stepped
into the corridor and abruptly fell back against the wall.
The overhead illumination grids were blinding to him.
Hands shielding his eyes, the young captain blinked
back painful tears and quickly made his way through the
wide passage. His heart was pounding frantically in beat
to the patriotic cant that still lingered in his memory.

Everything was so poignantly clear. The detail of the
deck plates, an organized mosaic of tiles along the corridor floor. Though indiscernible to the preoccupied mind,
he could see the variations in shade and texture. The illumination grid panels troubling him from overhead
were spaced exactly one and one half meters apart, two
meters in the corners where the corridors intersected,
and three meters where the passage led off to the enormous labyrinth of the officers' quarters. A sanitizing
chemical taint rose in the air, stinging his nostrils for the
first time as his heightened senses allowed him to experience, with fullness, the world around him.

Yes, everything was exquisitely clear to him, including
his plans for Lieutenant Leeds! He would call a complete escort of Imperial stormtroopers to accompany
him to the bridge. Then he would head directly to the
command center and he would arrest the ambitious
lieutenant in front of everyone. And at the expense of
several favors of his own, he would oversee the court-
martial procedures himself. Admiral Hennat, as yet a
keen friend of his, would gladly preside over the entire
affair, insuring a judgment of gross negligence against
the lieutenant. Leeds would become the scapegoat,
buried in a list of charges ranging from murder to trea-
son, while Vharing's own record remained perfectly
clean and clear.

After snapping the restraints on Leeds's wrists himself, the young captain would summon his com-scan officer, Lieutenant Waleran front and center. With great ceremony, befitting a field promotion in combat, he would advocate the industrious young officer to the rank of senior lieutenant in front of the entire bridge crew. And as Nolaan had done for him, Vharing would take Waleran under his wing, insuring him a place on the executive staff as his personal military aide.

At the end of the corridor, the turbolift was situated between an auxiliary maintenance shaft and a small storage room. Closing his eyes, Vharing rubbed at his neck, barely able to tolerate the excruciating pain, which seemed to intensify as he moved closer to the turbolift. His hands gently caressed the area under his throat and he felt the disfigured swelling of his larynx and the distended glands along the sides of his neck.

Nothing the medical droids can't see to, he told himself. His tongue was also swollen, all but blocking the airway to his lungs. Vharing paused, leaning against a heavy equipment chest. Loosening the collar of his uniform, he swallowed a cool draft of air, in the hopes that the chill might alleviate some of his discomfort.

Puzzled that he had not yet reached the turbolift, the captain fought off a bout of panic. His heart quickened as he opened his eyes. For every step he had taken, it appeared as if the lift entrance had moved three steps beyond him. Vharing closed his eyes again, rubbing the sensation back into them as the numbing cold of Tremayne's waiting room prevailed over his senses.

"Delirium," he whispered, willing the tension and anxiety to leave him.

When Vharing again opened his eyes, he was standing on the bridge of the *Interrogator*. What a breathtaking sight she was—a tribute to the perfection and dedication of the Imperial technicians that created her. Lieutenant Leeds was nowhere on the flight bridge. Vharing smiled with conceited satisfaction, reminding himself to pay a visit to the destitute officer, if only to offer a few choices as to his next career, as foreman in one of the Emperor's spice mines.

Vharing nearly laughed aloud at the thought. Brushing his hand reflectively over his lips, he took a deep breath and clasped his hands behind his back. He swayed rhythmically back and forth on his heels, conscious of the habit but too intrigued with the rapture of living to care.

Across from him, Lieutenant Waleran was speaking with the navigation team. A set of new insignias adorned his uniformed breast, casting a steady, proud glare over the dramatic gray of his formal command appointments. It pleased Vharing to see the newly promoted Senior Lieutenant so fully engaged in his work and enjoying it. He seemed well at ease on the bridge and from the atmosphere, the crew was at ease with him, too.

Ahead of them, the nebula was breaking up into fragmented sections of discernible stars and distant planets. The bridge crew was preparing to leave this sector, bracing themselves for the jump into hyperspace. When had the order been given? Shrugging off that uncertainty, Vharing straightened his broad shoulders. He wanted to pose for the crew to show his complete confidence in the new bridge officer. In his absence, Waleran must have received the orders and was prepared to carry them out.

Vharing raised his chin with a measure of pride. The action caused a crippling streak of pain to shoot through him. There was a literal explosion of sensory information at the base of his skull as his brain shuddered in agony. Gritting his teeth against the anguish, the captain forced his body into a rigid pose. Once he had given the order for the jump into hyperspace, he would officially turn the bridge over to Waleran and would retire immediately to the medical bay for a complete physical examination.

As the pilots signaled the all clear for the jump to hyperspace, Vharing opened his mouth to give the command—a loud, tortured wheezing escaped his throat. He tried to swallow but the tightness in his throat would not give. Lieutenant Waleran turned to him, as if looking through him, and then turned back to the pilots' station. Straightening his shoulders in a haughty imitation of his commanding officer, Waleran nodded to his subordinate and gave the order for the jump to hyperspace.

Vharing winced beneath the onslaught of the hyperdrive engines as the shriek of the motivators jarred his bones, right down to his teeth. There was a secondary explosion of light and color as the telltale points of stars elongated and stretched across the viewscreen, becoming the seamless fabric of hyperspace. As the radiant glow intensified, Vharing squinted, desperately afraid to close his eyes against the brilliance. For to close them would mean never to open them, never to see this world, or exist within it again. But the glare was too intense, the pressure at the base of his skull too powerful. He was forced to escape into a world where there was no light, no sound—just blackness.

Neck broken, his spinal cord pulverized at the base of his skull, Captain Jovan Vharing was dead. His head swung listlessly back and forth from his shoulders as two stormtroopers dragged his corpse from High Inquisitor Tremayne's waiting room.

Conflict of Interest

By Laurie Burns

Standing on the steps of the Verkuylian Imperial Governor's Hall waiting to present her fake credentials to the stormtrooper at the door, Selby Jarrad took another swipe at the sweat trickling down her temples and wished she'd been warned about the blasted stink.

Just another "minor" detail Intelligence had neglected to mention during the mission briefing, she thought. The city—the whole sweltering *planet*—reeked of alazhi being stripped, pulped and simmered for refinement into bacta. Of all the attacks that the New Republic team might face while helping Verkuyl's rebelling native workers oust the Empire, this obnoxious olfactory assault had never come up.

She slanted a glance at the tall, dark-skinned man beside her. Before landing, the stiff, formal collar of Major Cobb Vartos's business suit had been crisp and clean, but it had long since wilted in the suffocating heat. Grimy marks showed where he'd pried it away from his perspiring neck. Selby didn't even want to know what she looked like. Her own suit clung to her, and the thick auburn hair piled atop her head felt hot and heavy.

"I'm not sure which is worse," Vartos murmured to her, hooking a finger in his collar and giving it another yank. "Breathing through my nose and smelling the blasted stuff, or breathing through my mouth and *tasting* it."

Selby had a definite opinion on that, but just then the stormtrooper at the door barked "Next!" Vartos stepped up to the portal and handed the guard his forged ID. Carefully schooling her expression into the cool, professional mien of a corporate bidder—or at least as cool and professional as she could manage with hair sticking damply to her face and sweat trickling down her back—Selby did the same.

The stormtrooper scanned the cards. "Purpose of your visit?"

"My associate and I are here to present a proposal to His Excellency, Governor Parco Ein," Vartos told him. Since the Governor currently had a hall full of bidders waiting to present him with business proposals, Vartos didn't bother to add that the only proposal he and Selby intended to give Ein was: Surrender, or die.

When Ein had advertised he'd be considering bids for the construction of a new bacta refinery on Verkuyl, Intelligence had deemed the situation too good to pass up. The planet's native workers, encouraged by the slow but steady reduction in Imperial might in the three years since Endor, had finally indicated their willingness to openly rebel.

And in this case, the Republic's new allies would come with a bonus. Though Verkuyl was sparsely settled and a bit too far out on the Rim to be strategically valuable, Selby knew the New Republic considered military support of the coup a small price to pay to bypass the hassles of dealing with the bacta cartel and gain a direct pipeline to the medical resources. The Governor's Bid Party offered the perfect opportunity to insert an Intelligence team into his presence—combined with the military threat the fleet would present when it jumped into the system, orchestrating his surrender should be a snap.

Selby felt another drop of sweat meander down her spine as the stormtrooper seemed to spend an inordinate amount of time checking their credentials. His white armor gleamed brightly in the sun as they stood there, sweating under his blank, black-visored gaze for what seemed an eternity. The uneasy silence lengthened. She exchanged a glance with Vartos and knew he was thinking the same thing when suddenly a voice behind them broke in.

"Excuse me—is there a problem?"

She turned. The new arrival, a lanky, fair-haired man dressed in the dark blue uniform of an Imperial aide, regarded them quizzically from the sidewalk.

The stormtrooper snapped to attention. "Sir, they say they're here for the Bid Party, but I haven't been able to confirm their authorization to attend."

"I see," the man said, coming up the steps. "Your names?" He briefly consulted a small datapad. "You're on the list," he confirmed. "It's all right, Sergeant. Let them pass."

The stormtrooper nodded, stepping aside as the massive Hall door swung open. Inside, marvelously cool air welcomed them, and a copper-colored droid dotted with tiny green, rusty-looking specks glided forward to take their travel bags. *This awful humidity,* Selby thought. *Even the droids are affected.*

"I'm Daven Quarle," the man said, extending his hand first to Vartos, then to her. "I'm His Excellency's aide in charge of the refinery project."

Selby shook it, noting that Quarle's grip was firm, with hard calluses ridging his fingers. Not a mere bit-pushing bureaucrat then; this man was accustomed to work—and quite a lot of it.

Intelligent green eyes sized her up, as well. "So, you're the two from GalFactorial," he commented as they boarded the turbolift, en route to their rooms on the fifth floor with the other bidders. "Your company has a reputation for doing good work. But," he cocked an eyebrow as the lift started to rise, "I hear the refinery you people built on New Cov ended up coming in over budget. That true?"

"Of course not," Selby said, suddenly grateful that whatever omission Intelligence had made regarding the smellier aspects of refining bacta, she *had* been thoroughly briefed on her cover story. "Midway through construction, the client decided to change the venting system so the plant wouldn't vent to the outside. Obviously, redesigning at that point was difficult, but the client insisted, so the budget was readjusted and approved." She gave him a blandly professional smile. "In the end, the project actually came in *under* the revised budget."

"I see," Quarle murmured. "I'm glad to hear that. His Excellency always appreciates a creative bit of number-crunching."

Selby looked at him sharply, uncertain how to interpret the remark. She decided to change the subject. "If you don't mind me asking, how many other companies sent bidders for the project?"

That eyebrow quirked again. "Curious about the competition?"

Not really, she thought. *Concerned about innocent civilians.* Although the crowd gave them more opportunity for cover, she didn't like having to worry about the bidders' safety. The mission had been carefully planned to be as bloodless as possible, but accidents could—and frequently did—happen.

"A little," she answered out loud. "Actually, I wondered if there'd be an opportunity to present our bid to the Governor in person. I find it's beneficial to personally explain the numbers to prospective clients." She caught his eye meaningfully, held the look. "Our clients often find it rewarding, as well."

"Ah," Quarle said, inclining his head knowingly. He understood the covert language of a bidder wishing to

offer a bribe. "As it happens, you'll be able to meet His
Excellency later this evening, at a special reception
we've planned for the bidders. And those who wish to—"
he hesitated "—to *privately* discuss their bids with Governor Ein may make an appointment to meet with him.
Perhaps sometime tomorrow?"

Selby considered. Tonight, Claris would help members of the Verkuylian resistance set fuses around the
planet's main comm transmitter tower as her fellow operatives set in motion their own explosive plans at the
Hall. Tomorrow, she'd signal the fleet and then destroy
the Imperials' only means of calling for backup once
Selby gained entrance to Governor Ein's office to offer
him the New Republic's "bribe."

Which, being a savvy public official skilled in the art
of self-preservation, and further encouraged by the military might which would have just arrived to orbit persua-
sively overhead, His Excellency would, of course, accept.

She smiled at Quarle. "Tomorrow's perfect," she said.
"I'll look forward to it."

And if it weren't for the necessity of keeping up her guard,
she might have managed to relax and enjoy herself—
at least a little, Selby mused that evening as she and Vartos stepped into the Hall's open-air central courtyard
where the reception was being held. If Verkuyl's dubious
charms this afternoon had lived up to the planet's reputation as an Outer Rim backwater, their comfortable, well-
appointed rooms and this gracious gathering tonight
could do a lot to change her mind.

The sultry purr of smooth jizz poured over them, and
from the looks of the buffet table along the far wall, the
Governor was a generous, even lavish host. With sunset,
the jungle humidity had at last become bearable, and
the decorative tile underfoot and the fancy, fashionable
garb of the bidders would have been right at home in
any of the corporate ballrooms on Coruscant.

Except—it stank. Even in this beautiful setting, outside of the Hall's blessedly closed air system, the smell of simmering alazhi was impossible to escape.

"Let's split up, shall we?" Vartos murmured, eyes on the corner bar fountain spilling some kind of dark red drink into a shallow pool. "It'll be easier to slip out that way."

Not that he'd be slipping out for his reconnaissance of the Hall until he'd thoroughly reconnoitered the reception, Selby thought, amused. After all, they did have covers to maintain. "Sure," she agreed. "I think I'll check out that buffet myself."

Three hours, two plates, and endless bidder chitchat later, she paused under one of the courtyard's graceful archways to glance back at the swaying dance floor. It had steadily expanded in direct proportion to the shrinking bounty of the buffet table and the Governor's free booze supply. Bidders moving to the soulful wail of a bass viol filled nearly two-thirds of the courtyard, while the rest of the party had begun wandering through the arches and into the Hall proper.

Which made it a perfect time to do a little wandering herself.

She didn't dare use the turbolift beyond the fifth floor, where most of the Bid Party attendees had been given rooms. But even so, finding the Governor's office on the top floor proved no problem, as Intelligence had very thoughtfully provided a map. Shoes in hand, she crept up the Hall's quaint staircase, discovering and dismantling half a dozen security sensors before reaching her destination. It took only a moment to unfasten the tiny eavesdropping device, a silver-toned stud indistinguishable from the dozens of less useful ones decorating the neckline of her stylish blue evening gown. But getting the thing past the security sensors, sentry cameras, and the guard in front of Ein's office proved a bit more difficult.

In the end, she was reduced to enlisting the aid of a

housecleaning droid, which—having either not noticed the silver stud arcing through the air to plunk neatly into the Governor's wastebin or programmed not to care—obligingly carried it right past the guard and deposited it under Ein's desk. Selby waited until the droid finished its housecleaning, repacked its cart, and disappeared into the turbolift before she slipped back down the stairs to rejoin the reception.

She never made it.

Hurrying across the tenth floor's polished landing, Selby heard the turbolift's doors unexpectedly slide open behind her. *Burnin' stars,* she cursed, stomach sinking. *Did I miss a sensor?* Still meters away from the safety of the stairwell, with nowhere to go and no choice but to brazen it out, she turned to face the new arrival.

Daven Quarle.

They both stopped short in surprise. Green eyes swept over her, noting the shoes she held in her hand and lingering briefly on the gown's decorative neckline before settling on her bare feet. Selby, holding the hem of the dress nearly to her knees to facilitate her scurry down the stairs, hastily dropped it and covered her toes.

When Quarle looked up again, his eyes glinted—with suspicion, or amusement, Selby couldn't tell. "Bidder Jarrad," he said politely. "If you're looking for your room, I believe you have the wrong floor."

"Um, no. No, I don't," she said, thinking fast. That thumbpass in his hand—"I mean, I appreciate your concern, but I'm not really lost."

Quarle said nothing. She hurried to explain. "It's such a nice night, and the stars looked so pretty from the courtyard. I thought I'd go up on the roof and enjoy the view."

He raised an eyebrow. "Wouldn't taking the turbolift be easier?"

"Well, of course. But—" She shrugged and played her hunch. "It wouldn't take me all the way up, so I found the stairs and started walking."

"I see," Quarle said, eyes dropping again to the shoes dangling from her fingers. "As it happens, these stairs don't go up to the roof."

"Oh," Selby said, trying to sound disappointed. "Well . . . it was just a whim. Never mind." She started to turn away—

"Wait."

She glanced back. Quarle regarded her thoughtfully. "It *is* a nice night," he agreed. "And the view from the roof is spectacular. I can take you up there, if you like."

Selby studied his expression, wondering what was behind the offer. Did Quarle suspect her of lying, and want to get her someplace dark and private to quiz her more thoroughly—or worse? Or was it something far less sinister; just a simple invitation from a man to a woman to go stargazing?

It bothered her, a little, that it had been so long since the last such invitation that she could no longer tell when one was being offered. The demands of working Intelligence kept most people at arm's length—or farther. *I ought to at least find out what he wants,* Selby told herself. *If he is suspicious, the roof might not be such a bad place to deal with the problem.*

She made herself smile brightly at him. "Sure. I'd like that."

The short ride up to the roof was made in silence, and outside the air was still and stiflingly warm; a shock after the comfortably cool Hall. But overhead, a thousand-thousand stars glittered like tiny jewels strung on garlands in the heavens—a spectacular sight, as Quarle had promised.

They stood near the carved stone railing—Selby carefully keeping just out of his reach—and gazed out over the city. She located the main comm tower rising out of a small ring of lights about a kilometer away, and wondered if Claris and her team had finished rigging the explosives. If all went as planned, by this time tomorrow evening Verkuyl would be back in the possession of its original owners.

"Seem a long way off, don't they?" Quarle said.

"What?" She turned, looked at him sharply. "Who does?"

"The stars," he said, giving her an odd look. He waved his hand in a gesture that took in the jeweled sky. "They seem so far away, but in terms of interstellar trade, they're just a hop, skip, and a jump away—so close you can almost reach out and touch them."

"Oh," Selby said. Apparently he had brought her up here solely to stargaze. She looked up, too. " 'The miracle of hyperspace,' " she quoted, not sure what else to say. " 'Linking a hundred-thousand worlds together in a galactic village.' "

"That it does," Quarle agreed, gazing overhead. "Which one's yours?"

Selby scanned the night sky for a glimpse of Averill, but the starscape was completely unfamiliar. "I don't know," she confessed, surprised at the absurdly pleased feeling the small talk engendered. "It's out there somewhere."

He smiled, too. Without that reserved, watchful expression, he looked younger; perhaps only a few years older than herself. "Where are *you* from?" she asked.

"Here," he said. "Bacta bred, born, and raised. Never even been off the planet."

"Really," she said, mind clicking over his words. If Quarle was a native, then his parents had been among the original migrants who'd come to the planet as shareholders in Verkuylian BactaCo, a lone contingent which somehow managed to form its own enclave apart from the bacta cartels. Quarle's parents were probably among those workers who'd turned their backs on their colleagues and joined forces with the Empire when it had arrived to nationalize the company. And, given his position in the Governor's office, no doubt he was among the ones who had looked the other way as their former co-workers became little more than slaves, no longer producing bacta for their own profit, but for the imagined glory of the Empire.

In short, the kind of loyal Imperial citizen the rebelling workers she'd come to liberate widely regarded as a traitor.

Selby reminded herself that, given her fake ID and the convincing packet of professional lies that comprised her cover story, Quarle believed her to be a loyal Imperial citizen herself. "You're the right man to ask, then," she said, deliberately steering away from that topic of conversation. "Does it always smell this . . . this *bad* here?"

Quarle laughed out loud. "I barely notice it," he told her, "but then again, I've lived here all my life. I'm not sure I even have a sense of smell anymore."

"Lucky you." She grinned. "The first whiff out the hatch just about knocked me flat."

He laughed again. "Verkuyl will never attract the tourist trade, that's for sure." He paused, staring out over the city. "But while we won't ever be mistaken for the bright center of the universe, there are lots of things which could be done to improve the situation here," he said, abruptly serious.

"Such as?" Selby asked, curious in spite of herself. Just how did Verkuyl's Imperial masters envision molding the future of the planet they had stolen from its rightful owners?

Quarle looked at her a moment as if deciding how to answer. Then, apparently reaching a decision, he relaxed against the stone railing. Behind him the comm tower's distant lights cast reddish glints off his golden hair, and beyond the tower the absolute blackness of Verkuyl's vast alazhi jungle stretched to the horizon.

"The Governor has several ideas, most of which are very sound," he began, and though Selby had expected no less, she was somewhat disappointed when he went on to recite the standard Imperial line. She couldn't quite dismiss the nagging feeling he wasn't truly convinced though. So when he paused, she said, "Now. Tell me what *you* would do if you were in charge."

Quarle favored her with another of those long, assessing looks. Selby forced herself not to flinch as he stepped closer, narrowing the distance between them. "You really want to know?" he asked, voice low, standing so close their shoulders brushed.

Pulse abruptly pounding and all senses alert to any sign of attack, Selby nodded.

Quarle stared at her intently a moment more. Then, slowly, he folded his arms across his chest and eased back against the railing. "All right," he said, looking away. "What *I* think is that a new approach is needed— an aggressive expansion that'll ultimately offer Verkuyl more economic independence in the galactic community, give us more security, and address some of the concerns the workers have been voicing lately."

He glanced over, gauging her reaction. Intrigued, Selby relaxed against the railing herself and settled in to listen. Encouraged, he started to go on, but was interrupted by a discreet beep. "Excuse me a moment," he said, pulling a comlink from his pocket. "Yes, what is it?"

"Daven, it's Jorli," said a voice Selby recognized as belonging to a junior aide on Ein's staff. "I'm sorry to bother you, but the reception's pretty much wound down except for a few party-hards who won't take a hint. I turned off the fountain and got the droids stacking chairs, but they still won't leave. Should I call Security?"

"No," Quarle said with a sigh. "Leave them to me. I'll be down in a moment." Repocketing the comlink, he looked at Selby ruefully. "I'm going to have to cut this short. Duty calls."

"It always does," Selby said. She straightened up, too, wondering if perhaps—"Would it be all right if I stayed up here a little longer? It really is a beautiful view."

"Sorry, no," he said. "You'd need a thumbpass to get down the lift, and I don't have any extras. This one's keyed to me—nontransferable."

"Oh. Okay." Not that she'd really expected he'd give her free run of the Hall. Selby shrugged. "Well, then. Shall we go?"

The ride down was as quiet as it had been on the way up, the brief moment of camaraderie gone. Quarle courteously escorted her to her room, bid her a polite good evening, and strode away. Sternly resisting the urge to watch until he'd disappeared into the turbolift, Selby shut the door behind her. This was one of the worst parts of the job—when an enemy showed himself not as an adversary, but a decent-seeming person who just happened to be serving on the opposite side.

She sighed. In her line of work, it was easier to see everything in black or white, friend or foe, than to attempt sorting out all the shades of gray. Color blindness was often healthier, as well. Agents who hesitated to silence their foes often found that their newfound "friends" did not hesitate to silence them. Working Intelligence meant keeping the battle lines clear, and the enemy firmly fixed in your sights. There was no room for anything else.

Too bad, she thought. Something about Quarle—his concern for the workers, perhaps—told her there was more to him than met the eye. Not that it mattered, of course. She knew where her duty lay. She sighed again, turned around. From the doorway connecting their rooms, Vartos regarded her with a frown.

"Everything okay?" he asked. "You were gone quite a while."

"Fine," Selby reassured him. Walking over to the bed, she sat down and began pulling out the decorative combs that secured the neat crown of curls atop her head. Auburn locks slipped down about her shoulders. "We okay to talk here?"

"I checked it out. We're clean." He took a few steps further into the room. "Did you get it set?"

"Uh-huh." Selby inspected the combs on the coverlet

before her. Picking one up, she touched a fingernail to a certain spot and activated the receiver. They listened. Silence. She nodded in satisfaction. All quiet, as it should be. The eavesdropper awaited tomorrow.

Suddenly, a faint squeak broke the quiet. She and Vartos exchanged a glance. Another squeak, accented by the scrabble of tiny claws. Selby grinned. "His Excellency appears to have a skitter problem."

"Let's hope it doesn't have an appetite for shiny little snacks."

"They don't eat metal," she told him. "It's about the only thing they *don't* eat."

"Good." He studied her briefly. "So, what happened with that aide, Quarle?"

"He caught me coming back downstairs," she admitted. "I thought there'd be trouble, but it seemed to work out all right."

Vartos looked relieved. "Well, if you had to get caught, good thing it was him. He's in a good position to bail you out."

Selby frowned. "What's that supposed to mean?"

"Bail you out—cover for you. Make an excuse why you're someplace you shouldn't be." Vartos gave her an odd look. "Didn't he ask what you were up to?"

"I told him I was trying to get up on the roof to see the stars."

"And he bought it?"

"He seemed to." She looked at him, still frowning. "Why would he cover for me?"

"Wait, let me get this straight," Vartos said. "As far as you know he knows, you were just wandering around the Hall because—" he grinned "—you wanted to go stargazing?"

"That's what I said," she gritted. "What did you mean—"

"Sel, he's on our side," Vartos said gently. "He's with the Verkuylian resistance."

She caught herself before her jaw dropped. "He is?" It took another moment to digest the news. "Then he knows all about us," she said. "He knew the whole time what I was up to."

"No, I don't think so," Vartos said. "You know how these things are set up, Sel."

She nodded, still taking it in. Members of resistance cells almost always had nominal contact with each other, and limited knowledge of what was going on in order to reduce liability. That way, if one Rebel was compromised or caught, the damage to the overall group could be kept to a minimum.

She thought about it a little more, recalling her initial impression that Quarle wasn't quite what he seemed. "That takes nerve, playing both sides that way," she said, rethinking their conversation on the roof in light of this new information. "He's got a tough hull to patch passing himself off as a loyal Imperial."

"So do we," Vartos said, rather tartly. "And unless we absolutely need him for something, we're going to keep on treating him like he *is* one. Time enough *after* the coup to compare notes on your respective undercover careers, Sel."

The admonition was hard to miss. "Of course," she said, slightly hurt that he'd think anything else. "You can count on me to put the mission first, sir."

"I know." He studied her a moment longer, nodded once, and changed the subject. "So. Here's what the security setup on the lower levels looks like."

He launched into a description of sensor panels, guard posts, and hidden cameras. Selby listened, grateful her brain was kept busy visualizing the Hall layout rather than replaying that evening's encounter with Quarle. Wondering if the duplicity inherent in carrying off his masquerade gave him any difficulties. Whether it was . . . lonely . . . living a life split between ideals and duty, unsure who to call friend and who to call foe, but all too sure he could not let his guard down with either.

Realizing the direction of her thoughts, Selby forced

her mind back to the task at hand. As Vartos had said, time enough for that sort of thing later.

Or perhaps there would have been, if things had turned out differently.

Selby listened to the whispers from the tiny speakers concealed in her ornamental earsculpts as she sped up to the Governor's office the next morning. What she heard sent her stomach plunging as surely as if the turbolift's floor had suddenly dropped out from beneath her. Which, in a sense, it had. Claris, waiting at the comm tower for Selby's signal to hail the fleet, had just been captured.

And in the short space of time that it took Governor Ein to be informed of the arrest, and for Selby to overhear it before the eavesdropper's signal abruptly cut off, their carefully crafted plan went to pieces. The loss of Claris shattered it as effectively as a change in cabin pressure microfractured a ship's brittle hull.

For that first stunned moment, Selby felt panic freeze her mind as she watched the floor indicators flash past, carrying her ever closer to her meeting with the Governor. Claris captured, herself only seconds away from the stormtroopers sure to be awaiting her arrival at Ein's office—

Then a hot surge of adrenaline thawed the frost and sent her brain scrambling to find a way to salvage the situation. *Think,* she ordered herself, damning the eavesdropper for cutting out just when she needed an ear in the Governor's office the most. Was there any way she could stop the lift, get off it, and find a way to warn Vartos?

She bit her lip. Without a thumbpass, no. Not before first making a stop on the Governor's floor. The guard below had entered her destination, notified Ein's office she was on her way up, and keyed the lift for nonstop.

But there are other ways of making an exit, she thought,

glancing up to confirm the presence of a maintenance panel in the lift's ceiling. She could knock out the panel, climb into the shaft, and go . . . where? Her hand, reaching for the lift's controls, hesitated—

And then, suddenly it was too late. The doors slid open.

Selby froze. Two stormtroopers stood opposite the lift, blaster rifles resting imposingly on their white-armored shoulders in traditional parade-ground stance. She stared at them. They stared back, seemingly in no hurry to take her into custody. Inside, hope battled with caution. Could it be that they didn't know?

She couldn't just stand in the lift forever. Taking a deep breath, she stepped out. Boldly, she announced: "I'm here to see His Excellency."

The stormtroopers just stared at her without responding, but off to the side a golden-eyed protocol droid snapped to attention. "I'm sorry, but the Governor is unable to see you now," it apologized in an officiously smug manner that made Selby suspect it delivered this particular speech quite often. "Unexpected business has come up that requires his immediate attention. May I reschedule your appointment to another time?"

"Oh, I suppose," she said, trying to look annoyed at the delay. Still not quite believing her luck, she agreed to a time and re-entered the turbolift. As it sped back down to ground level, she steeled herself to tell Vartos there had been a change in plan. As the mission's commanding officer, it would be up to him to decide what course of action that change required.

For just a moment, she allowed herself to think about Claris, now in Imperial custody—an Intelligence operative's worst fear. Then the door slid open, and she set out in search of the generator room where Vartos waited for his signal to cut power to the Hall. If they hadn't been before, the Imperials were monitoring electronic communications now for sure. She'd have to deliver this message in person.

But as it turned out, she didn't have to. Vartos already knew.

Hands in the air and a grim expression on his face, he stood pinned against one of the humming power-relay boxes. He turned his head to look at Selby as she slipped in, and she had her own blaster out and in her hand before the situation really even registered. But the stormtrooper holding the blaster rifle on him didn't even glance her way. He didn't have to. Before she got her weapon up to firing position, a harsh voice from the side ordered her to drop it.

Selby froze midaim and slowly turned her head to look. A short distance away, Daven Quarle had his hands half raised as he stood between two rows of power relays. Behind him, the second stormtrooper's blaster rifle now pointed in her direction. "Drop it! Now!" the trooper repeated forcefully.

Selby risked another glance at Vartos. His eyes met hers, and in their grimly resigned depths she could see he understood her dilemma.

As it stood now, with the whole New Republic team captured and the fleet not called, the mission was doomed to certain failure. Without the fleet to encourage his surrender, Ein and his stormtroopers would simply crush the rebelling workers, and the three—no, the four of them, counting Quarle—would be interrogated and then most likely killed.

However, if she went ahead and took a shot at Vartos's captor, it would probably result in her commanding officer's immediate execution, but if—and it was a big if—Quarle over there was as quick-minded as he'd seemed and thought to divert the second stormtrooper, she just might manage an escape during the ensuing firefight.

And if she got free, there was still a chance she could—somehow—call the fleet.

You can count on me to put the mission first, she'd said to Vartos.

She'd meant it.

Raising the blaster, Selby fired.

The next few moments were a blur. As she dove behind

a metal control box that offered meager cover, the room lit up with blasterfire. Across the room, Vartos crumpled. Pinned in place and uncomfortably aware of the blaster bolts sizzling close all around, Selby kept shooting anyway until the first stormtrooper went down. Then, twisting to aim at his comrade, who was crouching behind a metal box of his own, a movement to the side caught her eye.

It was Quarle, edging stealthily along the wall toward their only means of escape, the door. Something else caught her eye as well—

"Daven—watch out!" she shouted, and fired. The bolt sizzled into a small panel on the wall a scant few dozen centimeters before him. The lights blinked out, blanketing the room in darkness.

And this was it—her only chance.

As if on cue the door slid open, illuminating her path to freedom. Momentarily silhouetted, Quarle slipped through to safety in the corridor beyond. Aiming a wild smattering of cover fire in the stormtrooper's direction, Selby got to her feet and darted after him.

She almost made it unscathed. Just as she reached the door, a blaster bolt grazed her outstretched arm, sending jagged claws of hot pain streaking up to her shoulder and forcing out an involuntary cry as she stumbled into the corridor beyond. The door slid shut behind her, the faint sounds of the trooper's fire slamming uselessly against the metal barrier.

Alerted by her cry, Quarle turned back. Suddenly nauseated, and dizzied by the burning pain, she faltered just outside the door and struggled to get her bearings. "Which way?" she managed from between gritted teeth.

Quarle hesitated, but far behind him down the corridor, two stormtroopers rounded the corner and the question suddenly became moot. Her arm felt engulfed in flames, but she managed to fire a few discouraging bursts their way before turning to run. As blaster fire echoed down the corridor, she felt more than heard Quarle close on her heels.

They hadn't gone more than fifty meters before he

pushed her firmly to the right and slapped at a door panel there. Selby let him guide her, bursting into a long, narrow room with no doors other than the one they'd just come through. "Where're we going?" she demanded, pain making the question come out harsh.

"Somewhere safe," Quarle said, just as shortly. He felt along the blank wall on the far end of the room while Selby restlessly prowled, scanning the room for possible avenues of escape. She was relieved to be out of the immediate line of fire, but with no apparent way out, that relief was sure to be short-lived. And the stormtroopers would be here any moment—

Turning back to Quarle, she was startled to see an old-fashioned swing door in the far wall where she was positive none had previously existed. "Hurry up," he said, and proved the door wasn't a mirage by pushing it open and stepping into the darkness beyond.

Selby hastened into the narrow passage beside him, and watched as he did something at a panel set in the back of the wall. The light streaming in the open door suddenly changed. When Selby looked through it to the room beyond, it was like looking through a gauzy curtain.

She flinched as the door at the far side burst open. One at a time, two stormtroopers leapt into the room with weapons at the ready. But astonishingly, they spared no more than a cursory glance at the far wall. She realized then that they must see the same blank wall she'd seen when first entering the room, and looked at the gauzy curtain with new respect. Holoflage—some of the best holoflage she'd ever seen—concealed the secret door from prying eyes.

"I'm impressed," she murmured tightly as Quarle shut the door, flicked on a glowrod, and led the way down the dark passage. Her arm throbbed with each step. "Very impressed. How did you know it was there?"

"Old family secret." He glanced briefly over his shoulder. "My grandfather was Corlin Quarle Deld."

A moment later, the name clicked. "Verkuylian

BactaCo's principal owner," she said, and he nodded. Selby nodded, too, as the pieces fell more neatly into place. No wonder Quarle masqueraded as an Imperial while secretly plotting revolt. His family had owned the whole planet before the Empire took it over.

She thought of the holoflage and felt a renewed stirring of hope. "Got any other family secrets I'd like to know about?" she inquired.

Quarle paused before a door. Beyond, the passage disappeared into darkness. Crouching, he shined the glowrod on a dusty keypad and punched in a series of numbers. A lock snicked, and he opened the door to reveal a tiny room.

"I might," he said finally, locking the door again behind them. "But we need to figure out what we're going to do here. It's obvious that whatever plan you and your partner came here with has fallen apart, and my cover's been blown as well. At this point, just getting out alive seems the best we can hope for."

"That's not good enough." Selby shook her head. "If I can get word to the fleet, there's a chance we can still pull this off."

Quarle looked at her sharply. "The fleet?"

"There's a small New Republic battle force nearby waiting for a signal from Claris—or rather," she amended, "a signal from me, before jumping in. Once it shows up, unless Ein has a Star Destroyer or two hidden in his back pocket, he'll have no choice but to surrender."

"I see," Quarle said slowly. He gazed off a moment, thinking, then slanted her a faint smile. "And no, he doesn't." The grin faded as his eyes went to her injured arm. "Why don't you tell me what's going on while we take care of that burn?" he suggested. "We'll figure out where to go from there."

The medpac he produced contained only the mildest anesthetic, so Selby was just as glad to focus on describing the mission as Quarle gently cleaned the burn and slathered a viscous green gel over it. "Unstabilized alazhi," he said at her doubtful look. "Not quite as effective as refined bacta, but it'll certainly help."

It did. The cool gel soothed the burn and, as it hardened, provided a protective coating which made bandaging unnecessary. Selby flexed the arm experimentally, relieved to find the movement elicited only a dull throb of protest. "So," she said. "What do you think?"

"It's *your* arm." Quarle raised an eyebrow. "What do *you* think?"

"The arm's fine," she said, giving him a faint smile in thanks. "I meant, what next? Can you get me access to a subspace comm unit?"

He pursed his lips thoughtfully and sat back. "Probably," he allowed, then paused. "One question, though. What were the fleet's orders if it never got a signal? Send someone to investigate, or just go on home?"

"They wouldn't abandon us," Selby said. "They'd try to find out what happened."

"So someone would eventually show up to find out why the signal never came?"

"They wouldn't abandon us," Selby said again, feeling a twinge deep inside that, on the uncertain chance she could salvage the mission, she had basically abandoned Vartos back there in the generator room. She knew that if she failed, Intelligence would eventually send someone to investigate, but at that point the mission would simply mean extracting the surviving team members, if there were any, and pulling out. Vartos and Claris would have been lost in vain, the rebelling Verkuylian workers would be purged, and the Empire would win—perhaps permanently. Without enough support from the workers who were left, the New Republic would probably not return.

"I see," Quarle said. "So it's call the fleet now, or never get another chance."

"Looks that way," Selby agreed. She hesitated. "I'm sorry—this could get a lot messier than originally planned. If Ein starts rounding up workers, using them as hostages . . . we can still win, but victory may come at a higher price."

Quarle's cheek twitched. "All things worth having usually do."

"There could be fighting, in orbit or on the ground," she warned. "Will it be worth it to you?"

He looked at her. In his eyes, she saw grim acceptance.

"I want what's best for Verkuyl," he said. "If bloodshed is what it takes—" He looked away. "I'll regret it, but I'll learn to live with it.

"Now." He abruptly changed the subject. "I can think of three subspace comms we might be able to get to. Let's figure out which one would be best to try for. . . ."

If she'd known of all the Hall's hidden passages last night, Selby reflected as she followed Quarle down a narrow corridor, getting up to the Governor's office undetected would've been as easy as shooting mynocks off a power coupling.

The Hall had proven a virtual warren of hidden passages. Quarle's grandfather had been a careful, one might even say paranoid, businessman—which was fortuitous, given the present circumstances. It meant they could move within the Hall with astonishing freedom, only needing to leave cover to call the fleet. Selby smiled to think that when the Imperials, no doubt monitoring outgoing subspace transmissions, came running to investigate the call, all they'd find were unconscious guards in an empty room. She and Quarle would slip back into hiding to await the fleet's arrival before confronting Ein.

"We're almost there," Quarle said quietly, pausing at an intersection. "Before we go any further, I want to check the situation outside, see what we're up against."

"Sounds good," she murmured back. "Lead on."

He hesitated, then turned to look at her. "I'd rather do it alone," he said. "I know the passage system. You don't. And this way, if I get caught there'll still be one of us left to finish the job."

Selby frowned. It made sense, but she did not particularly want to split up. Quarle didn't have a blaster and would be unable to protect himself if he ran into trouble. She felt another twinge, remembering Vartos. Team members were supposed to watch each other's backs. She briefly considered giving him her own blaster for the reconnoiter, but decided not to. Intelligence had taught her to watch her own back first.

Quarle's eyes dropped to the blaster, too, but when she didn't offer it, he didn't ask. "You wait here," he told her. "I shouldn't be gone too long."

Selby nodded. He looked at her a long moment more, as if wanting to say something else, but then merely nodded, too. Turning, he started around the corner—

"Watch your back," she said softly.

He glanced back, raised that eyebrow. "Always," he assured her, and strode away.

Once he was gone, Selby leaned back against the narrow passage's wall and sighed. Alone with her thoughts for the first time since the shoot-out in the generator room, she could not get Vartos's face out of her mind. Had it simply been incredibly bad luck, his being discovered by the stormtroopers? Or had Claris already been "persuaded" to talk about her fellow operatives?

Which reminded her—

She reached up, slipping off the now-useless earsculpt. Holding it in her palm, she stared at it thoughtfully.

Claris must have talked, she decided. For the eavesdropper to have cut out so quickly and unexpectedly after her arrest, the Imperials must have known exactly what to look for. She fingered the smooth curve of the metal, feeling it gently flex, then brought it up close to study the intricate scrollwork doubling as a tiny speaker.

When Quarle's voice sounded from it, she froze.

With hands that suddenly felt like ice, Selby held the device against her ear. Silence; only her pulse pounding in her head. She frowned, carefully flexed the earsculpt again, and this time whatever weak connection inside the receiver that had apparently caused it to cut out now held. She listened, growing colder with each word.

"—Tafno has promised backup within six hours," Ein was saying. "Two Dreadnaughts at least, maybe more. Convince her to delay making the call until then. When the Rebels arrive, they'll find a fleet with a little firepower of our own waiting for them—not the easy pickings they expect."

"Yes, of course, Your Excellency," Quarle said. "But how do you propose I convince her? We are nearly in position to make the call now. She'll want to know why we should wait."

A long pause. Selby could barely breathe for the tight feeling in her throat. "Tell her that we've imposed satellite silence," the Governor finally said. "Due to this terrorist threat, I've ordered a temporary ban on outgoing subspace comm traffic. Tell her the satellite relays have been shut down—but that a very old, unofficial relay placed in orbit by your grandfather will be within transmissible range in, oh, about six hours. And that you—*only you*—know how to access it."

Ein chuckled dryly. "You know, Daven, you may have hated the old man, but you must admit being Corlin Quarle Deld's grandson has put you in a unique position to realize his visions for Verkuyl."

"It's the only thing it ever *has* done for me," Quarle said. "The rest of the time, I'd as soon forget the tyrant ever existed."

"I shouldn't worry about it," Ein said. "No one holds it against you. You've already done more to make Verkuyl the success it is today than your grandfather ever could have. Your service to the Empire will long be remembered."

•   •   •

When Quarle rounded the corner, he found Selby waiting for him.

He stopped short at the sight of the blaster she held pointed at his chest. His eyes took in the steadiness of her aim, then brushed past to settle on her face. "Trouble?" he asked.

"How is it," she began conversationally, "that Corlin Quarle Deld's grandson ends up on the same side of the Empire that stole his home and destroyed his family's company?"

Quarle moved a few steps closer. Her aim did not waver. He stopped.

"BactaCo has hardly been destroyed," he said. "In fact, we currently have more business than we can handle. And the new refinery will increase both production and profits."

"I see," Selby said. Although determined to remain as cool about this as he, she felt her eyes narrow. "Then you don't care what the Empire does to Verkuyl, so long as the company gets its share of the credits."

He raised that eyebrow, and she had to fight back a sudden, violent urge to wipe that calm look off his face. "Those credits are what feed and clothe the workers, Selby. That's what a company is all about—providing goods or services for a price. To whom, it doesn't matter. Don't kid yourself that it was any different in my grandfather's day, and don't think your New Republic's motives are any more pure. When it comes to running a company, the accumulation of credits is the bottom line."

"At least your grandfather came by the company honestly," she bit out. "He bought the planet, built the refineries, brought in the workers. He didn't steal it from its rightful owners in the name of the Empire and enslave its workers. He—"

"Don't preach that Rebel propaganda to *me*," Quarle broke in sharply. "He *did* do that—and worse, he did it in the name of free trade. At least when the Empire took over, Verkuyl began giving something back to the workers, not just producing credits to satisfy my grandfather's greed."

He stopped, took a breath to compose himself. "Do you know how he got workers to come to Verkuyl?" he continued, a little more quietly. "Remember, this was before the Empire. People needed jobs, and they were willing to do almost anything to get them. To sell themselves into slavery, even. And so they did.

"In exchange for their passage here and the privilege of working in my grandfather's refineries, they signed on for ten-year terms, at the end of which they were promised a share of stock of the company they'd labored to help build. My grandfather called it indenture," he added bitterly, "but it was slavery."

Selby said nothing. Indentured servitude wasn't like being your own boss, free and clear, but it wasn't slavery, either. Both parties willingly entered into an agreement, and at the end of the contract—

"When the contract expired, most of the workers were so deeply in debt that even with their share of the stock, they couldn't get out," Quarle said. "Once they cashed out and paid off what they owed, there wasn't enough left over to leave. So they stayed."

She frowned. "How'd they get so far in debt?"

"The Company Store, of course," he said. "Most of the workers brought families with them, or married and started families once they arrived. My grandfather provided basic food and housing—soup kitchens and barracks—but anything else cost extra. A lot extra. It added up. By the time the Empire arrived to nationalize BactaCo, ninety out of every one hundred workers were so deep in debt they didn't even get credit vouchers on payday. The wages were simply transferred straight to their delinquent accounts."

He gave Selby a bitter smile. "If the Republic really wanted to *liberate* the workers, it should have been here twenty-five years ago."

Silence followed. "What happened when the Empire took over?" she finally asked.

Quarle's mouth twisted. "Well, I'll say one thing for old Corlin. If he couldn't have the credits, he didn't want anyone else to, either. When he realized the Empire wasn't just going to come in and oversee the operation—that they intended to boot him out and run it themselves—he started erasing company records. Client lists, production reports, shipping contracts—"

"And employee records." She nodded, beginning to understand. "The Empire didn't know about his arrangement with the employees."

"That's right," he said. "So when the Empire took over, Verkuyl stopped being a miserable little company planet run by a tight-fisted tyrant, and became what it was supposed to be: a place for these people to work and live. In the past twenty years, we've tripled our worker population and quadrupled our bacta production—and increased our profits by a thousand percent. Verkuylians are better off under the Empire than they ever were under my grandfather, so don't imagine you're doing us any great favors by *liberating* us."

It was true the Verkuylians had not clamored to be free of the Empire.

Indeed, it had only been in the last two years or so, when the New Republic chased the Empire out of the Core and triumphantly claimed Coruscant, that the resistance movement on Verkuyl had even begun. During her mission briefings, Selby had formed the impression the workers might have been cowed—or *content*, a small voice now whispered—to labor for the Empire forever if not for two things. One, that as Imperial strength ebbed, it provided less and less in the way of support to its smaller possessions such as Verkuyl; and two, the loss of a major medical supplier at Chennis last year had sent New Republic rabble-rousers to various Imperial-held suppliers to see what kind of rebellion they could stir up.

Verkuyl had stirred nicely.

But that doesn't mean the workers aren't sincere in their desire to be free, Selby told herself. *Just that it took our encouragement to give them the courage to revolt.*

She looked at Quarle. "If the Empire is forced to leave Verkuyl, you probably stand to inherit the bulk of the holdings. How can you possibly object to that?"

He shook his head. "You just don't get it, do you? I want what's best for Verkuyl—not what's best for myself, but best for the company and the planet. And I believe what's best for it right now is the Empire."

"The workers don't agree."

"The *workers* don't see the big picture," Quarle retorted. "They're laborers, not administrators. At the moment, they can't see past the promises the New Republic's dangling in front of them like nerfs being led to the milking shed.

"Independence—" He made it sound like a dirty word. "You tell me where, anywhere, workers don't dream of being their own boss. But they haven't got the faintest idea how to actually do it. Without the Empire's guidance, they'll run this company—their livelihood— right into the ground, or make juicy pickings for the bacta cartel. Then how much will their *independence* mean?"

"They'll be free," Selby said.

"Free to starve, maybe," he shot back bitterly.

She raised the blaster.

"Selby, *think* about it," he said warningly. "The Governor knows what's going on here. You can't win, but if you surrender now, I give you my word you won't be harmed."

He took a step forward, eyes earnestly searching her face. "Please, Selby. You won't get out of here any other way. It doesn't have to be like this."

In her mind's eye, Selby saw Vartos held at blasterpoint by the Hall stormtrooper. She thought of Claris, and the horror stories every Intelligence agent had heard of the fate that awaited them at the hands of Imperial inquisitors. She thought of Quarle, and that in doing what he truly felt best for his people, he had to betray their confidence, knowing full well that for many of them it meant certain death.

Black or white, friend or foe, she reminded herself. In this job, there was no room for anything else.

"Yes, it does," she said, and fired.

Thirty-four hours later, leaning against the stone railing of the Hall's roof and staring down at the dancing flames of a celebratory bonfire in the street below her, Selby reflected that, for having salvaged success from such certain failure, she should be in a much brighter frame of mind.

Listening to the revelry going on below, she wondered at the absence of her usual satisfaction at the successful completion of a mission. She didn't doubt the New Republic had done the right thing, bringing about the liberation of Verkuyl and restoring BactaCo to its native workers. A populace held in thrall, either to an Empire or a business dictator, needed to be set free.

But for the first time in her years of being involved in such liberations, it occurred to her to question whether the New Republic had done it because it was the best thing for the planet and its people, or because a direct pipeline to BactaCo was the best thing for the New Republic.

She could not forget Quarle's prediction: that the Verkuylians, faced for the first time with self-government and the running of a business, would be crushed under the weight of their new responsibilities. To help ease their transition, Selby had been told the New Republic planned to provide advisors to help the fledgling businessfolk find their economic feet in the galactic community. She frowned, bothered by this train of thought. New Republic "advisors" to Verkuyl somehow sounded too similar to the same sort of "advice" the Empire had dispensed.

She half wished Quarle, who had the experience to run the company and, by birth, the right, had chosen to stay and help. But released from the hidden passage where she'd left him bound, only a certain darkness in those green eyes betraying the feelings he kept from showing on his face, Quarle had elected to leave Verkuyl with the rest of the Imperial interlopers. Once the workers learned what he'd done, it was painfully clear that they would never trust him again.

"Sel?" A voice cut into her brooding. "It's almost time to go."

She turned. Vartos's dark skin blended into the shadows around the turbolift, but she could see the faint gleam where his eyes reflected the starlight overhead. Both he and Claris had survived their captivity, although Vartos had required a few hours in a bacta tank to fully recover. Selby found that somehow ironic. "Yes, sir," she replied. "I'll be right down."

Vartos nodded and stepped back into the turbolift, leaving her alone. Selby turned back to the railing, eyes again drawn to the bonfire below. Verkuyl celebrated its freedom tonight—but how long would its jubilation last under the pressures of its new responsibilities?

She sighed. She would not be around to find out. She had done her job—done it well—and now it was time to forget the things Quarle had said and move on to the next assignment.

Black or white, friend or foe, she reminded herself. Under the Empire, Verkuyl had been black. Under the New Republic, it would be white. It might be true that Verkuyl's future most likely held shades of gray—but in her line of work, it was best not to look at those shadowed colors too closely.

Turning away, Selby took a deep breath. She grimaced at the stink—the awful smell of the alazhi simmering in the refineries. It permeated everything, and after just four days on Verkuyl, she felt as if its stench had somehow soaked right through her skin and taken up permanent residence in her heart.

She feared it would stay with her forever.

No Disintegrations, Please

by Paul Danner

S*queak.*
  Squeak.
Squeak.

Most beings would have found the intermittent sound annoying. Some might have even gone so far as to blast the noisy repliwood sign into toothpicks. But the main street of the New Hope Settlement was currently devoid of life. There were only a few dust balls moving in accordance to the fickle will of the wind. The row of stores that flanked the main street stood silently, sealed up and forgotten. The rust-colored sands of Ladarra were already returning to reclaim the land it had lost years ago. . . .

And so the sign continued to squeak, hanging as it was by a single frayed duracable. The lettering was a bit faded, but the words were still legible: "The Ellstree Bar—Cold Lum; Droids Welcome; No Disintegrations, Please . . ." Like the rest of the shops in downtown New Hope, the bar looked to be long deserted. But as the old saying goes, "appearance and truth have as much in common as Jawas and Hutts."

The children sat in a semicircle around the man. There were at least a dozen of them, mostly human, but a few other species were represented as well. They were orphans and urchins, the last generation of a failed colony—too poor to book passage off Ladarra and unwilling or unable to face the difficulties of life in the few larger cities on the planet.

The man had no name as far as the children knew. They merely called him the Storyteller. He was dressed as they were, in ragged clothing scrounged from a dozen wardrobes and cobbled together into a free-form garment. The Storyteller was an older human, with a heavily lined face and a shock of white hair. He had the look of a man who had seen too much and his eyes were unable to stay focused on any one location for longer than a minute—as if they were constantly searching for any possible threat.

"You want *another* story?" he asked in a weary voice.

The children nodded in unison. They rarely spoke, and he wasn't sure all of them even knew how.

"How about the legend of the fearless young Jedi Knight who rescued a beautiful princess?"

A chorus of groans answered that question.

"Well, then. There's always the tale of the evil Imperial governor who wanted to conquer the innocent little world of—" He saw the looks on their faces and couldn't help but laugh. "No? My, but this is a tough crowd." He shook his head in mock irritation. "So what would you like to hear about?"

"Tell us a new one," one of the children said. She was a pretty little one, though it was hard to tell under all that grime.

"Come now, you've heard all of them at least once. Just pick the one you like."

The girl folded her arms and jutted out her lower lip.

He fought to keep a straight face. "Okay, okay . . ." He scratched his chin in dramatic fashion. "A new story. Let me see . . . ah, yes, I've got it!"

Their eyes lit up.

"No, no . . . that won't work."

The children frowned at him.

"Kidding, kidding," he chuckled for a moment, then quickly grew serious. "I do have one tale that I heard a long time ago. To my knowledge it has never been told again." He had their full attention. "How many of you have heard of . . ." His voice lowered to a dangerous whisper. *"Boba Fett?"*

Their eyes grew wide at the mention of the name, and one by one each little hand lifted into the air.

"Well, I happen to know a long-forgotten tale of the greatest bounty hunter who ever lived. Would you like me to share it with you?"

Every head in the room slowly nodded.

The Storyteller had his audience. . . . He smiled briefly, then settled back into the comfortable chair and slowly closed his eyes. He began the story after a moment of dramatic silence. The children listened with rapt attention.

As the shuttle's exit hatch slowly descended, the sudden hiss of escaping gases nearly caused Rivo to jump right off the platform. As it was, he barely regained enough balance in time to prevent himself from unceremoniously rolling down the ramp.

General Gaege Xarran gave a dramatic sigh to indicate his disgust and extended an arm to steady his brother as he stumbled down the ramp.

Xarran quickly glanced at the sharp line of stormtroopers that served as an honor guard. The squad remained at such rigid attention that he momentarily wondered if the Dark Lord of the Sith had suddenly emerged from the *Lambda*-class shuttle. The Empire's ivory-armored shock troopers weren't always the brightest specimens around, but at least they knew enough to keep their mouths shut and follow orders.

Unlike some people, the General thought as his gaze fell

upon Rivo. Xarran suddenly felt his body grow flushed with anger and his lips twitched into an involuntary sneer.

"How could you be so stupid?" he whispered. Not that it really mattered whether the stormtroopers overheard; they had been privy to conversations of much greater importance than the scolding of a sibling.

Rivo might as well have been one of the silent group of guards, for he acted as if his brother had never spoken. His eyes were still darting around wildly, searching for a possible threat in every shadow.

Xarran lightly cuffed his brother with an open hand, striking the back of his head. If there was one thing the General did not like, it was being ignored. "Answer me!"

Rivo's response was swift—Xarran was doubly shocked as he stared down the stubby barrel of a hold-out blaster. First of all, the General had never imagined his own brother would point a weapon at him, and second Rivo was supposed to have been relieved of his armaments. Someone was destined to die for the oversight, but the General intended to avoid being the unlucky party.

It was his brother's life, however, that appeared to be in the most immediate danger. . . .

The stormtroopers remained motionless, but somewhere in the span of an eye-blink nine blaster rifles had been expertly trained on Rivo.

The young man didn't seem to notice. His eyes held a blank stare that didn't quite focus on anything. The General wasn't even quite sure if Rivo still recognized him.

"It's only me, brother," Xarran said softly. "I'm the one trying to keep you alive." Slowly but steadily the General reached out with a gloved hand. The span was less than half a meter, but it took forever to close the distance between his fingers and the weapon.

When the General took hold of the blaster, Rivo's nervous energy drained out as if he were a leaking power cell. His entire body slumped down and the weapon spilled like liquid through his fingers until it was collected in Xarran's waiting hands.

"I'm sorry," Rivo managed through choked sobs. He wavered unsteadily, lost in his anguish.

Xarran pulled him into a hug, nodding to the guards over Rivo's shoulder. The gesture was unnecessary. Their blasters were already holstered.

The General cradled the back of his brother's head, in the same place where moments before Xarran had struck him. That now seemed like an eternity ago—it suddenly became clear to him how time, no matter how brief, could irrevocably affect one's entire existence. Every moment was a crossroad to infinite possibilities— Rivo's greatest talent besides drinking and gambling was picking the wrong path to travel. Fortunately the results, as bad as they were, had never ended with outright disaster. This time was different, however, for Rivo's latest mistake might end up costing his life.

Of course, it went without saying that Xarran would do everything in his power to prevent that occurrence. And as a General in the Imperial Army, that power was considerable.

Xarran gently supported his brother, helping him walk the long landing platform toward the garrison complex. The stormtroopers executed a crisp about-face and fell into line behind them. "You'll have nothing to fear anymore, brother. I doubt anyone could have tracked you here."

Rivo gazed up at his brother and for the first time, there was a glimmer of recognition in his eyes.

Heartened by the small gesture, Xarran continued. "And in the highly unlikely event that you were followed, one would have to be certifiably insane to even consider attacking an entire Imperial garrison."

In the distance, well concealed high in the cover afforded by the dense foliage, a silent figure lurked in the shadows.

He watched, though he held no macrobinoculars—

for a pair was conveniently built into his battle-scarred helmet.

He listened as easily if he were one of the stormtroopers, his broadband antenna descrambling the signal of their comlinks and effectively turning the silent soldiers into eavesdropping devices.

Once again, nothing escaped his notice.

Just as no one escaped him.

He climbed down from his perch among the trees with surprising grace considering the bulkiness of his battered gray and green armor.

By the time he finished his descent, darkness had begun to fall like a velvet blanket, and the twin moons of Vryssa were steadily rising in the northern sky.

He paused only once to stare at the towering silhouette of the Imperial garrison base. The massive structure remained in shadow for a few moments longer, then its powerful spot-lumas ignited. The harsh light was coldly reflected in the figure's mask.

General Xarran had unwittingly issued an arrogant challenge.

A challenge Boba Fett was more than ready to accept. . . .

The speeder bike patrol caught him unaware. He had just climbed down from his overlook and was checking his equipment. His motion sensors didn't go off until they were right on top of him. The bikes were so fast they didn't register with enough warning time.

As he dove for cover in the thick tangle of bush, Fett saw one of the scout troopers gesture in his general direction. His two partners immediately circled around, moving into standard Imperial flanking position. Their vehicles were newer models, pure scout bikes by the look of them—very fast, but without any armaments or protection.

Fett needed to know how much they knew. He activated his antenna. . . .

". . . Saw something through those trees. Hard to tell, though. Could have just been a buldobeast."

"Keep your positions. I'll check it out."

"Acknowledged."

"Should we contact the other patrol?"

"You want to listen to their jokes about getting spooked by a little buldo?"

"Negative."

"That's what I thought. Now, stand by."

Fett watched as the lead biker approached, giving his vehicle minimal throttle. The repulsorlift craft drifted a few meters above the ground as the scout trooper conducted a grid search of the area.

Ever so slowly, Fett rolled onto his back and snaked his right arm up through the thicket. He took a single deep breath and then his body froze. The hunter was so still it seemed as if he were made of ferrocrete.

The scout biker moved overhead, directly above Fett's hiding place. The hunter could feel the backwash from the repulsorlift engines pressing against him. The scout was leaning over his vehicle, examining the area closely. The trooper's head jerked back suddenly as if he had spotted something.

Fett flexed his wrist and the rocket-propelled dart housed in his forearm compartment streaked silently through the air. The hunter's aim was perfect. The dart jammed into the soft black bodysuit between the scout's helmet and chestpiece. The poison worked fast, starting with the victim's vocal cords. The man silently jerked forward and then tumbled from his seat, leaving the speeder bike hovering in place.

Moving quickly, Fett hopped up onto the bike and jammed the comlinks of the other two bikers. He opened up the throttle and veered off toward one of them. Without even a glance at the other, the hunter activated his armor's grenade launcher.

The trooper was shocked to see Fett streak past on the speeder bike going after his partner. Figuring he had the drop on the hunter, he gunned his bike forward—

just as Fett's grenade finished its arc and fell into his lap.

The bounty hunter felt the shock wave of the blast but didn't bother to look back. He was too busy concentrating on his final target. This trooper was taking no chances. The scout was hightailing it out of the vicinity in order to escape the jamming and get some help. He already had a sizable lead on the hunter and was rapidly increasing the gap. Fett knew he couldn't catch up—the trooper was more familiar with the terrain.

Steering the vehicle with one hand, the bounty hunter drew his modified blaster rifle. Scomp-linked to the macrobinoculars in his helmet, the weapon finally locked on target at three hundred meters. The scout trooper didn't even see the two angry crimson blaster bolts that slammed into his back and took him clean off his vehicle.

Fett slowed his bike to a stop and scanned the area for anyone else. The hunter was not happy—he had expended unnecessary time and energy. And now they would know for sure he was on the planet.

Perhaps that might be to his advantage. . . .

Rivo's voice cut the silence, though it was but a whisper. "He's here. Now."

"Impossible," Xarran said, barely keeping the disgust from his voice. The General did not like to see his brother cower. Especially in front of his men. "You give this bounty hunter too much credit, brother. Our sensors would have detected his ship's approach."

Rivo shook his head. "*This* bounty hunter is not the simpleminded scum you are used to dealing with. Boba Fett is different. He has never failed. They say he is the best that ever was. . . ."

Commander Tyrix checked his console. "The patrol *should* have reported in by now, sir."

"This confirms it!" Rivo said.

Xarran would have none of it. "There is no reason to

make any connection with your situation and this incident. For all we know—"

"Sir," Tyrix said. "Another patrol has found the remains of the missing unit. . . ." The Commander listened for a moment, pressing his headset against his ear. He paled considerably. "They're all dead."

The General was on his feet. "How?"

"Blaster, a grenade, and some sort of poisoned dart. The troopers' weapons were fully charged . . . none of the men even got off a shot."

Rivo let out a nervous giggle. "I told you . . . he's coming for me."

Xarran ignored him. "Commander, send out two detachments. If this bounty hunter is indeed here, then I want him found and brought before me. Preferably alive . . . although a body will do just fine."

"Two detachments, sir?" Tyrix swiveled his chair around to face the General. "For just one man?"

Xarran's face did not so much as twitch. "I'm sorry, Commander, did you say something?"

"No, sir," Tyrix said, hurriedly swiveling back to his console to activate the comlink.

Fett sat in the hunter's blind among a thick tangle of coilwood branches. He watched as the first wave of speeder bikes roared below him, buzzing along like bloodgnats. He felt the impact tremors as a pair of Imperial walkers lumbered by flanked by a half dozen of their comical AT-ST counterparts. He shook his head in amazement as squad after squad of stormtroopers marched into the underbrush. Their bright white armor was not exactly the best forest camouflage.

This massive show of force told the bounty hunter all he needed to know about his opponents. . . .

Two detachments meant they certainly knew he was here. And they were nervous.

Behind the tinted faceplate of his battered helmet, Boba Fett actually smiled.

•   •   •

Xarran leaned over the tactical screen watching proudly as his forces deployed into the forest. He listened to the excited comm chatter as his men moved into position and began an expertly coordinated, utterly systematic search. There would be no escape. Not from the might of the Empire. The General snorted and crossed his arms over his barrel chest. "He's as good as ours."

As he spoke, all communications went dead.

Boba Fett double-checked the comm jamming unit. It was an advanced prototype and very powerful. Unfortunately, its duration was also extremely short: 58 minutes. And then it would explode.

He set his chronometer to countdown mode. Seconds began to vanish. He had just under an hour to eliminate two Imperial detachments.

The hunter turned and hefted his blaster rifle. Fett only foresaw one problem: what to do with the three minutes he would have to spare. . . .

Perched on the edge of his seat in the walker's cockpit, Lieutenant Byrga smacked his lips in nervous anticipation. The AT-AT drivers exchanged a quick glance, but wouldn't dare to comment on the habit of a superior officer. Even if it was extremely irritating.

Byrga was staring so hard at the sensor readouts that his eyeballs were on the verge of jettisoning themselves free of his head. The Lieutenant didn't like the fact that they had lost communications. Despite all efforts, they could not make contact with the rest of their detachment or the garrison base. That made Byrga anxious. His lips were smacking on overdrive.

"Don't worry," he said trying to reassure the rest of the command crew, who had learned to ignore his rantings and still do their jobs effectively. "We are the best

the Empire has to offer. No one escapes us. We will find
this fool who dares oppose the will of Palpatine and
crush him in the iron grip of the—"

The magnetic grappler connected with the armored
underbelly of the AT-AT and locked into place. The
twenty-meter lanyard trailing behind it pulled taut and a
small armored figure emerged from out of the dense
underbrush. Fett calmly waited for the winch in his armored suit to elevate him up to the walker's stomach.

The hunter used the time to power up his wrist lasers.

Byrga's ramblings continued. The one good thing about
that, at least for the rest of the command crew, was when
his mouth was running there was a cessation of lip-
smacking. "Make me proud, men. I want to be the one
who finds this bounty hunter."

The Lieutenant abruptly cocked his head to one side.
"Did anyone else hear that?"

The drivers shook their heads.

Byrga turned toward the dark tunnel leading back
into the walker's passenger compartment. "That's strange.
We're not carrying any troops." He activated the blast
door and peered inside. After a moment's decision he
placed one hand on his holstered blaster and slowly
walked into the AT-AT's neck. "I'll be right back, men.
Carry on without me for a moment."

The drivers happily complied.

"I want all communications back on-line!" Frustrated, Xarran screamed into the internal comlink, "Immediately!"

Commander Tyrix sighed and gritted his teeth. "Uh,
sir . . . the blackout is affecting the comm as well." His
voice lowered to almost a whisper. "The engineering
teams can't hear you."

The General was at Tyrix's console in three strides.

Xarran's face was so close the Commander could count the veins bulging in the man's forehead.

Xarran spoke through gritted teeth, the words slow and precise. "Then get down there and tell them."

"Yes, sir!" Tyrix said as he dove into the nearest turbolift.

The AT-AT drivers were so entranced by the wonderful silence in the cockpit they didn't even notice the unusually long absence of their commanding officer. That was their first mistake. When the blast door finally slid open again they didn't even bother to look up from their consoles. As it turned out, that oversight was their last.

Boba Fett lowered his smoking blaster rifle and took a moment to admire his new mode of transportation.

Lieutenant Grejj sat back in his command chair, fingertips steepled in front of his face. The walker's command crew was doing a fine job considering the circumstances. He only hoped they could get communications back online as quickly as possible. Then they could eliminate the bounty hunter and resume normal duties. Grejj liked his routine. He did not like surprises.

"Sir! We're picking something up on sensors."

The Lieutenant leaned forward. "What is it?"

The driver shook his head. "Just another walker . . . must be Lieutenant Byrga."

"Let's go see if his hunting has been more successful."

"He must have already seen us," the driver said. "Here they come now."

Grejj nodded, reaching for the cockpit release lever. "With any luck this will be over soon."

As a matter of fact, it was.

The remains of Lieutenant Grejj's AT-AT and a pair of AT-STs that had stumbled onto the fight were scattered

along the ground. The two smaller walkers were so confused by the duel between their larger siblings that they
had actually opened fire on Grejj.

Fett guided his AT-AT through the smoking debris as
his sensors picked up a large grouping of stormtroopers
nearby. The hunter checked his chronometer and
noted that he was right on schedule.

"Communications have been restored, sir."

"Finally! Patch me through directly to our forces."
Tyrix's fingers flew over his console and he quickly signaled his success with a nod to the General.

Xarran reached for his comlink. "Xarran to Alpha and
Delta Groups. All units are to report status immediately."

There was silence.

Rivo gave his brother a meaningful glance, but Xarran ignored him and tried again. "I repeat, this is General Xarran ordering all units to account current status.
Alpha Group . . . report."

Nothing.

A bead of sweat trickled down the General's forehead. He leaned closer to the mike. "Delta Group . . .
report."

Again, there was not a sound.

Xarran stared accusingly at Tyrix. "You must have
been in error, Commander. The comm system is still
down."

"I regret to inform you, sir. It is functioning within
normal parameters. Our forces should be responding."

"Yet that is not the case." Xarran's voice had lost a bit
of its hard edge. "Why?"

Rivo answered with a plaintive wail. "Because they're
all dead!"

Xarran spun around, viciously backhanding his brother
across the face. "Will you shut up!"

The unexpected blow sent Rivo crumpling to the
deck, where he cringed, holding up his hands in suppli-

cation. Xarran's face softened with regret immediately. He helped Rivo up and said in a low whisper, "Forgive me, brother . . ."

"Wait a minute!" Tyrix nearly jumped from his console. "General, sensors are picking up one of our walkers at the outer perimeter."

Xarran beamed. "Put it on the viewscreen."

Tyrix complied and the image of a battle-scarred AT-AT filled the viewer.

"Returning in victory?" the Commander said.

"Let's find out." Xarran tried the comlink again. "Base to walker. Report."

A gout of fire suddenly bloomed on the underbelly of the AT-AT followed by a loud explosion that sent a burst of static over the comlink. The walker lurched forward, like a mortally wounded behemoth, then fell. Its chin connected with the ground, and then the rest of its body followed suit, causing the soil to rumble. Then the metal monster disappeared in a haze of smoke and flame.

"What was that?" Tyrix blurted out.

"A message," Rivo said softly.

The base control room was absolutely still. No one dared to move or speak. Everyone was staring silently at the terrible image that loomed on the viewer.

Everyone that is, except for Xarran. The General stood up and slowly walked into his office, boots clacking on the deck plates. His voice echoed through the room. "Someone turn off that blasted thing. . . ."

Tyrix shut off the screen, but as the rest of the base crew hurriedly resumed their duties he continued to stare at the dark viewer for a few moments. His gaze flickered across the room, and came to rest on Rivo. After thirty years of military service, the Commander had seen more than his share of horrible things, but the look of terror in Rivo's eyes sent a chill rippling down his spine.

·   ·   ·

Fett would have liked to have seen the General's expression when the AT-AT exploded. He probably shouldn't have wasted the thermal detonator, but the psychological effect on the man and his troops would be worth it.

Both sides had taken their feints and jabs—now it was time to move into the final round. Fett was almost sorry to see it come. The skirmishes before the main event always served as interesting diversions, especially since the outcome of his mission was never in doubt.

Boba Fett did not lose.

"What were you thinking, Rivo?" Xarran was seated in the plush replihide chair behind a desk that dwarfed most landspeeders.

Rivo sat across from him in a much smaller seat. His eyes had apparently found something interesting on the floor. "Money," he mumbled after a moment. He finally made eye contact with his older brother. "What else is there? I was blinded by greed, Gaege. I never figured that Jabba would be able to track me as the source of his data leak."

"You didn't think that someone like Jabba the Hutt would have his own expert slicers? I always told you that your ego would be your undoing, didn't I? You may be good, but there will always be someone better. And that's true no matter if you're a slicer, a soldier, or a bounty hunter."

"The funny thing is, I didn't even mean to slice into Jabba's records. It was a complete accident. But once I found out what I had stumbled onto, I couldn't resist."

"You never could pass up a chance to make an easy credit," Xarran sighed. "Especially if it didn't involve honest work."

"I didn't come here for a lecture, brother. I came here for help." He stared out the transparisteel window that overlooked the lush forests of Vryssa. "Although from the looks of it, maybe I came to the wrong place."

The General's face twitched slightly. "Perhaps you'd

have better luck out there by yourself. Feel free to leave anytime."

"Okay, so I messed up again. I apologize, Gaege. . . . I know you're doing your best. I just never thought I'd be on the run from Boba Fett."

"You stole sensitive information from one of the most dangerous scumlords in the galaxy and then sold it to the highest bidder . . . how much did Jabba lose as a result of your actions?"

"Over one-hundred-fifty thousand credits. But I don't think he really cares about the money. It's just the principle of the thing. The Hutt wants to make an example of me. And what Jabba wants, Jabba gets."

"Well, he isn't going to get you, brother. I don't care how many bounty hunters he sends."

"Do you really think Fett can be stopped?"

"The man is good. Very good. But I see his strategy now, and I refuse to play his game any longer. No more troops will leave the base. If he wants you, he will have to come here. And mark my words, no one can penetrate the 'death fence.' It's set for maximum voltage per my orders. The charge is so high the tiniest spark could fry a bantha in seconds." Xarran gave a thin-lipped smile. "No one gets out. And no one gets in."

Night had fallen on Vryssa.

Fett was crouched in the bushes, twenty meters away from the base's outer perimeter. The ten-meter-high wall surrounding the complex seemed to be alive, crackling as it was with azure arcs of electricity. The surges danced over the surface like writhing snakes.

The spot he had picked was a good distance away from the nearest gatehouse, though stormtroopers constantly patrolled along the fortified catwalks set back from the fence. Observation towers were spaced about one hundred meters apart along the catwalk, and a combination of flood lights, detection sensors, and droids were used to maintain security. Fett's current position

put him roughly fifty meters from the two flanking towers. It was a good distance, but he didn't think it would
be enough to avoid detection.

Fett activated his internal comlink. It was time for a
little distraction. . . .

Slave I roared over the treeline, screaming toward the
garrison base at full speed. Its sophisticated sensor-
jamming array was fully powered and the hull itself was
magnetically polarized to scramble and confuse enemy
scans. As it was, the base was taken by surprise.

On its first pass the ship delivered a frighteningly po-
tent volley of concussion missiles, proton torpedoes,
blaster bolts, and ion blasts. The attack was so fierce that
the base's powerful deflector shields fluctuated and the
entire structure shuddered with the impact.

"See?" Xarran shouted from the command center. "The
man has grown desperate! He knows there's no way in so
he resorts to a suicide run." He focused his gaze on Rivo.
"*Everyone* makes mistakes, sooner or later. And I will
make sure this one is his last."

Standing at one of the tactical stations, Tyrix turned
to his commanding officer. "All turbolaser turrets are
primed and ready, sir."

Xarran squeezed his gloved hand into a tight fist.
"Fire at will! Blow him out of the sky!"

As *Slave I* circled for another pass, six heavy twin laser
turrets mounted around the building opened fire, followed by the thunderous roar of the three heavy twin
turbolaser turrets from the upper level of the base. Unfortunately, the heavy weapons were slow to fire and
even slower to track such a swift target.

Fett's ship executed an amazing series of maneuvers
that allowed it to continue its strafing run while dancing
around the green swarm of angry laser bolts. Twisting,
turning, and rolling, *Slave I* delivered a vicious counter-

attack capped by a full spread of proton torpedoes that punched a gaping hole in the base's deflectors. In return, Fett's ship took some minor damage, but easily eluded any critical hits.

Slave I executed a quick Segnor's Loop and moved into position for another assault.

"It's not working," Tyrix said, slamming a hand onto his console. "That ship's just too fast for our turrets to track. We're barely touching him and he's already knocked three quarters of our shield generators off-line." The damage control screen flashed the grim news. "Another run like that and he'll leave us defenseless!"

"No one is that good," Xarran thundered. The General was shaking with rage. "Launch the entire squadron. I want every TIE we have in the air now."

Nodding, Tyrix punched the comm panel, calling for all pilots to report to their spacecraft. He turned to Xarran, "Should we sound the code alarm, sir?"

"No," Xarran said, his face flushing slightly. "I've served in the Imperial Army for most of my life and I will not be taunted into sounding full alert by one man, no matter how powerful he may appear to be. Besides, Fett will not breach the perimeter . . . the TIEs will see to that."

Tyrix paused a moment before responding—a sign of disapproval he would never dare to vocalize. "As you wish, sir."

Rivo shook his head. "Why won't you take the precautions? It won't hurt to—"

Xarran cut him off. "There isn't much good you can do up here, brother. Perhaps you should return to your quarters."

"But, I'm . . . fine." Rivo saw the look on Xarran's face and silently walked to the turbolift.

Slave I soared through the skies, taking potshots at the forty TIE fighters giving chase. Fett hated to see such an unfair fight, but there was nothing he could do about it. His ship was faster, more maneuverable, and bristled with twice as much weaponry as all the fighters put together. And unlike the TIEs, *Slave I* had shields. The Imperial fighters were hopelessly outmatched, even with the rather simplistic combat routines he had preprogrammed into the ship. The attacks on the garrison were typical Rebel strafing runs the Empire had so much trouble dealing with, while the evasive maneuvers against the TIEs were randomized according to sensor information. Fett avoided having *Slave I* be too aggressive with the fighters. Preprogramming was still no match for a live pilot.

All things considered, it was a good distraction, but would be over relatively soon. He was going to have to hurry.

Most of the stormtrooper patrols had cleared the catwalks—those that remained had their attention focused on the skies above.

Fett sprinted for the perimeter fence. When he closed half the distance he engaged his jet pack and soared into the air in a burst of flame. Elevating quickly, the hunter easily cleared the ten-meter-high fence, continued over the energy mine field between the fence and the base, and executed a perfect landing on the catwalk.

He checked his blaster rifle and quickly moved to the observation platform to his left. The first stormtrooper to step out caught a bolt in the helmet and went down. In midstride Fett sent a stun grenade arcing through the air and into the guardhouse. His faceplate tinted opaque as the flash-bang erupted, so the hunter didn't miss a beat when he dove inside the blast door on his stomach. Wild blaster bolts erupted overhead as Fett calmly picked off all five stormtroopers manning the tower.

He sealed the entrance behind him and walked over to the computer terminal. Fett entered the encryption codes he had purchased from an unsavory Bothan and went to work. The first thing he pulled up was a three-dimensional schematic of the garrison.

•   •   •

"Status?"

Tyrix glanced at the General and almost smiled. "We took heavy losses but the TIEs are routing him. Take a look."

The Commander stepped away from the tactical screen. Xarran studied the images for a few moments, watching as *Slave I* slowly led the TIE fighters away from the base. "It's a feint."

"What?"

"Fett's not on that ship."

Tyrix was confused. "Then where is he?"

"Here." It pained the General to say it. "Inside the perimeter by now, I'd venture. Sound the code alarm—reference an intruder alert. Go to full battle stations and step up interior patrols." Xarran quietly walked back to his chair and dropped down as if the weight of an AT-AT was set upon his shoulders.

Fett stood at the command console of Sub-Level 3. Over a dozen stunned or dead technicians were scattered around the room. The hunter studied the illuminated panels which controlled the base's main power, backup generators, tractor beams, and deflector shield generators. He went to work. . . .

Tyrix nearly fell out of his chair. "Sir! We have him!"

"What?" The General was by his side in seconds.

"Someone's accessing the main control units on Sub-Level Three." He called up the data. "See? He's using a code from last month, and the computer flagged it."

"It has to be Fett. He's trying to shut us down." Xarran contemplated his response. "Send three squads down to . . . no, wait. Seal off that room immediately. We'll flood it with Chemtrox gas and that will be the last of our little bounty hunter."

Tyrix's voice lowered. "But what if it's not him . . . ? And even if it is, he could have some technicians—"

Xarran pushed the Commander out of the way. His fingers flew over the console and a smile slowly dawned on his face. Fett was shutting down all systems and there was no time for moral debate. The race was on again and this time Xarran would win.

Fett whirled around as the heavy blast doors sealed and locked. He was effectively trapped. So, they finally discovered his trick and now knew where he was. It certainly took them long enough. Of course it was too late. Fett was about to cut the power.

He was so absorbed in his work that he almost missed it . . . luckily, his sound sensors picked up the recessed vents clicking open and the slow, steady hiss of gas being pumped into the room.

A quick scan revealed the substance to be Chemtrox— an extremely lethal agent. Fett had heard it delivered a particularly painful death. He didn't intend to find out firsthand if the rumors were true.

Fett activated his armor's enviro filter seal. It protected him from harmful or deadly atmosphere and there was a two-hour supply of air.

As the Chemtrox gas swirled around him Fett prepared to shut down the main computer.

"There . . ." Xarran wiped the sweat from his forehead and sat back in Tyrix's chair. "It's over. No one could have possibly survived that."

Everything went black. Every last bit of power in the entire garrison base. There was only darkness.

The Commander's voice rang out. "You were saying, sir?"

A blaster shot sent a crimson flash of light through the control room and Tyrix's body hit the floor. General Xarran activated a glowrod and hefted his blaster pistol.

His eyes danced wildly in the soft light, then focused on the corpse of his Commander.

The terrified faces of the base command crew stared back at him as if he had suddenly transformed into a mynock. Xarran fired three bolts into the ceiling. "Everyone out. Now!"

The crew quickly obeyed, stumbling over themselves to reach the emergency stairs. The General entered his office and sat down in front of his console. There was one system that would not have been affected by the loss of main or backup power. It ran off a special generator that only he knew about—well, he and Tyrix, but the Commander wouldn't be talking any time soon.

Xarran activated the panel and smiled as the base's self-destruct system lit up with crimson letters. The General lowered his head to accommodate the retinal scanner and began reciting the code to activate the countdown.

Fett moved through the darkened, deserted corridors of the base. Except for the steadfast stormtroopers, nearly everyone had fled the once-mighty garrison. With his sound, motion, infrared, and targeting sensors all activated, picking off the ivory-armored opponents was ridiculously easy.

Of course, the one person who mattered was also present . . . somewhere in the bowels of the garrison.

Fett had paid a small fortune to have the unwitting fool tagged with one of his special microscopic subdermal trackers back on Inat Prime. It was a wise investment.

Jabba had not placed an open bounty on Rivo Xarran; rather, His Bloatedness had offered the job solely to Fett . . . fifty thousand credits. Dead or alive.

Fett suspected the Hutt wanted to see just how good Fett really was. Jabba knew Rivo would run to his big brother for help and an entire Imperial garrison would stand between the hunter and his prey.

Fett didn't like the Hutt, but he paid well and on

time. That was more than he could say for most. Besides, one day Jabba would get what was coming to him. After all, justice was a patient hunter.

Fett knew the value of that particular virtue very well, so he continued his careful ascent through the garrison's main tower. There was no need to rush. The end would come soon enough. And no matter how novel the hunt had been, the conclusion was always the same.

With a high-pitched giggle, General Gaege Xarran, executive officer of the Imperial Garrison Base on Vryssa, moved down the stairwell. He had holstered his blaster in favor of a larger carbine. A spot-luma was mounted on top of the weapon, and a stubby microgrenade launcher barrel hung underneath. "Come out, come out wherever you are . . ."

Fett emerged from the stairwell on Level 5. His tracker unit informed him that Rivo was less than fifty meters away, in the barracks adjoining the base's recreation facilities. The hunter moved down the shadowed corridor, stopping at the last door. Fett imagined the slicer was hiding under the bed, probably clutching his hold-out blaster and promising that if he survived this situation he'd never do anything bad again.

Fett slapped a small explosive charge to the entrance and stepped back. He activated the detonator and watched as the door evaporated into a fine mist. The hunter paused for a moment, half expecting Rivo to fire a few desperate shots out the doorway.

Holding his rifle at the ready, Fett carefully made his approach. When his motion sensor alarm activated, the hunter froze and took aim, figuring Rivo was making a run through the door.

Fett was so intent on the situation, it took him a split second longer than usual to realize that the motion alarm had not come from in front of him. He whirled around, though even as he did, he knew it was too late. He braced for the impact.

The heavy blaster bolt took the hunter in his left side with such force that it knocked him off his feet. He landed hard—hard enough to knock the wind out of any ordinary man. But Fett was no ordinary man.

He was firing his rifle from the moment he recovered from the impact. The furious volley sent his attacker scurrying back around the hallway for cover. Daggers of pain began jabbing at his side, but the wound was not serious and would have to be ignored for the moment. Fett had more important things to worry about.

His attacker suddenly swung back around and began shooting. As Fett returned fire, he recognized Gaege Xarran's features. The exchange exacted a toll on both men . . . Xarran took a bolt in the left leg, sending him stumbling back behind cover; Fett was grazed in the right arm and his feeling in the limb abruptly tingled into numbness. The rifle tumbled from Fett's grasp and he had to make a choice. Quickly.

The hunter threw himself into the room just as a blaster bolt singed the floor where he had been microseconds before. Fett rolled into the large office and came up with his remaining wrist laser ready to go; however, his tracker unit told him that Rivo must be in the refresher. That door was closed, so Fett kept most of his attention focused on the room's entrance. He was suddenly sorry he had vaporized the front door.

Fett crawled over to the wall, pushing his back against it. His right arm still dangled uselessly at his side. Luckily his left arm was uninjured, allowing him to keep the wrist laser aimed at the doorway.

The bounty hunter didn't have time to admonish himself for carelessness. Time was too precious now. Rapid yet rational decisions would mean the difference between life and death, success and failure. He could feel his heart surging in his chest. The outcome was in doubt for the first time. Oddly enough, he rather enjoyed it.

Fett began with a quick appraisal of his situation. Rivo would have to be mostly ignored at the moment. Even if he did come out shooting, the man was not combat-trained. Gaege Xarran was trained, however . . . Fett had learned the General had once served as a member of the Imperial Royal Guard. And while the General might have been past his prime, he was still very well-armed.

On the other hand, Fett's armor had lost many of its secondary systems. While the basic suit was functioning, his sensor arrays were off-line and he could not direct any power to most of the weapons. The communication units were undamaged, but relatively useless at the moment. The only intact item that could prove helpful was his jet pack.

Things were not looking good. . . .

Without his sensors, he had no way of knowing if or when the General would come around the door frame firing. Even worse, Fett could not defend himself, other than in hand-to-hand combat. And at the moment he was short one hand.

Fett reached into one of his pouches and withdrew his final thermal detonator. He would not allow himself to be captured. He would take his enemies with him.

Then he saw it. . . .

Xarran's blaster had been equipped with a spot-luma. In his frenzied state, the General must not have realized that it also gave away his otherwise stealthy approach.

By watching the halo of light increase in intensity, Fett could estimate exactly how far away Xarran was at the moment. Fett quickly performed another analysis of the room and formulated a new plan. The bounty hunter barely resisted the urge to grin as he quickly set the delay on the thermal detonator.

He glanced up once more at the ever-brightening light outside the door and lowered his left hand, gently rolling the silver sphere toward the doorway.

A moment later, General Gaege Xarran whirled around the corner expertly scanning the room with his blaster. "It's over!" he screamed triumphantly, just as something clicked against his boot.

Xarran looked down at the thermal detonator in horror.

"Yes," Fett said. "It is. . . ." And a microsecond-long burst from his jet pack sent the hunter streaking across the room.

Before Xarran could even think about reacting, Fett was at the far end of the office and safely hidden behind a large desk.

The explosion that followed rocked the entire floor.

Fett's chosen cover was of typical Imperial design—big, bulky, and quite resilient. Just as he had hoped, the durasteel monstrosity absorbed most of the impact while his armor deflected any burning debris.

He brushed himself off and approached the refresher door. Rearing back, he kicked it open and prepared to beat Rivo into unconsciousness one-handed if need be. As it turned out he didn't have to. . . .

Where Rivo should have been Fett saw only a small holopad. There was a possibility the device was rigged, but the hunter didn't think that was the case. He swiveled the viewscreen forward and was greeted by the smiling holographic visage of Rivo Xarran.

"Hello, Fett. I'd ask you how you're doing, but the answer is sort of obvious. An encounter with my brother, perhaps?" Rivo paused. "Well, are you going to say something or just stand there?"

Fett was a bit surprised with the live feed . . . he had mistakenly assumed it was a recorded message: "What do you want?"

"Oh, yes. I forgot. You are a man of few words, aren't you? Well, as I'm sure you've figured out by now, I discovered your wonderful little tracker. I bet you'd love to know how. Sorry, I can't give away all my secrets. . . . I must say I am impressed. I never thought you'd actually foil an entire Imperial garrison," Rivo said with a sneer, "even if it was commanded by my idiot brother. Of course, there's no sense in taking any chances, either. Which is why I safely removed myself from your reach."

"For the moment," Fett said, studying Rivo's image. "You are not quite the sniveling coward you appear to be."

"No, I'm not. But neither am I a truly evil individual. My only weapons are my computer and my mouth. Unfortunately, they are both boon and bane at times." He waved a hand. "But enough about me. Let's get down to business. I cannot get back to my normal life with you chasing me around the galaxy, and I know you will not rest until you drag me or my corpse before the great Bloated One. Correct?"

Fett didn't reply.

"So, I propose a compromise . . . and to show my good faith, I'll even let you in on a little secret. My brother has set the garrison base's self-destruct system. Relax, you have ten minutes before it blows; however, I'll make this quick. You can tell Jabba that I died in the explosion, collect your fee, and go about your business. I will assume a false identity, go underground, and never, ever reveal what has transpired within this building so long as I live. We both win." Rivo's confident gaze faltered somewhat. "What do you say, bounty hunter? Is it a deal?"

After a moment, the bounty hunter nodded. "Very well. But one day I will find you, Rivo. And on that day, I will finish this job."

Rivo grinned. "Ah, yes. It may take longer than usual, but Boba Fett always wins. Very good, then. Until that day . . ." His image flickered away into darkness.

The hunter checked his chronometer. At least that was still working. He had better get moving. Fett had a feeling the little Sithspawn might have "accidentally" overestimated the countdown to detonation. As he headed for the roof, Fett sent out a beckon call to *Slave I.* . . .

The Storyteller stopped, enjoying the eager stares of the children.

"How does it end?" asked the little girl breathlessly.

Her question was taken up by the other kids as they demanded a resolution to the tale.

The Storyteller smiled appreciatively and continued. "Well, after many, many years Boba Fett managed to track Rivo down to a backwater planet in the Outer Rim Territories, to the very cantina where the slicer was hiding—" He paused for effect and then said softly, "—And then the greatest bounty hunter of all time finally completed his task. You see, Boba Fett *never* loses." He glanced at his chronometer. "Now, it's way past your bedtimes. Get off to sleep, all of you. And no bad dreams or no more stories before bedtime."

Satisfied, the children filed up the stairs to their rooms, still chattering about the story. All except for the little girl. She paused at the top of the steps with a quizzical look on her face. "Is Boba Fett a good guy or a bad guy?"

He considered that for a moment. "That's a question only you can answer," he said finally.

The girl shrugged her shoulders and bounded up the stairs, leaving the Storyteller alone with his thoughts.

Well, not quite alone.

"How long have you been sitting there?" the Storyteller asked.

"You tell me," came the flat, filtered response.

The Storyteller turned toward the shadowed booth from which a gray and green-garbed figure emerged. Boba Fett stood before the Storyteller, arms folded across his armored chest.

"After all these years you actually managed to find me." Smiling, the Storyteller stood up. "At least my little tale will be authentic now."

The bounty hunter slowly reached into one of his pouches and the Storyteller took a deep breath. Fett withdrew something silver and shiny and the Storyteller suddenly had visions of thermal detonators.

Fett casually tossed the object toward the man, who caught it out of reflex.

The Storyteller braced himself for the end, but when

it didn't come he looked at the object in his palm. It was a credit chit.

Fett was already walking toward the exit.

The Storyteller held it up, confused. "What is this?"

The bounty hunter didn't turn around. "Many things, Rivo. An end, a new beginning . . . and maybe even an answer to a little girl's question." Fett glanced back once, then disappeared through the doors.

The Storyteller (he no longer really thought of himself as Rivo) examined the chit. It contained fifty thousand credits. The exact bounty put on his head by Jabba. Suddenly, everything became clear. He grinned and ran outside.

Boba Fett was gone . . . vanished into the wastes of Ladarra.

The Storyteller stood there in silence. And realized something was wrong. For a brief moment, he couldn't quite figure it out—then it suddenly hit him.

There was no squeaking.

The Storyteller looked down . . . and found himself staring at the disintegrated remains of the bar's replica wood sign. He threw back his head and began laughing.

Day of The Sepulchral Night

by Jean Rabe

W onder what we'll find?" Solum'ke mused for what
I guessed was the half-dozenth time since we
set out.

"Maybe nothing," I replied—again. "It's just a legend,
after all. Don't get your hopes up."

"Well, Diergu-Rea Duhnes'rd, love of my life, I think
there's something to it," she persisted. She formed her
bulbous, mottled lips into a delightful pout. "The
Qwohog thinks so, too. Otherwise, he wouldn't have
talked us into renting this sail barge."

Talked you, I mentally corrected her. *Talked you into
spending the last of my credits during the Day of the Sepulchral
Night.*

If we'd stayed in the city—and on dry ground—we
could have booked passage on that Corellian corvette
occupying most of the port and got back into Imperial
lanes. There we could pick up a few leads on lucrative
contracts. I'd spent so many credits on our brief vacation
on this backwater world that I needed to turn a good
bounty to replenish my normally bulging account.

We'd come to Zelos II several days ago for a little
relaxation. The place is known for its tourist spots—
elaborate spas and cantinas that cater to all manner of be
ings and all manner of tastes and appetites. For the pas
several days I'd been lavishly doling out my credits or
the exhibitions and in the casinos, and—of course—or
the more-than-suitable accommodations in which I had
been romancing the lovely Solum'ke. Like me, she's a
Weequay, a tough-looking humanoid with alluring coarse
gnarled skin. Hers is an enchanting desert tan, shaded
darker in just the right places and relatively smooth
across her beautiful bald head. Mine is a dark gray
nearly the color of the magnificent wiry topknot that ex
tends to the center of my back. We make an attractive
couple.

We don't *have* to use words between us—not spoken
ones, anyway. Ours is the ability to excrete pheromones
that allow us to communicate our moods and desires
Right now my desire was to be elsewhere, but I kept my
pheromones in check so as not to give it away and dis
appoint her.

"Look at the moons," she breathed huskily. Her phero
mones said she was in a very romantic mood. "They're
beautiful."

We don't *have* to use words. But I like the sound of her
voice, and she knows it. I followed her gaze. Zelos II has
four moons, and I had read somewhere that moonlight
is an essential ingredient to an amorous environment.
That's one of the reasons I suggested we come to this
planet.

Unfortunately, it was also because of those four moons
that we were now on an understaffed sail barge skimming a meter above the Great Zelosi Sea and leaving
land uncomfortably far behind.

K'zk, the Qwohog piloting the rented barge, had
been sitting at a nearby table in the restaurant we had selected for dinner last night. He had looked small and out
of place among his humanlike Zelosian companions—
whom he was failing to convince to make this very trip.

In fact, he pretty much looked out of place away from water. That drew Solum'ke's attention, and she immediately became more interested in K'zk's diatribe than in my soft-spoken words of adoration and the grilled lemock haunch sizzling on her plate.

Qwohogs are bipedal amphibians. This one was pale green, almost matching the restaurant's drapes. He had silvery-blue scales atop his head, pointed ears, and long, thin fingers that he waved every time he uttered a word. His speech was funny and clipped, made harsh and nasally by the vocalizer mask he wore. I'd learned that Qwohogs normally communicate by sending vibrations through the water—freshwater—and need a mask to be understood above the waves. Saltwater isn't their preferred environment, but apparently this Qwohog and his fellows had swallowed their fears and were about to strike off across the Great Zelosi Sea. They just needed someone along who wasn't averse to maybe getting in the saltwater.

"Isn't this romantic?" Solum'ke whispered, interrupting my musings. She demurely leaned against the rail and stared at three of Zelos II's moons. They hung low in the sky, practically touching the sea. "The moons, the water, the breeze across my skin. Truly romantic."

"Not if you're a Zelosian," I said as I moved closer and placed my hand on the small of her back. "Right now it's midmorning, and under any other circumstance you couldn't see those moons. The fourth moon's aligned with the sun. The natives are superstitious enough as it is about the moons and night and day. But on this particular day their behavior is extreme—or so I can tell from the datachips I've skimmed. No wonder K'zk couldn't get any of the natives to come with him. Suicides, insanity, unfounded hysteria. In fact . . ."

"All right," she said flatly, the whimsy suddenly gone from her voice. "It's an eclipse. Nothing romantic about an eclipse, huh? At least not to you. Hysteria. Such a romantic word."

"The Day of the Sepulchral Night," I said, thinking I

should say something to get the mood back. I shouldn't have gotten analytical on her. "Not romantic in and of itself, certainly. But everything's romantic—and perfect—when you're with me."

She grinned, revealing a pearly row of wide, blunt teeth, and settled against me. "I'm so glad we came to this place."

I kept my pheromones in control, smiled, and thought about my credits, which were continuing to evaporate on sail barge rent with each kilometer of sea we crossed. "Nowhere else could we have seen this day of night," I answered as I held her close.

The Zelosians' culture is wrapped around day and night—we both learned that our first day on the planet. Light is good, darkness is bad, according to their philosophy. And during this extremely rare eclipse, the natives lock themselves indoors in abject terror. The cantinas and casinos close, the spas are boarded up, and only non-Zelosian ships in the port come and go. Even I had to admit the morning sky looked a little eerie.

The reflection of the three full moons, a sallow blue, a pallid violet, and a glimmering green a shade darker than K'zk the Qwohog, hit the small waves, sending patterns of light dancing toward the prow and the horizon.

I squinted at a spot far in front of us. Something was breaking up the light show.

"Wreck off starboard!" one of the four Qwohog crewmen called. It was a scant crew, the Zelosians who worked the barge taking the day off to hide. My rent had paid for the craft only—K'zk provided the crew.

"There, K'zk!" a stocky Qwohog shouted. "That wave-skimmer's busted good. Must've run aground on the rocks!" The Qwohog gestured wildly toward jagged shards of hull that floated on the dark water, scattered amid bits of torn sail and rigging.

A coral spike jutted defiantly out of the center of the refuse. The ruined wave-skimmer's masthead, a remarkably buxom Zelosian woman, was caught against the

pike and thumped hollowly like a beating heart with
each lapping wave. There were bodies, most bobbing
facedown, the life long since seeped out of them. A few
men were draped over the larger pieces of hull and
might still be alive. It was impossible to tell from this distance, and the matter was becoming moot. I spied a tiny
dome-shaped pate cut through the water—melk. The
scaly rodent-sized beast rose, rolled its eyes back and
opened its mouth. In an instant it had begun to feast on
one of the possible survivors. Other melk were appearing, about two dozen I guessed. I imagined the waves,
painted black by the eclipse, were becoming tinted red
with blood.

K'zk padded toward us and peered toward the coral
spike and slowly shook his head. "Too many shoals
around here. Tide's too low. Any skimmer captain worth
his water would have known better, wouldn't have taken
a skimmer into these parts." He ran his slender fingers
across his scales. "Lower the sails!" he called through his
mask. "Hold our position! I don't want us drifting any
closer." Softer, he said to the closest Qwohog, "Take a
sail raft over. See if there might be any survivors. I'll not
risk this barge going into those shallows for any man.
Diergu-Rea, do you mind going with him? Little short-
handed because of the eclipse, you know."

I scowled. I didn't like the water, but I knew how to
swim, so I wasn't afraid of hopping in a little sail raft. But
I didn't want our captain to spend the rest of the day
picking through bloating bodies. With so many melk
feasting, the odds of finding someone alive were about
as great as finding a veelgeg in a kemlish pulled from
Kryndyn's deep bay. Nil, in other words. I wasn't worried
about the melk looking to me for dinner. With so much
flesh in the water, they'd leave the sail raft alone. What
worried me was the waste of time.

We were here to find Zelosian's Chine—or not find it,
more likely—and return to the relative safety of the
Kryndyn spaceport. I thought about voicing my objec-

tion, since I was financing this little trip, but one of the Qwohogs cut me off.

"Found a couple of live ones, K'zk!" An alert Qwohog had a pair of macrobinoculars pressed to his eyes and trained on the water. He was gesturing with a spindly arm.

I let out a deep breath and headed toward the sail raft. "Yeah, I'll go."

"Me, too," Solum'ke added excitedly. Her phero mones told me she was honestly anxious to help.

We climbed into the raft, reached for the syntherope dispenser to lower it a bit, then we kicked on the repul sorlift switch. The tiny craft settled about a half a meter above the water. I glanced back at K'zk, who was check ing over the barge's repulsorlift unit.

Our Qwohog mate guided the sail raft among the refuse. From the looks of the broken deck plates and the floating, bent mast, I guessed the wave-skimmer had been a little less than half the size of the sail barge. Its lift mechanism probably wasn't powerful enough to float it high above the spires, and hence the skimmer had struck one and become crippled.

The smell of the bodies wasn't strong yet, suggesting the men probably died around dawn. Still, it was enough to make Solum'ke wrinkle her pretty nostrils. She pointed toward the two men the Qwohog had miracu lously spotted. Humans, not Zelosians like most of the unfortunates facedown in the water. They were clinging desperately to a couple of cargo crates lashed to another coral spike. It kept them out of the water and away from melk, but it was a precarious perch. The men waved frantically and called to us. The sail raft scraped against a ridge edging just above the surface as we made our way toward them. I glanced over the side, the moonlight re vealing a shallow reef. I could've stretched my arm over the side and touched it if I weren't afraid a melk would bite my hand off. If we'd taken the sail barge in to rescue these men, we might've run aground, too, and been melk food.

As we pulled alongside the crates, I helped the survivors into the sail raft. They were pale men with dark brown hair that was matted with blood. Their features hinted that they were Corellian—far from our home, but not at all that far from the Corellian corvette that was in port. If they were from that ship, they might be our free ride out of here—transportation in exchange for our saving their lives.

The older one looked to be in worse shape. His lip was split, and a deep gash along his leg was swelling, probably becoming infected. It looked like a melk had bit him and spit him back out. A primitive gaffhook at his side was crusted with blood and made me wonder if he had managed to take a piece out of the reptile.

"Thank the moons someone saw us," the younger man said. "We'd have been dead by evening if you hadn't come along."

"Anyone else alive?" Solum'ke asked.

The pair shook their heads and found a spot in the center of the sail raft, settling heavily onto the seat. "They're sleeping in the bellies of the melk," the eldest said. He extended his hand to me, and I shook it. It was terribly cold. He'd been in the water a while. He introduced himself as Hanugar, and the younger survivor as Sevik.

"What happened?" I found myself asking.

"A coral reef and a low tide because of the eclipse," Hanugar said. "The wave-skimmer we rented struck it late last night. Cracked the hull open and ruined the repulsorlift mechanism. It was a good ship, but the captain was nervous, wanting to get home before the Day of the Sepulchral Night. When we hit, we took on water too fast to do anything to save her."

"What were you doing so far from the coast?" Solum'ke wondered aloud.

Sevik shrugged. "Sightseeing. The regular tourist stuff."

The Qwohog steered the sail raft back to the barge,

while we listened to Hanugar and Sevik explain how they were barely able to tie the cargo containers together and hang onto a coral spike to escape being melk bait. They seemed genuinely thankful for the rescue, and volunteered to pay for our passage offworld. My hunch was right. They were from the big corvette in port.

Once on deck, Solum'ke looked over the Corellians' wounds. She has a knack for fashioning poultices and bandages—Sriluur knows she's had to bandage me plenty of times after I ended up on the wrong end of a cantina fight.

"What brought you out here so late at night?" Sevik asked us. It was a fair question—we'd asked it of him.

"Sightseeing. The regular tourist stuff," Solum'ke replied.

"Honeymooning," I whispered in answer so softly that he couldn't hear. I grinned and turned away, knowing Solum'ke wouldn't tell the Corellians the real reason we were out here—hunting for treasure that according to K'zk was buried in Zelosian's Chine.

From somewhere behind me, I heard K'zk order one of his fellows to bring the Corellians some food. As the pair devoured the meal, I listened to their idle banter. K'zk was telling them we were heading south, thinking about skimming toward the Bryndas Islands where the more exotic spas could be found. The Qwohog sounded convincing. Ha! I thought to myself. *He had tried to convince the Zelosians at the restaurant to come out on this fool treasure hunt with him. But they'd have nothing to do with it because of the eclipse. Then he turned his charms on Solum'ke and succeeded. Treasure appealed to her.*

I heard the flap of the sails rising and billowing above me, the rev of the repulsorlift engine. Time to be on our way again.

K'zk had told us he couldn't go after the treasure himself. It was the problem with saltwater. He couldn't breathe it, and being submerged in it could make his skin blister. Going after the treasure might entail getting wet—and hence his need for someone to help him. He said we'd split whatever we found fifty-fifty.

I felt the barge veer to the right to avoid another dangerous coral ridge.

K'zk claimed that according to Zelosian legend, during the Day of the Sepulchral Night the tides would be at their lowest point. Several miles offshore of the main continent, the crest of the sunken mountain ridge called Zelosian's Chine would poke above the waves. Supposedly great wealth rested within a cave inside the crest—treasure that once belonged to a merchant prince. According to the legend, nearly two hundred years ago during another rare eclipse, the prince's ship was caught in Zelos's gravity well and pulled into the atmosphere and crashed into the chine. The prince survived and directed his men to bury his treasure in a cave along the ridge. He intended to make a raft of part of his ruined ship, sail into a port, and purchase a ship that would take him back to his treasure and then offworld.

But according to the legend, he drowned before he got to shore. The melk probably ate him. And in the decades in between and since, no one had recovered the prince's treasure. Not the Zelosians, because they wouldn't go out during the Day of the Sepulchral Night. And not the tourists, because the legend was supposedly a closely guarded secret. K'zk wouldn't say how he came by the tale.

"The chine, K'zk! I see Zelosian's Chine!" one of the Qwohogs roared through his vocalizer mask.

I skeptically peered over the rail. Nothing but choppy water. I couldn't see what the Qwohog was so excited about.

"K'zk?" I heard a Qwohog prompt. "We goin' in?"

I felt the sail barge ease forward, then I looked past the bowsprit. There, a couple hundred yards out, something edged above the waves. At first glance I thought it was the spiny backbone of some great sea creature. I felt my hand drift to my blaster. But the backbone didn't move, and I relaxed a little. It was nothing more than another coral ridge.

Solum'ke was at my side. She had left Sevik and Hanugar and had silently snuck up behind me. "This has to be it," she breathed. "This has to be Zelosian's Chine."

"You don't know that," I gently warned. "There's lots of coral ridges around here and . . ."

Her dark eyes sparkled and her wide mouth fell open as we neared the ridge. The moons illuminated the peaks that jutted above the surface about a dozen feet or so. There were a few deep shadows amid the rocks—caves, I figured. The largest was round, like the eye of some immense beast, and it was toward the top. The smallest were just above the surface of the waves.

I heard the sails being lowered and the hum of the repulsorlift engine dropped to a whisper.

K'zk quickly explained he didn't want to chance the sail barge's hull on finding any dark rocks hiding just above the surface, said he didn't want it ending up like the Corellians' wave-skimmer.

"The legend of Zelosian's Chine," Sevik whistled.

"That's what you were out here after, wasn't it?" Solum'ke asked him.

The Corellian nodded. "Yeah, tourist stuff—just like you."

"Wonder what we'll find?" she mused aloud.

I shook my head. "It's a ridge, nothing more, with a few caves in it."

"The prince's treasure's in one of the caves," Solum'ke said. "Etren crystals as big as my fist, the legend says."

"*If* this is the right ridge, and *if* the legend about the merchant prince is true," I cautioned. "But the treasure might be gone—if there was any to begin with. Sevik and Hanugar are evidence enough we're not the only treasure hunters on the planet. And don't forget, a lot of years have passed. Sol, don't be too hopeful about this." My words and my pheromones were doing nothing to dampen her enthusiasm.

"Take the sail raft in as close as you can." K'zk had

moved up behind us. "Whatever you find—put in these sacks. Don't try to hide anything from me. We'll split it fifty-fifty."

"What about us?" Hanugar interrupted.

"You have your lives," Solum'ke said, a threatening tone laced into her sultry voice. "Fifty-fifty means two shares—ours and the Quohog's." Her pheromones backed up her threat, though the Corellians couldn't read them.

"Now, now," the Qwohog tsked, the noise sounding like an insect buzzing in his vocalizer mask. "We might spare them just a little bit if they lend a hand."

I grabbed a couple of glowrods, got in the sail raft, and helped Solum'ke climb in.

She was curious like a jarencat, and despite my best efforts I couldn't convince her to stay on the sail barge while I looked around. Sevik came along, and Hanugar took a one-man sail raft.

"Wonder what we'll find?" Solum'ke mused aloud, as I steered the sail raft closer. "Wonder what we'll find?"

"Maybe nothing," I said—again—as I tied the raft off on a rocky protrusion.

Hanugar had already landed, and was heading into the largest cave at the top, the one that seemed to look like a beast's eye. Let him have that one, I thought, as I watched him scramble inside. If I were hiding a treasure, I would put it in the least likely spot. And the least likely spot that we could see tonight seemed to be the cave I noticed closest to the water, a narrow crevice that looked like a big black wrinkle. It would be a tight squeeze. The other caves were too small to even consider. It was possible there were more caves beneath the surface.

Solum'ke nudged me forward. I hated enclosed places. And I hated treasure hunts. Give me a handful of contracts on pirates, spies, and failed smugglers—you'll get richer much faster.

Solum'ke passed a glowrod to Sevik. He still looked in sorry shape, despite her ministrations, but his eyes gleamed like hers at the prospect of wealth. Was I the only one being realistic about this? I wondered. Was I the only one who knew we would be sailing away empty-handed? Anything to humor Sol, though. Anything to make her happy. I felt her thick fingers brush my shoulder. She was right behind me. It was easy going at first, as there were few jagged edges to bite into our boots. The decades beneath the waves had smoothed the rocks' surfaces.

"Wonder what we'll find?" she whispered again.

I shrugged my broad shoulders and slid inside the crevice. The space was small, making me uneasy, and the glowrod Solum'ke held behind me lit the damp walls and sent shadows rollicking about the cramped confines. Our own silhouettes against the rocks seemed eerie and added to my queasiness. Still, I edged forward and down, following the natural shaft, then I stopped when I heard something crunch beneath my boot. I looked at the stone floor and blinked. Bones, humanoid ones from the looks of them. They were brittle with age, but white, picked clean by melk I guessed.

"Diergu-Rea?" Solum'ke's voice was tinged with just a touch of nervousness.

"What'd ya find?" Sevik called. He couldn't see anything around Sol's pleasantly stocky frame.

"What's left of earlier treasure hunters," I replied. Maybe they'd found the crevice on a Day of the Sepulchral Night decades ago and dallied too long, became trapped inside and drowned when the eclipse ended and the water rose. Or maybe something else had happened to them. I sped our course and wished we would have thought to buy rebreathers before we left port.

We must have been more than a dozen feet below sea level when the passage became tighter still and pools of saltwater swirled around my knees in the depressions. No wonder the Qwohog was afraid to come down here. The water had so much salt in it that even my thick skin was irritated.

To complicate matters, I felt trapped, like a caged beast. I almost signaled Sol to turn back, but something sparkled ahead, quickening even my doubting heart. I pushed myself between the shaft walls and cringed when my shirt ripped on a rock. I felt the stone cut across my shoulder blades and felt the warmth of my blood running down my back. My back would heal—Sol would see to that—but the shirt wouldn't. And it was expensive, a gift she gave me on our first night here.

"How much farther?" Sevik called.

I didn't know, so I didn't answer. I continued to squeeze through the shaft and edge downward still. The walls were slick with moisture, and I suspected the glowrod-light bouncing off the water was what caught my eye. I ran my finger along the stone in front of me and brought a drop to my lips. More saltwater. There must be cracks in the rocks someplace, letting a little bit of the sea in.

"There's nothing here," I whispered to Solum'ke. "Let's turn back and hope Hanugar was more successful."

I saw the dejected look on her face and read her pheromones that screamed disappointment, then her expression and mood instantly brightened. She was looking past me. I craned my neck and followed her gaze. Red crystals. A couple of shards sat on a ledge a little farther down. It was enough to make me forget my concerns and my claustrophobia and press onward.

"We found something!" Solum'ke passed on to Sevik. He let out a whoop behind her.

My boots crunched over more bones as I reached the niche with the crystals. Beyond, the shaft opened—as did my mouth. Myriad multicolored crystals littered the floor of a natural cavern, covering every bit of stone and twinkling merrily like fireflies in the light of the glowrod. Some crystals winked up at us from below the surface of small pools, making it impossible to tell just how deep the wealth lay. Urns, miniature statues, hammered metal idols, and more caught Solum'ke's attention. A

large wooden chest sitting amid the wealthy clutter
caught mine. I let out a low whistle and padded toward
it, my boot heels clinking across the crystals. I quickly
knelt before the old chest. The wood stank, rotten
with age.

"We're rich!" Solum'ke cried. "Oh, Diergu-Rea, I
knew there was something to the legend. I just knew it!
K'zk was right!"

I looked over my shoulder. She had set her glowrod
down and was scooping up crystals, letting them fall
through her fingers and clink against the floor. Sevik was
busy skirting the edges of the saltwater pools. He started
unrolling the canvas sacks K'zk had given us and was deciding what to fill them with first.

"These crystals are old, lover," Solum'ke said. She
was holding one, almost reverently. "We'll be set for the
rest of our lives." Bits of rotting leather were scattered
here and there, remnants of the sacks that the crystals
had once been stored in. She brushed the leather aside
and plunked the crystals into her own sack. "This'll buy
us our own freighter, a fleet of them, maybe a moon
somewhere."

I returned my attention to the chest. It had a large,
primitive locking mechanism that was rusted, as were
the iron bands that cut across the discolored wood. An
iron plaque on top had some type of inscription on it,
but it was in a language I couldn't read. I reached to my
waist and retrieved a Rodian throwing razor. Jabbing the
pommel at the lock made a hollow sound that reverberated around the chamber. The lock wouldn't give. But
the wood was old, and I redirected my attention to prying at it. It took me quite a while. How long I'm not certain, but eventually I cut a hole in the top of the chest. I
reached for a glowrod, peered into the cavity, and
sucked in my breath.

"Diergu-Rea, what'd you see?"

"Gems, crowns, the wealth of a prince, Sol," I answered hoarsely. My throat had gone dry. "Crystals not

quite as big as your fist, but big. We're going to be very rich."

She squealed with delight and passed me a sack. I thrust my hand in the chest's opening, my fingers closed around the gems, and I started pulling them out. The light danced across their facets, and I enjoyed the view for a moment before I dropped them in the sack. My arm worked faster, in and out of the opening, retrieving sparkling gems as black as a midnight sky, pale blue ones in the shape of tears, orange ones that brightened with the heat of my hand, and more. I dropped a green crystal necklace over Sol's head, and returned to scooping jewels into my sack. I let my thick fingers play along the surface of a large sunblaze, let myself get carried away.

I'm not sure how much time passed; time seemed irrelevant while there was all this loot about. But I know it was enough time to let me fill my canvas sack. I started stuffing my pockets full of the gems left in the bottom of the chest. I wasn't going to let even one bauble escape me.

"I can hardly lift this," Solum'ke grunted. She was a formidable Weequay, probably stronger than I, and the seams of her sack were threatening to split. "If this planet were more civilized, we could've rented droids to help us carry this."

"Not many droids on Zelos II," Sevik cut in. He was obviously strong, too. He had two bulging sacks, each tossed over a shoulder. "In fact, there's not many . . ."

His words trailed off when I waved at him. I cocked my head to the side and listened. Water. "Something's wrong," I said. My pheromones told Solum'ke I was worried. I shouldered my sack, took one of the glowrods, and eased my way by Sevik and into the tunnel.

I'd made it to the narrowest part of the shaft when I realized something was very definitely wrong. A rivulet of water was running down the rocky floor, the source of the noise. At first it looked like a trickle, but as I stared, the water spread out and was coming quicker, becoming a stream. It rushed into the pools of water that were in the depressions of the tunnelway, then came out the other side like a miniature waterfall.

"Sol! We've got to get out of here, now! Grab what you've got and let's go! Fast! I think the sea is rising!"

I heard Solum'ke scrabble across the crystals on the floor behind me. A glance over my shoulder revealed that Sevik's feet were rooted to the spot, his eyes transfixed on all the crystals we were leaving behind.

"Sol!" I shouted, nodding toward our guest.

She gave him a harsh nudge that seemed to snap him back to reality. He brought up the rear of our little entourage, carrying his sacks practically effortlessly. It was tougher going climbing the shaft. It was steeper than I'd realized, and the floor was slippery. As we neared the opening, the water came rushing in even faster, surging around our knees, then our thighs.

A moment later, my head poked out of the opening, and I balanced on the ledge to keep from falling into the sea—which was lapping at my waist now. I let the glowrod slip from my fingers—I didn't need it. The sky was lighter, the eclipse ending, the tides rising quickly. I started scrambling up what was left of the ridge, motioning Sol to follow me.

Hanugar's sail raft was heading toward the barge—along the deck of which all the Qwohogs stood. Our sail raft was ruined—there was a deep gash in its hull where the repulsorlift mechanism rested. The mechanism was a useless piece of history, shattered by being dashed against a sharp coral spike. The sail raft still floated—but like a primitive boat—on the water, not above it. And it was without any power.

A wave broke against my chest, threatening to push me under. The sea was rising even faster now, and within minutes I knew we'd be treading water—or drowning if we didn't drop the gems.

"When the sea gets a little higher, I'll bring the sail barge in!" K'zk hollered. He called something else, but his words were lost by the crash of a wave against the rocks around us.

The minutes seemed to crawl by as the sea rose up to our shoulders. We watched Hanugar tie his sail raft to the rail and climb onto the barge. Hanugar's raft was pulled up.

The raft! Our raft! My eyes searched about and locked onto our damaged one. It was drifting away from us. It would do to keep us above the water.

"Hurry!" I yelled to Solum'ke, as I gestured toward the raft. I'd sighted a couple of melk heads in the distance—naturally heading in our direction—and I desperately wanted to be out of their element, fast. I felt the sting of the saltwater against my back where I'd cut it, and I knew my blood was seeping into the sea. It would lead the melk straight to us.

"Where's Sevik?" Solum'ke shouted. She'd somehow managed to reach the raft and tossed her sack into its bottom. She hefted herself over the side and started using her arms as paddles to drag the crippled raft toward me.

The water was up to my chin now, and I had to point my head toward the lightening sky to keep my mouth above it. "There's no sign of him!" I answered. "He might have drowned!"

Within a handful of heartbeats, she was tugging my sack and me into the raft. I glanced at the sail barge, at Hanugar who was standing at the railing. Then my mouth dropped open as I saw Sevik climbing up the side of the ship, his two sacks still over his shoulders. It would have been physically impossible for him to have swum so far with the weight of the crystals. Unless . . . I looked closer, spotted a repulsorlift belt around his waist. "Why you slimy excuse for a Nimbanese jowl-preener . . ."

The rest of my words were drowned out by a wave crashing against the side of our raft. I saw the sail barge hover higher and glide toward us.

"Throw us a line!" I yelled.

"The crystals first!" Sevik called back as he leaned over the side with a length of syntherope.

"No!" Solum'ke and I shouted practically in unison. We clutched our treasures.

K'zk was next to Sevik, peering over the side, a blaster rifle trained on Solum'ke's beauteous face. His voice cracked through the vocalizer mask. "We'll take all of the crystals—one way or another."

Solum'ke made a move for her blaster. *What happened to fifty-fifty?* her pheromones asked.

"The saltwater," I whispered to her.

I heard her groan. Our blasters would be useless, ruined by our dip in the sea. I draped my arm around her shoulders, and she slumped against me, as we gave in and watched our sacks of gems and crystals rise into the traitorous Qwohog's sail barge.

"Just tell me," I called up to K'zk, "Were the Corellians involved in all of this? From the first? You obviously know them."

"Of course. Partners. Fifty-fifty," the Qwohog replied as he eased the sail barge a few meters away from our crippled raft. "I'd received a message they were marooned, so we had to pick them up before looking for the chine. *We were all looking for Zelosian's Chine*—they on the skimmer and me with the barge. Two ships would have a much better chance of finding it. They truly fell afoul of the ridge, lost some of our mates in the process. Our captain won't be pleased."

"But this should mollify him!" Sevik chuckled, as he held up a big crystal.

"So why'd you need us?" I sneered.

"Insurance in case they didn't find the ridge," came the Qwohog's curt reply. "Or in case I couldn't save any of my Corellian friends. Couldn't deal with the saltwater myself, you know. Besides, you made fine extra pairs of hands. Sorry to leave you stranded— you were good sports about the whole thing—even paid to rent the sail barge. But we can't have you turning us in to the authorities before we've had a chance to get offworld."

"The corvette."

The Qwohog nodded. "Our ship. And we'd best hurry. The captain's waiting for us. Thanks for your help!"

As the moons faded and the sun came out, chasing away all signs of the eclipse, we watched the sail barge become a spot on the waves and then disappear. Our little sail raft bobbed near the reef, still afloat, protecting us from the melk.

"We'll die out here," Solum'ke said. I'd never heard her sound so sad.

"We're not that far from the coast. Other barges will be out before the day is up—headed toward the spas on Bryndas Islands. Someone will rescue us."

"We lost everything," she continued to moan. "All that treasure. All those . . ." She dropped a hand to her neck, to the green crystal necklace I'd put there.

I reached into my pocket and pulled out a handful of sunblazes. "Every pocket is full," I said. "More than enough to pay our rescuers and buy passage off this place—buy us a small freighter, a new one maybe."

"And we still have our lives," she said, brightening a little.

"Very long ones," I added. She caught the gleam in my eye. "Maybe in another dozen or so decades we can come back here—during the next Day of the Sepulchral Night."

"Get what we left behind in Zelosian's Chine," she finished.

I drew her close, buried my nose against her still-damp neck. She smelled of the sea and of summer, intoxicating.

Solum'ke returned my embrace. "What are you thinking about?" she whispered after several quiet moments.

"A Qwohog."

"And two Corellians?"

"Shouldn't be too hard to find."

"Not for the best bounty hunters in the sector," she replied. "I think I hear another sail barge coming our way already."

Uhl Eharl Khoehng

by Patricia A. Jackson

Twin tridents of lightning surged across the low-lying skies of Iscera. The congested atmosphere bled through in clotted tones of red and orange, as volatile gases reacted with the charged violence of the storm. Torrential gusts of wind and wet snow buffeted the hull of the *Prodigal,* layering the freighter with a secondary armor plate of thick ice. Bearing no exterior signature or running lights, the YT-1300 sat alone on an exposed pad, isolated from the main traffic of the Iscerian spaceport.

Lightning briefly illuminated the interior of the *Prodigal*'s bridge. Fable Astin sat tentatively, contemplating the storm. Exhausted and sickened, the young Jedi ran her fingers through the matted tangle of her hair, draping the unruly mane over her shoulders. The tapered cut of her flight jacket accentuated her slender waist and the lengthy lines of her legs and thighs. She winced irritably, shifting position to relieve the pinch of her gray pirate leggings, which had gathered in the backs of her knees. The slight motion rattled the heavy blaster at her hip and caused the lightsaber to fall into the cushion beside her.

Fable flipped the comm switch for the tenth time, waiting for the computer to bring up the stored message from the ship's logs. The featureless image emerged from the miniholovid, realigning itself into the face and upper torso of a woman. Prematurely gray with the burden of command, auburn hair curled at the shoulders of her uniform, which bore the insignia of a Rebel Alliance officer. "Greetings Captain Astin and to your Harrier Infiltration team. This is Commander Beatonn of the Rebel frigate, *V'nnuk'rk*." Beatonn paused briefly, interrupted by the distant blare of a proximity alarm. "Your objective is very clear, Captain. The Empire has begun construction of a communications bunker on Nysza III. Your orders are to destroy the bunker before it can be completed. Good luck, Captain, and may the Force be with you." The holo-communication ended amid static discharge and interference.

Fable toggled the erasure switch, deleting the transmission. It was a duty long overdue. Nearly seventeen hours had passed since the completion of their objective, which had resulted in the untimely death of her technical officer, Arecelis Acosta. "Did you know that he was half human?"

"I'd heard rumors," Deke Holman replied. The auxiliary control lights cast a surreal aura over his handsome but grim face and the shock of fiery, red hair crowning his cumbersome head. A Socorran, he was dark-skinned and rugged, wearing the traditional gold hoop in his left ear lobe. Still damp from their misadventure on Nysza III, he leaned forward and stared into the holographic etching secured on the viewscreen. He recognized his own stout figure, framed on each side by his companions. On the right, his captain and friend, Fable Astin, smiled as he tickled her neck. To the left, Arecelis Acosta was playfully feigning a punch.

The Coynite was nearly 2.2 meters tall, powerfully built at the chest and shoulders. His body was covered with a fine blanket of blue-black fur, which was intricately braided around his neck and ears. In the etching, his thick fingers grasped at Deke's forearm, easily making the circumference of his flesh. Arecelis's other hand was balled into a fist as the Coynite feigned an incoming punch.

Deke shook his head, thoughtfully pursing his thick lips. "I'm really going to miss him." He sniffed disdainfully, slumping against the back of the acceleration chair. "No wonder there was no security in that bunker. Who would have thought a Jedi would be there?" Rubbing his forehead, he sighed, "At least you were with us."

"Didn't do Arecelis much good," Fable scoffed. Her body was bruised from her momentary encounter with Vialco, a dark Jedi assigned to the garrison. One feint and one block was all he needed to launch her across the width of the construction corridor. Trembling with rage, all Fable could do was stare up at him, as his mocking laughter echoed through the empty ceiling tiles above the complex. Her limited skills were no challenge to him, and she had undermined herself by drawing her lightsaber in anger, opening herself to the dark side.

"Smells like a gundark crawled into the nav computer and died. It reeks in here!" The exacerbated Jedi threw her gloves onto the console, acutely aware of the stench permeating the bridge. During their escape from the bunker, they had been forced to dive into a construction tunnel full of stagnant water. The scent was prolific. "We need to get out of here. Is there a bar or something in town?"

"This is pretty much a dry world, Capt'n," Deke replied. "But when I went to pick up those rations, I passed a little theater on the boulevard. Evidently, it's the last show before the winter break and the owners are giving away tickets."

"Did you get any?"

"Didn't have much of a choice. The kid nearl
knocked me down trying to give the last two away."

"What's it called?"

Posing valiantly, Deke stood up and put his hand ove
his chest. In a deep voice, he declared, " 'For the Want o
an Empire.' "

"Wonderful," Fable grumbled, leading the way out o
the flight cabin. "I can't wait to see this."

Against the elaborate backdrop of the stage, the clashin₉
of swords echoed from the inner recesses of the set. Th₍
dual ended abruptly, with the edge of one prop sword slic
ing cleanly through the other, detonating the small charg₍
inside to provide the dramatic effect of a lightsaber ex
ploding through metal. Panting and fatigued, the actor
separated, retreating to the far edges of the mock cave.

Fable focused on the mesmerizing movements of th₍
lead actor. A subtle trick in the theater lighting en
hanced the malevolence of his character, a tragic her₍
bent on destroying his one-time friend and companion
Captivated by the last moments of the scene, she sat o₎
the edge of her seat, waiting for him to speak.

The audience gasped as the sword sliced the air onl
millimeters from one actor's face, feigning the dreade₍
deathblow. As his rival died at his feet, the hero turne₍
toward the audience. "Come, my good fellows," he an
nounced in a clear, resonating tone, "let us part this sa₍
scene and, through our good company, make the jour
ney shorter." The curtain closed as the stage hand
emerged to reset for the final act.

Fable sat back in her chair. "Did you see that?" Sh₍
covered her mouth, laughing anxiously into her hand
"His technique is almost flawless." Scanning the gloss
holo-program, she whispered, "What's his name?"

"Jaalib Brandl."

"I want to meet him." Turning on the wary Socorran
she squeezed his knees tightly. "You speak Iscerian
don't you? Talk to the owner."

Grumbling under his breath, Deke moved away from his seat and toward the aisle. "I'll see what I can do."

Through most of the final act, Fable sat with the actor's image across her lap, comparing the picture with every minute expression of his youthful, almost adolescent face. The Force was with him and she felt it, moving through the audience with a tangible presence. She marveled at the dangerous parallel dimensions of reality and the play, where a young councilman began a slow rise into the inner circles of high government, only to discover corruption in every facet of its existence. In act two, he initiated a campaign to end the deterioration of the bureaucracy. But as his vision expanded in the third act, it became a ruthless autocracy, bent on exterminating its enemies and all who opposed it.

For the final scene, the hero stood alone in a splintered universe of his creation, devoid of hope, life, family, or friends. In a final affirmation, gazing out over the audience, he briefly met her eyes and held her captive. On his dying breath, he gasped, "For the want of an empire . . . all humanity was lost."

Collapsing to the stage floor, the hero perished amid a thunderous echo of applause. Fable was one of the first to stand, eagerly applauding the performance, and joined the audience's shouted accolades as the minor characters returned to the stage to take their bows. From the side wall, she spotted Deke waving for her to join him in the aisle.

"Come on," Deke whispered, leading her out of a side door. "Most of the actors stay and hobnob with the audience, but a stage hand told me that Brandl's already heading back to his quarters."

"There he is!" Fable shouted, as the door slammed shut behind them. "That's him!" she gushed, recognizing the actor's costume robes. "Brandl!" she shouted, sliding down the icy stairwell. "Jaalib Brandl?"

The actor hesitated as the young woman scampered across the ice toward him. She was moving too rapidly for the footing, sliding precariously with every stride.

Dropping his bag, Jaalib stepped forward as her legs slipped from beneath her, anchoring the young woman in his arms. "That was quite an entrance," he teased.

"That was quite a performance!" Fable countered. Flushing crimson with embarrassment, she stepped away from him and laughed nervously, covering her reaction with a smile. "Where did you learn to use a sword like that?"

"An actor needs a variety of exotic skills," Jaalib replied with a grin. "It's the only way to insure longevity in this profession." Retrieving his bag, he whispered, "Now if you'll excuse me, I have a long flight ahead of me tomorrow. Good night, Miss . . . Miss . . ."

"Fable. Fable Astin."

"Good night, Miss Astin." His smile deepened. "Fable."

"Good night," Fable sighed, watching the outline of his robes vanish in the shadows of the theater courtyard. Teeth chattering, she stared into the darkness for a long moment.

"Come on, Fable!" Deke complained. "It's freezing out here. Let's get back to the ship."

The pressure in Fable's lungs was building rapidly. Trapped by stormtroopers in the construction tube, she was desperate to find a quick escape for her infiltration team. They were fifteen minutes off schedule with a load of thermal detonators on their backs, each timed to go off in less than forty minutes, regardless of their safety. If they did not reach the objective site soon, no one would be alive to complete their mission.

Fable reached in front of her, tapping Arecelis on the shoulder. As the Coynite turned, his features began to distend and shift, blending into the harsh, angular jaw of Vialco, the dark Jedi they would later encounter in the command station. "Had you given yourself to the passion, he might still be alive," he taunted. "Your feelings can do little for him now."

Yanking the lightsaber from her belt, Fable lunged savagely. She faked a left feint, deftly bringing the lightsaber down and across to the right.

"That's it, girl! Anger is the control. Your fear is the power. And your fear is great, little one." His voice reverberated through the darkness, washing over her consciousness. "You have taken your first small steps toward the ultimate ecstasy. Now awake and open yourself to the true power."

He's in my room! Fable thought frantically, struggling with the nightmare. The lightsaber flared in her grip, burning her hand, and she dropped it to the floor. As the weapon clanked against the deck plates, Fable woke frantically to find herself standing in the center of her cabin. She recoiled in horror when she saw her seared palm. Dropping to the floor, Fable curled into a fetal ball on the floor and rocked from side to side, desperate to quell the pain. The young Jedi called on the power of the Force to control the injury, but the throbbing wound's anger did not subside, nor did she feel the sense of inner peace that came with the summoning of the Force.

Fumbling with the light control beside her bunk, Fable cradled her injured hand against her. She snatched the lightsaber from the deck and threw it into the mirror, shattering glass fragments across the small personal gear locker. Stumbling to the sink unit, she tripped the sensor, stifling a scream as the jets blew cool, moist air over the cauterized wound. As the soothing jets blew over her and her tears, she slumped to the floor. In one moment of grief, one step from the path of light, she had changed the course of her future, betraying herself, her love of the Jedi, and the teachings of her mother.

On the table beside her bunk, the holo-image of her mother grinned inanely at her. In the fragmented remains of the mirror, Fable saw that same face, younger and smoother; but there was something noticeably sinister about the features—her features.

"Fable!" She heard the frantic pitch in Deke's voice as the Socorran hurried through the cabin hatch. Pulling herself up from the floor, she slowly moved along with him as he guided her to the bunk. "What happened?" he gasped, examining the ugly wound carved into her flesh.

"It was him," Fable whispered. "He was here."

"Who?" the Socorran demanded, wrapping the burn in sterile gauze.

"Vialco. At least that's what he calls himself." She winced as the burn pulled at the tender skin. "He's coming for me. To turn me to the dark side. And there's nothing I can do to stop him!"

Ignorant of the Jedi's true troubles, Deke snarled, "You know I'll go down with you, Capt'n. What do you need me to do?"

Hiding her frightened face beneath the shadow of her long hair, she whispered, "Deke, I need you to run a background check on Jaalib Brandl. Do you have access to the civilian database?"

"Having access and getting access is the same thing to me. But how's that going to help, Fable?"

"Please Deke, I can't explain it right now," she whispered, perceiving the jealous glint in his eyes.

Deke nodded, rising to his feet. "I'm on it."

Heavy snow blanketed the exterior lots of the Iscera spaceport, throwing layer upon downy layer over the hulls of the freighters docked in the outer arena. The steady flow of large, cumbersome flakes cut visibility nearly in half, hampering Fable's efforts to see through the viewscreen into the internal docking bays nearby. "What have you found?" she asked, sitting down in the copilot's chair. A cup of soup warmed her good hand, bringing a small measure of strength to her exhausted body.

"Nothing out of the ordinary," Deke sighed. Staring into the terminal, he watched the information scroll across the screen. "The civilian logs don't show very much. Jaalib Brandl, seventeen years old, orphaned at age twelve. No known relatives within the Imperial sectors. Lived with a family friend, Otias Atori, and then left to pursue a career in theater. There were no records of him even existing before the age of twelve." He sat back in the chair. "That's when I got suspicious."

"Suspicious?" Fable probed. "Why?"

"The Imperials have a sneaky practice of creating people, swapping records to implant operatives among the populace. The only way to trace them is through their records. If you look hard enough, every once in a while," he smirked confidently, "you'll find a hole."

"Like no records before a certain age?"

"Uh-huh. So I started cross-referencing in that Imperial database we intercepted. Only I forgot to use his first name. Look what came up." The image of an older man appeared on the screen. There was a brooding, sinister edge to his handsome face, a piercing glare and an arrogant smirk that gave the impression that he was posing. "See any family resemblance?"

"Lord Adalric Brandl," Fable read the information. "An actor?"

"And this was his biggest and best role yet." Deke tapped the control panel. A restricted information bar flashed across the screen as he accessed the code.

Fable set her cup aside, afraid that her trembling hands might spill the hot liquid into her lap. "An Imperial Inquisitor? Brandl's father is a Jedi-killer?"

"The Alliance has official notices about this maniac all over the network. Avoid at all costs, executive order 2354. This guy was bad news."

"Was?"

"Evidently Brandl went rogue and took off, prompting a galaxywide manhunt. They found him," Deke shuddered, "following a string of corpses that he left from one sector to the next. And when they finally caught him, he went berserk and committed suicide." The status line scrolled over the image of Brandl's face, flashing the word "Deceased" across the screen.

"What's that?" Fable pointed to the corner of the terminal.

"It's an Imperial code about notifying next of kin. This one means the body was never recovered."

"Never recovered? Never recovered by the family or never found?"

"Can't tell you, Capt'n. Wasn't there."

Fable strummed her fingers lightly against her thigh, feeling the lightsaber's slight weight against her hip.

"I've seen that look before," Deke grumbled pensively. Fumbling with the control panel, he reached into the mass confusion of the circuitry boards beneath the shield generator controls and retrieved a dusty bottle of Socorran raava. "Here," he gave it to her. Then removing the earring from his lobe, he handed the golden hoop to her as well. "I noticed the port manager is Socorran. Give him the earring and tell him you need a ship. Then give him the bottle and let him know that he can discuss the terms with me."

Fable wiped at her cheek, feeling the moisture beneath her fingertips. "You're a good friend, Deke."

"That's what they tell me," he sighed, propping his legs against the console. "Now go on," he fussed, "before I change my mind."

Quietly, Fable walked into the corridor beyond the flight bridge.

"Fable?" Deke whispered, as she hesitated, lingering beneath the bulkhead. "If Brandl's alive, he's got nothing to lose."

"At this point, Deke, neither do I."

The hyperdrive cue pulsed, startling Fable to consciousness. She rubbed at the bruise swelling on her forehead where she had knocked it soundly against the canopy of the X-wing. "No bad dreams?" she sighed with a half smile. From above, an abrupt movement distracted her and before she could utter one sound, the body of Arecelis came crashing through the cockpit shield, bringing the icy grasp of space. As the air was drawn from her lungs, Vialco stood over her, straddling the cockpit and mocking her with his deep, throaty laughter.

Fable shrieked, slapping hysterically at the mutilated corpse cradled in her lap; but there was nothing there. Frantically craning her neck to get a full view of the outside canopy, she saw nothing but the brilliant lines and colors of hyperspace, as they began to retract into the telltale pinpoints of distant planets and stars. Reeling from the traumatic nightmare, she collapsed against the acceleration chair.

The emerald-gold face of Trulalis emerged before her as the X-wing materialized from hyperspace. Quickly engaging the engines, she braced for the atmospheric entry. Scanning her sensors, Fable checked the data screens, which were inundated with immediate life-sign readings. The sensors began tracing the ion signature, automatically pinpointing the trace of a light shuttle. Setting a similar course, she eventually landed outside the perimeter of a small settlement.

From the ground, Trulalis was breathtaking and majestic. Fable found herself captivated by the noble black trees whose leaves radiated a green hue when struck by direct sunlight. With massive, arching branches, the trees formed a shaded corridor above the overgrown trail. Enjoying the quiet walk, Fable rechecked her sensor information, confirming that the life signs she had received were mostly animal in nature. The settlement structures the computer had uncovered were void of any life. As she came closer, it was apparent why.

Strewn about the outskirts of the common, she found the remains of stormtrooper armor. There were no bodies inside, but the unmistakable blast scoring across the chests were disturbing evidence of a failed retaliation against the Empire, as were the skeletal remains of their victims, which were half buried in the loose topsoil nearby. At the settlement gates, she stared into the desolate streets where wreckage and debris were scattered from one end of the broad avenue to the next.

The body of a small bantha lay in the doorway of a narrow shelter. Shrunken and thin, its thick hide had been preserved by the nurturing Trulalis soil. Manicured gardens had gone to seed, spreading erratically over the front lawns and the dilapidated remains of the abandoned cottages. In one shelter, Fable found the transport shuttle, which had been assigned to Jaalib—she knew she was on the right track.

The only true survivor of the Imperial onslaught sat in the center of the settlement. Its shadow stood over her in silent testament of its endurance. Fable stared up and up, until her eyes could take in the enormity of the ancient theater. Blast scoring had scarred the pristine limestone obelisk, leaving a blemish of tragedy etched into the elaborate design. Hemmed in by stone fences and gates, the gardens were immaculately trimmed and manicured, tapered back from the winding garden paths, which wound and curved into the enormous entrance. Two stone pillars framed the central portal, casting grotesque, disembodied shadows over the archway.

Mustering her courage, she stepped into the immense antechamber. Her eyes took in the magnificence of tapestries and display cases, each showing the relics of prop swords, ornate jewelry, and costumes used in the various stage productions. She heard voices echoing from the right wing and followed instinctively, attuned to the familiar strength of Jaalib's voice.

"You are a thief, a liar, and a pawn!" Jaalib spat in a frantic voice. Fable hesitated in the doorway, staring across the darkened auditorium.

"A thief? A liar? A pawn?" another voice commented. "Are these not the greatest virtues of any good king?"

"Virtue—" Jaalib broke off, his face contorted in an uncharacteristic mask of rage.

"Your concentration is off," the stranger whispered. "Perhaps we're moving too quickly."

"No, it's me!" The despondent sound of his voice

echoed in the dusty spaces above the stage. "I keep see-ing you, hearing you play the part and then," he stum-bled, "I see my own clumsy attempts." Anxiously brushing a hand through his dark hair, he managed a weak smile. "Perfection is never easy, Father, especially when it's your perfection."

From his throne, in the shadowed backset of the stage, Adalric Brandl chuckled softly. The rustling of his cumbersome black robes sent whispering vibrations over the front rows as he stepped down from the raised dais. "Of all the tragedies ever conceived, *Uhl Eharl Khoehng* is the greatest," Brandl said with conviction. "The role of the Edjian-Prince is the most difficult and the actor who plays it," he paused, "is assured greatness."

"How old were you? The first time you performed it?"

"I was nearly thirty before Otias would even permit me to read for the part." Brandl snorted with warm plea-sure. "You are a young man, Jaalib." Placing a comfort-ing hand on Jaalib's shoulders, he whispered, "You were born for this part. Give yourself time to grow into it."

Recognizing Brandl's profile, Fable slowly walked down the center aisle toward the stage. Hands crossed shamefully in front of her, she met Brandl's curious eyes as his gaze fell over her. "Lord Brandl . . ." she faltered, staring into the shadows.

"Fable!" Jaalib hissed. Jumping down from the plat-form, he charged her, robes billowing from his shoul-ders. "What are you doing here?"

Fable could hear his voice, but only distantly. She could feel the harsh pinch of his fingers on her wrists, but felt no pain. Caught in Brandl's intense gaze, she could not move. His presence was overpowering and Fable found herself deeply intrigued by the somber charm and magnificence of this strange man, himself a tragic hero, trapped in the torrent of some inconceivable drama.

Her eyes cautiously traced the noble angle of his fore-head and brow, noting the gentle curvature of his nose, his mouth, and the regal set of his chin. Faint laugh lines framed thin, pale lips, fading into the surrounding tautness of his cheekbones. Waves of black hair betrayed streaks of silver running through the closely cropped sides, shadowing Brandl's solemn face. At his right temple, obtuse veins of scar tissue erupted from the otherwise smooth skin, winding a cruel path around the outer edges of his eye. Severely traumatized, the eye itself was damaged, sheathed in the pupilless, irisless remains of a clear, yellowed orb.

"Fable!" Jaalib shouted, shaking her.

"Jaalib," Brandl whispered, "mind your manners. An audience, even an audience of one, is always to be treasured and respected."

Glaring at her, Jaalib hissed, "You shouldn't have come here!"

Fable glanced at him briefly and then moved away, refusing to acknowledge that she agreed with him.

"An admirer, Jaalib?"

"Yes, Father, but she was just leaving." Before Jaalib could herd her back up the aisle, he felt the light restraint of his father's hands.

Drawn to the innocence of the young woman's frightened eyes, Brandl closed the distance between them. With hesitation, he caressed Fable's smooth cheek, gently lifting her chin to raise her eyes. Astonished by the strength in her gaze, Brandl smiled pleasantly. "There is no frailty here," he whispered with a narcissistic grin. His eyes narrowed dubiously as he took her bandaged hand, warming her cold fingers in the warmth of his touch. "The dark side beckons with the promise of easy gain, but there is always a price, always a tribute to its passion."

Fable swallowed, struggling to find her voice. "I . . . I," she stammered, "Lord Brandl, I need you . . . to . . ."

"Weigh your words carefully, young woman, do not waste time counting them." Turning to Jaalib, he gently pressed her toward his son. "Jaalib, take our guest to a comfortable room. She will stay the night."

Shoulders hunched in rage, Jaalib led Fable up the wide aisle, leading her out of the grand hall auditorium.

An excruciating cramp in her leg brought Fable to consciousness. She bolted frantically from the bed, scanning the shadows for signs of movement. Taking her lightsaber from beneath the pillow, she assumed the ready stance, waiting for the unseen phantom to strike. But there were no shadows to fight, except her own. "No bad dreams?" Stiff from the close quarters of the X-wing, she felt surprisingly well and rested. Snorting softly, Fable sat down on the bed. "No bad dreams!" she cheered into her pillow. Her optimism was short-lived as a knock sounded at the door. Momentarily, the latch cleared and the door parted. Pulling the blanket over her body, Fable swallowed a moment of fear, relieved when Jaalib's brooding face peered into the chamber.

"The morning meal is ready," he growled.

"I'll be right there." As the door closed, she hurried from the bed and dressed quickly. Ignoring her flight jacket, she pulled the fine linen shirt over her head and shoulders, leaving the long ends to hang over her leggings. In the darkened corridor outside her room, Jaalib was waiting. "This way."

As the sweet aroma of sausage and boiling cereal filtered through her nostrils, Fable's stomach rumbled appreciatively. Painfully aware of her hunger and of the young actor's annoyance, she waited for him to sit down at the small table. A series of large flame ovens lined the back of the room behind him. Fable waited until Jaalib took the first bite, then eagerly began filling her plate with steaming broth and several links of sausage.

Hearing only the clang of her utensils, she looked up to find Jaalib glaring at her. There was a deep-seated loathing behind his eyes. Gazing about the small, crude kitchen, she realized that they were alone. "Where is Lord Brandl?" she whispered, hoping he would ignore her.

"You shouldn't have come here!"

Piqued by his cruel tone, Fable slammed her fork against the plate. "Why don't you just butt out of it!"

"He won't help you," the actor snarled. "Others have come. Like you. So why don't you just get your things, and I'll walk you back to your ship."

"I said, where is he?" Fable hissed with premeditated venom.

"He's in the Barrows," Jaalib relented. "He's been waiting for you."

"The Barrows?" she questioned around a mouthful of hot broth.

"The graveyard."

Outside in the cold dawn, storm clouds swept the sky. Wishing for her flight jacket, Fable shivered, hugging herself as the cool breeze fluttered through her hair and the thin fabric of her shirt. Trotting up the back landscape of steps and garden porches, she wandered into the rear courtyards of the theater, needing no specific direction to follow the dark presence of Lord Brandl. She followed a short path to the outskirts of Kovit, where the ground rose and fell in an irregular series of earthen mounds and grassy knolls. Up the steepest mound, she halted on the crest, finding herself surrounded by wax cylinders, hundreds of them, mounted atop slender pedestals, which were buried in the soft ground. Metallic ball bearings were precariously perched on each cylinder, giving the appearance of small, blue flames.

Across from her, on the opposite mound, Brandl stood with his back to her, at the foot of an enormous sarcophagus. The grainy image of a woman had been carved into the lid, delicately outlining the lace and fabric of the gown she was laid to rest in. "The Jedi is his own worst enemy," Brandl declared. "The greatest conflict comes from within. Our Masters teach us, scold us," he hesitated, "command us to follow reason, not our emotions."

"You disagree?" Fable asked, stepping into the center of the wax cylinders.

"Where there is smoke, there is fire." Brandl straightened, staring down his nose at her for a long moment. "Vialco is a coward. His tactics are mere illusions, prey for the weak-minded."

Brushing off the possible insult, Fable shrugged. "But he is powerful." Shaking her head remorsefully, she whispered, "I can't beat him. At least, I don't think so."

"Losing is not an option . . . it's a conscious decision. You will not know until you try."

"Trying isn't good enough! I have to succeed or—"

"Or he may succeed in his attempts to lure you to the dark side? How do you know that I will not turn you?"

Fable felt a tremor down her back. "I don't."

"The student's greatest achievement is attained through succession," Brandl began, "a succession which requires the destruction of the Master. This is what the dark side teaches us. But what you must always remember is that when we embrace the darkness, we are already masters in the design of fate, humbling ourselves as students." He leaned heavily against the massive stone tomb. "When we seek the dark side, we seek our doom. Too often, we are successful."

"So you'll help me?"

"Vialco's undoing is inevitable. Even I have seen this."

"So I'll win, right?"

Brandl gently tugged at the clasp of his robe, loosening the collar. "If you're looking for visions, Fable, sit quietly and dwell on your past. Now prepare yourself. See the ball bearing directly ahead of you, sitting atop the wax cylinder? Draw your lightsaber and strike it. Destroy only the metal bearing. Leave the wax unharmed."

Fable hesitated, deliberately slow in assuming the ready stance. Breathing with effort, she stared at the ball bearing, her wounded hand tingling from her last experience with the lightsaber.

"The dark side's influence is stronger in moments of weakness. Do not let yourself be distracted. Now strike."

Fable drew the lightsaber from her belt, concentrating on its ignition. Swinging in a wide arc, she struck at the ball bearing, elated as it evaporated into nothingness, leaving the wax cylinder slightly scorched but unharmed. She disengaged the weapon and resumed the ready stance, unable to hide the arrogant smirk etched across her features.

"When climbing great mountains, it is always best to begin at a slow pace," Brandl remarked quietly. "Now strike for two."

Without waiting to focus on the pedestal's position, she ignited the lightsaber and struck two blows, swinging the blade toward the ball bearings and disintegrating them as the cylinders remained untouched. Overwhelmed with confidence, she again disengaged the weapon and resumed the ready position, eager to begin the next phase.

"No gain comes without a price. I will be your mentor and you my pupil. You will forever carry the distinguishment of my presence, as well as the taint," he stumbled over the word, "the traits of my own Masters."

"You mean the Emperor," Fable whispered, "don't you?"

"I chose the path that led me to this life," Brandl continued, "I will lead you on a parallel course, where I will show you the glories of the light and the majesty of the dark." He nodded, indicating the next alignment of wax cylinders. "Now strike for ten."

Fable faltered for a moment; then fresh with the assurance of her performance, she ignited the lightsaber and charged, working her way through the line. As she reached for the fourth cylinder, she felt herself floundering. Furiously struggling to the fifth, she sliced neatly through the cylinder and knocked the ball bearing at her feet. In a failed attempt to rally for the sixth, she tripped and fell into the wet earth, taking several stands and cylinders with her.

Brandl slowly descended from the mound, stepping just inside the perimeter of the training circle. Shamefully rising to her feet, Fable flinched as he drew his lightsaber and moved toward her. With a resonating power that spread out from it in all directions, the lightsaber became a smear of brilliance as Brandl worked his way through the wax cylinders. He destroyed one ball bearing after another, leaving no perceptible mark on the wax. Fable watched in awe as the weapon danced through a score or more of ball bearings before Brandl completed the cadence and disengaged the weapon. Gawking at the craftsmanship, she turned to Brandl. "You really are a Jedi Master."

"Only fools admire what they see," he hissed evenly, brushing past her. "I know . . . for once I was a fool." The first drops of rain began to fall, quickly covering the barrows with a slick film of water and loose earth. "You will continue this exercise until you have mastered it properly. Only then may you return to the theater."

"And if I can't," Fable insisted.

"You know where your ship is docked. Don't hesitate to go back to wherever it is you came from." He left her alone, with no further comment.

Nearly eight hours later, Fable walked through the stormy deluge of rain, listening to the frigid drops against her shoulders. Every chafing step brought her closer to the theater and closer to a temper tantrum of monumental proportions. Jaalib was waiting for her at the door with a modest smile and a warm blanket. "He asks the impossible!" she hissed.

The actor draped the blanket over her shoulders. "Your dinner's getting cold."

Fable pushed through the door of her room, startled to find a heavy plasteel tub in the center of the floor, steaming with hot water. "A bath?" she whispered wearily. "Oh," she groaned, stumbling across the floor, discarding boots, socks, and belt as she moved across the room. About to pull the muddy shirt over her arms, Fable hesitated, feeling a draft from the door, where Jaalib stood, watching her. "Do you mind?"

Flushing with embarrassment, he stepped back into the shadows. "I'll bring your dinner later," he stammered and closed the door behind him.

As its orbital axis began its seasonal tilt, Trulalis was thrust into a tempestuous season of torrential rainfall and thunderstorms. Dawn showers became steady downpours by the afternoon, flooding the gutted lowland with muddy water and the persistent rumble of thunder. Above the biting autumn breeze, the hum of a lightsaber was interrupted by the rattle of falling pedestals, wax cylinders, and ball bearings as Fable blundered through the exercise.

Brandl watched with mounting dissatisfaction. As the last pedestal fell to the saturated earth, he stormed down from his high mound. "You little fool! Do it again!"

Fable braced herself against the malevolent voice, glaring at the ground, too frightened to meet Brandl's cruel eyes. Despite a streak of improvement, she was steadily losing ground and his frustration was proof of that, as were the whispered obscenities spoken vehemently under his breath. She watched his broad, swaying shoulders as the Jedi Master started back up the mound to his stony, sarcophagus throne.

"How eager you young upstarts are to give yourself to the Force, demanding tribute from it, as if you were the source of the power. The Force does not thrive on the basis of whether you live or breathe! It exists because it has always been so! Begin again!"

Grateful to the rain for hiding her tears of humiliation, Fable tucked the lightsaber into her muddy leggings and started up the opposite mound. Defying Brandl's command, she headed for the dark solace of the theater, where Jaalib would be waiting for her with a warm blanket and a much-needed kind word.

Enraged by her failure to comply, Brandl pursued her, throwing accusations and threats of retribution. Though Fable had seen only traces of it, she recognized the temperament and arrogance that must have been the beginning of Brandl's descent into the Emperor's power. And though she felt numb from the onslaught of his dreary emotions, she had transcended his mental barriers and become an admiring witness to the dedication and devotion that had kept him whole through the trial of his life. He was a man who would stop at nothing to accomplish his goals and he would kill her in an instant, if it so suited his purpose. And the time they had spent together, learning and growing, would hold no bearing on his decision. Sickened by the thought, Fable found herself in a position to admire and loathe the fallen Jedi.

Fable slowly pushed through the door of the theater. It was early and Jaalib was not there as she had expected. Emotionally spent and demoralized, she nearly collapsed right there at the threshold, desperate for the young actor's support after yet another dismal day of training. As she stepped from the rain, Brandl was right behind her with another scathing assault. "The Force is your enemy! Turn your back on it and it will destroy you! It is your lover! Lust for it! Spurn it and it will devour you in fire. But go to it, as a child to its mother, make yourself humble before the omnipotence of its existence and it will guide you beyond the shallow confines of this mortal world!"

Alarmed by the commotion, Jaalib hurried into the antechamber, placing himself between Fable and his father. Bordering on obvious hysteria, she stumbled into his arms, dampening his shoulder with well-deserved tears. Putting the blanket over Fable's trembling shoulders, Jaalib gently sent her off to her room. "Your bath is waiting," he whispered quietly. "I'll be there in a moment."

Waiting for the girl's shadow to dissipate in the adjoining darkness, Brandl hissed, "She's impossible!"

"Odd," Jaalib chuckled, handing his father a steaming cup of broth, "she said the same about you."

"She is so charged with emotion and sentiment!" he growled, allowing his emotions to show through the aloof veneer. "It's as if your mother never—" his voice broke off abruptly, "as if your mother never left us."

"She didn't leave us," Jaalib replied matter-of-factly. "She died, defending me from stormtroopers. Stormtroopers and Jedi hunters who came looking for you." He sniffed at the absurdity of his mother's devotion to the man who had abandoned them, only to return eight years later, bringing the darkness of his life with him. "When they didn't find you, they found a way to justify the cost of their visit by obliterating the village."

"Courtesy costs little, Edjian-Prince, and discourtesy can rob even the richest man of his fortune."

Feigning anger, Jaalib drew away from his father, recognizing the famous line. "Courtesy?" he declared impishly. "Then no more call me Edjian-Prince. Dress me in rags and let me be a poor, rude man."

Brandl's face brightened with the spontaneous performance. "You've been practicing! Excellent! You're finding the right voice for the part. Come," he whispered eagerly, pulling Jaalib against him, "we should use this moment to complete the final act." Together, they vanished into the shadows of an adjoining corridor.

Relaxed and warm beneath the downy comforters, Fable resisted the notion of rising. She laid very still, waiting for the inevitable knock on the door. "Come in."

"You're awake?" Jaalib remarked, peering inside.

"I'm usually awake," she chuckled. "I just pretend to be asleep so you'll feel sorry for me."

"Why would you want me to feel sorry for you?"

"Come on," she rolled her eyes. "You're father is the most difficult man I've ever known, Jaalib." Sitting up on her elbows, she teased, "Look what I've been going through and then tell me you don't feel some sympathy."

"Consider yourself fortunate. He was a lot worse, believe me."

"Worse?" she scoffed. "What do you mean?"

"In the last five years, he had to be a father, a mother," Jaalib sighed sadly, "as well as a mentor. It changed him."

"I knew I would have to work hard," Fable said, "but I was certain that all the work would be keeping him from luring me to the dark side."

"Has he tried?"

"I don't think so. Every time I feel it coming on, he stops me and tells me to make the right choice. My choice." She yawned, throwing the comforter to the side. "I'd better go."

"My father's not here," Jaalib said. "He's going to be away for a few days; so there's no training, unless you do it on your own." He forced himself to face her openly, allowing himself only the solace of the shadows about them to conceal his apprehension. "I was hoping you might go on a picnic with me. To make up for my behavior."

"Your behavior?"

"You remember, when you first arrived." He laughed softly. "I all but attacked you. It was inexcusable."

"And perfectly justified. You were protecting the person who is most important to you. I would have done nothing less." Patting the side of the bed, she beckoned him to sit down beside her. "My mother was a Jedi. She trained my father and then watched him die at the hands of a rival. After that, we spent most of our time running from the Emperor." Fable shook her head sadly. "I was only a baby, but I remember it well. Living with a Jedi," she paused thoughtfully, "you learn to hide your emotions, especially the hurtful ones. My mother never knew how I felt." Fable sighed as the strain of those emotions returned. "Then one day, I picked up a lightsaber and let go!" She giggled. "I don't know who was more surprised, my mother or me. That's when I began my training, whether I liked it or not." Fable shrugged away the arduous memories. "Now about that picnic, I'm starving."

"We'll have to hike, I'm afraid. The Empire didn't leave much behind in the way of transportation. Not even a bantha. Do you mind?"

"It'll be relaxing. Come on."

The Khoehng Heights were located nearly five

kilometers outside the perimeter of the Kovit Settle
ment. Long overgrown by wild wheat, the trail leading
into the mountain pass had narrowed, no longer marked
with the footsteps of the farmers who once tended it. It
was a rare, clear morning. Storm clouds loomed in the
distance, held back by a persistent wave of warm breezes
blowing through the lowlands. From the Heights, Fable
scanned the panoramic view of the countryside. She
could see the winding trail that led into the base of the
lower mountains. The footpath climbed to give her
inquisitive eyes the full benefit of the view.

Fable sighed with immeasurable pleasure, her stomach full of warm sweet cakes and honeysticks. She en-
dured Jaalib's gentle caress at her cheek, as he playfully
wiped the excess sweet powder from her face. "I've been
in space too long," she whispered, taking a deep breath.
"It's so beautiful here."

"After they left," Jaalib whispered, "we were cut off.
No supplies, no medicinal goods, nothing. There was
plenty of food ready for harvesting, but there was no one
left to do it."

Fable hummed a melancholy tune. Shivering in the
mountain air, she turned to Jaalib and held his gaze
as he draped his cloak over her shoulders. "Why do
they call this place the Khoehng Heights? Is that Old
Corellian?"

"There's an outdoor theater built into the side of this
mountain," he replied, indicating a slight, stony ridge.
"This place is named for the first play ever performed
there nearly five hundred years ago."

"Five hundred years ago?" she gasped.

"*Uhl Eharl Khoehng. Khoehng* is Old Corellian for king.
The *eharl* comes from Socorran mythology." He shrugged
uncertainly. "It means elf or trickster."

Reminded of her Socorran companion, Deke, Fable
felt a pang of remorse for leaving him. Her thoughts
were abruptly diverted by a clap of thunder overhead.
The skies released a deluge of cold rain. Frantically gathering the blankets and remaining baskets of food, Fable

held on to to Jaalib's hand as they sprinted over the ridge. Their voices and laughter reverberated against the hollowed side of the mountain, as they slid down the precarious face of the moss-covered bank and into the shadowy protection of the antiquated theater.

An overhanging eave of solid rock covered the main stage and the first few rows of the audience pit. Cobwebbed and damp, the ancient structure stood in a silent tribute to its creators. Ragged tapestries hung from the rock walls, covered with mold, grime, and clay from the decaying structure. A few prop swords and robes were arranged on the inner panels of the stage and a multitude of candles and pedestals stood to either side of the audience pit, centuries-old relics left behind by a more playful, tolerant age.

"I used to come here as a boy," Jaalib confessed. Extending his arms to either side, he declared, "Now this was true theater, by candlelight, in an age which understood and coveted its artisans."

"*Uhl Eharl Khoehng,*" Fable whispered dubiously. "What's it about?"

"It opens on a distant world, in a kingdom built in the center of a dark forest. After many years of ruling this kingdom, the good, wise king dies and his handsome son," Jaalib winked, "the Edjian-Prince, takes the throne."

"I thought you said this was a tragedy."

"It is a tragedy," Jaalib scolded, "and that becomes apparent when the Edjian-Prince decides to expand the kingdom and begins sending expeditions into the forest to mark trees for felling. The men he sent never returned." He narrowed his eyes, moving his face very close to hers. "And that is when the older folk began whispering about *uhl Eharl Khoehng.*"

"Stop it!" Fable hissed, batting his hands away as he tried to frighten her.

"The Edjian-Prince was intrigued. He began sending daily messengers into the forest, carrying his invitation to the Eharl Khoehng to dine with him in the palace. None returned. When there were no more messengers, he sent small armies, keeping only the best and strongest warriors to guard the kingdom. They did not return. When the townspeople demanded a halt to this dangerous ambition, the Edjian-Prince ordered his remaining army to drive them all into the forest. None, not even the soldiers, were heard from again." Lighting two candles, he moved the pedestals into the center of the stage. "Only the Edjian-Prince and his faithful old hunt servant remained."

"He sent the old man?" Slapping Jaalib's thigh, Fable hissed, "This is a terrible story! What happened to the Edjian-Prince after the old man left?"

"When his servant did not return, the Edjian-Prince barricaded himself in the palace. Without his armies or his subjects, there was nothing to stop the Eharl Khoehng from attacking. One quiet night," Jaalib whispered, "the Eharl Khoehng did come, invading the Edjian-Prince's dreams. He promised safe passage through the forest. Eager to make peace, the Edjian-Prince went into the wood, where he remained for nearly a decade."

"What!"

"The Eharl Khoehng tricked him. While he did have safe passage through the forest, food, clothing, and shelter, the Eharl Khoehng held him prisoner, using illusions to trap him in the labyrinth of the forest." Jaalib blew out one of the candles. "Ten years of guilt took its toll. The prince thought he heard the voices of his subjects crying out to him. Then one day, he was startled by the spirit of his beloved huntsman. The old man reported that the Eharl Khoehng had turned the townspeople into trees and left them there in the woods, conscious, but unable to move or speak, except when the wind blew through their branches."

"And then?"

"And then," Jaalib whispered, "unaffected by the Eharl Khoehng's illusions, the huntsman led his master on a journey to the outer edge of the forest, where the Eharl Khoehng was waiting for them." A malevolent shadow fell over his face as Jaalib stepped into the center of the stage, posing beside the lit candle. " 'Worship me and call me master and all that I have shall be yours, including your kingdom,' the Eharl Khoehng said."

"And what did the Edjian-Prince do?"

"He went mad," Jaalib began in the narrative voice. 'He ran back into the wood and set fire to it. By the time he was finished, there was nothing left, not one tree. 'This is the only kingdom I deserve to rule,' he declared, and the only kingdom that the Eharl Khoehng can claim.' " Taking one of the blackened tapestries from the wall, he threw the thick material over his left shoulder and continued the narration. "Dressed in the rags of his former life, hands and face blackened with soot, the Edjian-Prince went before the Eharl Khoehng, falling to his knees in homage. In his loudest, most humble voice, he cried, 'Long . . . live . . . the king.' "

Visibly moved, Fable applauded, shaking her head with wonderment. "Your father played that part?"

"The Edjian-Prince was my father's greatest role," Jaalib said absently. "No one has been able to bring the same dignity to the role." He sat down on the edge of the stage. "And when the time is right, we'll produce it again and I will be the Edjian-Prince and he shall be my nemesis, uhl Eharl Khoehng himself."

Fable chewed anxiously at her lower lip. "Jaalib, why didn't you become a Jedi?"

"All I ever wanted to be was an actor," he remarked, swinging his legs against the stage. "And that's exactly what I've become. I've learned the lightsaber and other meditations of the Jedi, mostly to appease my troubled sense of loyalty. Beyond these, my father seems reluctant to teach me any more. And I'm reluctant to ask."

Staring at the rows of candles, Fable was reminded of the wax cylinder exercise. "The lightsaber exercise, the one using the ball bearings? Can you do it with candles?"

Jaalib shrugged. "That's how he taught me. I never used the wax cylinders until much later."

"Can you show me your secret? Your execution is almost flawless, elegant and equally effective."

Assembling the pedestals in the familiar circle, Jaalib motioned for her to step inside the exaggerated diameter. "May I?" he teased, gently embracing her from behind. He placed his hands on top of hers and ignited the lightsaber. The elongated shaft pulsed with magnificence and power, throwing light across the stage and the first few benches in the pit. Fable stiffened for a moment, feeling his body so intimately against her. But as he guided her through a slow rotation with the lightsaber, she relaxed and concentrated on his directives. "What do you see?" he whispered.

Staring down the line of unlit candles, Fable's eyes traced the straight, angular path. "No," Jaalib whispered, reading the expression of her body. "This is why you're having such a hard time."

"You've been watching me?" she hissed, elbowing him in the ribs.

Jaalib laughed softly. "You're trying to think in linear terms, spatial dimensions. It's not like flying a starship. You can train your eyes, which you've done quite well, but sooner or later, he'll catch you." Moving her gently to the side, he added, "You may let your eyes dictate where the lines begin, but let the Force guide you. It's not like clearing a room and then moving on to the next. There is no sequence, except the one you create as you move along. There are always several paths, right to left, top to bottom, any combination."

He removed the lightsaber from her hands and began the cadence. His movements were slow and deliberate so that she could follow him, but even these motions were faster than her most frenzied attempts to complete the exercise. As the lightsaber swept over the tops of the candles, the small wicks exploded with flame, but the wax tips remained unscarred by the weapon. Quickly moving around the circle to blow out the flames, Jaalib handed the lightsaber back to her. "Now you try."

Fable swallowed doubtfully, wondering how she would follow such a flawless performance. Igniting the lightsaber, her eyes traced the several lines of candles as they extended out in every direction. She arced swiftly through the circle, feeling the confidence of her former self return. Ten, fifteen, eighteen. As she reached the last movements of the cadence, she lost control, pitching forward as she spun frantically on her heels.

"Easy," Jaalib crooned, catching her in his arms. "You were doing wonderfully until you lost your concentration." Blowing out the candles, he said, "Try again. And this time, remember, the Force is a waterfall. Nothing can stop or turn it off. Nothing can divert the flow." Scolding her with a stern finger, he added, "Doubt and uncertainty form barriers, but only if you let them."

"Now you're starting to sound like your father."

In response, he bowed ceremoniously, then motioned toward the candles. This time, as she moved through the circle, Fable allowed the rain to guide and open her to the Force. The steady beat of the drops against the stone benches steadied her concentration and she completed the cadence without incident.

She disengaged the lightsaber, trembling slightly as she turned from the center of the circle. The Force was flowing through her, still channeling her conscious mind. Jaalib was behind her and Fable could feel his heart racing above the gentle vibrations of the Force. Before her nerve could fail, Fable turned and kissed him passionately.

"Shall we try it again?" he whispered.

"Rogue!"

Jaalib grinned, winking mischievously. "The cadence, I mean." His grin deepened as he stepped into the circle and began to blow out the candles.

The Force was with her and Fable felt it, flowing through her mind and body. She imaged the power channeling through her arms and hands and grasped the lightsaber from her belt. Visualizing the path in her mind, she moved through a series of precise parries and feints, disintegrating the first several balls with faultless execution. As she began the second half of the cadence, Brandl whispered, "Execute each motion as though it were your last. Someday, your life may depend on it. Or the lives of others."

For nearly two hours, Fable worked through the first cadence and was moving onto the second. Obviously fatigued, she began making poor judgment errors and scorched the tops of the last ten cylinders, slicing through the last one at the conclusion. She stepped back into the ready stance, gasping for breath.

"As you progress, you will learn the limits of your abilities," Brandl stated. "You are excused for the remainder of the day."

Bowing respectfully, Fable pulled her jacket from a nearby branch and started on the trail back to the theater. Jaalib was waiting for her with a sweet cake and the promise of a bath and a kiss. "How did it go?"

"I made it to the second cadence!" she whispered with excitement. "And Jaalib, I think I saw him smile."

"Now *that* is good news."

Glancing over her shoulder, she winked at him. "I think I'll go to bed early tonight, as a reward. Do you mind?"

"Not at all. Father and I are working on the last act of the play." He smiled pleasantly, betraying his affection. "See you in the morning."

Fable awoke to a terrible sense of foreboding. Quickly dressing, she sat tentatively at the edge of the bed, hugging her knees against her chest as she scanned the shadows. Something was terribly wrong and she could feel it. Cradling the lightsaber in her lap, she took a deep breath, assured that she was ready for the worst, whatever that may be, whenever it might come.

The familiar knock came at her door. "Come in," she

replied, eager to share her concerns with Jaalib. But as the door opened, she was greeted by the foreboding shadow of her mentor. "Where's Jaalib?"

"Jaalib is the one and only treasure left to my miserable existence," Brandl snarled. "I forbid this to happen. I forbid it!"

"Where is he? I want to talk to him!"

Advancing into the room, Brandl cornered her. "The theater on Iscera will be opening in a few days. I sent him there to make preparations for our production. By the time he returns, you will be gone."

Fable followed Brandl into the corridor with heavy, angry strides, allowing her emotions to seethe within her. On the verge of a temper tantrum, she braced herself as common sense called on her to reason. She had come to Trulalis to improve herself, to get an edge on the enemy who pursued her, and then to return, if possible, to her friends in the Rebel Alliance. Falling in love had no place in that design.

Brandl set a bowl of steaming broth at the end of the table and sat down on the opposite end. Fable slammed herself into the stool, barely able to curb her temper. "So what's it like to be a pawn for the Emperor!"

"I brought pleasure to my master through the tears of his subjects." Momentarily distracted by the sincerity of the spontaneous soliloquy, Brandl stared into his bowl. Recovering his cynicism, he glared across the small table. "The Emperor's ideas are quite noble. It's his methods which eventually offend those of lesser vision."

"Sounds like you're still loyal to him." Through narrowed eyes, she retaliated. "Why not, he only tried to kill you."

"In time, you will learn that an old friend is very much like a good mirror. The longer you stare into it, the harder it is to find the flaws."

A shrill whine echoed from high above, sending a peculiar reverberation through the theater. Fable felt a chill as her ears recognized the distinct sounds of a shuttle flying overhead. Its exhaust boosters could be heard above the whine of the ion drive, as the pilot circled looking for an appropriate place to land. "That's Vialco. Isn't it?"

Brandl closed his eyes and was silent. Fable straightened her shoulders as she rose from the table, turning her back on the Jedi. "No more bad dreams," she whispered with firm resolve and stepped from the shadows of the theater into the dawn. Her body knew every hollow and rise in the unmarked trail that led to the picturesque grounds of Kovit's graveyard. She stared across the entrance mound to where Vialco stood among the tarnished graves and markers. For a moment, the fear and horror of their first encounter returned in full force.

"You've matured much faster than I expected," Vialco declared. "I never imagined Lord Brandl to be such a gracious host."

Vialco walked among the raised tombs, brushing his gloved hands over the rough-hewn stone, as if drawing power from the shadows lurking at the site of each grave. His face was gangly and angular, unattractive, with gaunt cheeks and unusually large brows. Sensing her peripheral thoughts, he whispered, "No, no more bad dreams, girl. I've come for the harvest." A sinister determination shadowed his pallid face. "What shall it be, hmm?"

Fable shifted her weight to one foot, cocking her hip arrogantly. As Vialco ignited his lightsaber, she calmly drew her own, assuming the ready stance. She parried his first, preemptive attempts to break through her defenses, losing no ground to him, and met his surprise with a coy smile.

"We are much improved," he commented. "Have I left too much time for you to prepare?"

"Lord Brandl did say you were a coward," Fable taunted. "But I already knew that."

Vialco's face flushed with rage as he began a series of short lunges, forcing Fable to move back along the perimeter of the muddy basin. Feinting to the left, she swung around behind him, delivering a swift kick to Vialco's behind. Enraged by her insolence, Vialco turned on her, gripping the lightsaber tightly in his hands. Deliberately stretching her defenses, he attempted to penetrate her confidence.

"Fable?"

Fable heard the soft-spoken voice from the past, and without turning toward the shadowy image on the edge of her peripheral vision, she knew the illusion to be Arecelis. The image waved and laughed, sounding intimately like her dead friend. "No," Fable whispered, "no, I don't think so, Vialco. I saw what you did to him. I saw it!" she seethed. The tip of her lightsaber sliced easily through the shoulder of his cloak. "And that was your first mistake."

"And my second?"

"Letting me live to remember it!" She lunged savagely at him, knocking Vialco against the tomb of Brandl's wife. Breaking off the assault, she somersaulted back down into the depression. Disengaging her lightsaber, she stood there defiantly. "Shall I play with you like you played with him?"

"Wretched girl!" Vialco hissed, spittle flying from the corners of his mouth. "If you will not be turned, you will die!" Summoning the corrupt powers of the dark side, Vialco felt the energy coursing through him. He extended his arms, curling his fingertips as the first tendrils of lightning surged from his hands.

Fable flinched, awkwardly balanced as she tried to back away. The arc of lightning shot through her, ripping into her flesh. Screaming in pain, she dropped to the ground, curling into a fetal ball as the agony washed through her. Before she could collect herself, a second and third blow left her tortured body temporarily paralyzed.

"Have we come so far to fall so low?" Vialco taunted. "Tsk, tsk, what a pity," he smacked his thin lips.

Reeling with the corrupt power surge, Fable jumped to her feet. As Vialco took aim, she somersaulted, voicing a shrill squeal of effort as the pulse of electricity cuffed her shoulder. Wielding the lightsaber in both hands, she began the subtle movements of the first cadence. As each tendril of lightning arced at her, she swept the blade of the lightsaber across it, effectively deflecting it. She imagined that each arc was a new series of lines. Each point was the metal reflection of a ball bearing, the shiny wick of a candle.

Twenty, thirty . . . she lost count of the number of successful deflections. Even as the crescent of lightning arced behind her, slipping in above her head, she simply brought the lightsaber over her shoulder into its path. Never turning to look, her body reacted as her eyes designed the next path.

Fable fought her way to the top of the mound. Knocking Vialco from his feet, she pushed him down into the depression. She watched in horror as the tendrils of lightning rebelled against their master, burning through his clothing and flesh. He lurched for his lightsaber and fumbled, knocking the weapon out of reach. "Have we come so far to lie so low?" Fable mocked. She slid down the face of the mound, raising her lightsaber to finish him.

Vialco cowered below her, writhing in the mud. Something in his groveling manner made Fable hesitate, dropping her arms to chest height, as the lightsaber hummed insistently in her hands.

"Will you give him the chance to betray you again?" Keeping her eyes on Vialco, Fable felt the dark presence of her master. "Kill him and be done with it," Brandl whispered. "Only then will you know that the nightmare is over."

Fable disengaged the lightsaber and turned to her Jedi mentor. "It is over. Why kill him?"

"Remember what he is and what he has done. He will betray your dreams, as he has done before, and use them to his advantage. End the nightmare, Fable. Kill him."

Fable heard the pulse of the lightsaber before she saw it. Wondering how Vialco had gotten hold of his weapon without her sensing it, she whirled, igniting her lightsaber. Vialco arced his blade toward her vulnerable legs. In a wild strike, she severed his head from the shoulders, never losing momentum. But as he fell, she clearly saw his empty hands. The lightsaber was still on the ground, several meters from his body.

"Who's tricking who?" Fable hissed, enraged by Brandl's careful deceit. Lunging toward her mentor, she met the abrupt thrust of his lightsaber. Dominating and powerful, he knocked Fable off of her feet and drove her back into the opposite mound. "You lied to me!" she gasped, weakly rubbing her bruised cheek. "What have you done?"

"I have set your place at the Emperor's table," Brandl replied. "Soon, I shall again stand at my master's side and you shall stand beside me." He glared down at her, mocking the injury in her eyes. "You knew there would be a price."

"What price?"

Brandl smiled, posing arrogantly for his small audience. Offering his hand, he whispered, "Worship me and call me master and all that I have shall be yours, including Jaalib's affections. There's no use fighting it, Fable. Accept and you will be well cared for, this I promise you." Brandl turned to leave. "Don't bother running to your ship. Thermal detonators are rather effective tools." Gently caressing the scars at his temple, he chuckled, "I should know."

Locked in her room, Fable rocked quietly from side to side, wiping tears on her sleeve. Her fingers were blood-covered and black with grime, the nails shredded from a recent tantrum at the site of her X-wing. In an attempt to avoid her impending fate, she had fled to the vessel and found the gutted remains of her starfighter in a blackened blast diameter. Only the central frame of the X-wing had survived the initial blast. Vialco's shuttle was also consumed by the explosion, strewn across a sunken depression of scorched earth. Cursing Brandl, she rocked faster and harder, desperate to find some way to escape him.

The door opened slowly, a small crack that grew larger as the hunched figure skulked into the room. Fable's eyes brightened immediately, recognizing the face. "Jaalib," she whispered, swept into his arms. "Your father's—"

"Shh, I know," he hushed. Sitting down on the bed beside her, he gently pulled her trembling body against him. "I just happened to go over my ship's backup logs and discovered my father's side trip to Byss."

"Byss?"

"The Emperor's pleasure world. I hurried back as soon as I could and found what was left of your X-wing. Wasn't hard to figure out the next scene." He picked up a small satchel of her things and threw it over his shoulders.

"What are you doing?"

"You're leaving," he replied curtly. "Don't talk. Don't think. Don't even breathe heavy or he'll find us."

"He'll know eventually, as soon as we step outside this theater."

"And that doesn't give us much time," he argued. "So just run."

Following the trail out of the settlement, Jaalib jogged toward the mountain range, using the jutting lip of the Khoehng Heights as a guide beneath the moonlit skies of Trulalis. Fable matched his earnest strides and together they ran the short kilometer to the wheat field, where a familiar ship was waiting for them.

"The *Prodigal*!" she screamed. "Deke!"

"Heard you got yourself in a spot of trouble," the Socorran grumbled with relief. "Didn't think I'd let you go down alone, did you?" Hearing a proximity alarm from within the ship, Deke nodded to Jaalib. "I set the sensors just like you said." He eyed his ship dubiously. "Something or somebody just tripped the perimeter sensor."

"It's him," Fable trembled, casting her gaze to the far-off theater steeple.

"Then you had better go," Jaalib whispered.

"What about you?" Fable protested. "Come with us."

"He's my father, Fable. It's not that easy."

"And you call this easy?" she croaked, tears in her voice. Seeing the denial in his eyes, Fable pleaded, "Jaalib—"

Cutting off her objections with a kiss, Jaalib gently crowded her toward the ship. "For once in your life, listen, and go before he gets here."

"But—"

"No, Fable!" Jaalib hissed. "You're nothing but a consolation prize to the Emperor!"

"He's right, Capt'n," Deke insisted. "Time to bail."

Desperately appealing to her defiant eyes, Jaalib grinned, anxious to subdue her temper. "I was born to play this role, remember? I am the Edjian-Prince." Swallowing his sorrow, he embraced her warmly. "It's the last act, Fable. I have to burn the forest down now."

"Then burn it," she sobbed, cradling her head against his shoulder.

"I can't. Not while you're still here."

Fable stumbled up the ramp and cued the hatch controls. Leaning heavily on the secured door, she wiped absently at a tear, sensing the warmth of Jaalib's touch on her cheek.

Shielding his eyes from the freighter's exhaust, Jaalib stepped back into the swaying fields of wheat. Engines glowing red with the strain of sudden acceleration, the *Prodigal* banked sharply against the foot of the mountains, carrying Fable away. Lightning signaled her departure, bringing on a deluge of cold, cold rain. Jaalib took a deep breath, bracing himself for the wrath of the brooding presence slowly moving up behind him.

Brandl briefly glanced up, searching for some signs of Fable—his squandered prize. There were none and his austere gaze fell heavily on Jaalib. "Arrogant, deceitful child," he snarled.

Feeling the subtle constriction of his throat, Jaalib resisted panic as his windpipe contracted, seized by invisible fingers. "No less arrogant than my father," he rasped. Desperate for air, he dropped to his knees, slowly losing consciousness as the grip tightened about his throat. His father abruptly released him and the cool, damp air flowed into his body.

Staring after the retreating figure of his father, Jaalib staggered precariously. Compelled to follow, he screamed, "Long . . . live . . . the king!"

The Last Hand

by Paul Danner

"Sabacc!"

Doune's resounding laughter echoed through the gambling hall, the Herglic's huge body shaking with the effort. "You lose again, boy."

Vee-Six, Doune's droid, quickly calculated his master's winnings and enthusiastically reported the total for all to hear.

The gathered crowd cheered as the Herglic claimed the pot, leaving Nyo with a single credit to his name.

The young man lowered his head in disbelief, fighting back tears. *How could I have been so stupid?* Nyo thought as he stared at the lone cred chip that constituted all the money he had in the galaxy. Now, all hope was gone.

"Doune . . . the great gambler. Able to steal the money from a poor farmboy with ease. I suppose you are equally skilled at firing your heavy blaster on unarmed opponents."

The bold words silenced the room.

The Herglic looked up in shock, searching the syco-phantic circle of admirers who always clung to winners for the dissonant voice.

The spectators parted for the cloaked figure as if he were a thermal detonator. A large hood kept the stranger's face in shadow, but the dark visage was obviously focused on the Herglic.

"You think you could do better, friend?" Doune asked, a dangerous edge in his deep voice.

The figure gestured to the crowd. "I wouldn't want to embarrass you in front of all your . . . friends."

"I never turn away anyone so obviously willing to lose his money to me," Doune chuckled. "Sit down."

The stranger paused for a moment, then slid into the empty seat. "Very well. I must warn you, though . . ."

The Herglic cocked an eyebrow. "Wait, don't tell me. Let me guess." Doune gestured dramatically. "You're the greatest gambler who ever lived, right?"

"Actually, I was just going to say that I don't have any money on me, but now that you mention it . . ." The stranger lowered his hood, eliciting a collective gasp from the spectators. "I am."

The stranger's close-cropped hair was white, though streaks of silver snaked their way through the ivory. His eyes were pale violet, like tropical flowers that had withered and lost their luster. A jagged scar wound its way around his lip, cutting an unnatural line up past his nose. With stony features reminiscent of a royal statue, the man was undeniably handsome; however, that wasn't the reason for the crowd's reaction.

The whispers had begun, and the buzzing made it seem as if a colony of insects had descended upon the room. Throughout the snatches of conversation in the multitude of languages, two words were repeated with frightening frequency.

Kinnin Vo-Shay.

Doune's thick flesh had begun to mottle, a sure sign the Herglic was agitated.

"This is nothing but a trick, Master." Vee-Six leaned forward, eyes flashing as his databanks began recalling information. "The *Ashanda Ray* was reported lost in the Tyus cluster half a century ago. If Kinnin Vo-Shay had survived, which is highly unlikely, he would be well over one hundred standard years old. The man was lucky, but he was no Jedi."

"It would seem you are not who you appear to be, after all." Doune seemed to calm down a bit, his usual predatory smirk returning to his face. "I must admit, though, the resemblance is uncanny. You must have paid a fortune on cosmetic alterations. No wonder you're broke."

A nervous chuckle escaped the crowd.

"For such a renowned gambler, Doune, you're a much faster dealer of opinions than cards." The stranger leveled his piercing gaze. "Perhaps you win by talking until your opponents die of sheer boredom."

"The one thing I never deal in is charity," the Herglic said, a note of irritation creeping into his voice. "Until you ante up, there will be no game."

That drew a mixed reaction from the crowd. Many wanted to see if the stranger really was telling the truth, and there was only one way to decide that. . . .

"But, Doune, what if he really is Vo-Shay?" one brave soul asked.

The Herglic had had enough, and his blubber shook with fury. "I don't care if he's Jabba the Hutt. Without money, he doesn't play!"

A single credit spun through the air, shimmering in the dim glowlights. Without blinking, Vo-Shay plucked the cred from its flight with practiced ease. He slowly turned to face his surprise benefactor.

Nyo started to say something, but Vo-Shay offered a wink that was so quick the young man was scarcely sure he saw it at all.

"From one loser to another . . . how appropriate. Are you ready, then?" Doune demanded.

Vo-Shay's face lost all expression, resembling a droid that had been abruptly powered down. Those strange eyes took on a faraway look, as if they were staring into eternity. He spoke only a single word, but it sent a chill down the spine of every being present who had one.

"Deal," Vo-Shay said.

The room grew deathly quiet.

And the game began. . . .

Doune slid a blubbery fin across his forehead, which was glistening with perspiration. The Herglic examined his cards and grunted softly. His pile of credits was steadily decreasing, while Vo-Shay's lone credit had gained thousands of friends in less than an hour. He glanced up at his opponent, but the human gambler's face may as well have been carved out of ferrostone.

Only Vo-Shay's right hand was in motion, absently twirling the obsidian stone pendant hanging from his neck. When he had first removed the bauble from underneath his shirt, a collective gasp resounded from the crowd. The necklace that was rumored to be the source of the legendary gambler's astonishing luck. It was yet another piece of evidence that suggested that this man was really who he claimed to be.

The Herglic watched his shifting sabacc cards and nearly grinned. The Four of Coins had reformed into the Mistress of Staves, with a value of thirteen. He already held the Nine of Staves. Doune dramatically pushed the metallic cards into the neutral stabilizer field. "Twenty-two."

Vo-Shay began laying out his cards. The Ace of Flasks, the Master of Flasks, and the Nine of Flasks. A total of thirty-eight. A low murmur rippled through the crowd. Nyo winced and looked away. The gambler was about to go bust.

Chuckling, the Herglic reached for the pot . . . fifteen thousand credits.

Vo-Shay played one more card into the neutral field. The Evil One. Negative fifteen. That brought his hand down to twenty-three. "Sabacc," he said, grabbing Doune's hand just as it reached the thick stack of credits at the center of the table. "I believe that's mine."

The Herglic snarled. "Your luck cannot last forever, impostor."

But it did.

In another hour, Vo-Shay held over one hundred thousand credits. The crowd not only began to believe, they had completely shifted allegiance. Vee-Six was the lone supporter remaining in Doune's corner, and the droid was not exactly encouraging. "Please, Master," Vee-Six implored, "you must end this before—"

"Shut up!" the Herglic roared, shoving the droid away. He slammed a cred stick onto the table. "One more, human . . . double or nothing."

"Don't risk it," Nyo whispered, eyeing Vo-Shay's winnings. "Let's just cut and run."

The gambler smiled, his pale violet pupils dilated with excitement. "I never back down from a challenge." He eyed his opponent. "Ready?"

Doune nodded, nostrils flaring.

The gambler spun the obsidian pendant on its chain, and the stone danced as if it were alive. More than one observer found himself transfixed by the sight as Vo-Shay reached for his cards. . . .

Nyo and Vo-Shay walked out of the gambling hall with nearly a quarter of a million credits.

The young man was so excited, he couldn't stop talking. "If I hadn't seen it with my own eyes, I never would have believed it."

"Well, Doune actually played the game and I'm betting he still isn't sure what happened." The gambler patted the youth on the back and handed him the small electronic stick containing two hundred thousand credits.

"All yours, my boy. I kept the change for expenses . . . hope you don't mind."

"Are you kidding?" Nyo's hand was shaking as he held the cred stick. "I can't thank you enough for this . . . you've literally made my dreams come true."

"That's a lot of money you've got there." Vo-Shay studied the young man. "You obviously don't frequent places like that, so I'm assuming you were trying to win for a reason."

Nyo glanced off into the distance, shuffling his feet uncomfortably.

"Sorry . . . I have a bad habit of sticking my nose in where it's not welcome. Curiosity is just one of my many vices, but it gets me in trouble more than any of the others." The gambler squeezed Nyo's shoulder. "Whatever it is, I hope it works out for you."

Vo-Shay pulled up the hood of his cloak and effortlessly slid into the crowd.

"Wait!" The gambler turned, just as the youth caught up. "If you hadn't been nosy back there, I'd be walking home with one credit in my pocket . . . can we talk?" Nyo glanced around the bustling street. "In private?"

Vo-Shay shook his head and laughed. "Now you've gone and done it. I never could pass up a good confidential chat." The gambler gestured to a dingy cantina in the distance. "After you . . ."

The duo sat at a booth in the rear of the cantina, with a bottle of Corellian whisky and a good deal of space between themselves and the next patrons. Vo-Shay blended in so well with the shadows that it seemed as if Nyo was sitting alone at the table.

The gambler downed another shot of the tangy drink and stared at his companion. "Well, have you imbibed enough liquid courage, yet? Or am I going to be sitting here all night?"

Nyo chuckled, then grew serious. "Are you really Kinnin Vo-Shay?"

"Last I heard."

"Then how is it that you're—"

The gambler held up a gloved hand. "I thought we were here because you wanted to reveal *your* secrets. . . ."

"Point taken." The young man took a drink and then a deep breath. "The reason I need the money is—promise not to laugh?"

"I never make promises, son. I only deal in cards. Not words."

Nyo didn't respond. He was staring into his glass, as if mesmerized by the smooth contours. After a few more moments of silence, he finally spoke. His voice was a whisper. "I want to buy a lightsaber."

The gambler's eyes widened. "Really?"

"You think it's stupid."

"No! That's just the last thing I expected to hear. I figured it was something more mundane . . . a sick family member in need of an expensive operation, a beautiful girl you couldn't afford to marry, maybe a debt to a nefarious crime lord."

Nyo shook his head. "No, nothing like that."

"So where do you intend to pick one up? They're not exactly standard stock for equipment shops, you know."

"I've heard about a black-market dealer who has one for sale."

"Where?"

Nyo was obviously reluctant to answer.

"Come on, son," the gambler said, reaching for his glass, "it's not as if I'm going to race there ahead of you and snatch it up. . . ."

"Nar Shaddaa."

Vo-Shay nearly spat out his drink. "The Smuggler's Moon!" The gambler narrowed his eyes and gave the young man an appraising glance. "Just how old are you, anyway?"

"Twenty standard years," he said proudly.

"And you've lived here on Morado all your life. Have you ever been offworld before?"

"Well, no . . . but I've seen plenty of holos—"

Vo-Shay burst out laughing.

"What's so funny?" Nyo said, obviously annoyed.

"Nothing! What could possibly be funny about a boy who's never been off his home planet traveling by himself to one of the most dangerous hives of scum and villainy in the galaxy with two hundred thousand credits on him to purchase an illegal weapon from a shady black-market dealer?" He leaned forward. "Are you even carrying a blaster?"

The young man's silence answered his question.

The gambler wiped tears from his eyes. "By the Force . . . you must be either an overconfident fool or a half-wit. Your star may be fiery, but it isn't going to burn long in this galaxy if you keep up this sort of behavior."

Nyo abruptly stood, slamming his fist against the table. "I don't need a lecture! Especially not from somebody who's supposed to be dead because he was too lazy to pilot his ship around an extremely dangerous area of space . . ." The young man started to leave, but wasn't through yet. "And you may be the greatest gambler who ever lived, but you have a lot to learn about dealing with people. See you around." With that, Nyo promptly stormed out of the cantina.

You never change, do you, Shay? The disembodied voice was hauntingly beautiful, caressing the gambler's cheek like a cool breeze.

"Listen," Vo-Shay took a final swig directly from the whisky bottle and walked to the door, "if you want to put your two credits in, just leave them on the table . . . I don't have change for a tip."

"So, how much for passage to Nar Shaddaa?"

The Barabel captain quickly calculated his figure, then grinned at Nyo. With all those sharp teeth, it wasn't a comforting sight. "Twenty-five thousand. Paid in advance. No refund under any circumstances . . ."

The young man stumbled over his words. "I . . . I don't know. That seems like an awful lot."

"That's because it is."

Both the Barabel and Nyo looked up at the new voice. Vo-Shay stood at their table, arms folded across his chest. "The boy could get a better deal from a Jawa . . . and on something far nicer than the garbage scow you're passing off as a tramp freighter."

Enraged, the captain stood, towering over the gambler. "You insult me. . . ."

"No. You insult *him*," Vo-Shay said, indicating Nyo. "And if you want to live to prey an another easy mark, I suggest you leave immediately. Or else you'll be insulting *me*."

Barabels, however, are not easily intimidated. "And why should I care about that, little man?"

Vo-Shay shifted his position slightly, flashing the two hold-out blasters he held tucked under arms.

The captain snorted and took a threatening step forward, "I could make you eat those."

"If you *were* that good, you'd have already done it instead of just talking about it," the gambler said, refusing to give up a centimeter of ground. "Now go; find some nerfs to herd."

The Barabel shoved past Vo-Shay and slipped into the crowd milling around the bar.

Still chuckling, the gambler slipped the blasters into his cloak and dropped into the vacated seat.

"What do you want now?" the young man asked.

"Just to talk."

Nyo started to get up. "I don't have anything else to say to you."

Vo-Shay reached out and quickly yanked him back into his seat.

"Hey! Lemme go . . ."

"Not until you've heard my offer."

"What kind of offer?"

"I'll fly you to Nar Shaddaa."

Nyo couldn't believe it. "Why would you do that?"

"To make sure you get there without dying," the gambler said, rocking back in his chair. "And so you can pay me ten thousand credits."

It didn't take him long to consider the offer. "Deal," Nyo said, smiling.

"Let's get going, then."

The young man was already headed for the door, giddy with excitement. "I can't believe this. . . ."

Vo-Shay shook his head as he followed Nyo out. "Join the club," he said softly.

"There she is." The gambler's voice was filled with the pride only a parent or ship captain could ever know.

Nyo stepped into Docking Bay 49 and his mouth promptly fell open. "The *Ashanda Ray*. . ."

The two men circled the graceful curves of the light freighter. Vo-Shay carefully slid a hand along her smooth underbelly. "She was designed by a good friend of mine . . . a Mon Cal engineer with a great eye."

Like most ships designed by the Mon Calamari, the *Ray* was a model of efficiency, structural strength, and aesthetic appeal. More than a spacecraft, it resembled a handcrafted piece of art. With myriad pods, bulges, and bumps, the ship almost appeared organic rather than constructed—like a great ocean-dwelling creature.

"She can be a headache for maintenance and repair, but other than that . . ."

"Quite a beauty," Nyo agreed, "but I don't see any weapons . . . or sensors. Or anything."

"What would an exotic woman be without her secrets?" The gambler laid an arm around the young man's shoulders. "Now come on . . . let's go get your lightsaber."

Exhausted from his exploits, Nyo spent most of the trip in one of the *Ray*'s extremely comfortable bunks.

Vo-Shay was resting in the cockpit, half asleep himself. The ship would warn him if anything came up, and the smoothly accelerating starlines of lightspeed always made the gambler drowsy. When he heard the lilting voice, he wasn't sure if he was dreaming or not.

You definitely have your moments.

His eyes popped open. Definitely not dreaming . . .

"Was there ever any doubt in your mind?"

Do you want me to be honest, or nice?

"Nice," Vo-Shay grinned. "So, what's the word?"

It's hard to say right now. I need more time.

"Don't we all."

He's coming.

Vo-Shay craned his neck up over the top of the chair. "Well, well. Look what the gundark dragged in. . . ."

Nyo entered the cockpit, still rubbing the sleep out of his eyes. He unceremoniously plopped down into the copilot's seat. "Are we there yet?"

The gambler checked his displays. "Almost. You get some rest?"

The young man nodded, surveying the cockpit.

"Good." Vo-Shay leaned back in his chair, absently twirling his pendant. "You'll need to keep your eyes wide open in a place like Nar Shaddaa. Bad things can happen to people faster than you can even think about pulling your blaster."

"That's okay," Nyo answered with a grin. "I don't have one, remember?"

The gambler chuckled. After a few moments, he grew serious and turned to face Nyo. "You never told me why you wanted a lightsaber."

"You never told me how you survived your untimely demise in the Tyus cluster," the young man countered evenly, "or how come you're not over a hundred years old."

"An even exchange, huh? Okay, but I asked first."

The gambler immediately recognized that distant look that crept into Nyo's eyes. It was the one that always prefaced the resurfacing of a lifelong dream and usually culminated in trouble.

"I want to become a Jedi Knight," the young man said in a voice just above a whisper.

The gambler was silent for a moment. "I thought they built their own lightsabers when they were actually ready to wield one. . . ."

That seemed to deflate Nyo slightly, but he quickly recovered. "I just wanted to have something . . . connected with them. I mean, it's not like there's anyone around to train me. I don't know. . . ." He stared out the viewport, at the stars rushing past. "I guess I thought that if I felt a lightsaber in my hands, there'd be some kind of magic, you know? You have to take your first step somewhere, and this was the only path I could find."

Well spoken, young one.

"Huh?" Nyo snapped out of his reverie and glanced back at Vo-Shay. "Did you say something?"

"Wasn't me," the gambler said with a wink.

"So, I held up my end of the bargain . . . now, let's hear your story."

Something caught Vo-Shay's eye. "It'll have to wait."

"Why?"

The gambler's hands were already dancing over the controls, abruptly dropping the *Ray* out of hyperspace. "Because we've got company. . . ."

"I've got a bad feeling about this." Vo-Shay tracked the three incoming ships on the *Ray*'s sensors.

"Who is it?"

"They haven't introduced themselves yet, but somehow I don't think it's a welcoming committee." The gambler eyed the display and frowned. "One Ghtroc freighter and two Z-95 Headhunters. Could be worse, I guess. . . ."

"How? We're already outnumbered."

"But never outclassed." The comlink sounded its shrill call, drawing Vo-Shay's attention "It sounds as if they want to talk. That's always a good sign."

"This is Captain Yarrku of the *Night Raider*. . . ." came the filtered voice.

"He sounds familiar," Nyo said.

Vo-Shay grunted. "It's that Barabel from the cantina."

"Are you sure?"

"I never forget a voice."

"What could he possibly want?"

"Only one way to find out," the gambler said, then engaged the comlink. "Is there a problem, Captain?"

"There will be unless you hand over all the credits you stole from Doune."

"Stole? From Doune? Hah! That blubberpot Herg must be going senile. . . . I won that money fair and square at a sabacc game."

"Doune does not share your view of the situation. He believes you cheated him, and he has hired us to retrieve his money. If you hand it over, there will be no damage to you or your ship. Otherwise . . ." The Barabel's voice trailed off ominously.

"Doune is nothing but a poor loser. And as far as I'm concerned, he's going to stay that way."

"You know, I was hoping you'd say that," Yarrku said with an unfriendly chuckle. Then there was only static.

The two Z-95s broke off into standard flanking formation as frighteningly powerful laser bolts erupted from the Ghtroc freighter.

Vo-Shay executed a quick barrel roll and then pointed the *Ray*'s nose into a power dive. The two bolts screamed past, cutting through the space that the ship had occupied microseconds before.

Nyo couldn't believe it. "That thing's got a pair of quad lasers!"

"So much for talking," Vo-Shay grumbled as he swung the *Ray* around to face an oncoming Headhunter.

"This ship *does* have weapons, right?" Nyo asked.

The gambler merely grinned and touched one of the control screens.

One of the pods on the *Ray*'s belly spiraled open, revealing a large triple-barreled laser cannon. The turret swung around, locking onto the approaching Headhunter.

A thunderous volley of laser bolts tracked the Z-95 as it tried to execute an evasive turn. The blasts "walked" right up the ship's exposed starboard side, shredding the shields, and finally exploding the ship's wing.

Without the starboard stabilizers, the Headhunter began to spin out of control, harmlessly veering off into the distance.

"Does that answer your question?" the gambler asked with a smug grin.

His smile faded when one of the *Night Raider*'s quad laser bolts slammed into the *Ray*'s port side. The impact spun the light freighter around sharply and Vo-Shay found himself fighting to keep her steady.

The other Headhunter was closing in, with all blasters blazing away mercilessly.

Unable to evade the attack, the *Ray* was forced to take a considerable pounding from the Z-95's strafing run.

The ship bucked and shook under the assault, knocking the two men around in their chairs. The gambler cursed under his breath as he steadied his wounded craft.

"We just lost half our shields!" Nyo cried out in alarm.

Acting as if he didn't hear, an enraged Vo-Shay brought the *Ray* into a hard bootlegger's turn that sent a structural groan through the ship. He closed the distance with impossible speed. Nyo felt as if a giant invisible hand was pressing against his chest. "I didn't know freighters could move this fast."

"Most can't. This one can."

Thanks to Vo-Shay's expert piloting, the *Ray* mirrored every last maneuver the Headhunter executed. It was as if the two pilots were of one mind. No matter what tactic it tried, the Z-95 could not shake off the larger ship. A sustained burst of heavy blaster fire quickly turned the Headhunter into a flaming star-burst.

"Gotcha!" Vo-Shay shouted.

"And I got you," came Yarrku's filtered voice over the comlink. It was followed by another bone-jarring impact as another quad laser blast found its mark.

"Shields are gone," Nyo cried out in alarm. "And the hyperdrive's been damaged."

The gambler quietly brought the *Ray* around to face the *Night Raider*. The big Ghtroc freighter hung there in space, waiting, with its big quad lasers brought to bear. The two idle ships looked like gunfighters, each one waiting for the other to draw. . . .

Yarrku's voice broke the silence. "Your shields are gone. Another hit from my weapons and you'll be nothing but debris. Do the sensible thing and hand over the money. Before it's too late."

"So we give you the credits and you'll leave us alone?" Vo-Shay asked.

"You have my word."

He's lying.

Vo-Shay and Nyo spoke at the same time. "I know." The two men exchanged a quick look, though Nyo seemed more than a bit bewildered.

The gambler keyed the comlink. "Deal. I'll put the credit chip in a probe and launch it over."

"Minimal contact, minimal need for trust. Yes, that would be satisfactory. However, any tricks and I'll blow you to microns."

Vo-Shay shut off the comlink and reached for the controls.

"We're not really going to give it to him, are we?" asked a flustered Nyo.

The gambler grinned. "Oh, we're going to give it to him, all right."

Three of the small forward pods on the Ray slid away to reveal darkened launch tubes.

"All yours," Vo-Shay said over the comm as he punched the control panel.

A trio of proton torpedoes simultaneously screamed out of the *Ray*'s tubes, streaking toward the *Night Raider*.

In response, the Ghtroc opened up with both quad lasers.

Nyo shut his eyes.

The quad laser bolts reached the *Ray*, and impacted . . . against the ship's shields.

"Nooo!" That was the final transmission from the *Night Raider*, before the torpedoes converged and turned the ship into a giant, blossoming fireball.

The young man slowly looked around, utterly amazed to be alive.

Vo-Shay flashed a grin.

"But . . . our shields were gone," Nyo said in disbelief.

"One of the miracles of Mon Cal engineering, son. Redundant shield systems. Of course, half-witted opponents don't hurt, either." The gambler took the controls and engaged the sublight engines. "Nar Shaddaa, here we come. . . ."

"I don't have it," the dealer said. "How many other ways can I say it?"

"What do you mean you don't have it?" Nyo repeated for the fourth time.

Vo-Shay arched an eyebrow, leaning on the counter. "I think my associate is just curious as to the reason why you no longer have the lightsaber."

The chubby businessman grinned, bearing diamond-white teeth. "Because I already sold it."

"But I put down a deposit so you wouldn't."

"What can I say?" the man said simply. "A better offer came along."

Nyo looked just about ready to kill the fat merchant. Vo-Shay was suddenly glad the kid was unarmed.

"Well, who did you sell it to?" the young man demanded.

"Sorry. That's privileged information."

Nyo swept a hand across the bare warehouse that served as the dealer's shop. It was currently empty except for the three of them. "There's no one else here. Maybe I can cut a deal with the buyer. I swear I won't say a word."

"It's not going to be to hard to figure out who gave you the information." The dealer shook his head. "Can't do it. Now, if there's something else you'd be interested in . . ."

Nyo seemed to be on the brink of exploding at the man, but thought better of it. He spun around and stormed out of the shop. The gambler shrugged and followed him out.

"Sorry, kid," Vo-Shay said as they boarded the *Ray*. He squeezed Nyo's shoulder. "The galaxy can be a cruel place sometimes."

"I know," the young man said softly, "it's just that I wanted that saber so much."

"Well, you never know—" The gambler's voice abruptly trailed off as he saw the flashing light on the display.

"What is it?"

"A message . . ." Vo-Shay tapped the control.

A holo-recording crackled into the air, taking the shape of a certain Herglic gambler.

"Doune." The word tumbled from the gambler's lips like a curse.

"Greetings, farmboy. And to you as well, O legendary one. It seems as though the attempt to recoup my losses failed miserably. Ah, well . . . life can be surprising, can it not?" The Herglic held up a long, silver haft and smiled.

Nyo's eyes had grown to the size of thermal detonators threatening to explode.

"As I'm sure you've guessed by now, it was I who purchased this elegant little weapon you so craved. And

I would not be loathe to part with it—under certain circumstances."

"Come on, get to the point, you bloated bag of wind," Vo-Shay mumbled.

"What I am proposing is simple. One last hand of sabacc between myself and Vo-Shay. If the gambler wins, you can have the lightsaber. If I win, I get the source of the gambler's uncanny luck—the obsidian necklace. If you accept, meet me at the Nygann Cantina three hours from now. . . ." The holographic image faded.

Nyo and Vo-Shay exchanged a look.

"You've done so much for me already," the young man began. "I would never ask you to do this—especially if it means you could lose your necklace."

"I won't. Lose, that is . . ." The gambler grinned. "Besides, I told you . . . I never could resist a challenge."

Doune and Vo-Shay faced off once again, this time in a private gambling room at the back of the cantina. The only other beings present were the dealer droid, Nyo and Doune's droid, Vee-Six.

"One last hand decides it all, correct?" asked the Herglic.

The gambler nodded slowly, never taking his eyes off his opponent.

The dealer droid sent five sabacc cards to each player, then obediently waited for the two men to look over the hands they'd been dealt.

"Sabacc!" With a thunderous laugh, the Herglic abruptly shoved his cards into the interference field and glowered in triumph. "Beat that?"

Nyo paled as he glanced at Vo-Shay, who was nervously twirling his pendant.

The gambler looked up from his cards and slowly inserted them into the field. First was the Idiot card. Then came the Two of Sabers. A three of any suit would give Vo-Shay an Idiot's Array.

And a winning hand.

The Herglic took in a sharp breath, his skin mottling furiously. . . .

The gambler fingered one of his remaining cards, then slipped it into the field. For a moment, his hand covered the surface, then finally moved clear.

The Five of Staves. For a total of eight.

Vo-Shay had lost.

Nyo blinked once, then his mouth fell open. He tried to meet the gambler's eyes, but Vo-Shay had turned away as if he had found something incredibly interesting on the floor.

The Herglic roared his approval and then extended a flipper. "I believe you have something that now belongs to me. . . ."

Vo-Shay carefully slipped the obsidian pendant from his neck and handed it over without a word.

Ecstatic, the Herglic snatched it up. "So, the unbeatable one has fallen at last. With this, I will be unstoppable." He grinned at Nyo. "Congratulations, boy . . . you have just witnessed the death of an old legend and the birth of a new one." Doune got to his feet and started for the door, Vee-Six trailing behind him. The Herglic paused at the door, and almost as an afterthought, tossed the lightsaber onto the table. The weapon scattered the sabacc cards. "Here! It's not as though I need it. . . ." With a final terrible chuckle, the Herglic and his droid left.

Nyo stared first at the saber, then at Vo-Shay. "I . . . I don't know what to say. . . ."

The gambler looked up, brandishing a wide smile. "Well, you could start with 'thank you.' " He flipped over one of the sabacc cards he hadn't played. . . .

The Three of Sabers.

The young man was stunned. "You had the Idiot's Array! You won!" Then it hit him. "But why didn't you play it?"

"First of all, considering how badly Doune reacted to

my winning his money in the first place, do you really think he would have let us just waltz out of here with the lightsaber even if I did win it fair and square? Plus, I counted at least a half-dozen mercs nursing glasses of lum on our way in here. My guess is that all they were waiting for was Doune's order."

"I see your point, I guess. But you didn't have to sacrifice your pendant!"

"Listen, kid . . . that particular bauble was given to me a long time ago by a tenacious old girlfriend who wanted more of a relationship than I was ready for at the time. This girl refused to give up, no matter what I said or did. The only reason I considered it lucky was because the day she gave it to me, we finally broke up. I kept the thing and discovered that when I played with it during a game, it did a wonderful job of distracting my opponents. So you see, it really has no mystical power. I make my own luck. As do we all. . . ."

A smile crept onto Nyo's lips. "Doune's in for quite a surprise, then."

"Exactly why we should get going," Vo-Shay said, tossing him the lightsaber.

Nyo caught it easily and couldn't believe he was holding the one thing he had dreamed about for so long. He turned the haft over in his hands, caressing the smooth lines and imagining himself swinging that beautiful bright blade through a graceful arc. . . .

Vo-Shay abruptly reached back inside the room and yanked the starstruck young man after him.

Nyo awoke to a soft, humming sound. It varied in pitch almost constantly, and for a moment, he thought some sort of insect had crawled into his head during his nap. He was momentarily disoriented, but slowly recalled being on the *Ashanda Ray*, headed away from Nar Shaddaa.

Far away.

Then he saw the odd glow reflected on the ship's bulkhead. Quietly making his way back to the passenger compartment, Nyo peeked around the corner.

Vo-Shay stood in the *Ray*'s lounging area, deftly swinging the bright orange energy blade through a series of amazing thrusts and parries. After a few moments, the gambler sensed he was being watched and powered down the saber. He turned to Nyo, extending the weapon handle-first to the young man. "I hope you don't mind. I just couldn't resist."

"How do you know how to do that?" Nyo demanded. Then the young man suddenly grinned. "And can you teach me?"

The gambler plopped down onto one of the lounge chairs. "I guess I still owe you my story, right?"

The young man nodded, taking the seat opposite Vo-Shay's.

"Well, the legends surrounding my disappearance were correct. The *Ray* was indeed caught in the Tyus cluster, and at the center of that mass of ugly black holes, time was nonexistent. Many others had been trapped there before me, though none had survived. Except for one . . . a Jedi Master. She helped me escape, and even taught me a little about the Force."

"That's a pretty short summary. . . ."

"I'll save the whole story for another day," Vo-Shay said dismissively. "After all, we'll have plenty of time together when you sign on as my first mate."

"Do you mean it?"

"I never say what I don't mean, kid. Welcome aboard."

"So, you'll teach me about the Force?"

"Me? No . . . I'll teach you how not to lose everything to a Herglic at the sabacc table. *She'll* instruct you in the mysterious ways of the Force."

Nyo looked around, not understanding, until a shimmering blue figure appeared next to Vo-Shay. Even dressed in simple robes, the woman's beauty was not lost.

"This is Aryzah," Vo-Shay said by way of introduction, "the lovely Jedi Master who saved my life."

Greetings, Nyo. May the Force be with you.

"And just between the two of us, kid," Vo-Shay said with a wink, "you're gonna need it."

Simple Tricks

by Chris Cassidy and Tish Pahl

"Well, Cap'n," the port mechanic drawled, running a filthy rag between his blackened hands. "You've done quite a number on your ship here."

"I didn't do anything to my ship!" Fen Nabon barked. "A power flux ripped us out of hyperspace! It fried the drive, cooked the backup, and melted the stabilizers and motivator on its way out!"

Fen knew she should have patched the hyperdrive together with spit and engine tape and coaxed the *Star Lady* into Nad'Ris City, Prishardia's planetary capital. But the planet guide glibly guaranteed a "standard-class starport with all amenities" in Lesvol, Prishardia's second-largest city. On landing in the agricultural backwater, Fen realized she was more likely to find the promised "excellent accommodations and dining opportunities" in the molten core of Hoth.

The pasture of some smelly, indeterminate ruminant ringed the spaceport. More ominous, Fen noted, were the rusted swoops and ancient, gutted freighters which littered the cramped landing pad. She doubted anything in the port had operated under its own power in the last sixteen years. And the greaseball now droning on was likely personally responsible for the disrepair.

"Gibb," as the name stitched on his coveralls proclaimed him, paused to spit expressively onto the baked dirt, wisely missing the *Lady*'s extended ramp, then withdrew a datapad from a grimy pocket. "This is the inventory of replacement drives we can get, from here or from Nad'Ris."

As she reviewed the meager list, Fen realized why she had to pry the pad out of Gibb's shaking hands. There was a very old, very overpriced Horizon-Hopper. The SoroSuub would entail a repair even Fen wouldn't attempt. Several new Lifesaver 1000s were also handy, death wish included free of charge. There wasn't even a quick-and-dirty substitute that was safe enough and cheap enough to get her to a decent shipyard.

The bulge in the little man's throat rose and fell. "We don't have anything else," he choked.

Fen shoved the pad back at him. Space, there wasn't even anything worth stealing. "How long?" she growled.

"We can order an Avatar," Gibb stammered.

"How long?" Fen repeated, a little closer and a lot louder.

"Corellia is a long way, even at . . ."

"How long?" Fen was so close she could smell the chew that hung on him.

Gibb whispered, "A month, maybe two."

"One month," Fen ordered.

"Yes, Cap'n," Gibb squeaked before rushing off.

"Fen, you should teach diplomacy," a cultured voice scolded. Ghitsa Dogder emerged from the shadows of the *Star Lady*'s ramp.

"I didn't hear you offering to help," Fen retorted.

"Why would you need a con artist when your intimidation and yelling were so very effective?" Brandishing a datapad, Ghitsa continued. "I decided to read about our temporary home instead."

"The rube who wrote that backgrounder is a dead man," Fen gritted. "I'm gonna get a drink in the ship. You coming?"

"No, I think I will investigate for a little while."

Fen shrugged and headed up the *Lady*'s ramp. At the hatch she turned back to say something, but her partner had already disappeared into the decaying spaceport building.

Ghitsa's ambiguous statement set off a muted alarm in Fen's head. It wasn't as if she was worried about her partner's safety. Even in an unfamiliar place the con always took care of herself. No, the real big worry was that Ghitsa's sharp eye had probably spied something in the backgrounder on Lesvol. Something Fen missed.

"Sith," Fen muttered, scraping some of the pasture from her boot tread. Digging her fists into her pockets, she went in search of the bottle of Corellian Reserve she kept for really bad days. Whatever the crisis, Corellia had the cure.

Fen was into her third drink, cursing fates and the universe, when her partner finally returned carrying a fist-sized, bright orange fruit.

As Ghitsa set it down on the table, Fen eyed the fruit suspiciously. There were several explanations, each worse than the last. "I don't suppose you picked that up for a snack?"

"Of course not, Fen," Ghitsa sniffed haughtily.

"That's right. You haven't had a nonliquid meal since the Battle of Endor," Fen called as Ghitsa retreated toward her cabin. Against her better judgment, Fen climbed slowly to her feet and followed.

"Ghits, what are you up to?" Fen asked as she leaned against the open hatch to Ghitsa's quarters, nursing her drink.

"Just a way to pass the time and refresh the coffers while we wait for your beloved Corellian parts," came the muffled reply. Only Ghitsa's hindquarters, sticking out from a stowage closet, were visible. Fen had to resist the urge to administer a swift kick.

Ghitsa emerged a moment later, shaking out her prize.

Fen felt her jaw drop. "No," she said sternly.

Ghitsa responded by pulling on the simple robe.

"You must be joking!"

"Fen, you know I have no sense of humor." A metal cylindrical handle appeared from the robe's deep pocket. Ghitsa experimentally flicked the switch on and off. Nothing happened, of course.

Ghitsa pushed past her partner, headed for the main cabin. Fen once again trailed behind her.

"I'm surprised that after all these years you haven't been able to con a real one from someone," Fen mumbled.

Ghitsa was suddenly quite serious. "Given what we've heard recently about the Jedi Academy from the Fringe, I would not be surprised to see lightsabers showing up on the black market." Ghitsa stared at her, waiting, expectantly.

Fen hedged. "What?"

"You know what," Ghitsa said impatiently. "That rigged sabacc deck and the repulsor remote. Where are they?"

It was hopeless. Settling back into her seat with a resigned sigh, Fen said, "They're in the weapons closet, third shelf, in the back."

"How quaint," Ghitsa cooed, returning with Fen's lockbox. She set it on the table and sat across from Fen, helping herself to a glass of the Reserve. In the time it took Fen to pour herself another, Ghitsa had jimmied the box open.

"This is a really bad idea," Fen finally said.

Ghitsa picked up the fruit on the table and began drilling a delicate hole in it with her pocketknife. "I confirmed what was in the backgrounder. There are thousands of people in Lesvol and the only legal authority is more than two thousand kilometers away. It's chaos out there. I'd be providing them an invaluable service."

"For target practice," Fen grumbled. "Don't you remember what happened last time?"

Ghitsa nodded, but continued her carving.

"Can I just point out that the *Lady* is out of commission? We don't have any way of getting out of here once they figure out you're a fraud."

"We shall just have to make sure they don't figure it out then, won't we?"

Fen swirled the golden liquor in her glass, admiring the way the contents clung to the sides before surrendering to gravity. "I'm not helping you this time," she declared, knowing her resistance was as futile as her drink's, but still feeling the need to make a token stand.

From across the table, Ghitsa handed her the remote's tiny control. "Of course you will."

Fen developed hate relationships with many places in the galaxy. She loathed Socorro during the hot season, detested Mos Eisley during the dusty season, and her irritation with the exhorbitant prices of Coruscant during Fete Week was a matter of public record. But Lesvol on market day earned a whole new level of disdain.

With a deep breath Fen plunged into the throng of peasants and animals crowding the market square. Squeezing between an oversized vegetable cart and a booth of wheel-sized cheeses, Fen then swerved to avoid a shaggy something smelling vaguely of nerf. When a gap-toothed woman in shapeless black thrust a squawking bird in her face, Fen almost cooked both poultry and purveyor with a blaster bolt.

In contrast to Fen's mad dashing and darting through the market, Ghitsa's progress ahead was unhurried. Crowds and livestock magically parted for the woman in the brown robe. She walked serenely, the lightsaber handle swinging freely and conspicuously at her side. They were in the market barely ten minutes when Fen began hearing the whispered word of awe and respect: "Jedi."

Fen circled around, seeing Ghitsa find her target. Two quarreling men, one as short as the other was fat, had attracted a crowd. Words and spittle flew, with fists sure to follow, to the smaller man's disadvantage. A groat stood between them, oblivious, complacently chewing her cud.

"Friends," Fen heard Ghitsa say. "May I assist you?"

A hush fell as all eyes turned to the Jedi woman. "Who are you?" the larger man demanded.

"Jedi!" someone called from the back.

"Don't look like no Jedi," the man snarled.

Ghitsa smiled patiently. "Size and sex are not the measure of a Jedi, friend." She gestured to a nearby fruit stand. "I do not approve of casual use of the Force," her voice rang out. "But the gentleman here requests some verification."

Ghitsa held out her right hand. Her left, Fen knew, concealed a tiny remote which controlled the repulsor. A bright orange fruit rose from atop the mounded produce display, circled above the stunned crowd, then fell into Ghitsa's waiting palm.

She gathered the growing crowd with her eyes and authoritative presence. "I ask again, do you require the assistance of a Jedi?"

"I ask for Jedi mediation," the small man stammered, with a feisty glare at his combatant. "Baxendahl here sold me a breeding groat, but she's barren."

Fen turned away and began pushing against the throng, shaking her head in disgust. Ghitsa would wield her negotiation skills as others used weapons and push the men to some settlement involving cost of a groat's care, earning potential of a groat's milk, and value between a breeding and a barren groat. The grateful participants would then pay her for the trouble in some local currency or good. By the end of the afternoon, with another piece of floating fruit and a few "I can read your mind" sabacc tricks, the Lesvol community would think Jedi Master Skywalker himself had come to pay a visit. Force forgive her, but Fen didn't want to stay around to watch.

The moment would go down in the annals as one of the best of Fen's life. Twenty-nine days, fourteen hours, and twenty-seven minutes after a power flux forced her into the Maker-forsaken Lesvol, the brand-spanking-new Corellian Avatar-10 hyperdrive finally arrived.

"Cap'n, she's a beauty."

"That she is, Gibb." Fen sighed happily and gazed adoringly at the glistening drive, the stabilizers, the motivator, and the converters, spread out carefully and ordered. "I just wish we found the cause of that flux."

Gibb's small shoulders shrugged in his oversized uniform. "I've seen it on old YTs before, especially the ones with so many custom features and special modifications. At least you know you won't blow the Avatar when you put it in."

A month's close observation revealed that Gibb was a pretty fair mechanic. Fen hadn't asked, nor had Gibb explained, where he became so well acquainted with old-model starfighters and Corellian freighters. Everyone had a past and the secrets that go with it.

Gibb was right, though; these things did sometimes happen and the best you could hope for was that they don't kill you when they did.

Fen bent down, picked up a rock, and pitched it at a groat wandering too close to her new hyperdrive. With a frightened bleat the animal bolted across the landing pad.

"Jedi Ghitsa doesn't like it when you do that to her pets," Gibb warned, glancing about nervously.

"Well, she can just use her powers to stop me," Fen

groused. With her busy social and negotiation schedule, Ghitsa wasn't there, but that didn't stop even the sensible Gibb from worrying what the All-Knowing Jedi would see. The whole con was going to Ghitsa's head and really getting to Fen. Apart from Ghitsa's solemn pontifications, the spaceport and ship filled with farm animals, sickly fruit wines, and other homegrown products—all gifts that grateful but very poor clients gave their revered, dealmaker Jedi.

"I'm gonna pull the readings off the old drive," Fen said, pulling her favorite scanner from her back pocket.

Gibb nodded. "I'll finish prepping the ship." He disappeared into the *Lady*, the tools on his belt clanking noisily.

They wrestled the old drive out of the ship and set it on the grass next to the landing pad. With a few well-aimed rocks, Fen scattered the birds—more gifts to Jedi Ghitsa—that had taken to roosting on the drive.

Squatting down, Fen gently turned the first section over and clicked on the scanner. She dusted off bits of blackened char between the two and three couplings, then continued down the drive shaft. And stopped.

Fen thumbed the scanner off and rocked back on her heels. The good news was that she had just found, buried in the most inaccessible part of the drive, what had caused the power flux. The bad news . . .

The timid, "Uh, excuse me," so startled Fen that she reflexively hurled the nearest spanner in the direction of the voice.

Fen scrambled to her feet. The uninvited visitor hit the ground to avoid swallowing her thrown tool. "Ever heard of knocking?" she snapped. As he stood slowly, Fen took in the simple brown robe he wore and the untouched metal handle at his waist.

"Where?" He shrugged and looked about expressively. They were, after all, outside, on a spaceport landing pad.

Fen checked the grin. "Right . . ." *They sure started*

them young at Skywalker's ranch, Fen mused. *This one couldn't be a day over twenty.* But then, wild rumors about the Jedi Academy had been flying for months in the Fringe. *Could this soft-faced, shaggy-haired youth really be a fully trained Jedi Knight? By all accounts, probably. And she could just guess what brought a Jedi Knight to the wilds of Lesvol.*

"Well, well," she said with a low whistle. "Could it be one of the ascetic Luke Skywalker's little followers in the flesh?"

He straightened with her challenge but stumbled over the words. "Yes, I'm from Master Skywalker's Academy. I'm Zeth Fost."

"Fenig Nabon. You can call me Fen." Another matter demanded her attention, one even more urgent than exploring what a real Jedi was doing here and what she was going to do about it. Fen crouched down again at the drive.

"I don't suppose the Force can tell you what these char marks between the couplings mean?"

Zeth squatted next to her. "It doesn't really work like that."

"Too bad." Fen pulled a magnifier from her front pocket and began crawling up the length of the drive shaft. There. Between the eighth and ninth couplings.

"What is it?" a soft voice asked, too close to her ear. She almost slugged him, just out of reflex.

"Here," she said and handed him the magnifier.

"It looks like a . . . wire?"

"It's an old saboteur's trick. You create a complete circuit by connecting the couplings of a hyperdrive. A piece of wire as thin as a hair will do the job. Then send a spark up the drive shaft and it'll arc, from one coupling to the next. Fry the entire system." She waved at the drive's far end. "Somewhere in there I'll find the remains of a relay or battery that generated the power surge."

Zeth cleared his throat. "Do you know why?"

Fen slowly stood. "Yeah. Probably. Someone's likely gunning for my partner, Ghitsa Dogder."

There was a sharp but not very surprising intake of breath. "She's why I've come," Zeth said quickly, rising as well. "We've heard she is a very powerful Jedi and is doing much good here."

"Well, she's got a lot of enemies, too."

Fen was very proud she did not choke when Zeth intoned, "Those who do good things often have many enemies." His young face turned somber. "And those with untrained Force powers can be manipulated. Where is she?" he asked, now sounding more urgent.

As soon as he meets Ghits, the gig will be up, Fen thought. *That alone would be worth the admission price.* "I don't know," she finally said, making her decision. "She had a negotiation today. But Gibb will know where she is."

"Why didn't you catch a shuttle?" Fen complained from the passenger seat of Zeth's rented landspeeder.

"I didn't know where to go," Zeth responded. His eyes wandered about the bucolic landscape. "Everyone within a thousand kilometers was talking about the wonderful Jedi Ghitsa, but no one knew where she was."

Fen drummed her fingers on the console. They had sabotaged the ship on Chad, known her route, and set the drive to blow in the first inhabited system. But who? And why?

"A Force-sensitive would be a very powerful asset to a criminal organization," Zeth interrupted.

"Stay out of my head, spoonbender," Fen snapped.

"I wasn't in your head, Fen," Zeth said calmly. "Just making an obvious observation."

"Keep it that way, then." Wanting to be conciliatory, but not apologetic, Fen added, "Lots of bad guys seem real determined to kidnap you Jedi types."

Fen hadn't expected Zeth to flinch so obviously. "What is it?" she asked.

He shook his head. "Nothing."

"Turn right up ahead," she instructed. He drove through a battered and ancient gate and they both fell silent.

Feeling the speeder steadily accelerate, Fen glanced at Zeth. He was staring ahead. She gave up trying to shake the anxiety mounting since they drove on to the property.

They rounded a blind turn and the farmhouse was only a few meters farther. Fen was out of the speeder before Zeth coaxed it to a stop. It wasn't just the look of grim concern on his face or the silence which alarmed her. No, it was the clenching feeling in her gut. She'd felt the same way when she'd returned to that Ord Mantell cantina and found the man who had been her father dead on the floor.

She yanked out her blaster and ran to the farmhouse. The door was open, ajar and askew. At the door's threshold lay a Jedi robe.

"I'm assuming it's someone from off-planet," Fen jabbered as they whizzed back through Lesvol. "I wonder why it took them so long?"

"They may have thought once your drive failed you would go to Nad'Ris," Zeth said. "And when you didn't, they looked the same way I did. A planet is a big place to search for a single person."

As the speeder banked hard on a turn, Fen was gratified Zeth was driving only slightly slower than she would be. "Gibb is checking for reports of any strangers. He may know something by the time we get back."

"What's next then?" the Jedi asked.

"Listen, Zeth," Fen began. "I appreciate the help, but I can handle this on my own."

When Zeth smiled, years seem to fall from him. "Jedi have a responsibility to Force-sensitives, especially those like Ghitsa who have a real gift others would exploit." His expression darkened abruptly. "It's hard to explain, but the Force guided me here. I'd like to see it through."

"Well, who am I to argue with cosmic fate and destiny?" Fen grumbled.

Gibb ran out to meet them when they pulled up at the port. Ignoring Zeth's reprimanding frown, Fen again clambered out before he stopped the speeder. "What've you found, Gibb?" she asked, forcing calm into her voice as they jogged to the port building.

"Not much, Cap'n. I got a couple reports of a skiff going really fast toward Nad'Ris."

She and Gibb pushed into the tiny port administration building. "How long ago?"

Fen grabbed a chair, but in hands not quite still it slipped from her grasp and clattered to the floor. Gibb waited until she righted it before responding. "Couple of hours."

Zeth's voice came from the door. "Why did they notice the skiff at all?"

Gibb eyed the Jedi, as if weighing where his loyalties lay. "It was big, new, fast. Nothing like that around here."

Fen cracked her knuckles and smirked inwardly when Zeth winced at the sound. "Okay, Gibb, I need to slice into the Nad'Ris spaceport records. I'm looking for the incoming ship registry."

The mechanic blanched, looking from Fen to Zeth and back again. "But Captain . . ." he stammered.

"Now Gibb," she began, popping her finger joints one at a time. "Just 'cause a self-appointed guardian of good is watching is no time to get all moral on me. The only way to figure out where Ghitsa's gone is to look at where they probably took her, got it?"

Gibb nodded reluctantly, still eyeing the Jedi skeptically. Zeth winked and held out his hands in a "Who am I to argue?" gesture.

Fen scooted up to the data console. After several minutes of work she spun back around with a growl. "Gibb, why do you keep fidgeting?"

"Well, Captain. That will work eventually, but . . ." Gibb glanced at Zeth, face creased with worry. "I know a quicker way."

Zeth laughed. "Don't worry, Gibb. I won't tell."

Gibb wilted with relief. Thirty seconds later they were scrolling through the Nad'Ris port entries.

"I need to see the ship names," Zeth announced suddenly, crowding them at the terminal.

Throwing Zeth an annoyed look and an elbow in the ribs, Fen shot back, "And I need to see what flight plans and cargo they registered."

Gibb keyed a command and three columns of information appeared. Fen began anxiously searching.

"There!" Zeth suddenly exulted.

He shrank back as Fen pinned him with a favored glare from her extensive repertory. "And why do you think so?"

"Just the name, *Rook*," Zeth hedged. "I have a feeling about it."

"A feeling? Sorry, Jedi, but we need something solid." Fen turned back to study the screen. "I don't suppose your feeling noticed the *Rook* arrived the day after I did, registered a flight plan from Chad and Nal Hutta, and made no customs declaration, even though a ship that class has over two thousand metric tons of cargo space?"

"Cap'n," Gibb said, new worry coloring his tone. "See that blinking indicator? The *Rook* filed clearance to leave."

Fen felt cold dread settle in her stomach like the local brew. "How long?"

"An hour, maybe two."

Zeth moved in closer, studying the flashing light. "It'll take us all night to get back to Nad'Ris, unless you've got something faster than my speeder."

There wasn't anything else. They all knew that. The *Lady*'s drive was still in pieces. Nothing in the port could run, much less fly. Fen began working furiously on the console's keypad. "If you've got any tricks, I could use 'em," she said to Zeth.

"I told you, it doesn't work that way."

Why was a hermetic Force zealot barely out of his teens so gloomy? Fen pushed aside the thoughts clouding her rapid-fire keystrokes.

"Well, good thing I've got a few tricks," she said.

Behind her she heard Gibb's low chortle. "That'll keep them here into the next growing season, Cap'n."

Fen pushed out of her seat. Seeing Zeth grinning at her handiwork on the terminal, she felt the satisfaction of being able to impress a Jedi.

She tugged on Zeth's arm. "Come on. Let's move."

Songs of lovers lost or left behind and the intoxicants consumed to forget them were woven into the fabric of every culture built around spacefaring and alcohol production. Corellia had a million such madrigals; Fen knew half of them, and had lived the other half. When she'd been a small, dirty-faced child, singing the off-color lyrics in a busy spaceport was a sure way to earn a few extra credits or even a hot meal. Now, thirty-some years later, she sang them when she was nervous, excited, or drunk.

Fen dashed about the *Lady*'s main cabin gathering her gear. "Best I can hope for is a long life and a merry one. A quick death and an easy one." Singing slightly off-key, she snapped the last drawer closed.

Zeth stood patiently, saying nothing as Fen added two more detonators to the pile on the table in front of him.

"A fast ship and a sturdy one," Fen sang with more gusto about the ship than the easy death. She began methodically tucking the toys and gadgets into her flightsuit pockets. "A tall ale and another one," she finished with a flourish.

Fen dropped a vibro-shiv into each boot and added

her lucky hold-out blaster to yet another pocket at her sleeve. With a satisfied sigh she began checking the settings on her heavy blaster.

Zeth ran a hand over his mouth to keep from smirking. He then removed his belt, placed it on the table, and shrugged out of his Jedi robe. Balling it up, he tossed the robe into the corner. He again donned his belt, unclipped the lightsaber hanging there, and slipped it into a pocket at his side. "Well?" he finally asked. "Do I pass?"

"Take that earnest expression off your face and it just might work."

The smile finally broke out, and he glanced away to hide it.

"You have a sidearm?" Fen asked, circling around him for a more thorough inspection.

"I don't need one."

"Wait. Don't tell me. The Force will protect you."

"Actually, I figured you were carrying enough firepower to defend me and Coruscant." When the only reply was Fen's evil eye, Zeth amended; "I have my lightsaber . . . and the Force."

"This is my Force power. It's called a blaster." She sent the weapon in its home at her hip. "Let's go."

Fen was usually about as communicative as a Gamorrean. But charging along a dark thoroughfare to rescue someone who didn't deserve saving seemed to inspire confidences. So as she slammed down bottle after bottle of a carbonated, highly charged drink, appropriately dubbed Rush, the words tumbled out of her with a speed rivaling that of their headlong race into the night.

She told Zeth about her youth on the streets of Coronet and even a little bit about Jett.

Zeth's tale, like hers, began haltingly, then flowed. On learning he had been on Kessel, they spent the past hour trading Moruth Doole stories.

"So, anyway," Zeth said, taking another long pull on

his bottle. "I never would have gotten off Kessel if Han hadn't shown up."

"Solo?" Fen choked back a swallow of her Rush.

"Yeah," Zeth waited a beat before adding, "You know him."

"Stay outta my mind, Jedi," she warned.

"I wasn't in it," he shot back. "But I can't help it if you broadcast your feelings like an emotional holovid."

"Guess I'll just have to think quieter around you, won't I?" Fen clamped her mouth shut.

"You have deep feelings and strong loyalties," Zeth pontificated. "Why do you try hiding them?" Not put off by her stony silence, he pushed, "Because if you don't, then why are we going after Ghitsa, anyway? Space, you don't even like her."

"Because she's my partner, that's why," Fen finally burst out. "And no one harms any partner of mine. Except me."

"Did someone harm Jett?" Zeth asked gently.

Fen laughed, short and bitter. "If you call a vibro-shiv through the neck harm, then I guess so."

"I'm sorry, Fen," he said softly.

She wanted to hold on to the anger, as she would a blaster or a lover. But instead, with Zeth's unsolicited and compassionate sincerity, she felt the hurt drain away without the energy to maintain it. "Thanks," she said and sarcasm was the best she could muster. "That's mighty Jedi of you."

Fen looked quickly enough to see Zeth smile.

"So from where does this disdain for Jedi spring?" he asked. "Your denigration approaches an art form."

"Oh, I don't know," Fen replied, matching his lighter tone. "I just have a problem with authority and earnest self-righteousness."

"No Sith," Zeth retorted.

"Watch your mouth, junior. That kind of language could get you in trouble."

Zeth laughed. "You're right. If I go back swearing like a smuggler, they'll never let me out again."

Fen smirked in spite of herself. "Just tell them you learned it all from a great master."

His laughter abruptly stopped. Zeth turned away to stare moodily into the darkness.

They rode in silence as Fen tried to work out what she had said to provoke Zeth's capricious reaction. Giving up, she tried the blunt approach. "So, as long as we're spilling our souls all over the deck here, what's this bantha on your back? Did you drop a rock on another spoonbender or something?"

Zeth remained mute, as if weighing what to tell her. His voice was distant and sorrowful when he finally spoke. "I used my power as a Jedi . . . for revenge."

Fen glanced at Zeth. He was staring down at his upturned palms as if they were somehow dirty. She tore her eyes from the sight to concentrate again on the road. Vengeance was something she could certainly understand, but Fen suddenly didn't want to hear any more of this young man's tortured story. Before she could say anything, Zeth continued.

"In my arrogance I thought the ends justified the means." Zeth's voice dropped to a whisper. "My brother and many others paid the price for my fall to the dark side."

Fen gasped as the pieces began to fall into place. The wild rumors she had heard, the things he had said. When the answer finally popped into her consciousness, she'd never be sure if she deduced it herself or if he had planted it there. "Carida," she breathed. Millions dead, billions, an entire star system wiped out of existence.

She swerved the speeder to the side, slamming on the brakes as her mind screamed again. *Carida!* Aghast, she turned to see the Jedi staring out the window, fighting the tears clinging to his lashes. He nodded ever so slightly.

She was sharing a landspeeder, her life, with the most notorious mass murderer since Palpatine. This innocent looking man, this kid, was another Vader. A butcher. *He killed billions.*

Suddenly claustrophobic in the close speeder, Fen fumbled for an escape. A cool breeze flooded in as she shoved the hatch open. Fen staggered across the road, feeling the universe buckle under her feet. *Billions dead.* And she liked him. That was the worst of it. She had fallen completely for his wide-eyed innocence, the shy smile.

The incongruity hit her like a nova. She lost the battle to control her spiraling emotions and the waves of nausea splashing over her. Falling to her knees, Fen emptied her stomach into the soft, tilled field.

The universe had just stopped spinning when she heard him come up behind her. Fen struggled to her feet.

"So, you're Sithin' Durron?" she demanded. "Kyp Durron?"

"Yes."

"You lied to me." Fen straightened up and shoved her hands into her pockets, staring down at her feet. She needed new boots, she noted, then mentally kicked herself for allowing such a thought now.

"Yes," Kyp responded after a long pause.

"They have a word for what you did. It's called genocide."

"I know," Kyp replied, his voice breaking slightly.

Fen spun around, blind wrath overcoming self-preservation. She poked her index finger in the center of his chest. "Then tell me, Jedi," she choked on the word. "How come you're allowed to roam the galaxy recruiting others, recruiting my partner, to follow in your footsteps?"

Kyp remained silent, shoulders hunched, staring at the ground.

"Why aren't you in jail?" she demanded. Giving him another, much harder shove, she shrieked, "Why weren't you executed?"

He fell to the ground in an unresisting heap. "I don't know," Kyp said, his voice ragged. "I should be. I should be dead."

Fen went for the reassurance of her blaster, bitterly cold to the touch. She raised it, taking aim at the filth before her. She had killed better than this before and for less than crimes against the galaxy.

He finally looked up at her, and she could see tears glistening on his face. "No one would ever blame you, Fen, for killing the murderer of billions of sentients."

Fen felt an itching in her fingers. *He wants me to kill him,* she abruptly realized.

Please, Fen, came the wail in her mind. He outstretched his hands to her.

Fen was moved, but not to pity. "You're a real black-hearted coward, Jedi," she snarled, thrusting the blaster back in her holster. "Trying to get me to do something you don't have the courage to do yourself."

She hauled him to his feet. "Listen, you Sith Lord." She forced as much venom into the invective as she could and had the pleasure of seeing him wince at an epithet that was no longer amusing. Fen vowed she would never use the curse again. "I don't give ten credits whether you live or die. I'd gladly cut you down and rid the universe of your miserable existence." She roughly grabbed him by the elbow, propelling him to the speeder. "But not until after we get my partner out. Got it?"

"And I'm telling you again," Ghitsa responded patiently. "I've never heard of this before."

Culan Brasli's blow knocked her out of the chair. Bound at the hands and ankles, Ghitsa managed to twist her body so only muscle met the unyielding ship deck.

"That's not what we hear, Counselor," Brasli sneered.

Ghitsa had been beaten many times before. It was an occupational hazard working for the Hutts. On a scale of one to ten, Brasli's efforts were about an eight, maximizing pain while minimizing long-term damage. *A true artisan.* She curled up into a ball, making a smaller target for the inevitable kick. Brasli really put his weight into it as his heavy foot slammed into her, again and again. . . .

Dawn was less than an hour away. Fen followed the speeder's map through Nad'Ris to the spaceport and an alley that ran along the back of the port. She maneuvered the speeder down the narrow passage, weaving back and forth between the trash and broken, pitted pavement.

They hadn't exchanged two sentences since Kyp's revelations on the darkened roadway. She eased the speeder into a sheltered alcove and shut it down. When he still didn't say anything, Fen asked, "You coming?"

Kyp hopped out of the speeder but remained mute.

The back port wall loomed above them, slimy, dirty and a full five meters high. Scanning up and down the alley, Fen found the hoped-for service entrance. "I'm going to try getting it open," she indicated with a nod. "You stand watch, okay?"

Fen pulled a palm-sized device from a pocket and set it over the door's security lock.

"Is that what I think it is?" Kyp asked.

Fen cocked an eyebrow at his disapproving voice. "If you think it's an Opirus Model FD Sixty-Two security descrambler, then it's exactly what you think it is."

"Aren't those illegal?"

"So's murder," Fen scoffed.

It was several moments before Kyp asked quietly, "Did you murder everyone you thought was responsible for Jett's death?"

Fen almost dropped the descrambler. She could tell where this was going; being on the moral high ground was a rarity she wasn't anxious to give up.

"Did you?" Kyp repeated.

"Yes," she finally said, as slowly as the descrambler was working.

"If more people had been responsible, would you have retaliated against them, too?"

"You killed billions!" Fen burst out. She glanced nervously around, but the alley remained deserted.

"I know," Kyp moaned. "I relive it every day. But given the power and means, wouldn't you have done the same to avenge Jett?"

The answer wasn't nearly as simple as it should have been.

The sound of a slick-as-grease human voice woke her. "Brasli, please seat the Counselor."

Ghitsa craned her neck but got only lancing agony for the trouble. Brasli roughly yanked her up from the deck and shoved her into a chair.

Across a table from her sat a young, well-dressed man. "I apologize for Brasli's enthusiasm." He waved his hand, fingering a datacard between his fingers. Ghitsa noticed a datapad on the table that hadn't been there before. "Untie her, Brasli."

Ghitsa gasped as he loosened the bonds, feeling blood rush to her feet and hands. Although he commanded even Brasli's obedience, the man who gave the unquestioned order was too young and unpolished to have occupied the position very long. His suit indicated more wealth than taste.

"Do your Desilijic Clan masters know your Coruscantan accent is faked?" Ghitsa asked through a split and bleeding lip.

He flushed. "No one mentioned the Desilijics, or indeed the Hutts, at all."

"Brasli and I have met before. And I've been aboard the *Rook* several times." Ghitsa felt a warm trickle and impatiently wiped the blood from her chin. "Admittedly the circumstances were different."

"No doubt during the time your Hutt clan methodically stripped my own."

With his appropriately calm, detached response,

Ghitsa conceded that the Desilijics had not sent some-one completely green for this assignment. She needed more information if she was going to talk her way out of this one. "Counselor, I do not know your name."

He continued flipping the datacard in his fingers as if it were a sabacc card. *A sabacc card,* Ghitsa mused. *He started as a gambler.*

"I am Counselor Ral," he said decisively, sliding the card into the pad on the table. "And now, Counselor Dogder, we will discuss Durga the Hutt's investment in the Orko Consortium."

"I wouldn't have done it," Fen said. She modulated the descrambler again, but it was one year too old and the door was one year too new.

"I know," Kyp replied from where he stood watch. "But you did think about it?"

"Yes." She truly had. In her grief and despair over Jett's murder, Fen acted more violently than at any other time in her life. But still, she wouldn't have gone as far as her Jedi lookout.

"I hate what I did. There are days when I think the guilt will drive me mad," Kyp said, his voice wavering. "It would be easier if I were locked up somewhere."

"Or dead," Fen offered helpfully.

"As you said, that's the coward's way out."

Fen pocketed the descrambler and brushed her hands off on the front of her flight suit. "This isn't going to work. We have to find another way in."

Kyp slumped against the wall, hanging his head mis-erably. His bangs again fell over his eyes. "They didn't lock me away, and I'm not dead." He choked on a dry sob. "What am I supposed to do, Fen?"

"How should I know?" Fen retorted, angry that she actually felt sorry for him. Fen Nabon as judge, moralist, and confessor? If it weren't so comical it would be grotesque. Other priorities were more pressing than a murderer's atonement.

She cleared her throat roughly. "I guess you just make sure it never happens again."

Kyp drew his arms protectively around himself. "What if that's not enough?"

"You do what the rest of us do." She lifted his chin with her forefinger, forcing him to look at her. "The best you can."

"But if I fail . . ." he trailed off.

"I'll hunt you down and kill you myself." Their eyes met, and then Fen tore away from his grateful stare. "Come on. Time for Plan B."

·   ·   ·   ·

"Your sources err," Ghitsa said, with a patience she didn't feel. "I haven't worked for Durga's clan for over three years."

The blast of a voice over a comm at the cabin door startled all of them. "Counselor?" the disembodied and deferential speaker asked.

"I told you not to interrupt us," Ral snapped. Striding to the comm, he adjusted the controls so Ghitsa could not overhear the apparent orders and counterorders.

"I'll be right up," Ral said curtly. He awarded her a dark glare. "It seems that Nad'Ris Customs refuses to lift the quarantine placed on our ship for suspected biological contagions."

"Indeed?" Ghitsa queried blandly, heart leaping. Slicing into the Nad'Ris records to embargo the ship would be classic Fen.

"It is remarkable since the *Rook* declared no cargo," Ral mused. He nodded to Brasli. "Clean her up. Customs will be inspecting the ship. Then lock the good Counselor in here, so she may refresh her recollections undisturbed." She remained impassive under his thoughtful stare, but Ral was as shrewd. "And Brasli, alert your team. We must be ready for any uninvited guests."

·   ·   ·   ·

"We should be within a bay or two of where the *Rook*'s docked," Fen commented. They hid behind a trash heap in the alley. The port's back wall towered above them.

"We're going to have to hurry," Kyp said, turning toward her. His serious countenance suddenly changed, a smirk appearing where solemnity had been. His eyes flickered up to her face.

"What is it?" Fen growled, brushing a loose strand of hair away with her elbow.

"There's something you should know."

"What now?"

"There's a big smudge of dirt on your forehead."

Fen felt her face redden and warm. She wiped her forehead with her glove and saw a large smear of black grease. Groaning, she remembered working on the *Lady*'s drive a lifetime ago. "It's been on there since you met me at the ship, right?"

The smirk was now a full-blown grin. "Uh-huh."

"You could have said something," she accused, still wiping.

"I just did." Kyp raised his hand, touching her temple, "You missed a spot."

Oddly, Fen didn't shudder at his touch. "Is it gone?" she asked, rubbing her face again.

He nodded and turned back to study the wall. "We could climb it."

Fen reached a quick decision. "Kyp, there's something I should tell you."

He glanced at her quizzically. "Do I have food stuck in my teeth?"

"It's about Ghitsa."

"I know already, Fen," Kyp interrupted.

Rage swept through her again. "You were reading my mind!" she accused.

Kyp rolled his eyes. "I didn't need to. I've been searching through the Force since I landed. I would have sensed someone with Ghitsa's reputed skills pretty quickly, especially once she was kidnapped."

"You've known all along?" she stammered. "And you were still gonna help me spring a cheap con who finally got what she had coming to her?"

"I know you don't like to hear it, but the Force guided me here." He took a deep breath. "I think I'm beginning to see why."

Fen digested that fact and finally felt an easier truce settle between them. She scrambled to her feet. "Why don't you try using the Force to throw the rope and grappling hook over the wall?"

Kyp nodded and rose with the rope they brought from the speeder. He swung the hook up in a smooth arc. They heard a gentle clatter. Kyp tested his weight on the line, then clambered up the wall as easily as an insect.

Fen's ascent was not nearly as graceful. She was grunting with the effort when something suddenly scooped her up and deposited her on the top of the wall.

"Easy," Kyp muttered, lending a steadying hand as Fen teetered on the narrow ledge.

To her annoyance, he seemed perfectly balanced five meters above the ground. Fen glared at him, but Kyp was neither intimidated, nor apologetic. He only shrugged. "Force grip."

"Oh. Thanks," Fen managed. She quickly scanned the port. "There." She pointed at a hulking Ghtroc freighter two docking bays over.

They ran lightly across the top of the wall, a race against the coming dawn and prying eyes. From the wall Kyp leaped to a rung on the ship's hull and climbed up to the *Rook*'s top hatch. Fen was right behind him.

Kyp gave the hatch lever a strong pull. It didn't move. "It's locked!"

"Of course it is." Fen withdrew another device from her pockets of tricks.

"Let me guess," Kyp asked. "An illegal shipjacking kit?"

She set the decoder over the hatch lock, and it began rapidly scrolling through security combinations, one digit at a time. "I bet you keep all your ships unlocked on Yavin Four, don't you?" Fen swallowed the remainder when she saw his stricken expression and remembered why he might be sensitive to ship thieving. "Forget it. Sorry."

Fen heard the gentle whirring of gears, then a soft snap. "Are we clear down there?" she demanded, returning the device to her pocket.

Kyp nodded. With her left hand on the hatch, Fen drew her blaster with her right.

"Wait," Kyp ordered.

Now she was really angry. "What?"

"Your blaster," Kyp said, very earnestly.

"If you think I'm going in there without my blaster . . ."

Kyp shook his head vigorously. "No, of course you should. But, Fen, you've got to put it on a stun setting."

"Don't go getting all Jedi on me."

"Fen, killing them won't bring Jett back."

He said it so gently she had to fight through a bantha-sized lump in her throat to respond. "And not killing them won't bring your brother back."

Kyp looked at the lightsaber clutched in his hand. "I know. And I'll help you, Fen, regardless. But don't make me go down there knowing that more might die when I could have done something to prevent it."

He had found her vulnerability and twisted it for all it was worth. "Stun may not stop what they throw at us," she warned.

"I know," Kyp said. "But it's the right thing to do."

"No good being right if you're dead," Fen retorted. They'd wasted enough time, she told herself, as she thumbed her blaster to a stun setting. She popped the hatch open; warm, yellow light poured out.

Kyp dropped down. Fen was less adroit, grabbing the sides of the hatch and hoisting herself into the hole. What should have been a fall felt like a slide through feathers, and she landed lightly and soundless. *Convenient thing, that Force grip.*

Kyp glanced around quickly, then pushed a pressure plate on the wall. A door slid open and they scurried into the dark cabin. "How should we look for her?" he asked.

"Can't you just sense her, or something?" Fen said, as she quickly studied the room.

"No, I've tried. There are a lot of fearful humans on this ship." Kyp suddenly moved back to the door. "Someone's coming!" he announced.

"Really? Well, I've never been afraid to ask for directions."

Kyp eased the cabin door open as heavy footfalls moved passed. They slipped out silently and Fen exulted in the reunion.

"Hello, Brasli." Fen underscored her cheery greeting by ramming her blaster muzzle into the thug's back.

Brasli stopped abruptly.

"That's right," Fen cooed. "Put your hands up and away from that nice blaster at your side."

"I figured you'd show up for that Sithin' partner of yours, Nabon," Brasli sneered, slowly turning around to face her.

"No swearing around Jedi," Fen remonstrated as Kyp relieved Brasli of his weapon. "Now, are you going to tell me where she is, or is this Jedi going to have to go into that mass of pathetic neurons you call a brain and pull it out?"

When she and Kyp burst into the cabin, with Brasli at the end of a blaster muzzle, Ghitsa's exclamation of "Fen!" encompassed relief and a question, all in a single word.

Fen roughly shoved Brasli into a chair. "Sit." To Ghitsa she said, "Got anything to tie him up?"

"What Brasli used on me will work admirably on him," Ghitsa said, snapping a length of cord in her hands.

There was an ugly bruise across Ghitsa's face, but she was mobile. "You okay?" Fen blurted as she let go of the mental image of another partner's blood staining the floor.

"Nothing that a week in a spa won't cure." As Ghitsa trussed and gagged Brasli, the man's grunts reflected her enthusiasm for the task. Ghitsa let the moments beat by, then, as her cunning eyes slid over Kyp, added, "So Fen, you've found a real Jedi."

Reluctant to disclose his secret, Fen was relieved when Kyp stepped forward. "I'm Kyp Durron."

Ghitsa started. "Durron? Jedi Kyp Durron?"

"Save it for later," Fen broke in. Ghitsa had worked for Hutts; she'd be able to handle rescue by a mass murderer.

"I sealed the door," Kyp offered.

"Then how will we get out?" Fen countered.

They all jumped as a new, commanding voice burst into the cabin. "Brasli, report!"

Ghitsa pointed at the comlink affixed to Brasli's collar. "It's Counselor Ral. He's running this operation."

Fen strode to the bound man, tore the gag from his mouth and aimed her blaster squarely between his eyes. "You are going to answer your comlink. You try being cute and I'll blow you apart."

Brasli nodded. "What is it, Ral?" His voice was rough but otherwise normal.

"Where are you?"

"Tell him you're here," Fen mouthed.

"I'm with Counselor Dogder," Brasli rasped.

"Good," the other voice barked. "Stay there. We may have been boarded. We're searching the ship now."

The other voice clicked off. As Fen crammed the gag back in Brasli's mouth, Ghitsa plucked the comlink from his uniform and affixed it to her own collar.

"Fen," Kyp called.

"Yeah?"

He was studying the cabin wall. "This is an exterior bulkhead, right?"

"There's about a half meter of reinforced hull between you and the big, bad galaxy, if that's what you mean. What are you . . ."

Fen's words died in her throat and Ghitsa's sharp gasp was abruptly drowned out by the low hum of the bright violet blade in Kyp's hand.

A Jedi Knight and a lightsaber. It was almost holy, harkening back to an era long gone in her lifetime. Impossibly it lived again in the cramped cabin of a Hutt freighter.

Kyp laughed. "Now, Fen, don't you start. I'll just cut through and we'll be out of here." He pivoted to Ghitsa and offered her the shimmering lightsaber. "Unless you would like to do it?"

"No, wait!" Fen cried as Kyp raised his lightsaber. "If you cut through there, it'll set off the hull breach alarms. They'll be on top of us before we can get out of here."

"I could cover you," Kyp asserted.

"Both of us? For how long?" Fen responded. *And with how many dead?* she added silently for Kyp. When he nodded slightly, Fen knew he understood. "It's still a good idea though." She strode over to the cabin's control panel and tore off the cover.

Her partner was already anticipating Fen's plan. "Do you have something that can generate a continuous loop?" Ghitsa asked.

"Yeah. I think we can rig one of the no-shows I brought." Fen reached into a pocket at her thigh and pulled out the device. She handed it to Ghitsa. "See what you can do with it."

"What's a no-show?" Kyp asked over her shoulder. He had, Fen noticed, shut down the lightsaber.

"Something else you wouldn't approve of," Fen said lightly.

"It's a passive field generator," Ghitsa explained. Fen heard a snap as the no-show split in Ghitsa's hands. "Wearing one makes you invisible to most detection technologies."

"The cabin's sensors for things like hull integrity al'
run through this circuit," Fen said, working a pair of cut
ters out of another pocket with one hand and pointing
to the wiring in the wall. "From here it feeds into the
ship's computer."

"So you are going to slice into it and use the no-show
to create an uninterrupted feed from here to the com
puter?" Kyp's voice indicated he wasn't quite cut out for
this sort of skullduggery.

"More or less," Fen responded, sorting through the
multicolored wires in the panel. *Which one was for
hull integrity again?* She shrugged the doubt away,
jammed the cutters between her teeth, and began teas
ing green wire out of the panel. "Ghits," she mumbled
through a mouthful of tool, "you got that gen rigged
yet?"

"Yes."

As her partner clamped the generator onto the wire,
Fen commented, "I've never seen a hairpin used like
that before."

"Don't talk with your mouth full, Fen."

Fen spit out the cutters and sliced into the circuit. She
held a ragged breath, but no alarms sounded. "That
should keep them off our backs."

They both pivoted about on hearing the hum as Kyp
again ignited his lightsaber. He swung the blade over his
head and began slicing through half a meter of metal
like a boot through mud.

"You know, Fen," Ghitsa commented, staring at the
young Jedi now deliberately sawing through ship hull.
"I don't want to see a lightsaber on the black market.
Ever."

Kyp was through in a few edgy minutes and closed
down the lightsaber. "There's a skin of metal still holding it on. We'll have to push our way out."

Fen put a shoulder to the makeshift door.

As Ghitsa hesitated, Fen chided her, "Come on.
Here's a use for those shoulder pads."

"I was just wondering what we do once we break out of the ship?"

Fen looked at Kyp. He shrugged. "Run?"

Chuckling, Fen started the count. On her "Three!" the hull plate buckled, then clattered to the ground. Fresh air and light streamed in. "Anyone around?" she asked Kyp.

He shook his head. "For now, no. But we don't have much time."

"One more thing," Ghitsa injected, with a nod toward the wide-eyed Brasli, still tied to the chair. "Shouldn't we dispose of him?"

Fen understood from where that desire for revenge came. Brasli obviously worked over her partner pretty hard, judging from the bruises and busted lip.

Kyp solved the problem by jumping out the door to the ground some two meters below. "Come on," he gestured.

She jumped down and Ghitsa followed. They landed in the shadow of the *Rook*'s underbelly, concealed by a landing skid.

Kyp gestured to the docking bay's entrance on the other side of the landing pad. "I think that's the only way out."

"And it's in the line of their laser cannons," Fen noted, heart sinking.

Ghitsa pursed her lips. "I bet they've security coded the door, too."

Kyp pushed the hair out of his face again, a gesture that was part need and part unconscious habit. "Fen, if you can take whatever comes out of the ship, and Ghitsa, you work the door, I'll handle the rest."

"Just like that?" Fen challenged.

The Jedi Knight nodded. "Just stay behind me."

They had covered half the distance between the ship's bow and the docking bay exit. Fen was beginning to think maybe no one would notice when Kyp started yelling.

"Get to the door," he called.

Behind them, Fen heard the earsplitting whine of laserfire. She instinctively ducked and pushed Ghitsa forward to the entrance, but couldn't place what the ricochet sound was.

Fen whirled around and, for a second, reflexes honed by years of dodging and answering blasterfire failed her.

Kyp, the kid of a Jedi, was standing alone in the middle of the docking bay. Laserfire poured from the *Rook*'s forward guns. And like some weird children's toy, Kyp caught the green killing bolts on his lightsaber and tossed them away.

"Fen!" she heard Ghitsa shout. She spun about. Her partner was under the entrance's marginal cover. "It is locked. You'll need to hold them off a few minutes."

A few minutes. It was a lifetime in moments like this. She ran back to Kyp. Methodically, even calmly, he deflected each burst of fire. The blasts bounced off the lightsaber, ricocheting at crazy angles.

Out of the corner of her vision, Fen saw movement, flickers at the top of the *Rook*'s ramp, inside the ship. From behind Kyp's protective cover she crouched down, steadied her blaster on her knee and caught each of the Hutt henchmen in a blue wave of stun blasts as they emerged from the ship.

Her mind had been ticking off the seconds. She knew, rationally, they had not been under fire for more than a minute. It seemed an eternity. Ghitsa was good at locks, but they were only two people against an entire ship. If Kyp started to get tired, or faltered just once . . .

The wail of repulsors suddenly filled the docking bay. *What the . . .* Fen glanced up, wondering why it had gone so dark. A freighter hovered overhead. It was obviously piloted by someone who was really angry, and a friend, Fen concluded with surprise, as the ship poured cannon fire into the *Rook*.

The *Rook* shuddered, helpless on the ground. Fen

tared again at the ship, noticing the distinctive bow markings, the equipment standard on no other YT. The *Star Lady?* What was her ship doing here?

Fen's personal comlink burst to life. "Cap'n, this is Gibb. I figured you might need some help." He underscored the point with another deafening volley into the rounded ship.

The roar of the *Rook* coming to life drowned out 'en's shrieking invective at the reckless mechanic. The *Rook's* repulsors screamed, blowing dust in the landing bay. Threatened from above, the ship abandoned her ictims on the ground and surged up. Fen felt her heart top as the *Rook* swerved and narrowly missed the hovering *Star Lady*. Free of the docking bay, the *Rook* shot nto the sky.

"Gibb!" she screeched into the comlink. "You bring ny ship back! Don't you dare . . ." But Gibb did dare, larting after the retreating *Rook*.

"It's all right Cap'n. She's running now. I've called Nad'Ris Customs. They'll intercept."

Fen yanked a pair of macrobinoculars out of another pocket and glued her eyes to the scene.

"Who's that piloting the *Star Lady?*" she heard Ghitsa ask.

"Gibb," came Kyp's weary voice.

With a supreme effort Fen tore herself away from the ision of the *Lady* chasing the much bigger, and better rmed, Ghtroc.

In a tone full of disbelieving admiration, Ghitsa dded, "It really was good of you to let Gibb fly the *Lady* ere."

Fen could only nod weakly. To Kyp, she managed, You did great."

Kyp smiled back and pushed sweaty hair off his forehead. "I'm just glad we didn't have to kill any of them."

"Actually . . ." Ghitsa began.

Frowning, Fen asked, "What?"

"Well, they have no way of knowing about that hole Kyp cut in the hull. If they get too high up."

Kyp turned gray. "Gibb!" Fen yelled into the comlink. "Back off! Tell Nad'Ris Customs not to chase them. That ship's not spaceworthy. She'll blow if she goes much higher."

Ghitsa looked bewildered. "What's the problem?"

"Later, Ghits." To Kyp she said, "Can't you do something so they turn back?"

Kyp was looking up, into the space of sky the ship were heading. "Even if I could, the Force shouldn't be used that way."

His piercing sorrow made Fen ache.

Ghitsa humphed, then unclipped the comlink she'd taken from Brasli and thumbed it on. "I'm warning you though, it won't work."

"Try!" Fen demanded.

"Counselor Ral, this is Dodger." She smoothly cut off his sputtering rage. "Yes, as you have surmised, I have Brasli's comlink. Now, Ral, I am quite serious here. You have a hull breach. You'll never clear the lower atmosphere. You have to come back."

They heard laughter. "He's a gambler," Ghitsa explained. "He thinks I'm bluffing."

"Try again," Fen urged.

Staring into the sky, Kyp murmured, "Customs still thinks the ship is under quarantine. They'll try to stop it."

Fen brought the macrobinocs back up to her face. She could just make out the *Rook.* Per her orders, Gibb had not pursued. But Fen could see two smaller ships moving fast and firing wildly at the retreating *Rook.*

"Ral, this is Counselor's oath," Fen heard Ghitsa say. "I swear you have a hull breach."

"Too late," Kyp whispered.

From the comlink they heard a scream, then a burst of static. Through the macrobinocs, Fen saw a flash. And the *Rook* was gone.

·   ·   ·

was the one place in the galaxy Fen thought she would ever go. They landed on a humble pad at the base of an enormous stone structure. A temple, Fen guessed, built by some ancient and subjugated race. A rather odd race for a Jedi Academy, she thought.

Through the cockpit viewport they could all see a cluster of very somber, brown-clad beings of varying sexes and species. "Welcoming committee?" she asked Kyp, forcing a quip.

Kyp shook his head, shrugging out of his seat restraints. "Something's going on."

Fen slid out of her seat, but Ghitsa remained glued to her chair.

"You're not coming?" Kyp asked her.

Ghitsa looked away from the grave Jedi outside the ship. "No, Kyp," she said slowly. "I don't think so." Confirming that the experience had not irrevocably sobered her, she added, "Not even if I could pick up a few pointers for next time."

Kyp's mouth turned up in the beginning of knowing grin. "Be true to yourself, Ghitsa Dogder. That's the only pointer you'll ever need." He slipped out of the cockpit. With a final glance back at Ghitsa, Fen followed him out.

In a show of initiative that could become irritating if it were habitual, Kyp had already opened the ship's hatch. A whoosh of hot, humid air surged into the cabin, leaving Fen momentarily breathless.

Kyp trotted down the ramp to his friends, or whatever they were, Fen thought sullenly. She followed, refusing to be cowed and annoyed that these priests could probably divine how nervous she really was.

He exchanged a few words with them and the other Jedi dispersed. One woman, however, remained, exuding to Fen's eye a proprietary protectiveness. Fen leaned indolently against a landing-ramp strut, returning the suspicion with a sardonic glare of her own.

Kyp hurried back, his face, Fen thought, a bit drawn. "Something wrong?" she asked.

"Tionne says Master Skywalker has been injured."

"Again?"

He smirked. "They've just broken orbit and should b[e] in shortly." Kyp shifted, uncomfortably, as if he coul[d] feel the hot ground through his boots. "I should . . ."

Fen waved him off. "I hate good-byes," she sai[d] gruffly, wondering why her eyes were misting. Must b[e] something in the wretched jungle air. "Get going. We'[ll] see ourselves out." She turned, only to stiffen as a gent[le] hand at her shoulder brought her back around.

Kyp ducked his head, then glanced up through bang[s] that really needed a trim now. "I'll miss you, too, Fen[.]" He let his hand fall from her shoulder, blushing shyly [at] the bold move. "You sure you don't want to stay for a fe[w] days?"

"Positive. You're needed here." Fen glanced at th[e] woman who must be Tionne, still patiently waiting. "An[d] the Academy certainly doesn't need me."

She held out her hand, wishing now that the word[s] weren't sticking in her craw. "But if lifting big roc[ks] doesn't work out, there's always a place for you on m[y] crew."

He stared at her offered hand for what seemed fo[r]ever, then slowly took it, wrapping it in both of his ow[n.] "Thanks, Fen. For everything." As Kyp stumbled f[or] something to say, Fen pulled away.

"You too, Jedi." She pivoted on a heel and heade[d] back up the ramp without looking back. Kyp final[ly] found the words that had eluded him when she hear[d] softly in her mind, "The Force is with you, too, Fen."

They cleared the Academy airspace in half the time [it] had taken to get into it. Fen ignored the inquisitive hai[l] from the inbound Corellian freighter and space yach[t.] As soon as they jumped, she fled to her quarters.

A half hour of composure later, Fen rejoined he[r] partner in the main cabin. With ceremonial solemni[ty]

Ghitsa was depositing her brown robe and lightsaber handle in the ship's waste disposer.

Ghitsa finally broke the silence and joined Fen at the gaming table. "It's not as much fun anymore."

"I'm not sorry to see it go." Fen scowled. "This whole trip has been a bust."

"Yes, it has." Ghitsa inserted a datacard she had been fingering into a datapad and slid it across the table. "I lifted this from Ral. What do you think?"

"Orko SkyMine? Never heard of it."

"That's what the Desilijic wanted me for," Ghitsa explained. "They were looking for someone who could tell them what Durga was up to." She rubbed her cheek where the bruise was just beginning to fade. "They were disappointed I hadn't heard of it, either."

"So what?" Fen shrugged. "It's probably just some new Hutt corporate interclan espionage."

"Scroll down a little further."

Fen moved down the pad, stopped, studied it, and then studied it again, and whistled. "Whatever Orko is, they're raking it in and pouring it out again. It looks like the Hutts are up to something really big if this data is real."

Ghitsa slid out of the booth to pace restlessly. "The Desilijic Clan believed it enough to track us down, sabotage your ship, and kidnap a former Counselor from Durga's clan."

Fen stared again at the readout on the datapad, an idea forming. "Ghits," she began slowly, "this would be worth a lot of money to an information broker."

Her partner visibly wilted and slumped into a cabin chair. "I was afraid you'd suggest that." She burrowed manicured fingertips into her forehead to massage the creases there. "Who? New Republic Intelligence?"

Fen snorted. "We'd have to explain way too much to a low-level flunkie. And end up in their blaster sights for the trouble. And NRI won't pay top credit. No, I'd take this to Talon Karrde."

Ghitsa opened her eyes wide in surprise. "Karrde? He hates me."

"Most of the Fringe hates you, Ghitsa. But he'll pay good money for reliable information."

"That's not really the issue though, is it?"

"No," Fen said carefully. "It's whether you are finally willing to turn your back on the Hutts." She rose. "Think about it. It's your decision."

As she was heading out of the cabin, Ghitsa stopped her.

"Fen?"

She turned slowly around, knowing that her partner of eight years was at a cusp. Even after all this time, Fen had no idea which way this would go. *Be true to yourself,* the Jedi had told Ghitsa. *What did that mean to a woman who was a con to her core and had worked for Hutts most of her life?*

"What do those numbers on the datapad look like to you?"

"They're not what I would expect as a front for a smuggling operation or criminal syndicate."

Ghitsa raised her eyes, and caught and held Fen's gaze. "No, they weren't. Numbers of that magnitude are only found in a military budget." She hoisted herself out of her chair, moved over to the table, and removed the datacard from the pad. "Jabba made the same mistake, you know."

"What's that?" Fen asked, taking the disk.

"Politics. Tangling with the wrong people. Not being content with dominion in the criminal Fringe." Ghitsa shook her head. "Call up your contact. Tell him we've got something Karrde will be very interested in."

"Karrde's got some good contacts within the New Republic." Because there was nothing so demeaning as a futile sacrifice, Fen added, "He'll make sure this gets to the right people."

As she headed forward, Fen mused there should have been some acknowledgment to mark the occasion. In he twisted path of a lifetime in the moral ambiguity f the Fringe, somehow both she and Ghitsa were doing he right thing. She supposed, she thought sourly, it ame from meddling with Jedi. There was nothing imple to a Jedi's tricks. Nothing simple at all.

About the Authors

Kathy Burdette lives in Williamsburg, Virginia, where she is a manuscript editor for the Institute of Early American History and Culture. Although she has co-written several source articles for the *Star Wars Adventure Journal* with a mysterious, bearded rogue, this is her first solo attempt. When not fighting dangling participles in the name of academia, she enjoys spending time with said rogue and playing alternative country music through a Les Paul and a tube amplifier that goes to eleven.

Former journalist and magazine owner/publisher **Laurie Burns** now edits publications for students at a community college in California. When not working, she enjoys writing, riding horses, and gallivanting about with her husband in the mountains around their home. Her short story, "Retreat From Coruscant," appeared in a previous Bantam Spectra anthology, *Star Wars: Tales from the Empire*.

Chris Cassidy is a freelance writer who has worked for more than ten years in corporate communications and video production. "Simple Tricks" and "Hutt and Seek" (written with co-conspirator Tish Pahl) are her first ventures into the realm of intentional (as opposed to corporate) fiction. She has spent the last three years moving about from Toronto to Guatemala to Oregon to Toronto to her current location in Colorado Springs, which is oddly enough in Colorado. She and her husband, Bob, are owned by a loony border collie/terrier. She is currently enrolled at the University of Colorado, working toward a second degree in psychological anthropology. Chris is a longtime Star Lady and a founding member of the Club Jade listserve.

Paul Danner originally wanted to write *The Empire Strikes Back,* but he was only eight at the time and Mr. Lucas wouldn't return his calls. So he waited fourteen more years to carve out a little niche in the *Star Wars* universe with "One of a Kind" for the *Official Star Wars Adventure Journal.* He would go on to write five more stories for the *Journal,* as well as *Wretched Hives of Scum and Villainy,* a game sourcebook for West End Games. A recent graduate of the University of Miami with a bachelor's degree in screenwriting and creative writing, Paul spends his free time playing basketball and trying to pass himself off as Darth Maul. He hopes to one day make a name for himself writing both novels and screenplays. Are there any gold statuettes in his future? Difficult to see. Always in motion is the future. . . .

George Bernard Shaw once stated, "There is always danger for those who are afraid of it." **Patricia A. Jackson** agrees ardently and assures that there is nothing to fear from the dark side . . . so embrace it! "Uhl Eharl Koehng" is a continuation in the saga of her dark side family and her driving obsession to rid dark Jedi (as well as the Galactic Empire) of their unwarranted bad press. Chivalry does occasionally come dressed in black. Patty has recently stepped down from school administration to take the battle of education and creativity to the front lines in the classroom where it truly counts. This fall she will begin a new saga as an English teacher at William Penn Senior High School in York, Pennsylvania.

Tish Eggleston Pahl is a food and drug attorney practicing in the Washington, D.C., area. Her previous publications include professional journal articles, technical manuals, labeling and advertising copy, legislative drafting, and congressional testimony. With her co-author, Chris Cassidy, "Hutt and Seek" and "Simple Tricks" mark Tish's first foray into the realm of science, rather than legal, fiction. She lives in Bethesda, Maryland, with her husband, the long-suffering Tom, their young son, Tom, Jr., and two Labrador retrievers, Ghitsa and Zozo. In her not-so-copious spare time, she is the postmistress to the America Online Star Ladies.

Jean Rabe is the author of ten fantasy novels and a dozen short stories—among the latter a few *Star Wars* offerings published in the *Star Wars Adventure Journal.* A longtime *Star Wars* fan, her office features an old Darth Vader speaker phone; an R2-D2 cassette player that usually belts out steel drum music; a miniature *Millennium Falcon;* and a stuffed Ewok. Her other *Star Wars* memorabilia is carefully stored in the basement, which has come to resemble the cluttered inside of a Jawa sandcrawler.

Michael A. Stackpole is the *New York Times* bestselling author of several *Star Wars* novels, including the Rogue Squadron series and *I, Jedi.* "Interlude at Darkknell" is his second story collaboration with fellow author Timothy Zahn, the first being "Side Trip" in *Tales from the Empire.* Mike has also worked on and scripted several story arcs for Dark Horse's *Star Wars* X-Wing *Rogue Squadron* comics. In his spare time he writes BattleTech novels and fantasy novels, including *Once a Hero, Talion: Revenant,* and *A Hero Reborn.*

Timothy Zahn is the author of eighteen novels, including five *Star Wars* books: the Thrawn Trilogy (*Heir to the Empire, Dark Force Rising,* and *The Last Command*) and the Hand of Thrawn Duology (*Specter of the Past* and *Vision of the Future*). His most recent book, *The Icarus Hunt,* was published last August by Bantam Books. He contributed several short stories about Grand Admiral Thrawn and Talon Karrde to the *Official Star Wars Adventure Journal.*

The World of
STAR WARS Novels

In May 1991, *Star Wars* caused a sensation in the publishing industry with the Bantam Spectra release of Timothy Zahn's novel *Heir to the Empire*. For the first time, Lucasfilm Ltd. had authorized new novels that *continued* the famous story told in George Lucas's three blockbuster motion pictures: *Star Wars, The Empire Strikes Back,* and *Return of the Jedi.* Reader reaction was immediate and tumultuous: *Heir* reached #1 on the *New York Times* bestseller list and demonstrated that *Star Wars* lovers were eager for exciting new stories set in this universe, written by leading science fiction authors who shared their passion. Since then, each Bantam *Star Wars* novel has been an instant national bestseller.

Lucasfilm and Bantam decided that future novels in the series would be interconnected: that is, events in one novel would have consequences in the others. You might say that each Bantam *Star Wars* novel, enjoyable on its own, is also part of a much larger tale.

Here is a special look at Bantam's *Star Wars* books, along with excerpts from the more recent novels. Each one is available now wherever Bantam Books are sold.

The Han Solo Trilogy:
THE PARADISE SNARE
THE HUTT GAMBIT
REBEL DAWN
by A. C. Crispin
Setting: Before *Star Wars: A New Hope*

What was Han Solo like before *we met him in the first STAR WARS movie? This trilogy answers that tantalizing question, filling in lots of historical lore about our favorite swashbuckling hero and thrilling us with adventures of the brash young pilot that we never knew he'd experienced. As the trilogy begins, the young Han Makes a life-changing decision: to escape from the clutches of Garris Shrike, head of the trading "clan" who has brutalized Han while taking advantage of his piloting abilities. Here's a tense early scene from* The Paradise Snare *featuring Han, Shrike, and Dewlanna, a Wookiee who is Han's only friend in this horrible situation:*

"I've had it with you, Solo. I've been lenient with you so far, because you're a blasted good swoop pilot and all that prize money came in handy, but my patience is ended." Shrike ceremoniously pushed up the sleeves of his bedizened uniform, then balled his hands into fists. The galley's artificial lighting made the blood-jewel ring glitter dull silver. "Let's see what a few days of fighting off Devaronian blood-poisoning does for your attitude—along with maybe a few broken bones. I'm doing this for your own good, boy. Someday you'll thank me."

Han gulped with terror as Shrike started toward him. He'd lashed out at the trader captain once before, two years ago, when he'd been feeling cocky after winning the gladiatorial Free-For-All on Jubilar—and had been instantly sorry. The speed and strength of Garris's returning blow had snapped his head back and split both lips so thoroughly that Dewlanna had had to feed him mush for a week until they healed.

With a snarl, Dewlanna stepped forward. Shrike's hand dropped to his blaster. "You stay out of this, old Wookiee," he snapped in a voice nearly as harsh as Dewlanna's. "Your cooking isn't *that* good."

Han had already grabbed his friend's furry arm and was forcibly holding her back. "Dewlanna, no!"

She shook off his hold as easily as she would have waved off an annoying insect and roared at Shrike. The captain drew his blaster, and chaos erupted.

"Noooo!" Han screamed, and leaped forward, his foot lashing out in an old street-fighting technique. His instep impacted solidly with Shrike's breastbone. The captain's breath went out in a great *houf!* and he went over backward. Han hit the deck and rolled. A tingler bolt sizzled past his ear.

"Larrad!" wheezed the captain as Dewlanna started toward him.

Shrike's brother drew his blaster and pointed it at the Wookiee. "Stop, Dewlanna!"

His words had no more effect than Han's. Dewlanna's blood was up—she was in full Wookiee battle rage. With a roar that deafened the combatants, she grabbed Larrad's wrist and yanked, spinning him around and snapping him in a terrible parody of a child's "snap the whip" game. Han heard a *crunch,* mixed with several *pops* as tendons and ligaments gave way. Larrad Shrike shrieked, a high, shrill noise that carried such pain that the Corellian youth's arm ached in sympathy.

Grabbing the blaster from his belt, Han snapped off a shot at the Elomin who was leaping forward, tingler ready and aimed at Dewlanna's midsection. Brafid howled, dropping his weapon. Han was amazed that he'd managed to hit him, but he didn't have long to wonder about the accuracy of his aim.

Shrike was staggering to his feet, blaster in hand, aimed squarely at Han's head. ''Larrad?'' he yelled at the writhing heap of agony that was his brother. Larrad did not reply.

Shrike cocked the blaster and stepped even closer to Han. ''Stop it, Dewlanna!'' the captain snarled at the Wookiee. ''Or your buddy Solo dies!''

Han dropped his blaster and put his hands up in a gesture of surrender.

Dewlanna stopped in her tracks, growling softly.

Shrike leveled the blaster, and his finger tightened on the trigger. Pure malevolent hatred was etched upon his features, and then he smiled, pale blue eyes glittering with ruthless joy. ''For insubordination and striking your captain,'' he announced, ''I sentence you to death, Solo. May you rot in all the hells there ever were.''

SHADOWS OF THE EMPIRE
by Steve Perry
**Setting: Between *The Empire Strikes Back*
and *Return of the Jedi***

Here is a very special STAR WARS story dealing with Black Sun, a galaxy-spinning criminal organization that is masterminded by one of the most interesting villains in the STAR WARS universe: Xizor, dark prince of the Falleen. Xizor's chief rival for the favor of Emperor Palpatine is none other than Darth Vader himself— alive and well, and a major character in this story, since it is set during the events of the STAR WARS film trilogy.

In the opening prologue, we revisit a familiar scene from The Empire Strikes Back, *and are introduced to our marvelous new bad guy:*

He looks like a walking corpse, Xizor thought. *Like a mummified body dead a thousand years. Amazing he is still alive, much less the most powerful man in the galaxy. He isn't even that old; it is more as if something is slowly eating him.*

Xizor stood four meters away from the Emperor, watching as the man who had long ago been Senator Palpatine moved to stand in the holocam field. He imagined he could smell the decay in the Emperor's worn body. Likely that was just some trick of the recycled air, run through dozens of filters to ensure that there was no chance of any poison gas being introduced into it. Filtered the life out of it, perhaps, giving it that dead smell.

The viewer on the other end of the holo-link would see a close-up of the Emperor's head and shoulders, of an age-ravaged face shrouded in the cowl of his dark zeyd-cloth robe. The man on the other end of the transmission, light-years away, would not see Xizor, though Xizor would be able to see him. It was a measure of the Emperor's trust that Xizor was allowed to be here while the conversation took place.

The man on the other end of the transmission—if he could still be called that—

The air swirled inside the Imperial chamber in front of the Emperor, coalesced, and blossomed into the image of a figure down on one knee. A caped humanoid biped dressed in jet black, face hidden under a full helmet and breathing mask:

Darth Vader.

Vader spoke: "What is thy bidding, my master?"

If Xizor could have hurled a power bolt through time and space to strike Vader dead, he would have done it without blinking. Wishful thinking: Vader was too powerful to attack directly.

"There is a great disturbance in the Force," the Emperor said.

"I have felt it," Vader said.

"We have a new enemy. Luke Skywalker."

Skywalker? That had been Vader's name, a long time ago. What was this person with the same name, someone so powerful as to be worth a conversation between the Emperor and his most loathsome creation? More importantly, why had Xizor's agents not uncovered this before now? Xizor's ire was instant—but cold. No sign of his surprise or anger would show on his imperturbable features. The Falleen did not allow their emotions to burst forth as did many of the inferior species; no, the Falleen ancestry was not fur but scales, not mammalian but reptilian. Not wild but coolly calculating. Such was much better. Much safer.

"Yes, my master," Vader continued.

"He could destroy us," the Emperor said.

Xizor's attention was riveted upon the Emperor and the holographic image of Vader kneeling on the deck of a ship far away.

Here was interesting news indeed. Something the Emperor perceived as a danger to himself? Something the Emperor feared?

"He's just a boy," Vader said. "Obi-Wan can no longer help him."

Obi-Wan. That name Xizor knew. He was among the last of the Jedi Knights, a general. But he'd been dead for decades, hadn't he?

Apparently Xizor's information was wrong if Obi-Wan had been helping someone who was still a boy. His agents were going to be sorry.

The Bounty Hunter Wars
Book 1: THE MANDALORIAN ARMOR
Book 2: SLAVE SHIP
by K. W. Jeter
Setting: During *Return of the Jedi*

Boba Fett continues the fight against the legions of circling enemies as the somewhat hot-tempered Trandoshan Bossk attempts to re-establish the old Bounty Hunter Guild with himself as its head. Bossk has sworn undying vengeance on Boba Fett when his ship, Hound's Tooth, *crashes.*

In the excerpt that follows, Bossk attempts to kill Boba Fett in a violent confrontation:

Fear is a useful thing.

That was one of the best lessons that a bounty hunter could learn. And Bossk was learning it now.

Through the cockpit viewport of the *Hound's Tooth,* he saw the explosion that ripped the other ship, Boba Fett's *Slave I,* into flame and shards of blackened durasteel. A burst of wide-band comlink static, like an electromagnetic death cry, had simultaneously deafened Bossk. The searing, multi-octave noise had poured through the speakers in the *Hound*'s cockpit for several minutes, until the last of the circuitry aboard Fett's ship had finally been consumed and silenced in the fiery apocalypse.

When he could finally hear himself think again, Bossk looked out at the empty space where *Slave I* had been. Now, against the cold backdrop of stars, a few scraps of heated metal slowly dwindled from white-hot to dull red as their molten heat ebbed away in vacuum. *He's dead,* thought Bossk with immense satisfaction. *At last.* Whatever atoms had constituted the late Boba Fett, they were also drifting disconnected and harmless in space. Before transferring back here to his own ship, Bossk had wired up enough thermal explosives in *Slave I* to reduce any living thing aboard it to mere ash and bad memories.

So if he still felt afraid, if his gut still knotted when Boba Fett's dark-visored image rose in his thoughts, Bossk knew that was an irrational response. *He's dead, he's gone . . .*

The silence of the *Hound's* cockpit was broken by a barely audible pinging signal from the control panel. Bossk glanced down and saw that the *Hound's* telesponder had picked up the presence of another ship in the immediate vicinity; according to the coordinates that appeared in the readout screen, it was almost on top of the *Hound's Tooth.*

And—it was the ship known as *Slave I.* The ID profile was an exact match.

That's impossible, thought Bossk, bewildered. His heart shuddered to a halt inside his chest, then staggered on. Before the explosion, he had picked up the same ID profile from the other side of his own ship; he had turned the *Hound's Tooth* around just in time to see the huge, churning ball of flame fill his viewscreen.

But, he realized now, he hadn't seen *Slave I* itself. Which meant . . .

Bossk heard another sound, even softer, coming from somewhere else in his own ship. There was someone else aboard it; his keen Trandoshan senses registered the molecules of another creature's spoor in the ship's recycled atmosphere. And Bossk knew who it was.

He's here. The cold blood in Bossk's veins chilled to ice. *Boba Fett . . .*

Somehow, Bossk knew, he had been tricked. The explosion hadn't consumed *Slave I* and its occupants at all. He didn't know how Boba Fett had managed it, but it had been done nevertheless. And the deafening electronic noise that had filled the cockpit had also been enough to cover Boba Fett's unauthorized entry of the *Hound's Tooth;* the shrieking din had gone on long enough for Fett to have penetrated an access hatch and resealed it behind himself.

A voice came from the cockpit's overhead speaker, a voice that was neither his own nor Boba Fett's.

"Twenty seconds to detonation." It was the calm, unexcited voice of an autonomic bomb. Only the most powerful ones contained warning circuits like that.

Fear thawed the ice in Bossk's veins. He jumped up from the pilot's chair and dived for the hatchway behind himself.

In the emergency equipment bay of the *Hound's Tooth*, his clawed hands tore through the contents of one of the storage lockers. The *Hound* wasn't going to be a ship much longer; in a few seconds—and counting down—it was going to be glowing bits of shrapnel and rubbish surrounded by a haze of rapidly dissipating atmospheric gases, just like whatever it had been that he had mistakenly identified as Boba Fett's ship *Slave I*. That the *Hound* would no longer be capable of maintaining its life-support systems wasn't Bossk's main concern at this moment, as the reptilian Trandoshan hastily shoved a few more essential items through the self-sealing gasket of a battered, much-used pressure duffel. There wouldn't even *be* any life for the systems to support: a small portion of the debris floating in the cold vacuum would be blood and bone and scorched scraps of body tissue, the rapidly chilling remains of the ship's captain. *I'm outta here,* thought Bossk; he slung the duffel's strap across his broad shoulder and dived for the equipment bay's hatch.

"Fifteen seconds to detonation." A calm and friendly voice spoke in the *Hound*'s central corridor as Bossk ran for the escape pod. He knew that Boba Fett had toggled the bomb's autonomic vocal circuits just to rattle him. "Fourteen . . ." There was nothing like a disembodied announcement of impending doom, to get a sentient creature motivated. "Thirteen; have you considered evacuation?"

"Shut up," growled Bossk. There was no point in talking to a pile of thermal explosives and flash circuits, but he couldn't stop himself. Under the death-fear that accelerated his pulse was sheer murderous rage and annoyance, the inevitable-seeming result of every encounter he'd ever had with Boba Fett. *That stinking, underhanded scum . . .*

The scraps and shards left by the other explosion clattered against the *Hound*'s shielded exterior like a swarm of tiny, molten-edged meteorites. If there was any justice in the universe, Boba Fett should have been dead by now. Not just dead; atomized. The fury and panic in Bossk's pounding heart shifted again to bewilderment as he ran with the pressure duffel jostling against his scale-covered spine. Why did Boba Fett keep coming back? Was there no way to kill him so that he would just *stay* dead?

THE TRUCE AT BAKURA
by Kathy Tyers
Setting: Immediately after *Return of the Jedi*

The day after his climactic battle with Emperor Palpatine and the sacrifice of his father, Darth Vader, who died saving his life, Luke Skywalker helps recover an Imperial drone ship bearing a startling message intended for the Emperor. It is a distress signal from the far-off Imperial outpost of Bakura, which is under attack by an alien invasion force, the Ssi-ruuk. Leia sees a rescue mission as an opportunity to achieve a diplomatic victory for the Rebel Alliance, even if it means fighting alongside former Imperials. But Luke receives a vision from Obi-Wan Kenobi revealing that the stakes are even higher: the invasion at Bakura threatens everything the Rebels have won at such great cost.

STAR WARS: X-WING
By Michael A. Stackpole
ROGUE SQUADRON
WEDGE'S GAMBLE
THE KRYTOS TRAP
THE BACTA WAR

By Aaron Allston
WRAITH SQUADRON
IRON FIST
SOLO COMMAND

By Michael A. Stackpole
ISARD'S REVENGE
Setting: Three years after *Return of the Jedi*

The Rogues have been instrumental in defeating Thrawn and return to Coruscant to celebrate their great victory. It is then they make a terrible discovery—Ysanne Isard did not die at Thyferra and it is she who is assassinating those who were with Corran Horn on the Lusankya. *It is up to the Rogues to rescue their compatriots and foil the remnants of the Empire.*

The following scene from the opening of Isard's Revenge *takes you to one of the most daring battles the Rogues ever waged:*

Sithspawn! When his X-wing reverted to realspace before the countdown timer had reached zero, Corran Horn knew Thrawn had somehow managed to outguess the New Republic yet one more time. The Rogues had helped create the deception that the New Republic would be going after the Tangrene Ubiqtorate Base, but Thrawn clearly hadn't taken the bait.

The man's incredible. I'd like to meet him, shake his hand. Corran smiled. *And then kill him, of course.*

Two seconds into realspace and the depth of Thrawn's brilliance became undeniable. The New Republic's forces had been brought out of hyperspace by two Interdictor cruisers, which even now started to fade back toward the Imperial lines. This left the New Republic's ships well shy of the Bilbringi shipyards and facing an Imperial fleet arrayed for battle. The two Interdictors that had dragged them from hyperspace were a small part of a larger force scattered around to make sure the New Republic's ships were not going to be able to retreat.

"Battle alert!" Captain Tycho Celchu's voice crackled over the comm unit. "TIE Interceptors coming in—bearing two-nine-three, mark twenty."

Corran keyed his comm unit. "Three Flight, on me. Hold it together and nail some squints."

The cant-winged Interceptors rolled in and down on the Rogues. Corran kicked his X-wing up on its port S-foil and flicked his lasers over to quad-fire mode. While that would slow his rate of fire, each burst had a better chance of killing a squint outright. *And there are plenty that need killing here.*

Corran nudged his stick right and dropped the cross-hairs onto an Interceptor making a run at Admiral Ackbar's flagship. He hit the firing switch, sending four red laser bolts burning out at the target. They hit on the starboard side, with two of them piercing the cockpit and the other two vaporizing the strut supporting the right wing. The bent hexagonal wing sheered off in a shower of sparks, while the rest of the craft started a long, lazy spiral toward the outer edges of the system.

"Break port, Nine."

As the Gand's high-pitched voice poured through the comm unit, Corran snaprolled his X-wing to the left, then chopped his throttle back and hauled hard on the stick to take him into a loop. An Interceptor flashed through where he had been, and Ooryl Qyrgg's X-wing came fast on its tail. Ooryl's lasers blazed in sequence, stippling the Interceptor with red energy darts. One hit each wing, melting great furrows through them, while the other two lanced through the cockpit right above the twin ion engines. The engines themselves tore free of their support structure and blew out through the front of the squint, then exploded in a silver fireball that consumed the rest of the Imperial fighter.

"Thanks, Ten."

"My pleasure, Nine."

Whistler, the green and white R2 unit slotted in behind Corran, tooted, and data started pouring up over the fighter's main monitor. It told him in exact detail what he was seeing unfold in space around him. The New Republic's forces had come into the system in the standard conical formation that allowed them to maximize firepower.

THE COURTSHIP OF
PRINCESS LEIA
by Dave Wolverton
Setting: Four years after *Return of the Jedi*

One of the most interesting developments in Bantam's STAR WARS novels is that in their storyline, Han Solo and Princess Leia start a family. This tale reveals how the couple originally got together. Wishing to strengthen the fledgling New Republic by bringing in powerful allies, Leia opens talks with the Hapes consortium of more than sixty worlds. But the consortium is ruled by the Queen Mother, who, to Han's dismay, wants Leia to marry her son, Prince Isolder. Before this action-packed story is over, Luke will join forces with Isolder against a group of Force-trained "witches" and face a deadly foe.

HEIR TO THE EMPIRE
DARK FORCE RISING
THE LAST COMMAND
by Timothy Zahn
Setting: Five years after *Return of the Jedi*

This #1 bestselling trilogy introduces two legendary forces of evil into the STAR WARS literary pantheon. Grand Admiral Thrawn has taken control of the Imperial fleet in the years since the destruction of the Death Star, and the mysterious Joruus C'baoth is a fearsome Jedi Master who has been seduced by the dark side. Han and Leia have now been married for about a year, and as the story begins, she is pregnant with twins. Thrawn's plan is to crush the Rebellion and resurrect the Empire's New Order with C'baoth's help—and in return, the Dark Master will get Han and Leia's Jedi children to mold as he wishes. For as readers of this magnificent trilogy will see, Luke Skywalker is not the last of the old Jedi. He is the first of the new.

The Jedi Academy Trilogy:
JEDI SEARCH
DARK APPRENTICE
CHAMPIONS OF THE FORCE
by Kevin J. Anderson
Setting: Seven years after *Return of the Jedi*

In order to assure the continuation of the Jedi Knights, Luke Skywalker has decided to start a training facility: a Jedi Academy. He will gather Force-sensitive students who show potential as prospective Jedi and serve as their mentor, as Jedi Masters Obi-Wan Kenobi and Yoda did for him. Han and Leia's twins are now toddlers, and there is a third Jedi child: the infant Anakin, named after Luke and Leia's father. In this trilogy, we discover the existence of a powerful Imperial doomsday weapon, the horrifying Sun Crusher—which will soon become the centerpiece of a titanic struggle between Luke Skywalker and his most brilliant Jedi Academy student, who is delving dangerously into the dark side.

I, JEDI
by Michael A. Stackpole
Setting: *During that time*

Another grand tale of the exploits of the most feared and fearless fighting force in the galaxy, as Corran Horn faces a dark unnatural power that only his mastery of the Jedi powers could destroy. This great novel gives us an in-depth look at Jedi powers and brings us inside the minds of the special warriors learning to use the Force:

I switched to proton torpedoes, got a quick tone-lock from Whistler and pulled the trigger. The missile shot from my X-wing and sprinted straight for her ship. As good as she was, the clutch pilot knew there was no dodging it. She fired with both lasers, but they missed. Then, at the last moment, she shot an ion blast that hit the missile. Blue lightning played over it, burning out every circuit that allowed the torpedo to track and close on her ship.

I'm fairly certain, just for a second, she thought she had won.

The problem with a projectile is that even if its sophisticated circuitry fails, it still has a lot of kinetic energy built up. Even if it never senses the proximity of its target and detonates, that much mass moving that fast treats a clutch cockpit much the way a needle treats a bubble. The torpedo drove the ion engines out the back of the clutch, where they exploded. The fighter's hollow remains slowly spun off through space and would eventually burn through the atmosphere and give resort guests a thrill.

CHILDREN OF THE JEDI
by Barbara Hambly
Setting: Eight years after *Return of the Jedi*

The STAR WARS characters face a menace from the glory days of the Empire when a thirty-year-old automated Imperial Dreadnaught comes to life and begins its grim mission: to gather forces and annihilate a long-forgotten stronghold of Jedi children. When Luke is whisked aboard, he begins to communicate with the brave Jedi Knight who paralyzed the ship decades ago, and gave her life in the process. Now she is part of the vessel, existing in its artificial intelligence core, and guiding Luke through one of the most unusual adventures he has ever had.

DARKSABER by Kevin J. Anderson
Setting: Immediately thereafter

Not long after Children of the Jedi, *Luke and Han learn that evil Hutts are building a reconstruction of the original Death Star— and that the Empire is still alive, in the form of Daala, who has joined forces with Pellaeon, former second-in-command to the feared Grand Admiral Thrawn.*

PLANET OF TWILIGHT
by Barbara Hambly
Setting: Nine years after *Return of the Jedi*

Concluding the epic tale begun in her own novel Children of the Jedi *and continued by Kevin Anderson in* Darksaber, *Barbara Hambly tells the story of a ruthless enemy of the New Republic operating out of a backwater world with vast mineral deposits. The first step in his campaign is to kidnap Princess Leia. Meanwhile, as Luke Skywalker searches the planet for his long-lost love Callista, the planet begins to reveal its unspeakable secret—a secret that threatens the New Republic, the Empire, and the entire galaxy:*

The first to die was a midshipman named Koth Barak. One of his fellow crewmembers on the New Republic escort cruiser *Adamantine* found him slumped across the table in the deck-nine break room where he'd repaired half an hour previously for a cup of coffeine. Twenty minutes after Barak should have been back to post, Gunnery Sergeant Gallie Wover went looking for him.

When she entered the deck-nine break room, Sergeant Wover's first sight was of the palely flickering blue on blue of the infolog screen. "Blast it, Koth, I told you . . ."

Then she saw the young man stretched unmoving on the far side of the screen, head on the break table, eyes shut. Even at a distance of three meters Wover didn't like the way he was breathing.

"Koth!" She rounded the table in two strides, sending the other chairs clattering into a corner. She thought his eyelids moved a little when she yelled his name. "Koth!"

Wover hit the emergency call almost without conscious decision. In the few minutes before the med droids arrived she sniffed the coffeine in the gray plastene cup a few centimeters from his limp fingers. It wasn't even cold.

THE CRYSTAL STAR
by Vonda N. McIntyre
Setting: Ten years after *Return of the Jedi*

Leia's three children have been kidnapped. That horrible fact is made worse by Leia's realization that she can no longer sense her children through the Force! While she, Artoo-Detoo, and Chewbacca trail the kidnappers, Luke and Han discover a planet that is suffering strange quantum effects from a nearby star. Slowly freezing into a perfect crystal and disrupting the Force, the star is blunting Luke's power and crippling the Millennium Falcon. *These strands converge in an apocalyptic threat not only to the fate of the New Republic, but to the universe itself.*

The Black Fleet Crisis
BEFORE THE STORM
SHIELD OF LIES
TYRANT'S TEST
by Michael P. Kube-McDowell
Setting: Twelve years after *Return of the Jedi*

Long after setting up the hard-won New Republic, yesterday's Rebels have become today's administrators and diplomats. But the peace is not to last for long. A restless Luke must journey to his mother's homeworld in a desperate quest to find her people; Lando seizes a mysterious spacecraft with unimaginable weapons of destruction; and waiting in the wings is a horrific battle fleet under the control of a ruthless leader bent on a genocidal war.

THE NEW REBELLION
by Kristine Kathryn Rusch
Setting: Thirteen years after *Return of the Jedi*

Victorious though the New Republic may be, there is still no end to the threats to its continuing existence—this novel explores the price of keeping the peace. First, somewhere in the galaxy, millions suddenly perish in a blinding instant of pain. Then, as Leia prepares to address the Senate on Coruscant, a horrifying event changes the governmental equation in a flash.

The Corellian Trilogy:
AMBUSH AT CORELLIA
ASSAULT AT SELONIA
SHOWDOWN AT CENTERPOINT
by Roger MacBride Allen
Setting: Fourteen years after *Return of the Jedi*

This trilogy takes us to Corellia, Han Solo's homeworld, which Han has not visited in quite some time. A trade summit brings Han, Leia, and the children—now developing their own clear personalities and instinctively learning more about their innate skills in the Force—into the middle of a situation that most closely resembles a burning fuse. The Corellian system is on the brink of civil war, there are New Republic intelligence agents on a mysterious mission which even Han does not understand, and worst of all, a fanatical rebel leader has his hands on a superweapon of unimaginable power—and just wait until you find out who that leader is!

The Hand of Thrawn
SPECTER OF THE PAST
VISION OF THE FUTURE
by Timothy Zahn
Setting: Nineteen years after
Star Wars: A New Hope

The two-book series by the undisputed master of the STAR WARS novel. Once the supreme master of countless star systems, the Empire is tottering on the brink of total collapse. Day by day, neutral systems are rushing to join the New Republic coalition. But with the end of the war in sight, the New Republic has fallen victim to its own success. An unwieldy alliance of races and traditions, the confederation now finds itself riven by age-old animosities. Princess Leia struggles against all odds to hold the New Republic together. But she has powerful enemies. An ambitious Moff Disra leads a conspiracy to divide the uneasy coalition with an ingenious plot to blame the Bothans for a heinous crime that could lead to genocide and civil war. At the same time, Luke Skywalker, along with Lando Calrissian and Talon Karrde, pursues a mysterious group of pirate ships whose crew consists of clones. And then comes the worst news of all: the most cunning and ruthless warlord in Imperial history has returned to lead the Empire to triumph. Here's an exciting scene from Timothy Zahn's spectacular STAR WARS novel:

"I don't think you fully understand the political situation the New Republic finds itself in these days. A flash point like Caamas—especially with Bothan involvement—will bring the whole thing to a boil. Particularly if we can give it the proper nudge."

"The situation among the Rebels is not the issue," Tierce countered coldly. "It's the state of the Empire *you* don't seem to understand. Simply tearing the Rebellion apart isn't going to rebuild the Emperor's New Order. We need a focal point, a leader around whom the Imperial forces can rally."

Disra said, "Suppose I could provide such a leader. Would you be willing to join us?"

Tierce eyed him. "Who is this 'us' you refer to?"

"If you join, there would be three of us," Disra said. "Three who would share the secret I'm prepared to offer you. A secret that will bring the entire Fleet onto our side.''

Tierce smiled cynically. "You'll forgive me, Your Excellency, if I suggest you couldn't inspire blind loyalty in a drugged bantha.''

Disra felt a flash of anger. How dare this common soldier—?

"No,'' he agreed, practically choking out the word from between clenched teeth. Tierce was hardly a common soldier, after all. More importantly, Disra desperately needed a man of his skills and training. "I would merely be the political power behind the throne. Plus the supplier of military men and matériel, of course.''

"From the Braxant Sector Fleet?''

"And other sources,'' Disra said. "You, should you choose to join us, would serve as the architect of our overall strategy.''

"I see.'' If Tierce was bothered by the word "serve,'' he didn't show it. "And the third person?''

"Are you with us?''

Tierce studied him. "First tell me more.''

"I'll do better than tell you.'' Disra pushed his chair back and stood up. "I'll show you.''

Disra led the way down the rightmost corridor. It ended in a dusty metal door with a wheel set into its center. Gripping the edges of the wheel, Disra turned it; and with a creak that echoed eerily in the confined space the door swung open.

The previous owner would hardly have recognized his one-time torture chamber. The instruments of pain and terror had been taken out, the walls and floor cleaned and carpet-insulated, and the furnishings of a fully functional modern apartment installed.

But for the moment Disra had no interest in the chamber itself. All his attention was on Tierce as the former Guardsman stepped into the room.

Stepped into the room . . . and caught sight of the room's single occupant, seated in the center in a duplicate of a Star Destroyer's captain's chair.

Tierce froze, his eyes widening with shock, his entire body stiffening as if a power current had jolted through him. His eyes darted to Disra, back to the captain's chair, flicked around the room as if seeking evidence of a trap or hallucination or perhaps his own insanity, back again to the chair. Disra held his breath. . . .

STAR WARS®

THE FORCE IS WITH YOU
whenever you open a *Star Wars* novel
from Bantam Spectra Books!

The novels of the incomparable
Timothy Zahn

___29612-4	HEIR TO THE EMPIRE	$5.99/$6.99 Canada
___56071-9	DARK FORCE RISING	$5.99/$6.99
___56492-7	THE LAST COMMAND	$5.99/$6.99
___29804-6	SPECTER OF THE PAST	$5.99/$7.99
___57879-0	VISION OF THE FUTURE	$5.99/$8.99

The original Star Wars *anthologies*
edited by Kevin J. Anderson...

___56468-4	TALES FROM THE MOS EISLEY CANTINA	$5.99/$7.99
___56815-9	TALES FROM JABBA'S PALACE	$5.99/$7.99
___56816-7	TALES OF THE BOUNTY HUNTERS	$5.99/$7.99

...and by Peter Schweighofer...

___57876-6	TALES FROM THE EMPIRE	$5.99/$7.99

STAR WARS®

THE FORCE IS WITH YOU
whenever you open a *Star Wars* novel
from Bantam Spectra Books!

The breathtaking X-wing series by Michael A. Stackpole...

___56801-9	ROGUE SQUADRON	$5.99/$7.99
___56802-7	WEDGE'S GAMBLE	$5.99/$7.99
___56803-5	THE KRYTOS TRAP	$5.99/$7.99
___56804-3	THE BACTA WAR	$5.99/$7.99
___57903-7	ISARD'S REVENGE	$5.99/$8.99

...and Aaron Allston

___57894-4	WRAITH SQUADRON	$5.99/$7.99
___57897-9	IRON FIST	$5.99/$7.99

*The fantastic new Bounty Hunter War series
by K. W. Jeter*

___57885-5	THE MANDALORIAN ARMOR	$5.99/$7.99
___57888-X	SLAVE SHIP	$5.99/$7.99

STAR WARS®

THE FORCE IS WITH YOU
whenever you open a *Star Wars* novel
from Bantam Spectra Books!

Don't miss the exciting Han Solo trilogy
by A. C. Crispin

___57415-9	THE PARADISE SNARE	$5.99/$7.99
___57416-7	THE HUTT GAMBIT	$5.99/$7.99
___57417-5	REBEL DAWN	$5.99/$7.99

And these bestselling adventures

___57413-2	SHADOWS OF THE EMPIRE, Steve Perry	$5.99/$7.99
___57517-1	PLANET OF TWILIGHT, Barbara Hambly	$5.99/$7.99
___29803-8	AMBUSH AT CORELLIA, Roger Allen	$5.99/$7.99
___29805-4	ASSAULT AT SELONIA, Roger Allen	$5.99/$7.99
___29806-2	SHOWDOWN AT CENTERPOINT, Allen	$5.99/$7.99

Look for all of these exciting Star Wars *novels, now available wherever
Bantam Spectra Books are sold, or use this page for ordering.*

- -

Please send me the books I have checked above. I am enclosing $____ (add $2.50 to
cover postage and handling). Send check or money order, no cash or C.O.D.'s, please.

Name _____

Address _____

City/State/Zip _____

Send order to: Bantam Books, Dept. SF 11, 2451 S. Wolf Rd., Des Plaines, IL 60018.
Allow four to six weeks for delivery.
Prices and availability subject to change without notice.   SF 11 2/99
®, ™, and © 1997 Lucasfilm Ltd. All rights reserved. Used under authorization.